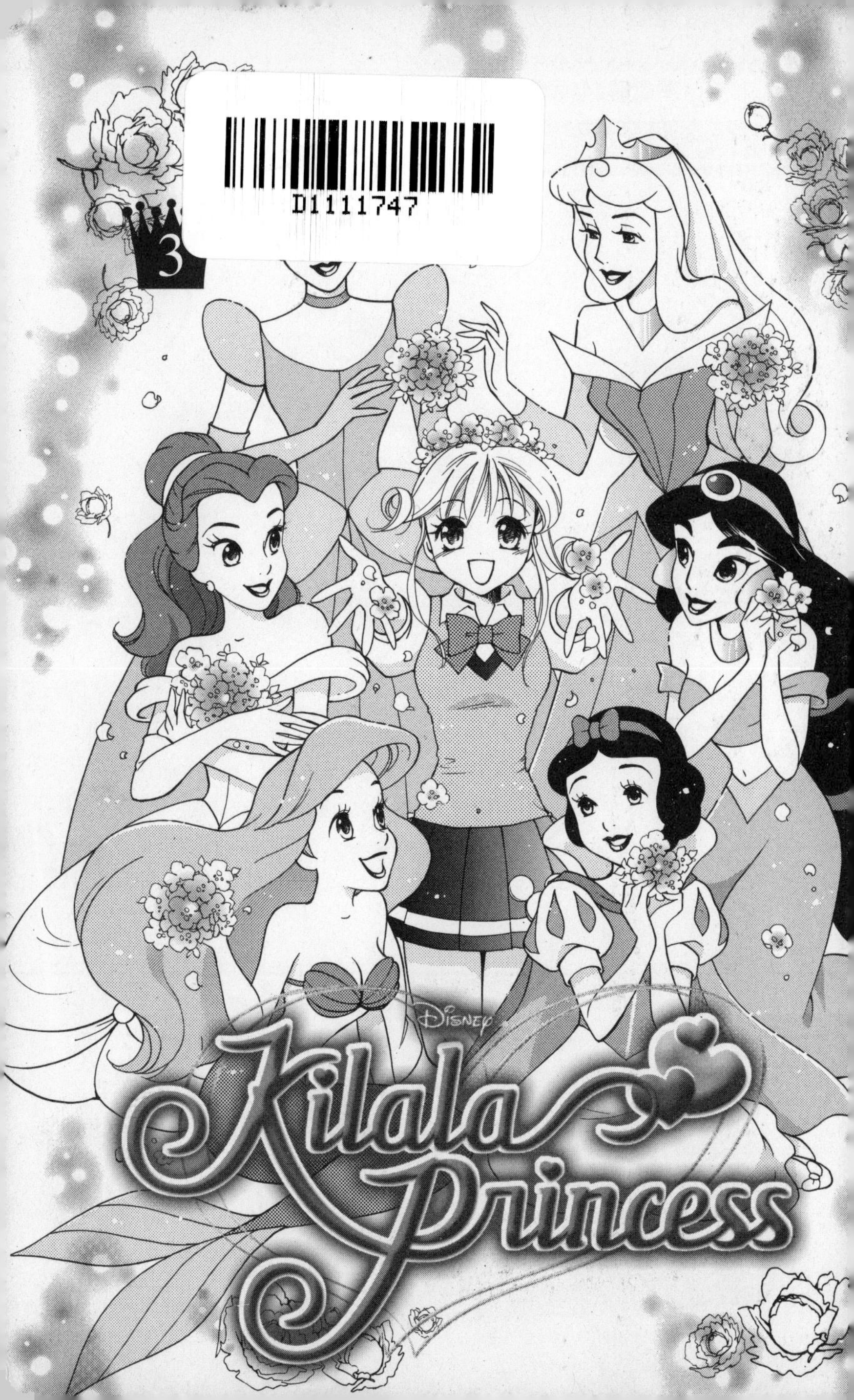
3
Disney
Kilala Princess

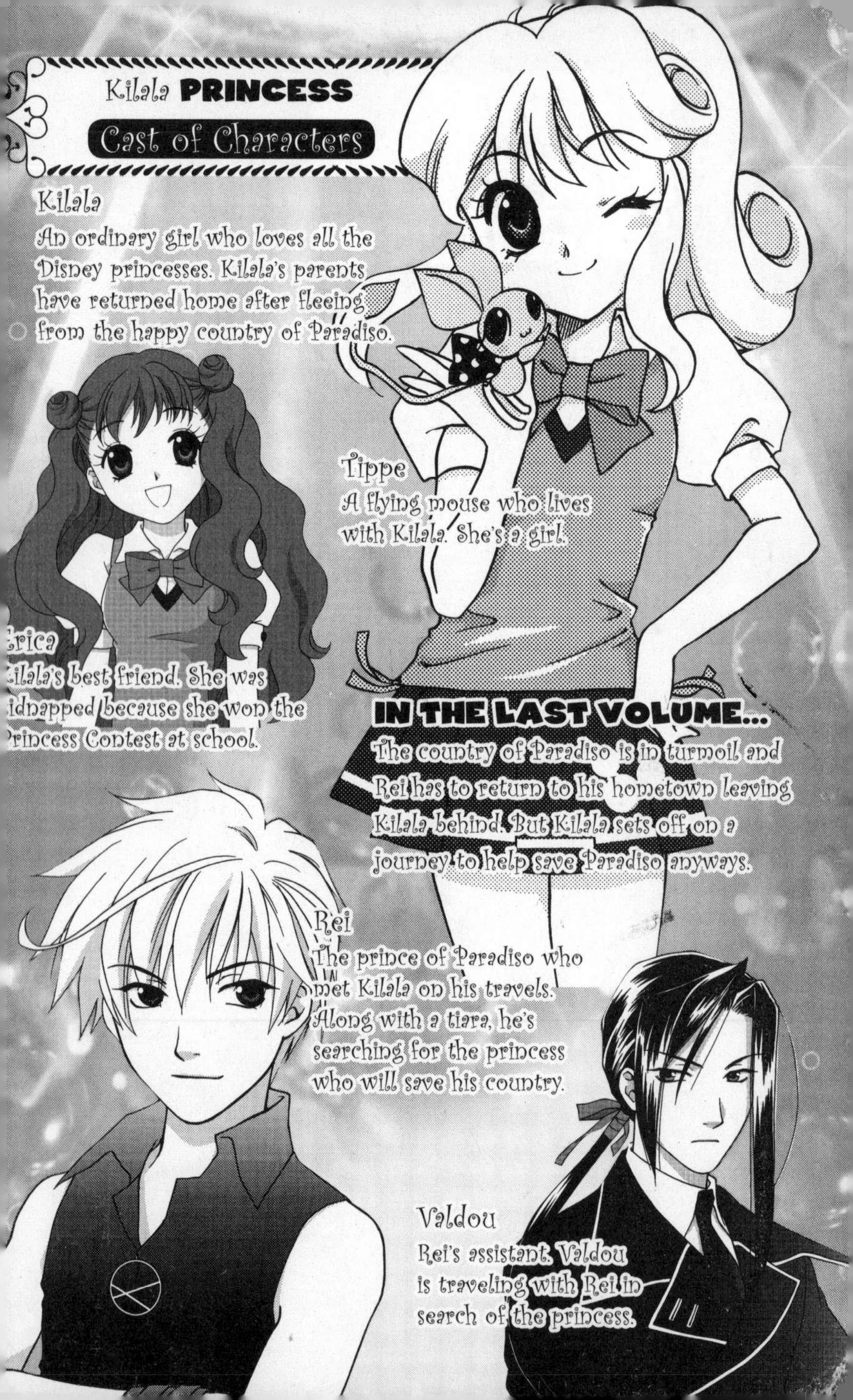
Kilala PRINCESS
Cast of Characters
Kilala
An ordinary girl who loves all the Disney princesses. Kilala's parents have returned home after fleeing from the happy country of Paradiso.
Tippe
A flying mouse who lives with Kilala. She's a girl.
Erica
Kilala's best friend. She was kidnapped because she won the Princess Contest at school.
IN THE LAST VOLUME...
The country of Paradiso is in turmoil and Rei has to return to his hometown leaving Kilala behind. But Kilala sets off on a journey to help save Paradiso anyways.
Rei
The prince of Paradiso who met Kilala on his travels. Along with a tiara, he's searching for the princess who will save his country.
Valdou
Rei's assistant. Valdou is traveling with Rei in search of the princess.

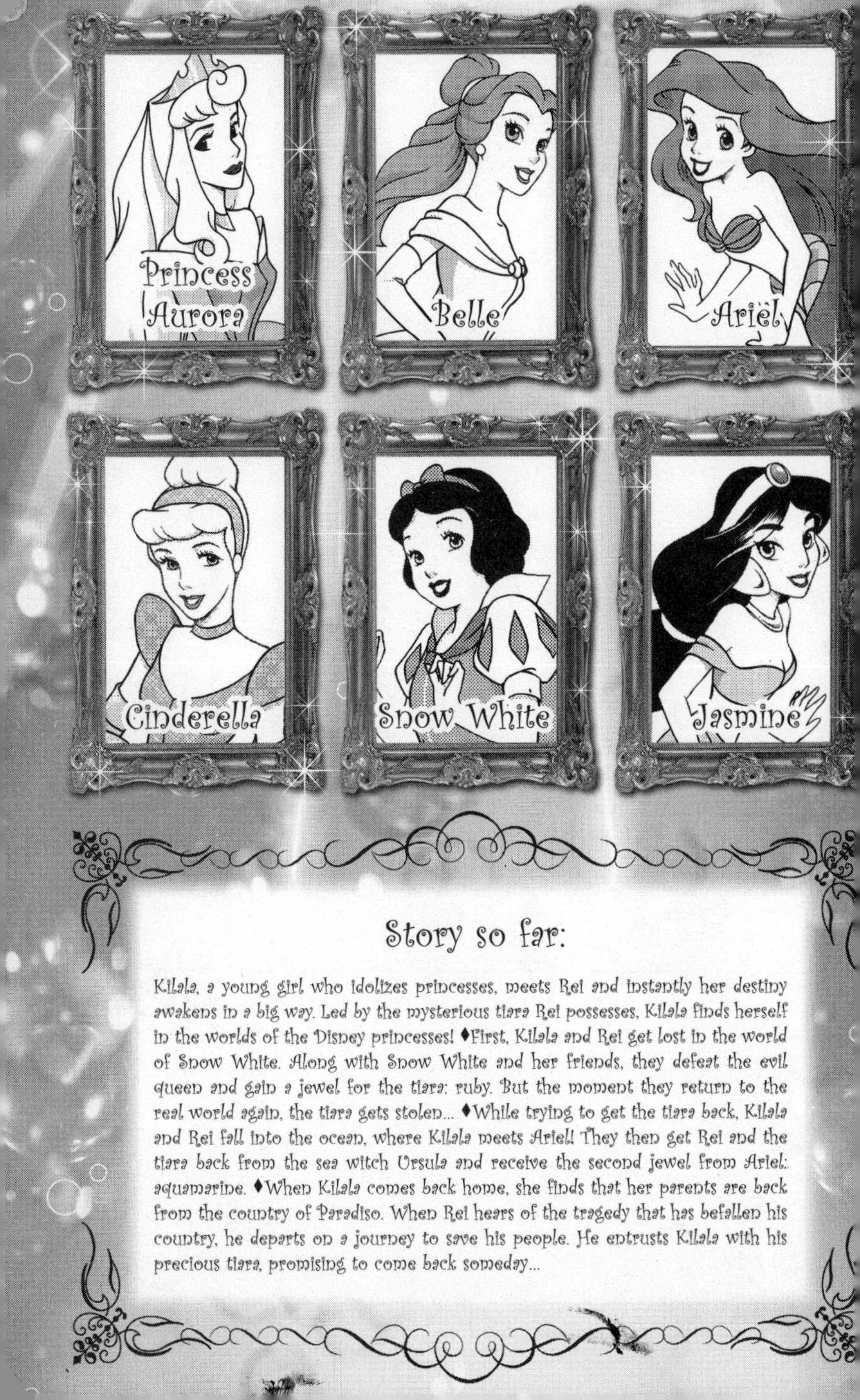
Ariel
Belle
Princess Aurora
Jasmine
Snow White
Cinderella

Story so far:

Kilala, a young girl who idolizes princesses, meets Rei and instantly her destiny awakens in a big way. Led by the mysterious tiara Rei possesses, Kilala finds herself in the worlds of the Disney princesses! ♦First, Kilala and Rei get lost in the world of Snow White. Along with Snow White and her friends, they defeat the evil queen and gain a jewel for the tiara: ruby. But the moment they return to the real world again, the tiara gets stolen... ♦While trying to get the tiara back, Kilala and Rei fall into the ocean, where Kilala meets Ariel! They then get Rei and the tiara back from the sea witch Ursula and receive the second jewel from Ariel: aquamarine. ♦When Kilala comes back home, she finds that her parents are back from the country of Paradiso. When Rei hears of the tragedy that has befallen his country, he departs on a journey to save his people. He entrusts Kilala with his precious tiara, promising to come back someday...

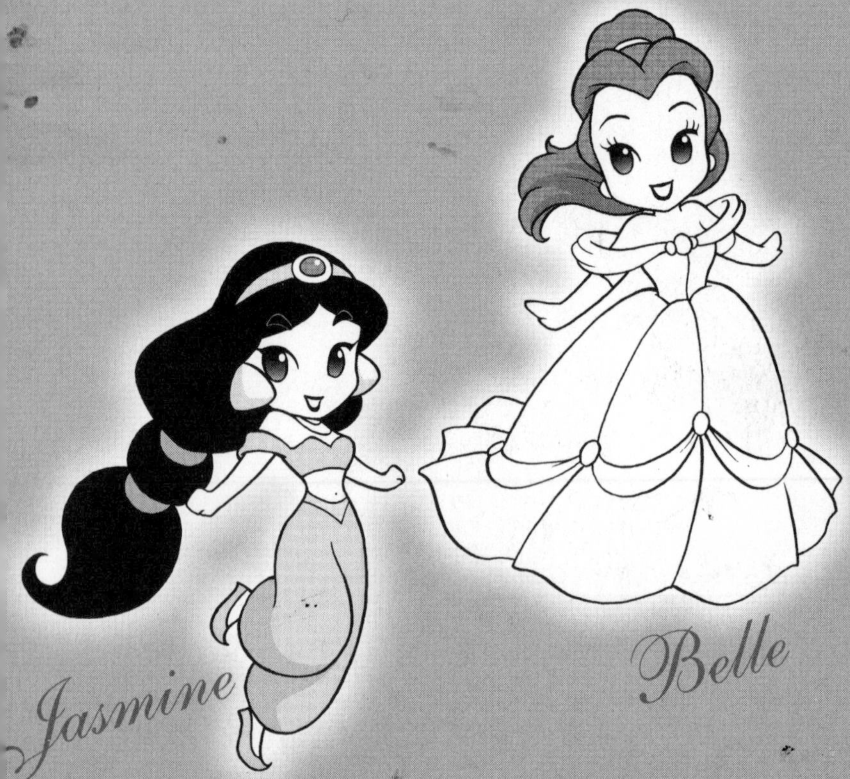
Belle
Jasmine

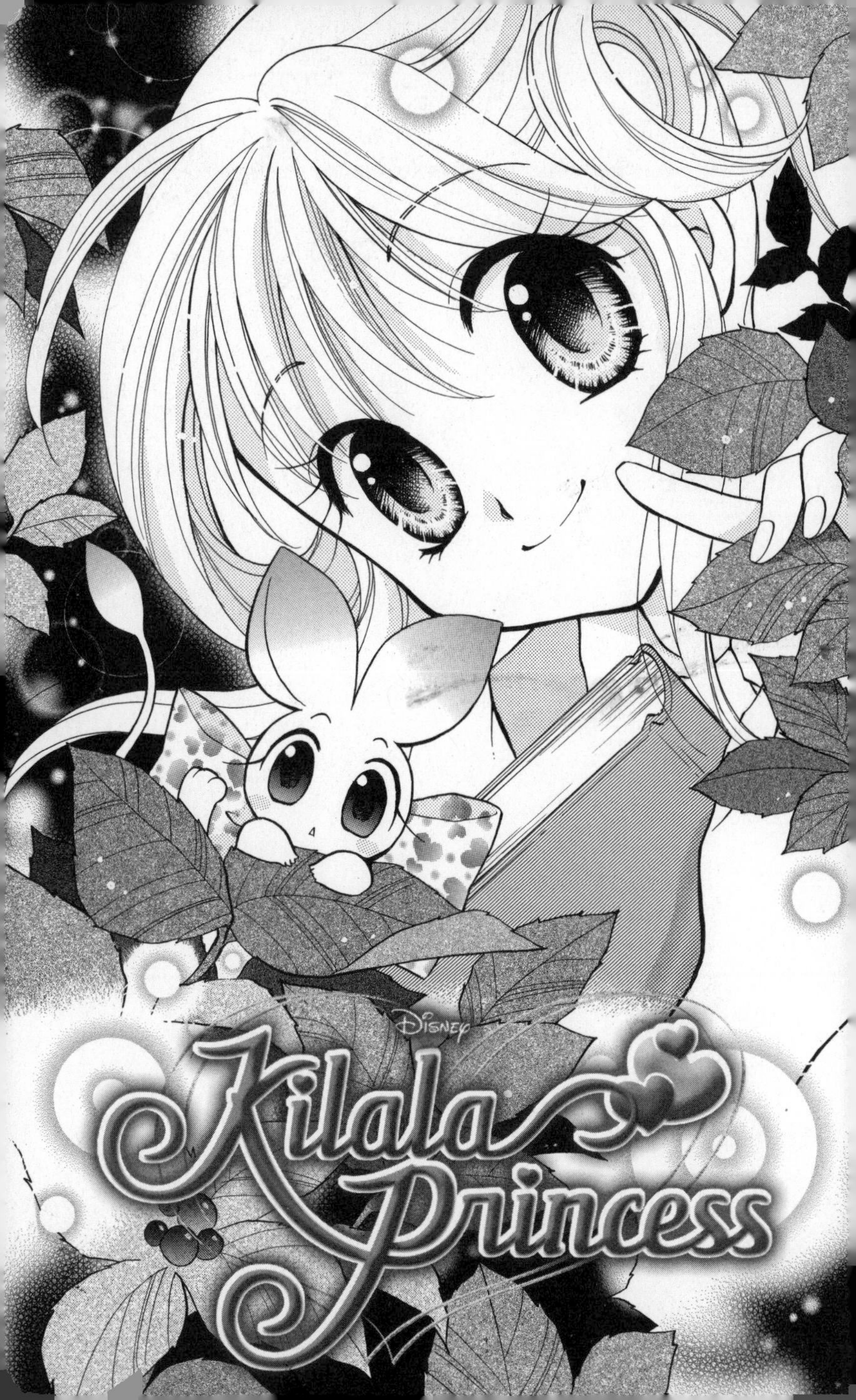
Disney
Kilala Princess

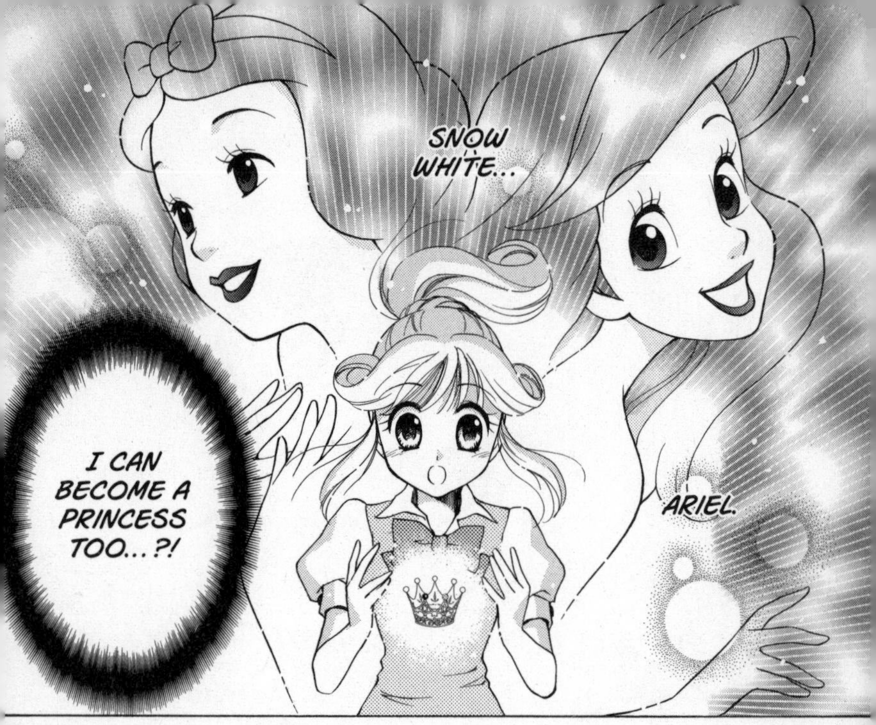
SNOW WHITE...
ARIEL.
I CAN BECOME A PRINCESS TOO...?!
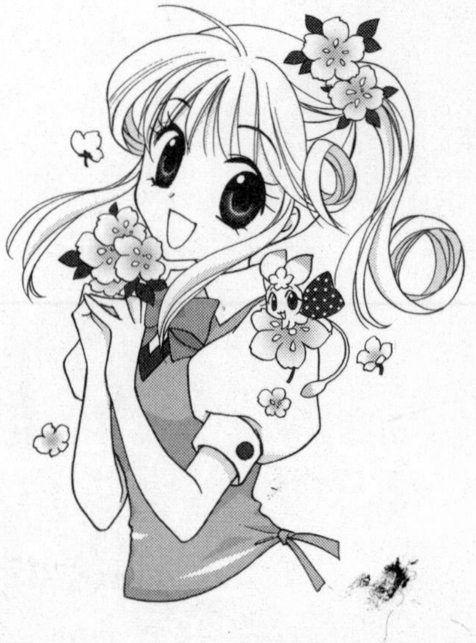

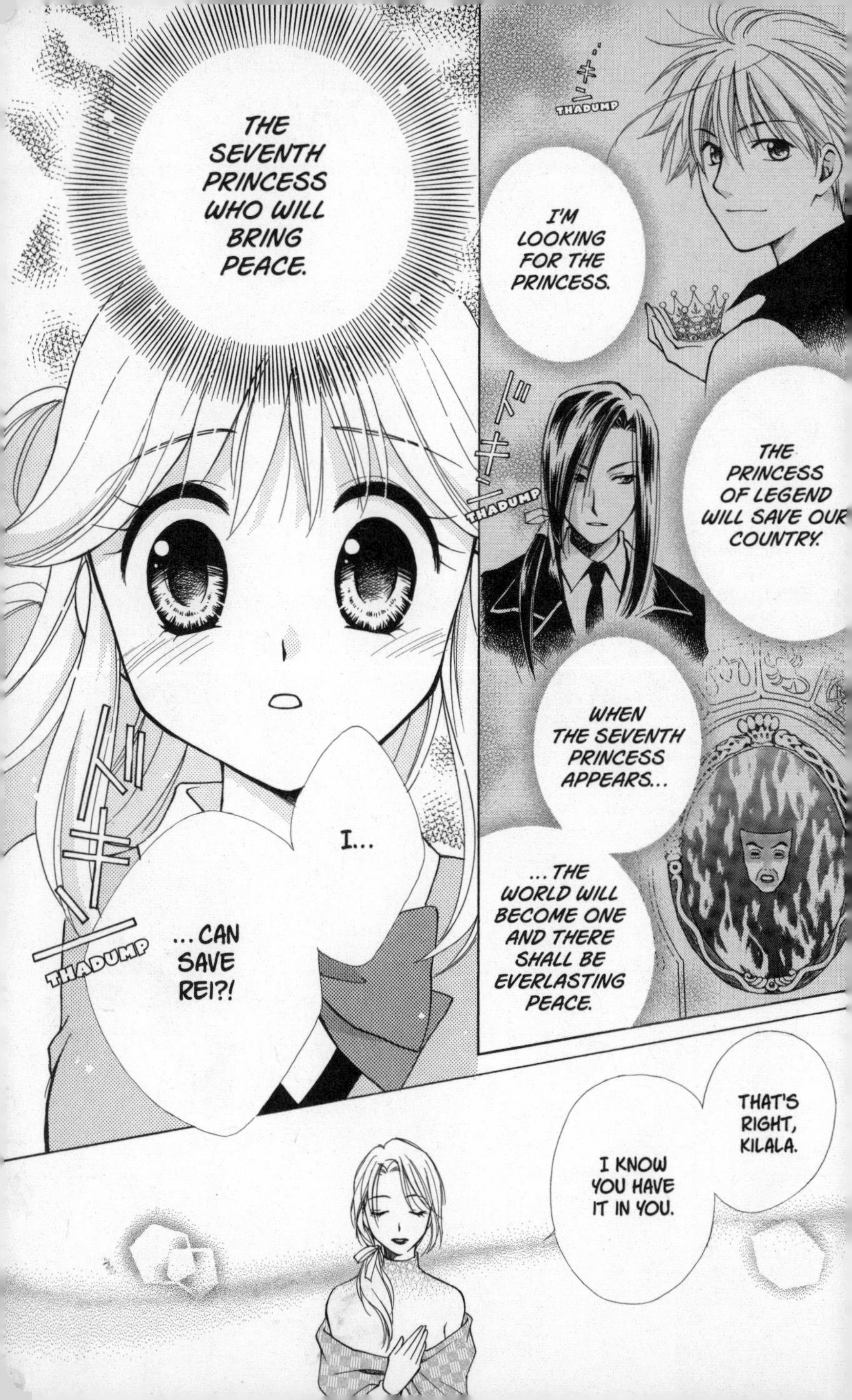
I'M LOOKING FOR THE PRINCESS.
THADUMP
THE PRINCESS OF LEGEND WILL SAVE OUR COUNTRY.
THADUMP
WHEN THE SEVENTH PRINCESS APPEARS...
...THE WORLD WILL BECOME ONE AND THERE SHALL BE EVERLASTING PEACE.
THE SEVENTH PRINCESS WHO WILL BRING PEACE.
I...
...CAN SAVE REI?!
THADUMP
THAT'S RIGHT, KILALA.
I KNOW YOU HAVE IT IN YOU.

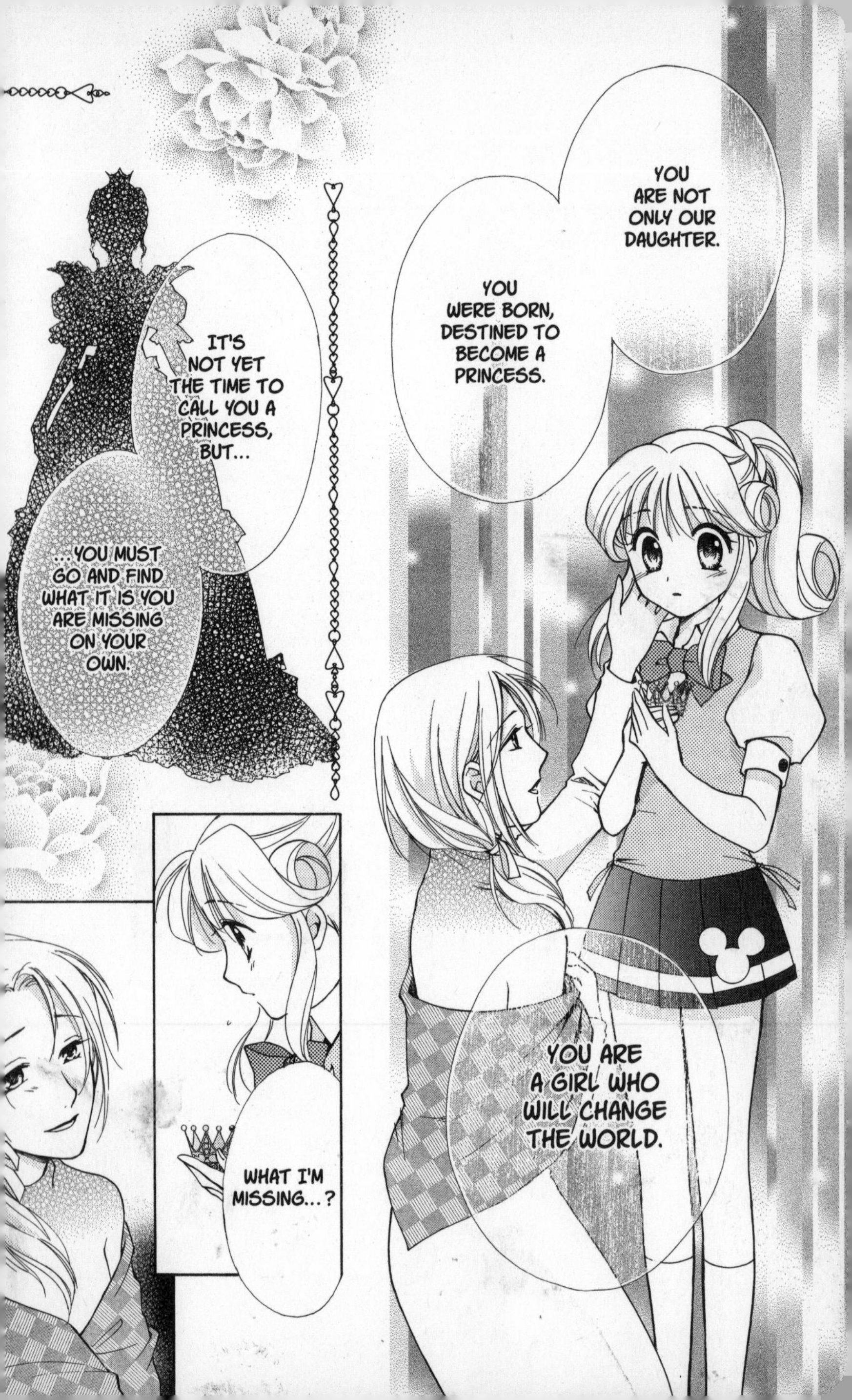
YOU ARE NOT ONLY OUR DAUGHTER.
YOU WERE BORN, DESTINED TO BECOME A PRINCESS.
YOU ARE A GIRL WHO WILL CHANGE THE WORLD.
IT'S NOT YET THE TIME TO CALL YOU A PRINCESS, BUT...
...YOU MUST GO AND FIND WHAT IT IS YOU ARE MISSING ON YOUR OWN.
WHAT I'M MISSING...?

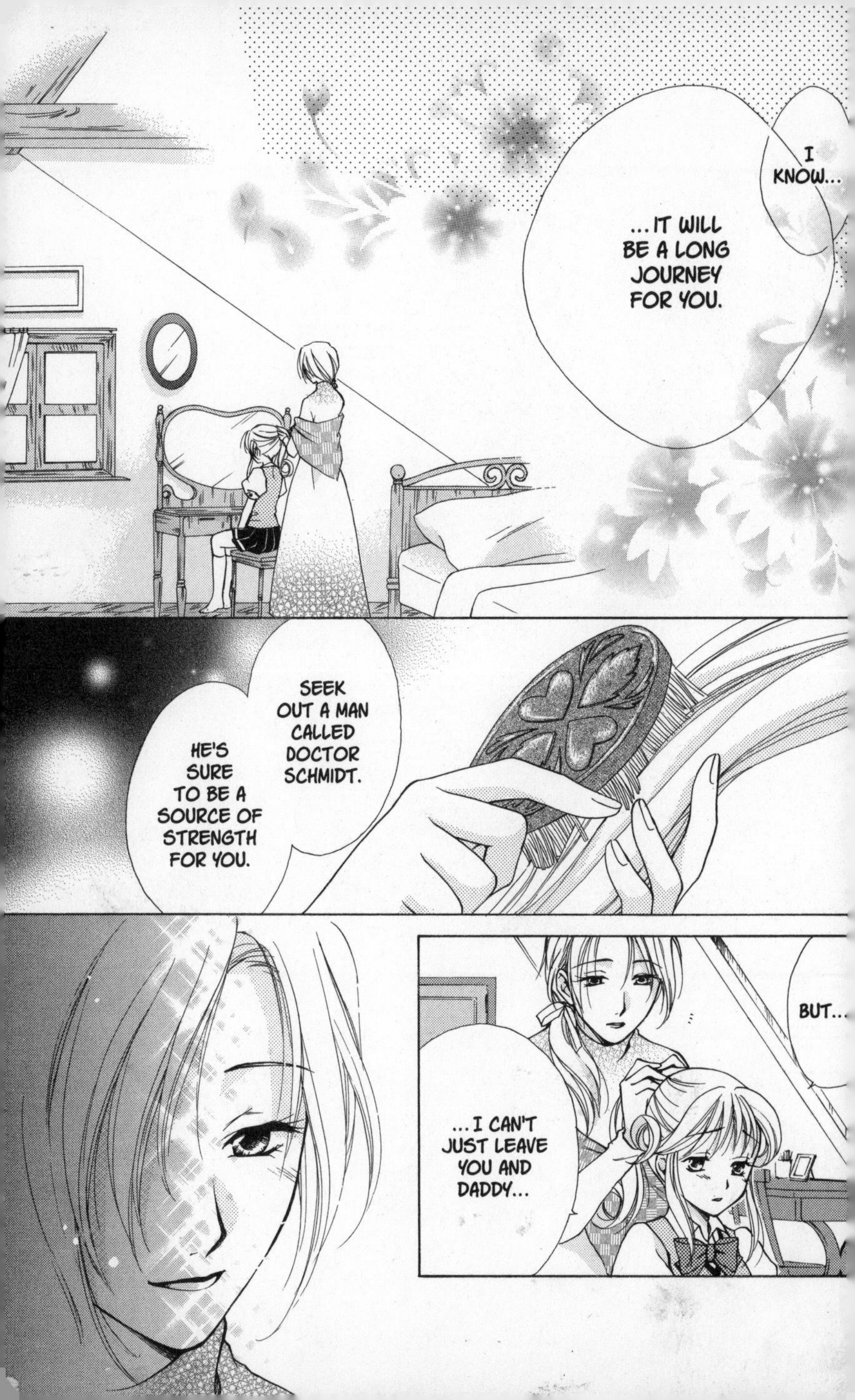
I KNOW...
...IT WILL BE A LONG JOURNEY FOR YOU.
SEEK OUT A MAN CALLED DOCTOR SCHMIDT.
HE'S SURE TO BE A SOURCE OF STRENGTH FOR YOU.
BUT...
...I CAN'T JUST LEAVE YOU AND DADDY...

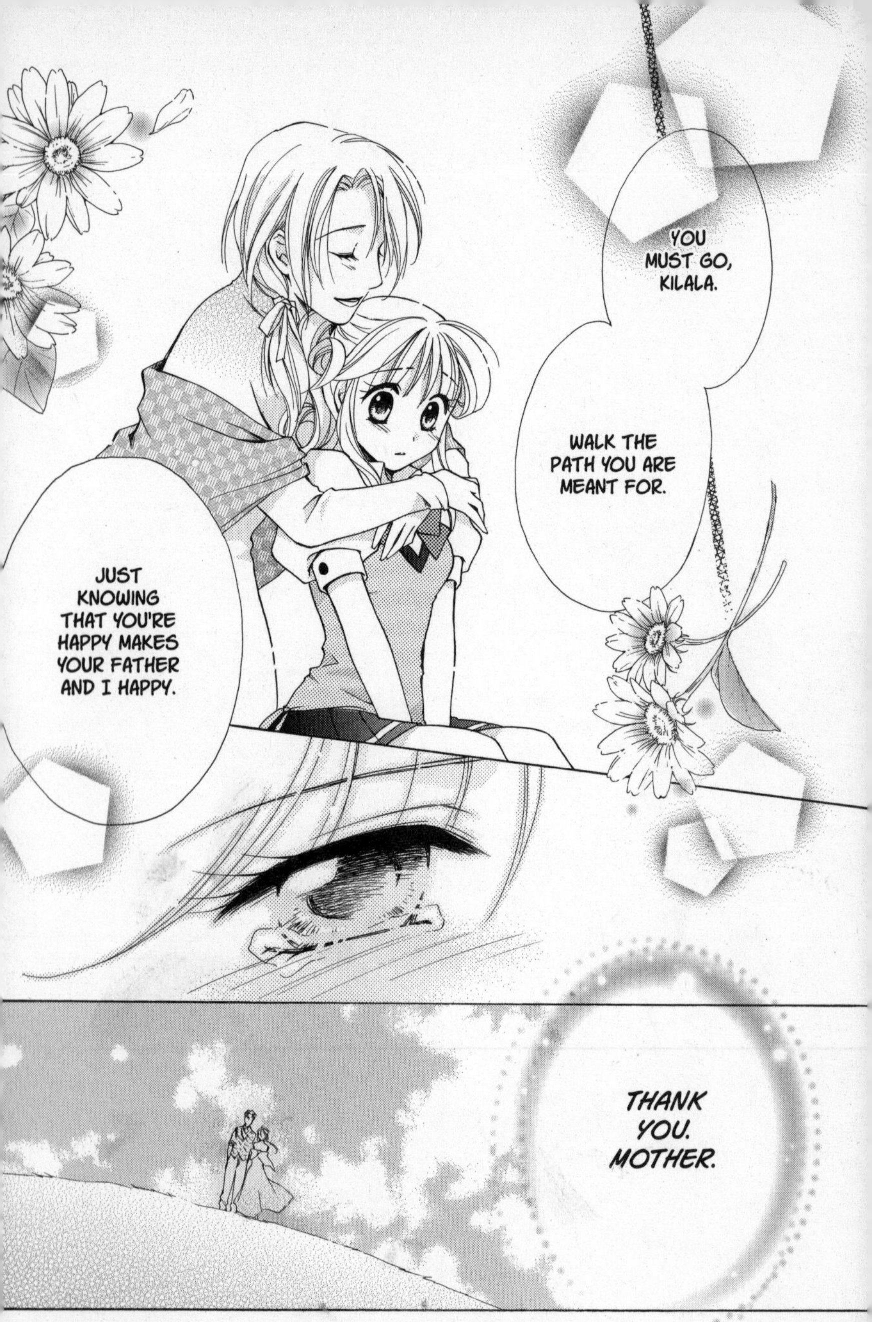
YOU MUST GO, KILALA.
WALK THE PATH YOU ARE MEANT FOR.
JUST KNOWING THAT YOU'RE HAPPY MAKES YOUR FATHER AND I HAPPY.
THANK YOU. MOTHER.

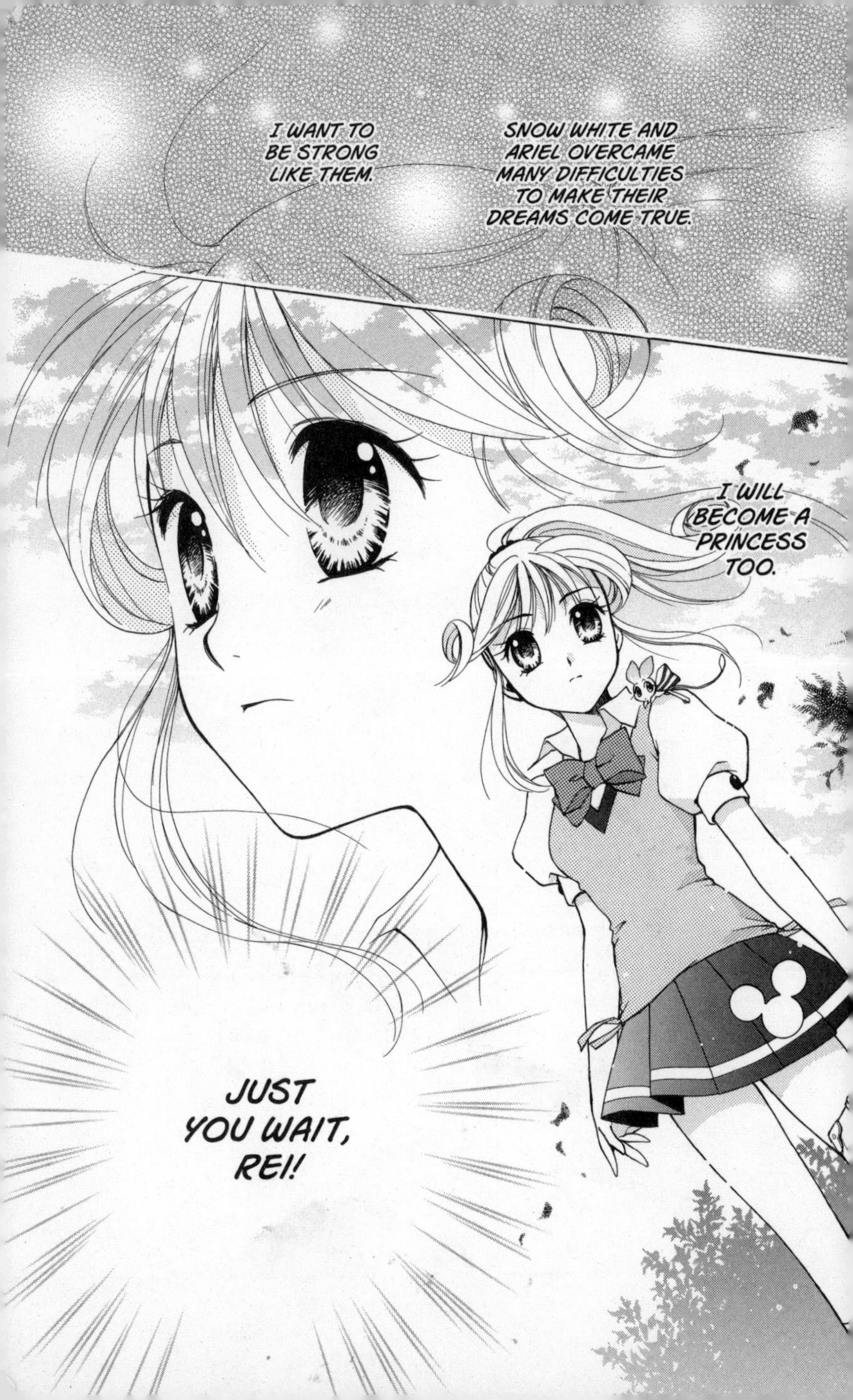
SNOW WHITE AND ARIEL OVERCAME MANY DIFFICULTIES TO MAKE THEIR DREAMS COME TRUE.
I WANT TO BE STRONG LIKE THEM.
I WILL BECOME A PRINCESS TOO.
JUST YOU WAIT, REI!

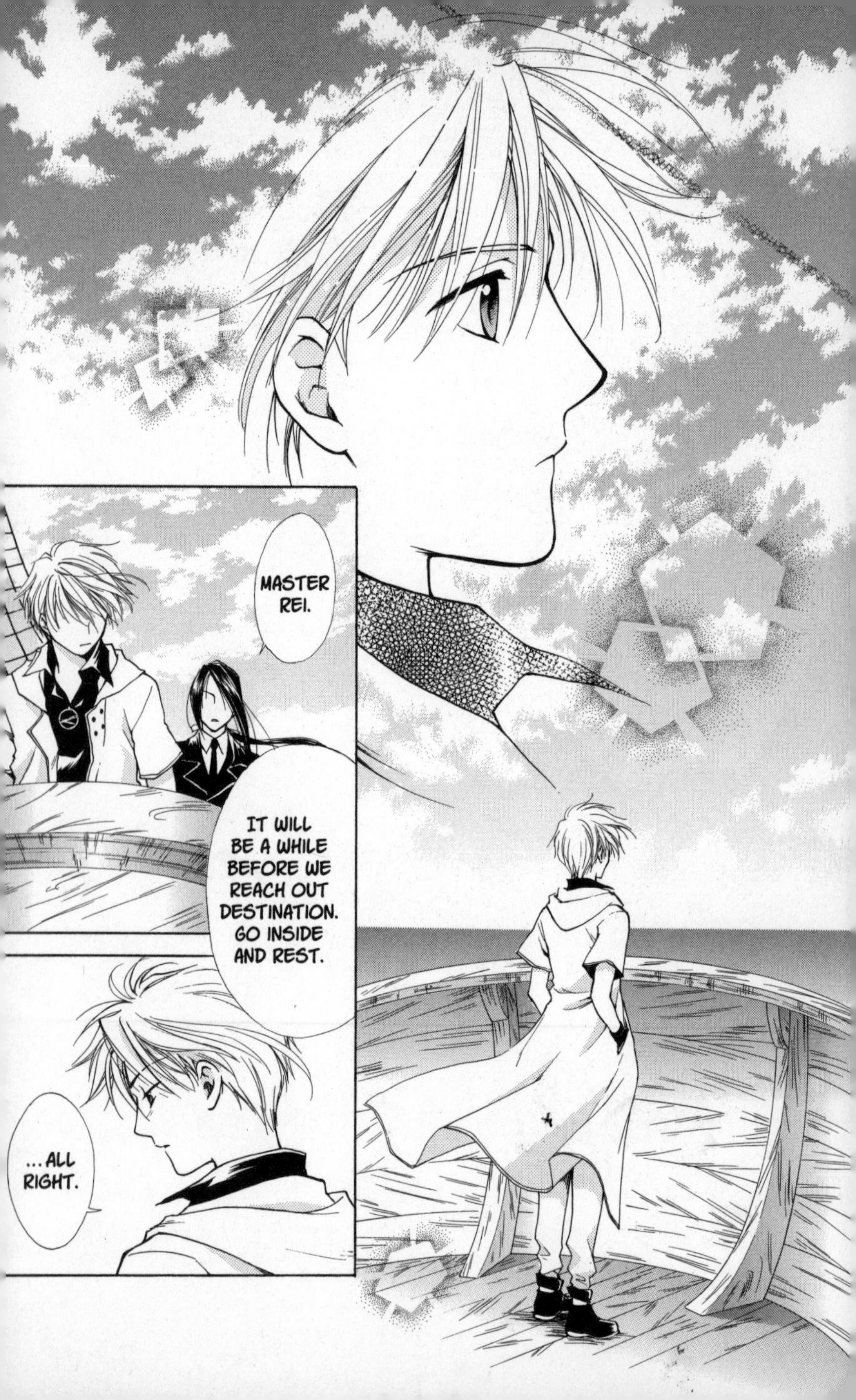
MASTER REI.
IT WILL BE A WHILE BEFORE WE REACH OUT DESTINATION. GO INSIDE AND REST.
...ALL RIGHT.

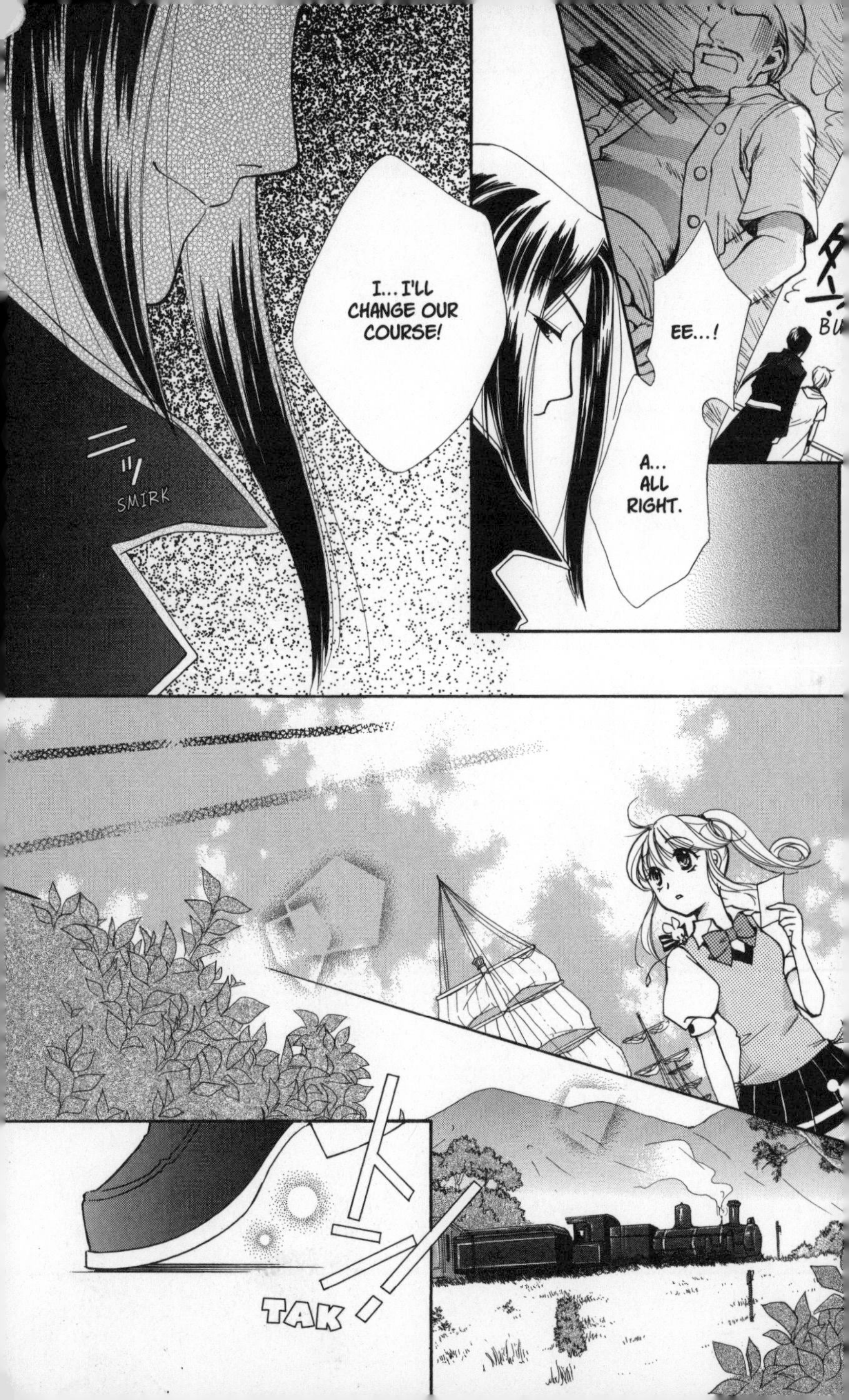
BU
EE...!
A... ALL RIGHT.
I... I'LL CHANGE OUR COURSE!
SMIRK
TAK

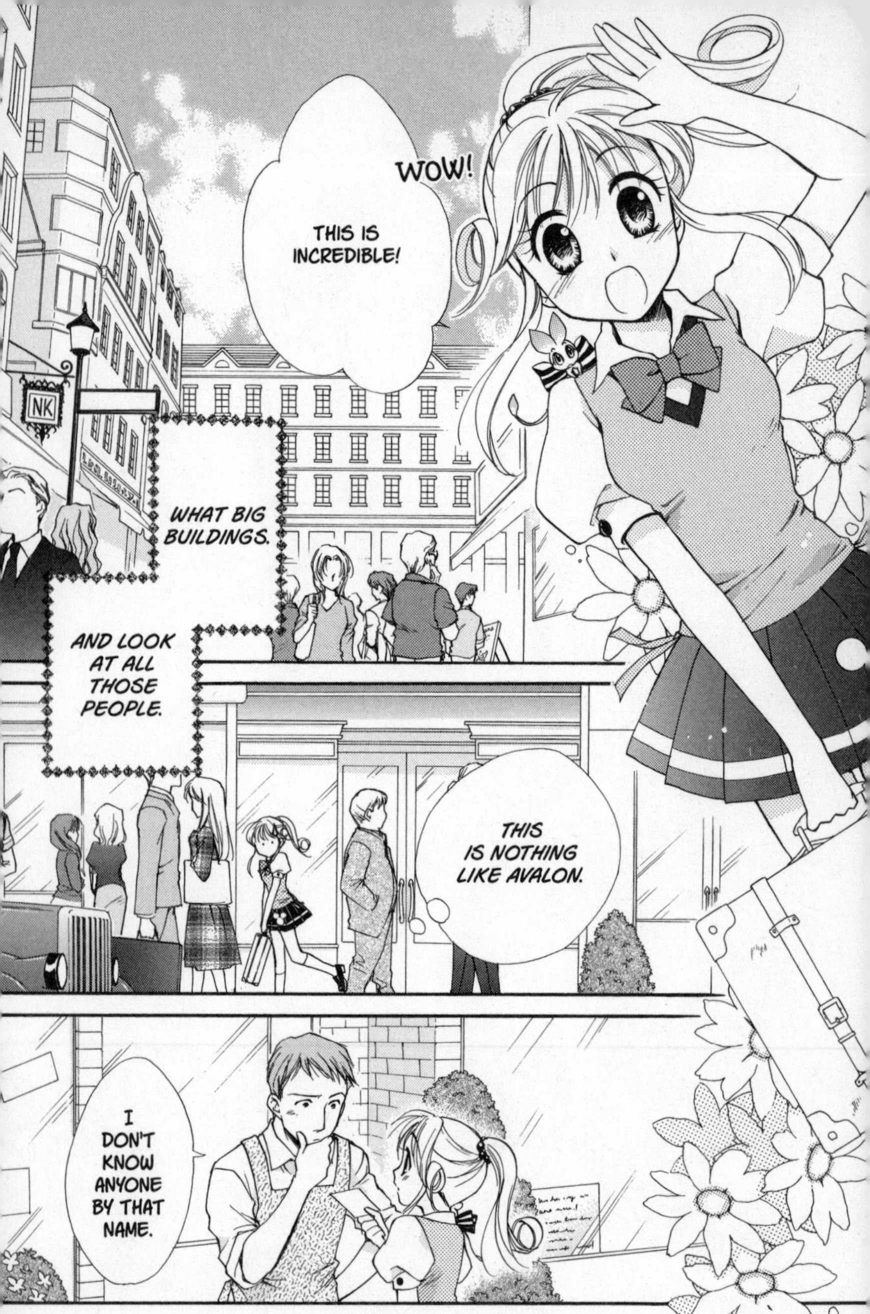
WOW!
THIS IS INCREDIBLE!
WHAT BIG BUILDINGS.
AND LOOK AT ALL THOSE PEOPLE.
THIS IS NOTHING LIKE AVALON.
I DON'T KNOW ANYONE BY THAT NAME.

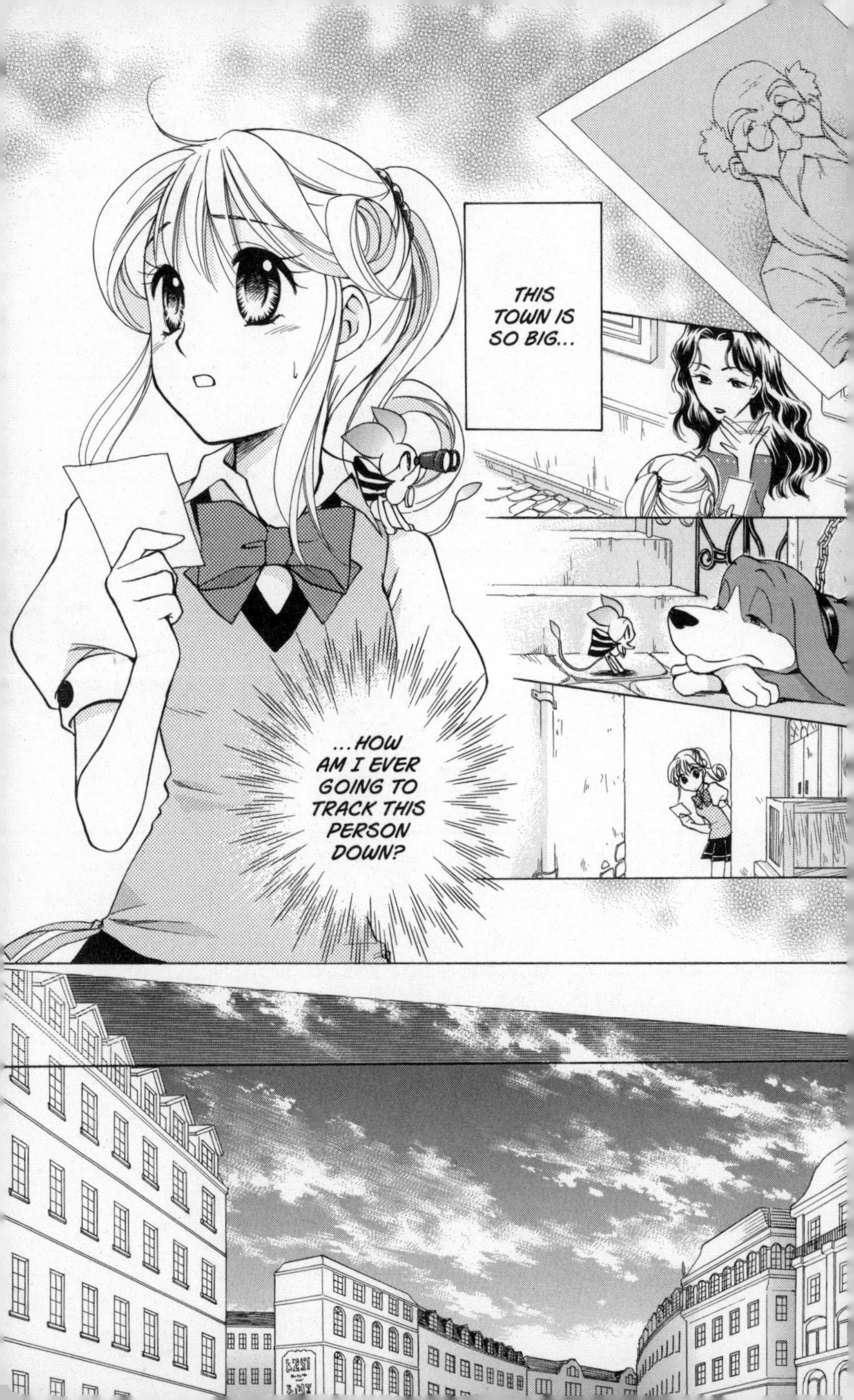
THIS TOWN IS SO BIG...
...HOW AM I EVER GOING TO TRACK THIS PERSON DOWN?

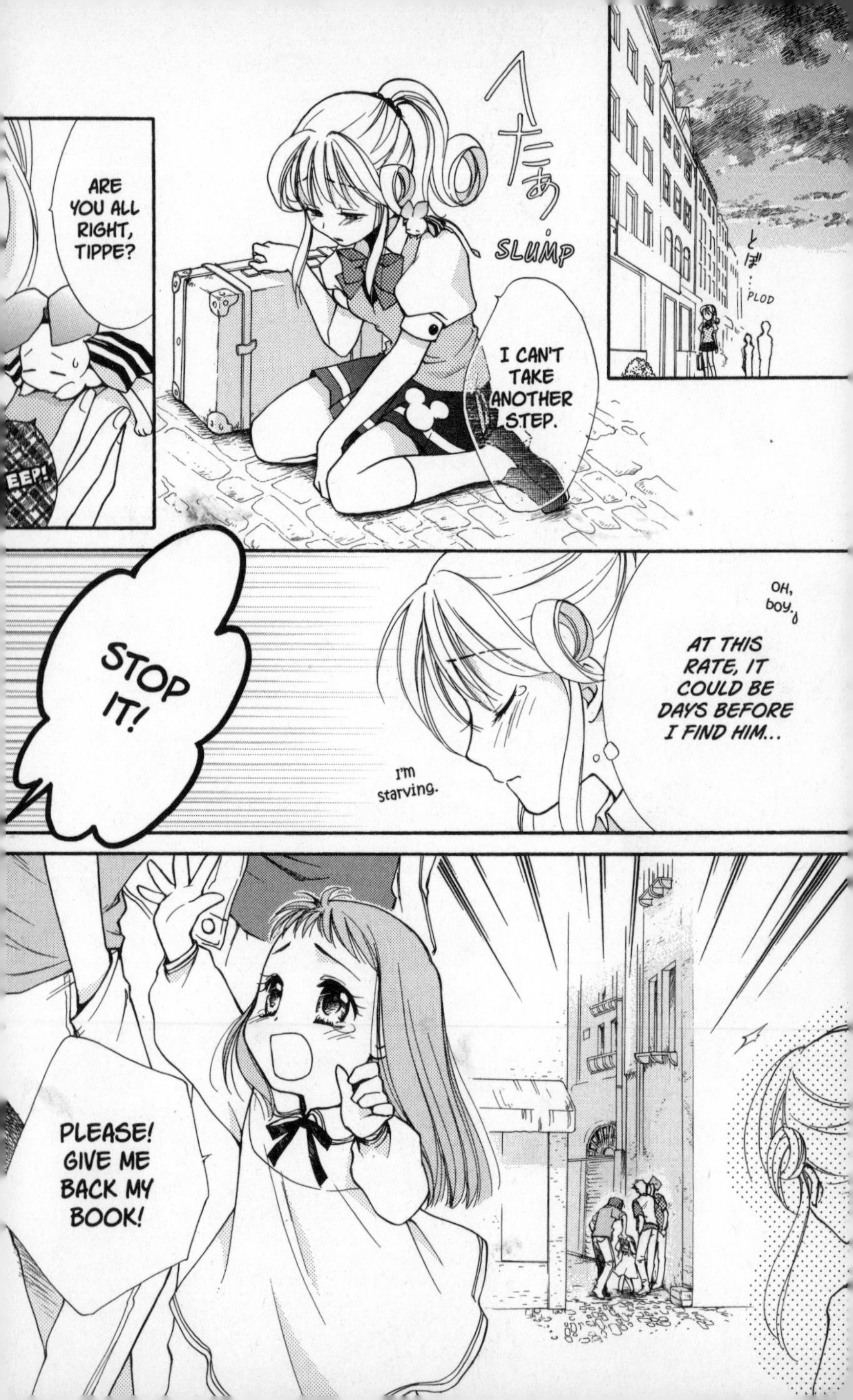

とぼ…
PLOD
へたぁ
SLUMP
I CAN'T TAKE ANOTHER STEP.
ARE YOU ALL RIGHT, TIPPE?
EEP!
OH, boy.
AT THIS RATE, IT COULD BE DAYS BEFORE I FIND HIM...
I'm starving.
STOP IT!
PLEASE! GIVE ME BACK MY BOOK!

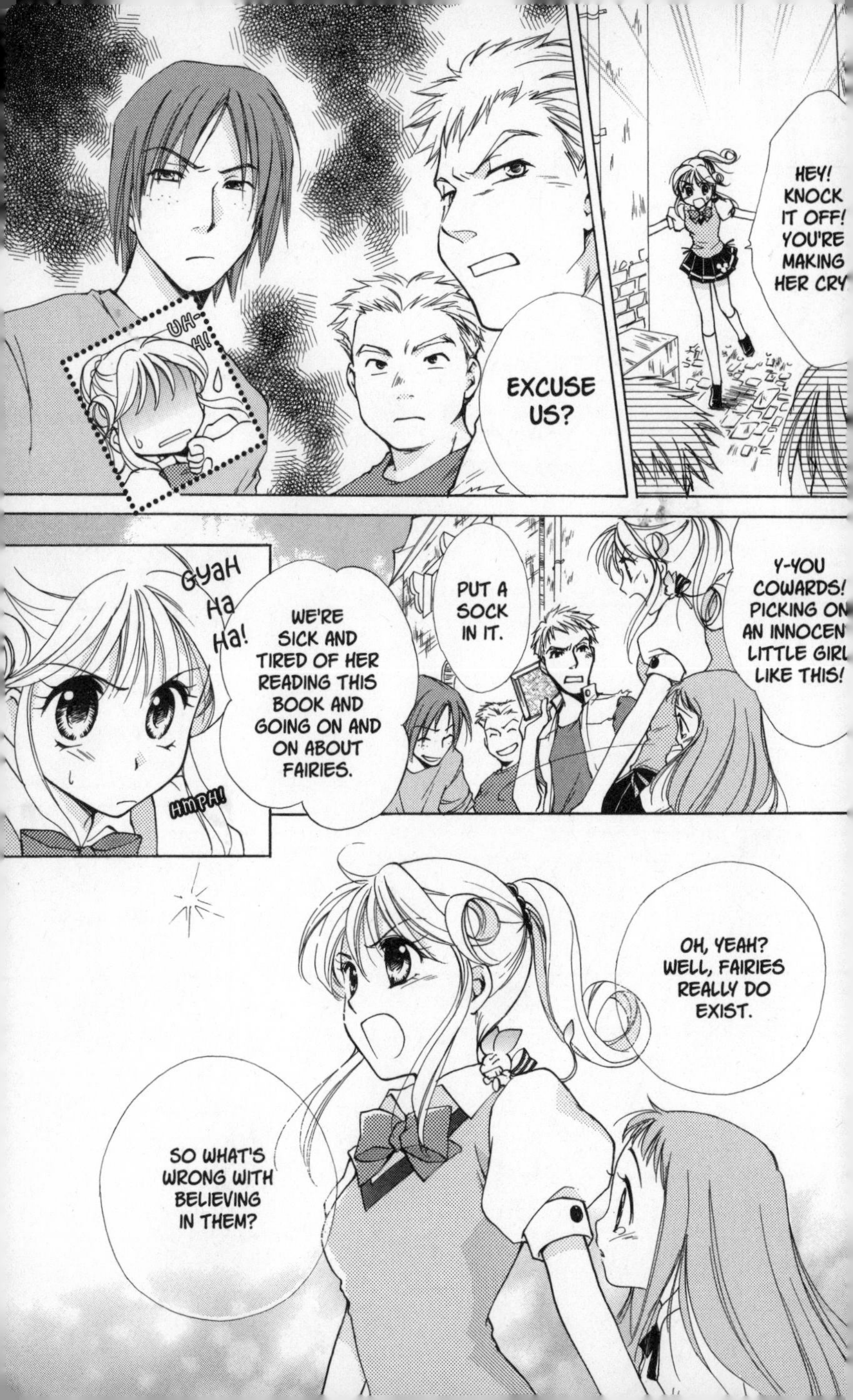
HEY! KNOCK IT OFF! YOU'RE MAKING HER CRY
EXCUSE US?
UH-H!
Y-YOU COWARDS! PICKING ON AN INNOCEN LITTLE GIRL LIKE THIS!
PUT A SOCK IN IT.
WE'RE SICK AND TIRED OF HER READING THIS BOOK AND GOING ON AND ON ABOUT FAIRIES.
GyaH Ha Ha!
HMPH!
OH, YEAH? WELL, FAIRIES REALLY DO EXIST.
SO WHAT'S WRONG WITH BELIEVING IN THEM?

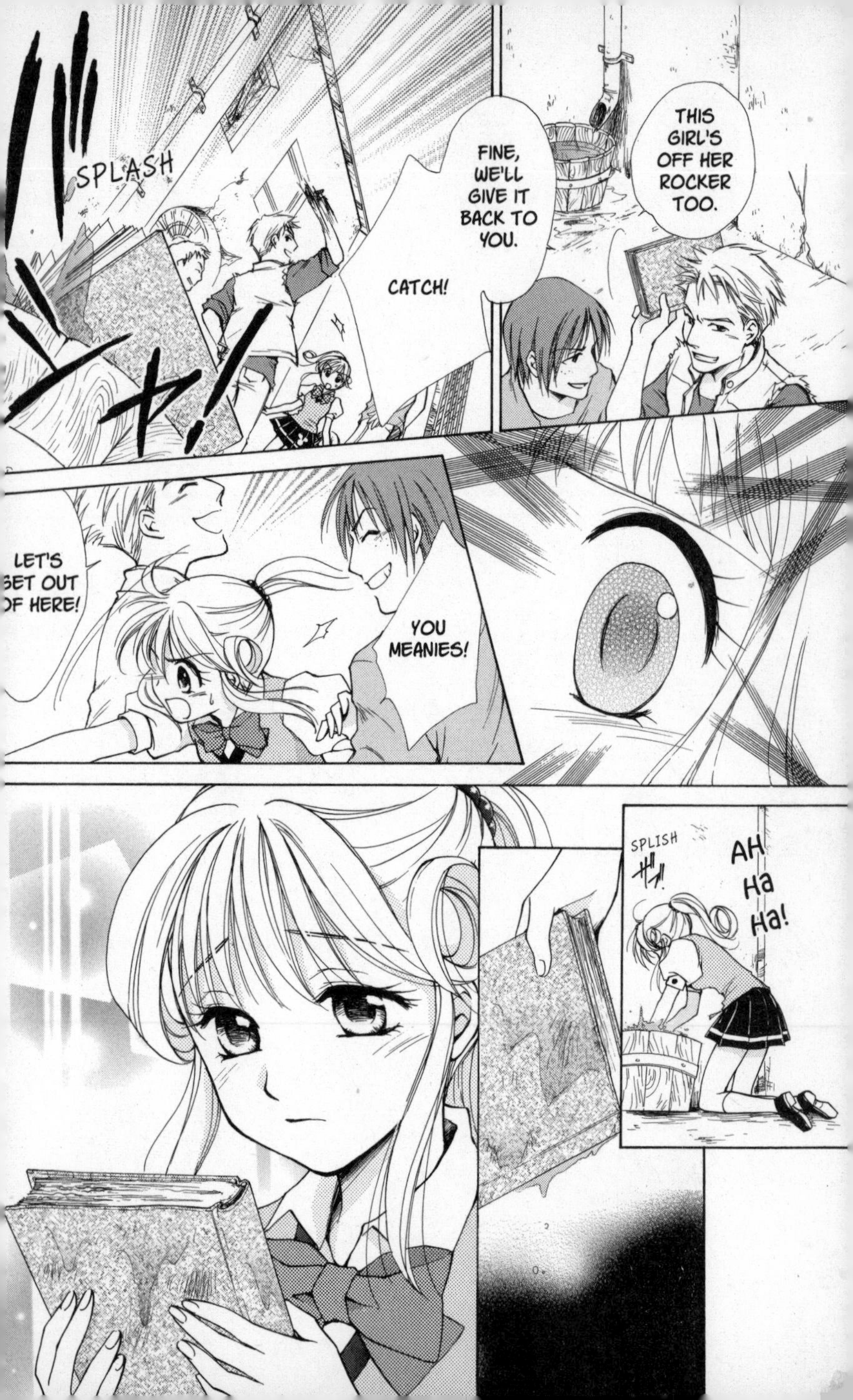
THIS GIRL'S OFF HER ROCKER TOO.
FINE, WE'LL GIVE IT BACK TO YOU.
CATCH!
SPLASH
YOU MEANIES!
LET'S GET OUT OF HERE!
SPLISH
AH Ha Ha!

READ THIS WAY

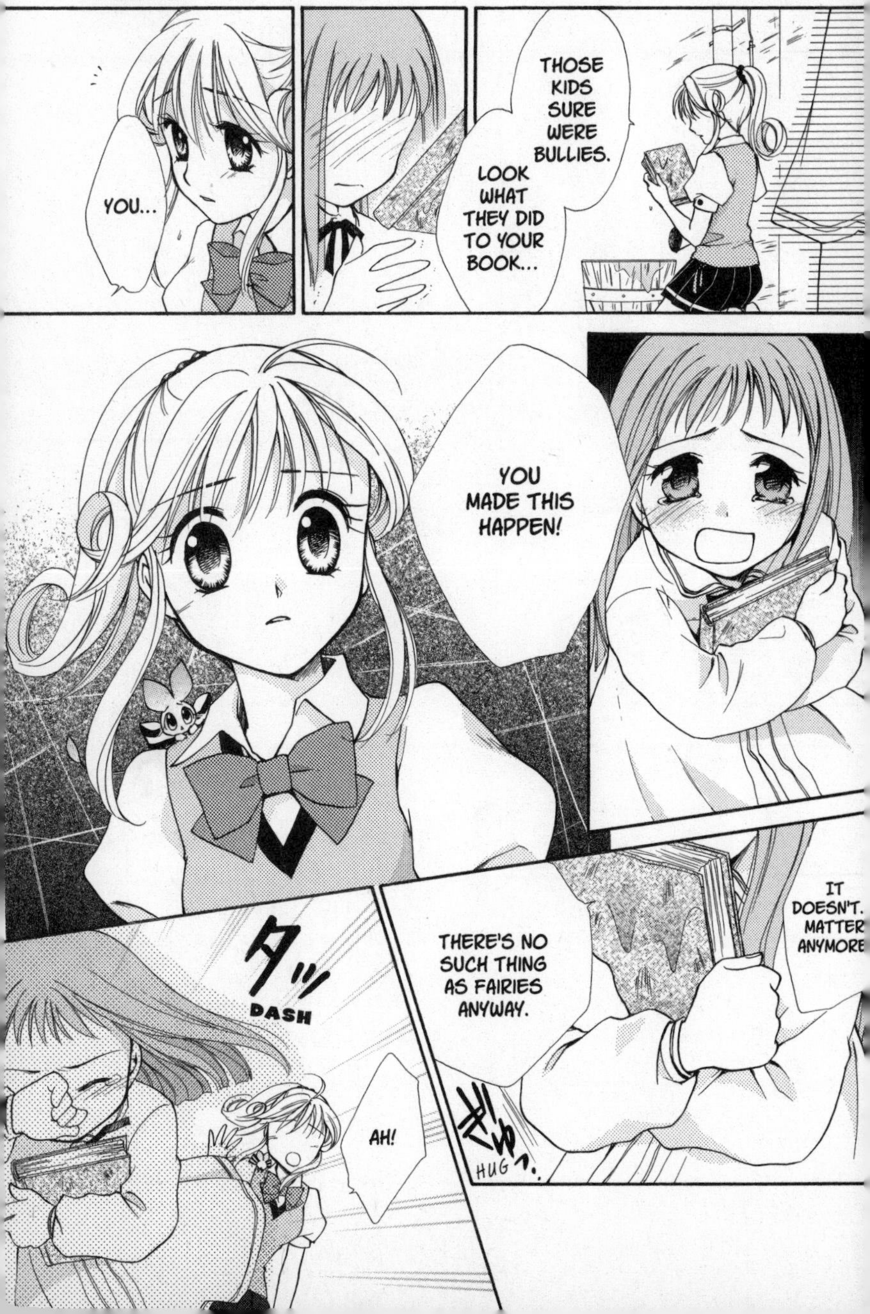
THOSE KIDS SURE WERE BULLIES.
LOOK WHAT THEY DID TO YOUR BOOK...
YOU...
YOU MADE THIS HAPPEN!
IT DOESN'T. MATTER ANYMORE
THERE'S NO SUCH THING AS FAIRIES ANYWAY.
HUG
DASH
AH!

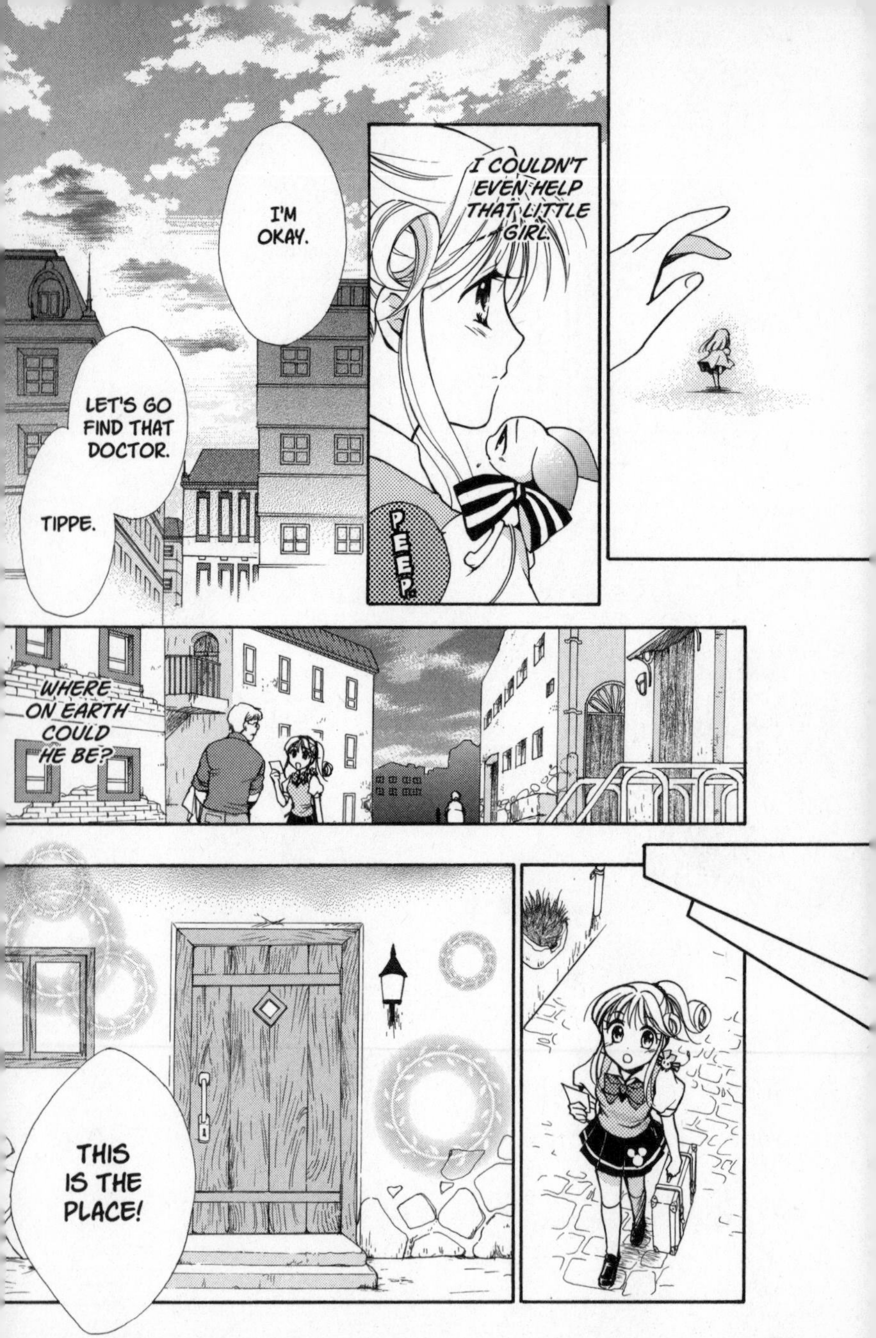
I COULDN'T EVEN HELP THAT LITTLE GIRL.
PEEP
I'M OKAY.
LET'S GO FIND THAT DOCTOR.
TIPPE.
WHERE ON EARTH COULD HE BE?
THIS IS THE PLACE!

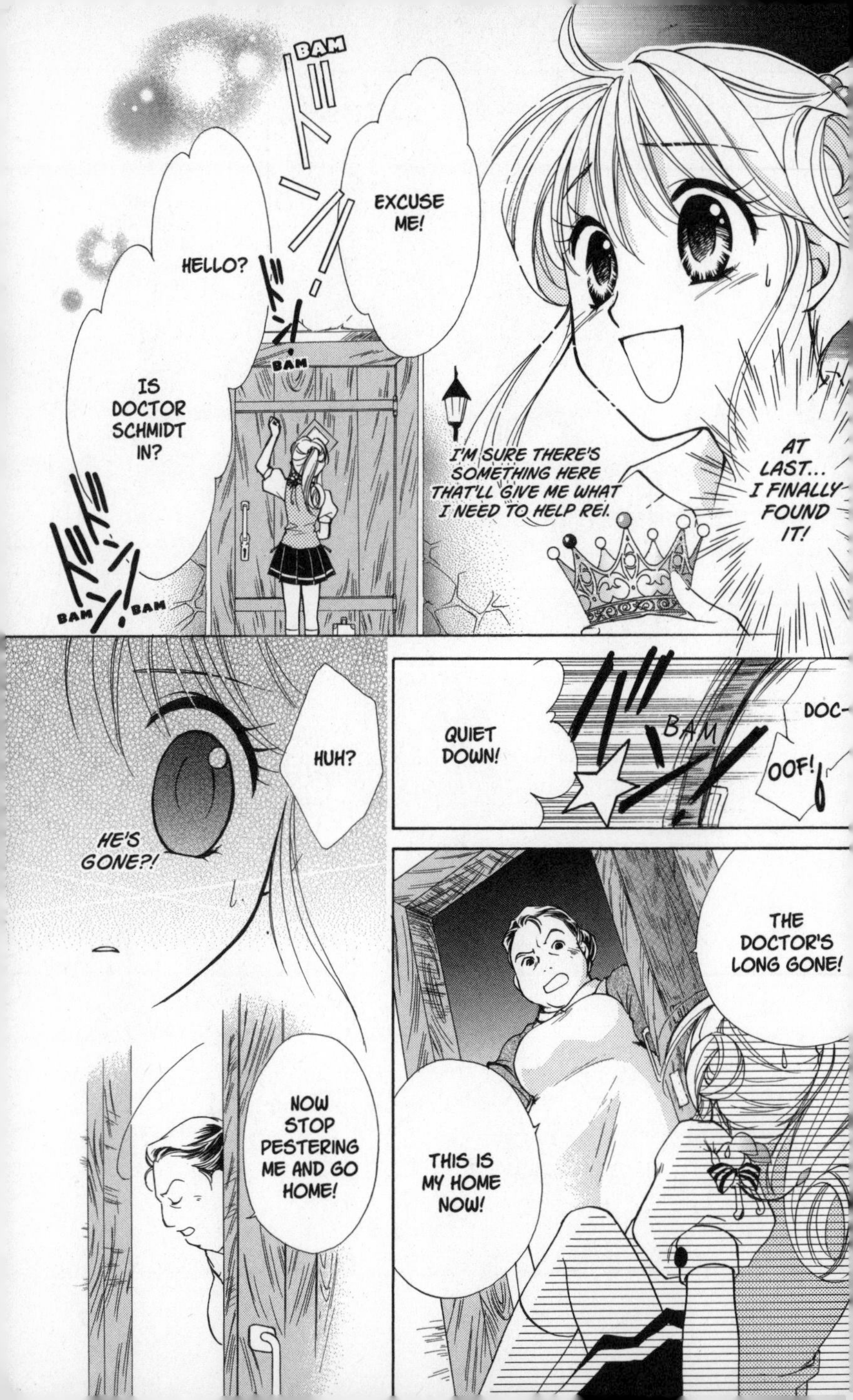
AT LAST... I FINALLY FOUND IT!
I'M SURE THERE'S SOMETHING HERE THAT'LL GIVE ME WHAT I NEED TO HELP REI.
EXCUSE ME!
BAM
HELLO?
BAM
IS DOCTOR SCHMIDT IN?
BAM
BAM
DOC-
OOF!
BAM
QUIET DOWN!
THE DOCTOR'S LONG GONE!
THIS IS MY HOME NOW!
HUH?
HE'S GONE?!
NOW STOP PESTERING ME AND GO HOME!

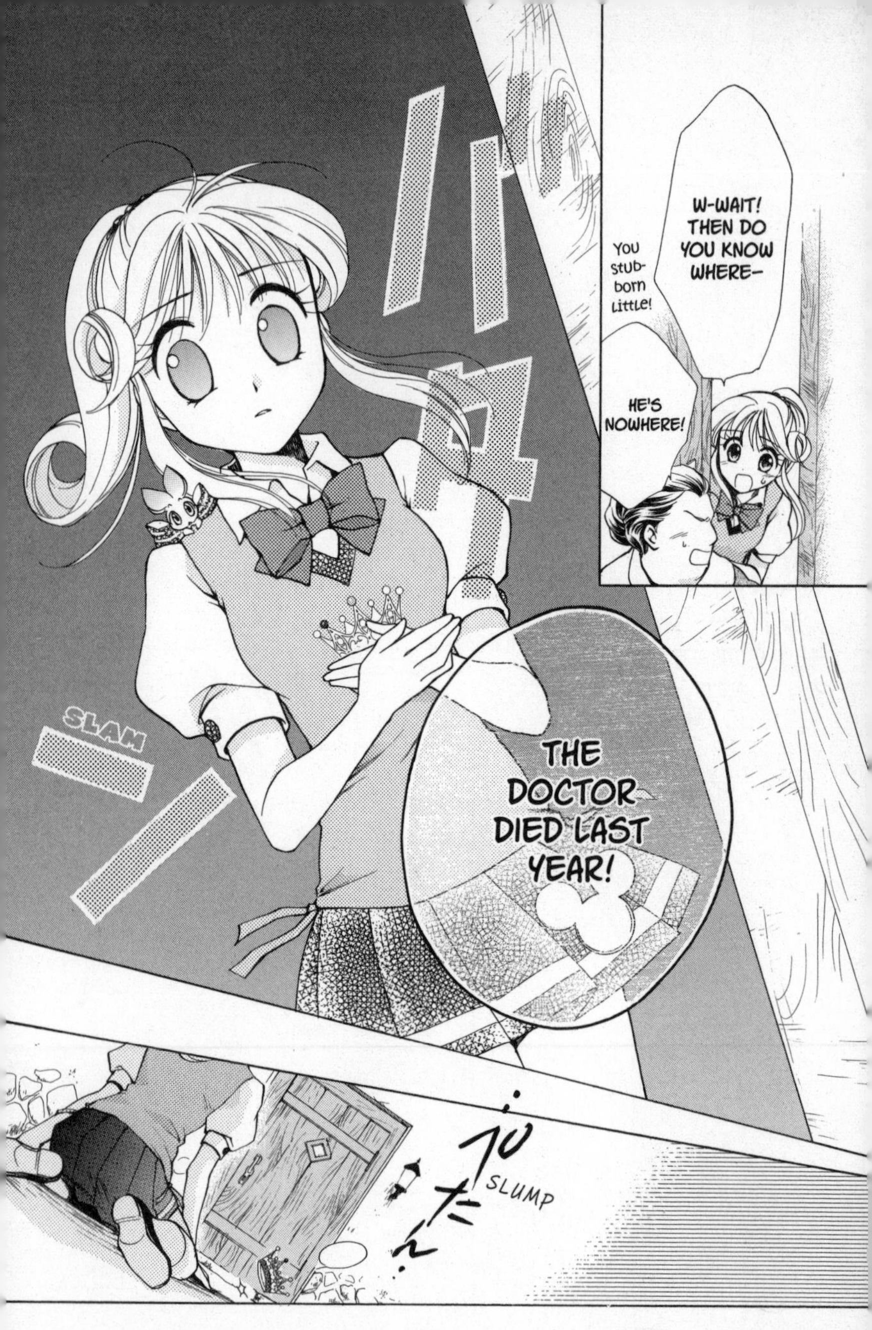
W-WAIT! THEN DO YOU KNOW WHERE-
You stub-born little!
HE'S NOWHERE!
THE DOCTOR DIED LAST YEAR!
SLAM
SLUMP

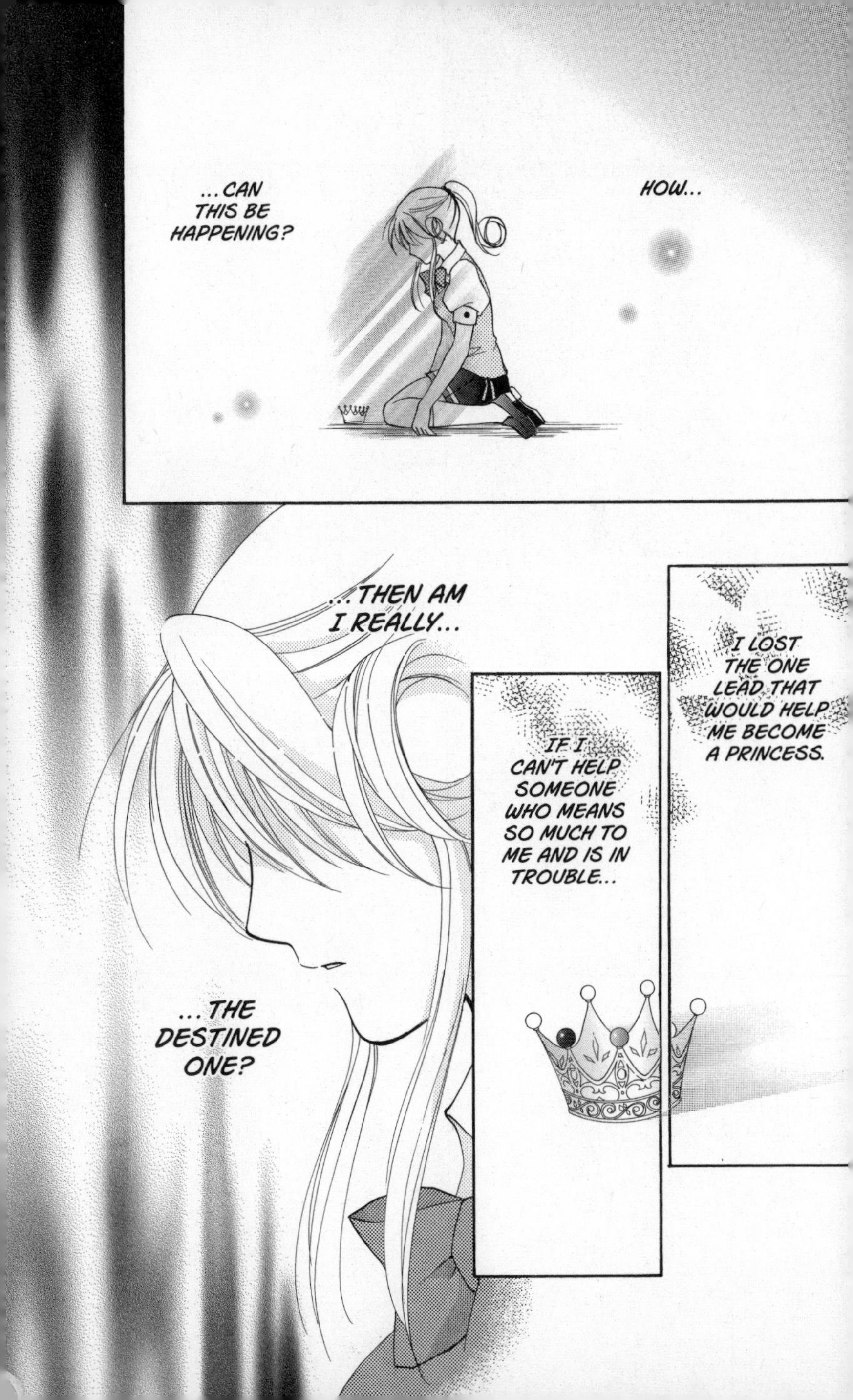
HOW...
...CAN THIS BE HAPPENING?
I LOST THE ONE LEAD THAT WOULD HELP ME BECOME A PRINCESS.
IF I CAN'T HELP SOMEONE WHO MEANS SO MUCH TO ME AND IS IN TROUBLE...
...THEN AM I REALLY...
...THE DESTINED ONE?

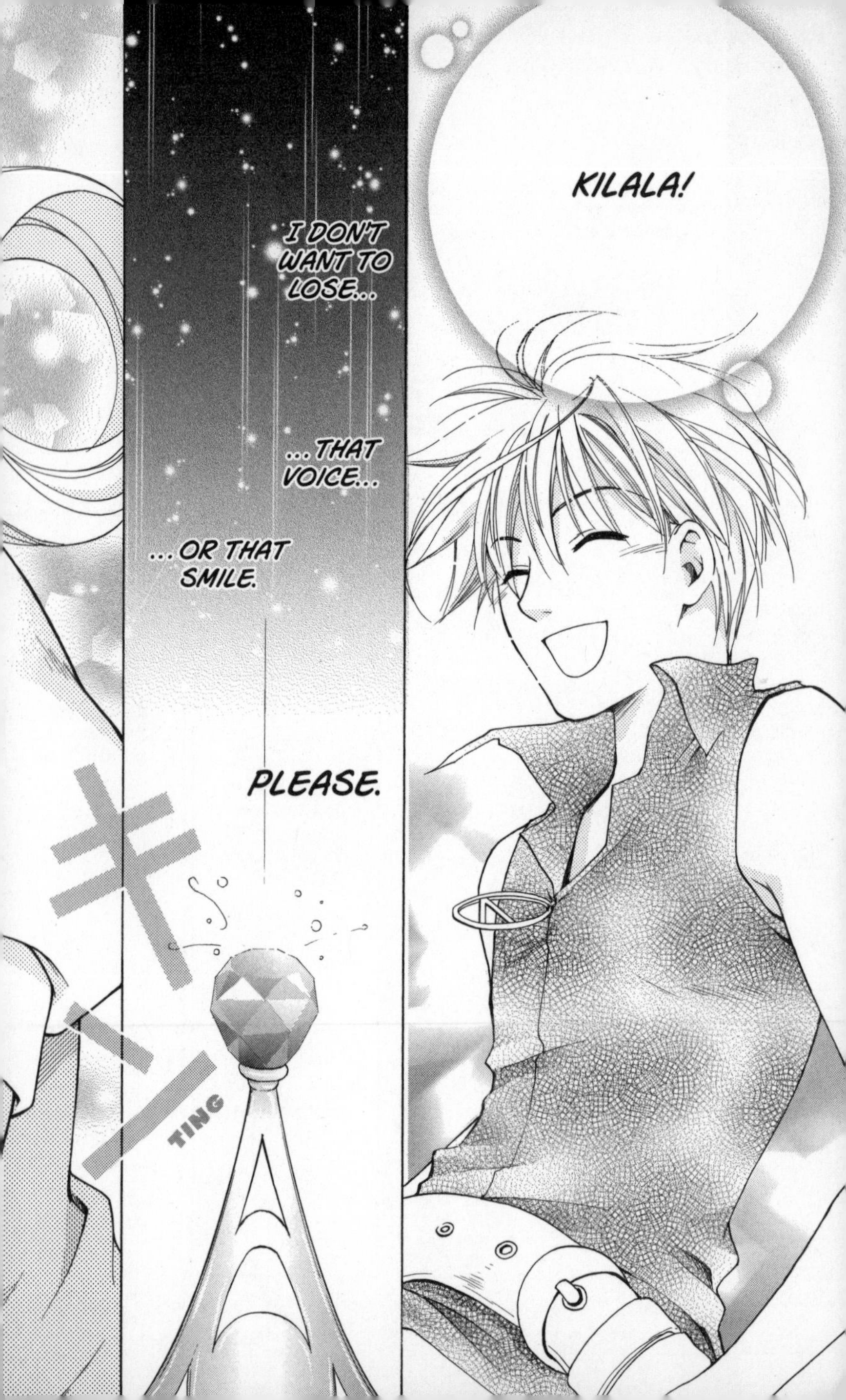
KILALA!
I DON'T WANT TO LOSE...
...THAT VOICE...
...OR THAT SMILE.
PLEASE.
TING

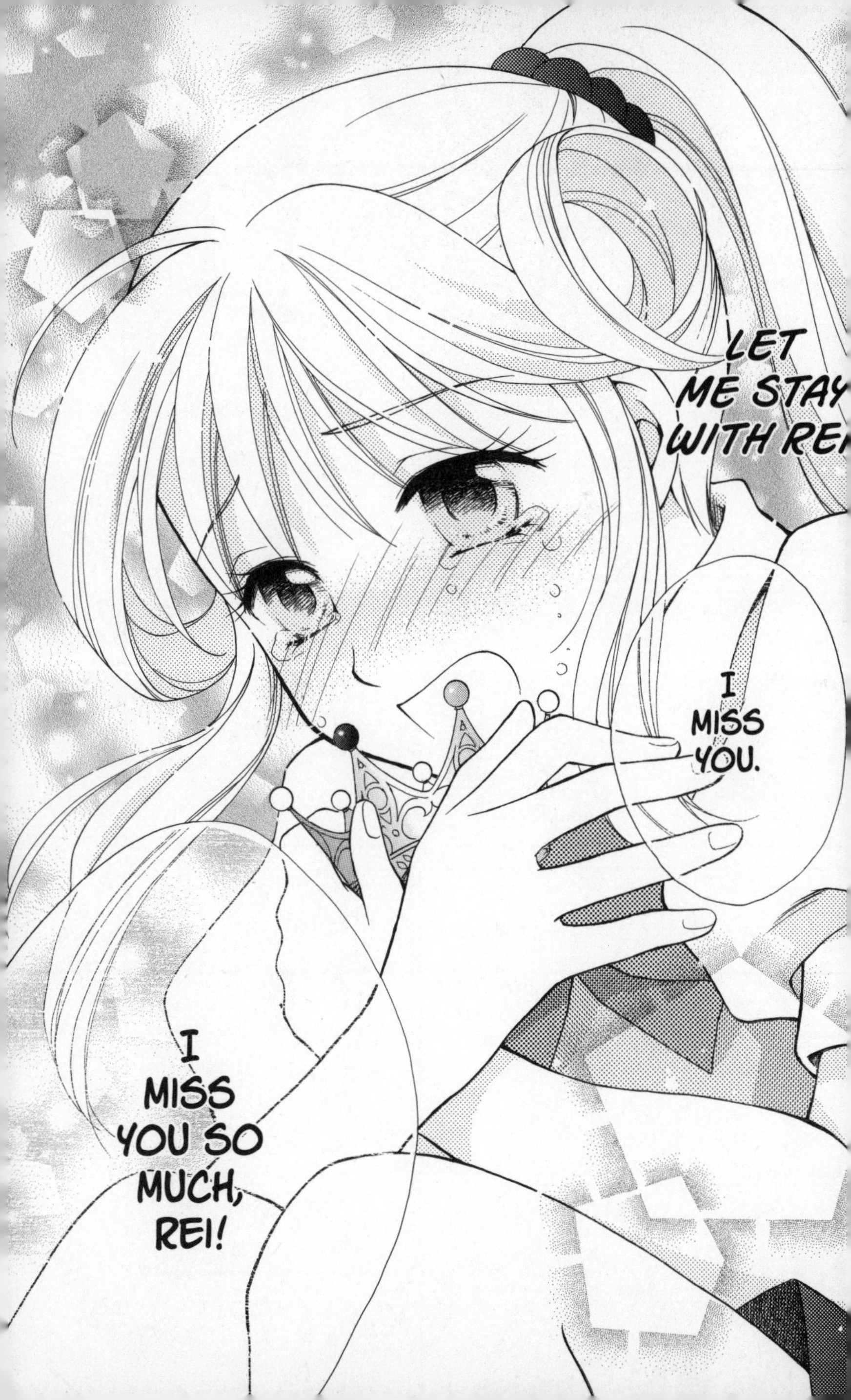
LET ME STAY WITH RE
I MISS YOU.
I MISS YOU SO MUCH, REI!

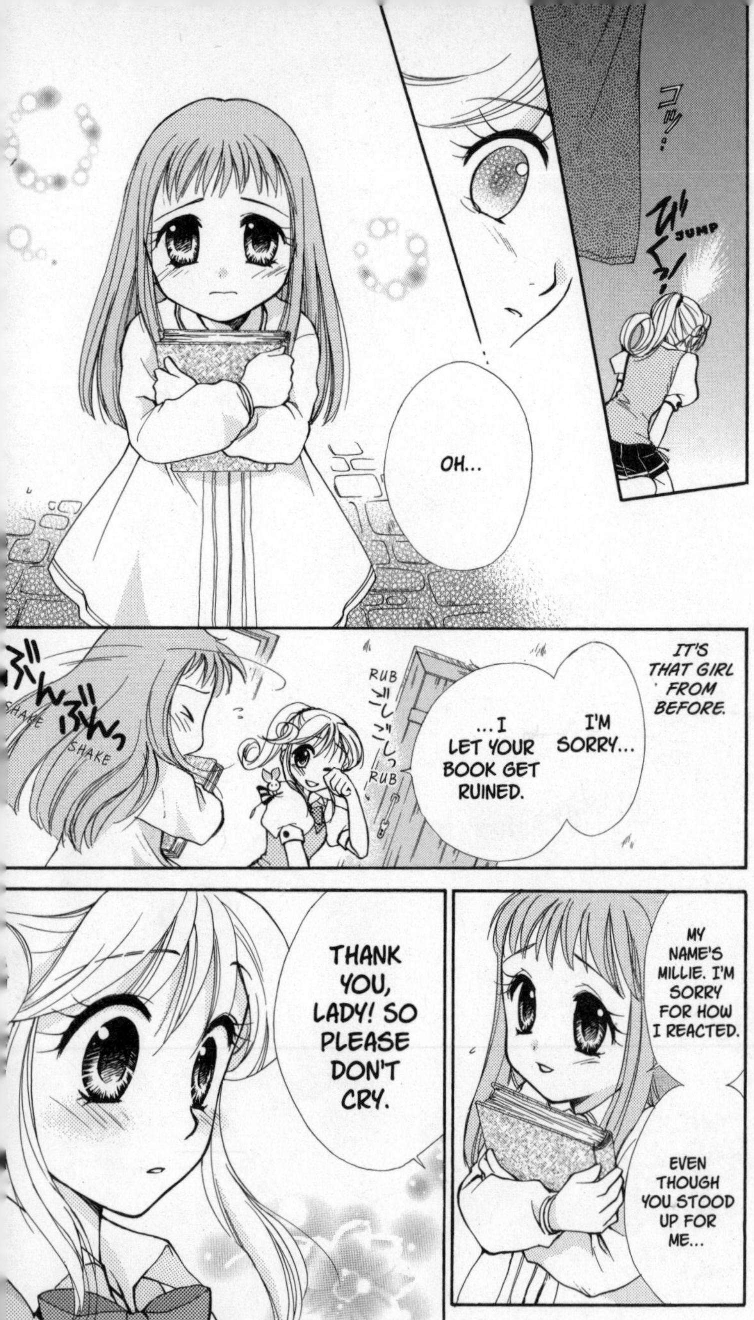
JUMP
OH...
IT'S THAT GIRL FROM BEFORE.
I'M SORRY...
...I LET YOUR BOOK GET RUINED.
RUB
RUB
SHAKE
SHAKE
MY NAME'S MILLIE. I'M SORRY FOR HOW I REACTED.
EVEN THOUGH YOU STOOD UP FOR ME...
THANK YOU, LADY! SO PLEASE DON'T CRY.

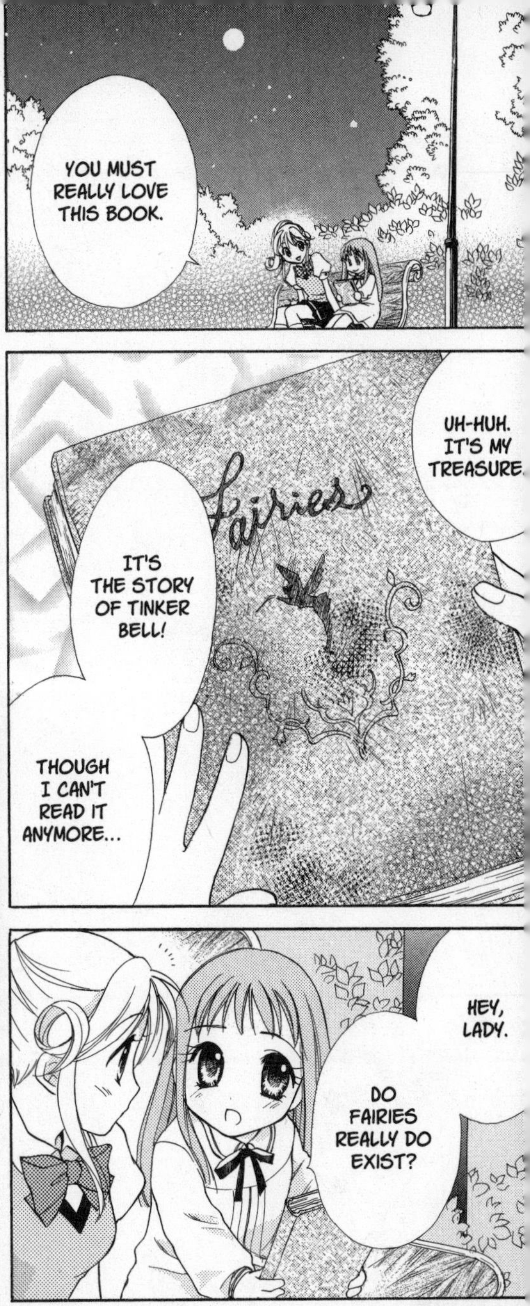
YOU MUST REALLY LOVE THIS BOOK.
UH-HUH. IT'S MY TREASURE.
Fairies
IT'S THE STORY OF TINKER BELL!
THOUGH I CAN'T READ IT ANYMORE...
HEY, LADY.
DO FAIRIES REALLY DO EXIST?

TIPPE HELPS OUT

1

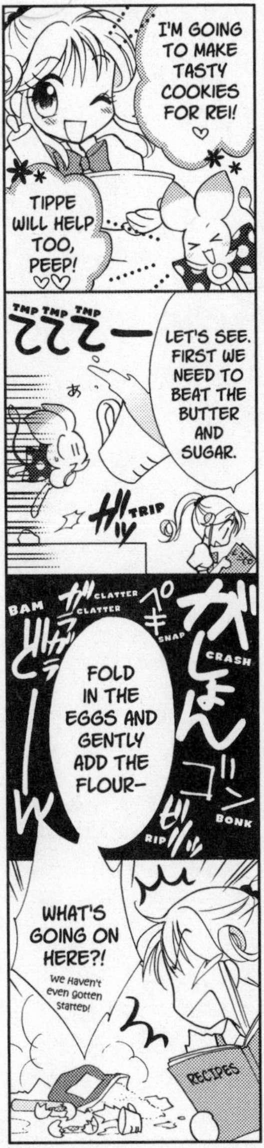
I'M GOING TO MAKE TASTY COOKIES FOR REI! ♡
TIPPE WILL HELP TOO, PEEP! ♡♡
TMP TMP TMP
てててー
LET'S SEE. FIRST WE NEED TO BEAT THE BUTTER AND SUGAR.
あ
TRIP
BAM
CLATTER CLATTER
SNAP
CRASH
FOLD IN THE EGGS AND GENTLY ADD THE FLOUR–
BONK
RIP
WHAT'S GOING ON HERE?!
We Haven't even gotten Started!
RECIPES

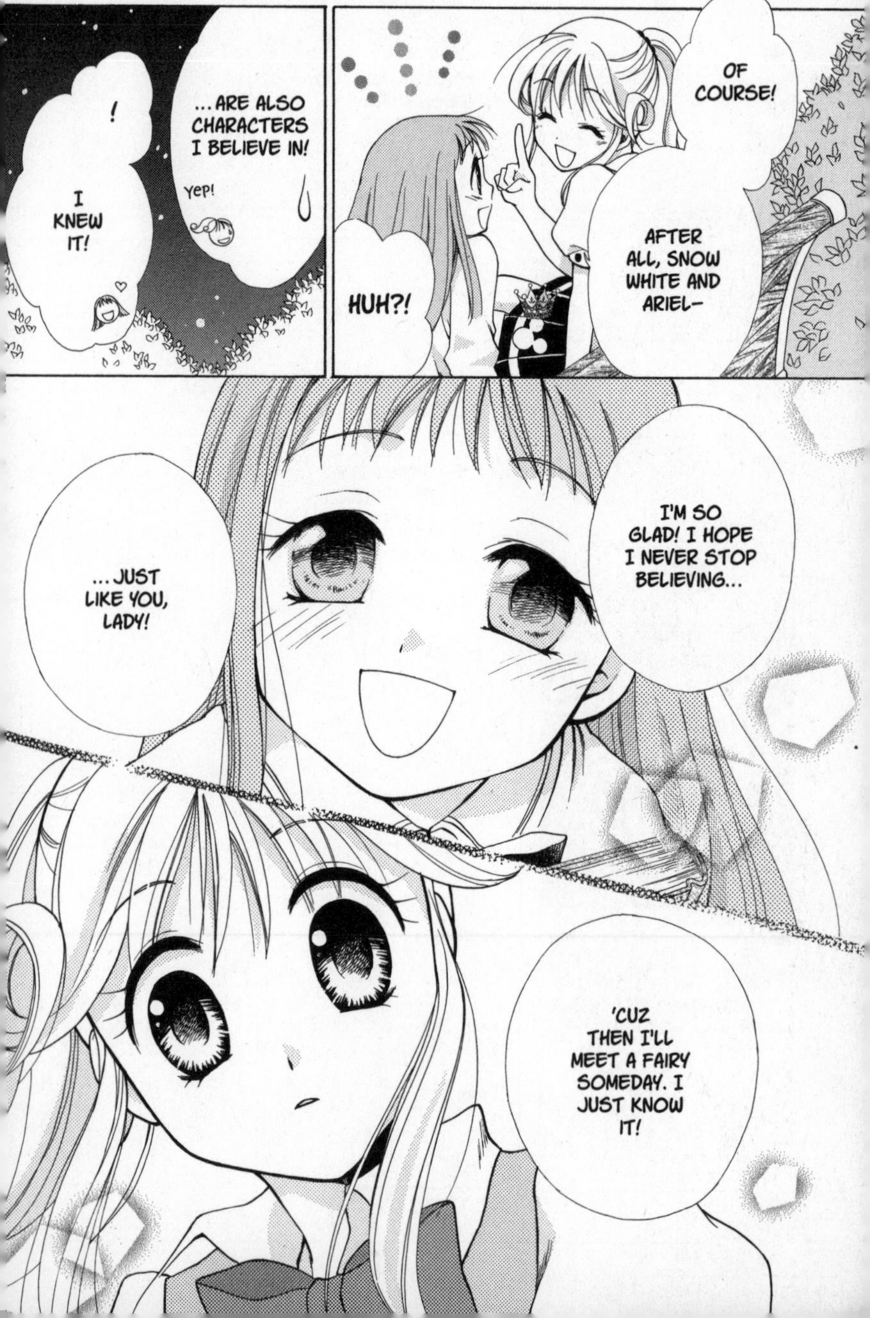
OF COURSE!
AFTER ALL, SNOW WHITE AND ARIEL–
HUH?!
...ARE ALSO CHARACTERS I BELIEVE IN!
Yep!
!
I KNEW IT!
I'M SO GLAD! I HOPE I NEVER STOP BELIEVING...
...JUST LIKE YOU, LADY!
'CUZ THEN I'LL MEET A FAIRY SOMEDAY. I JUST KNOW IT!

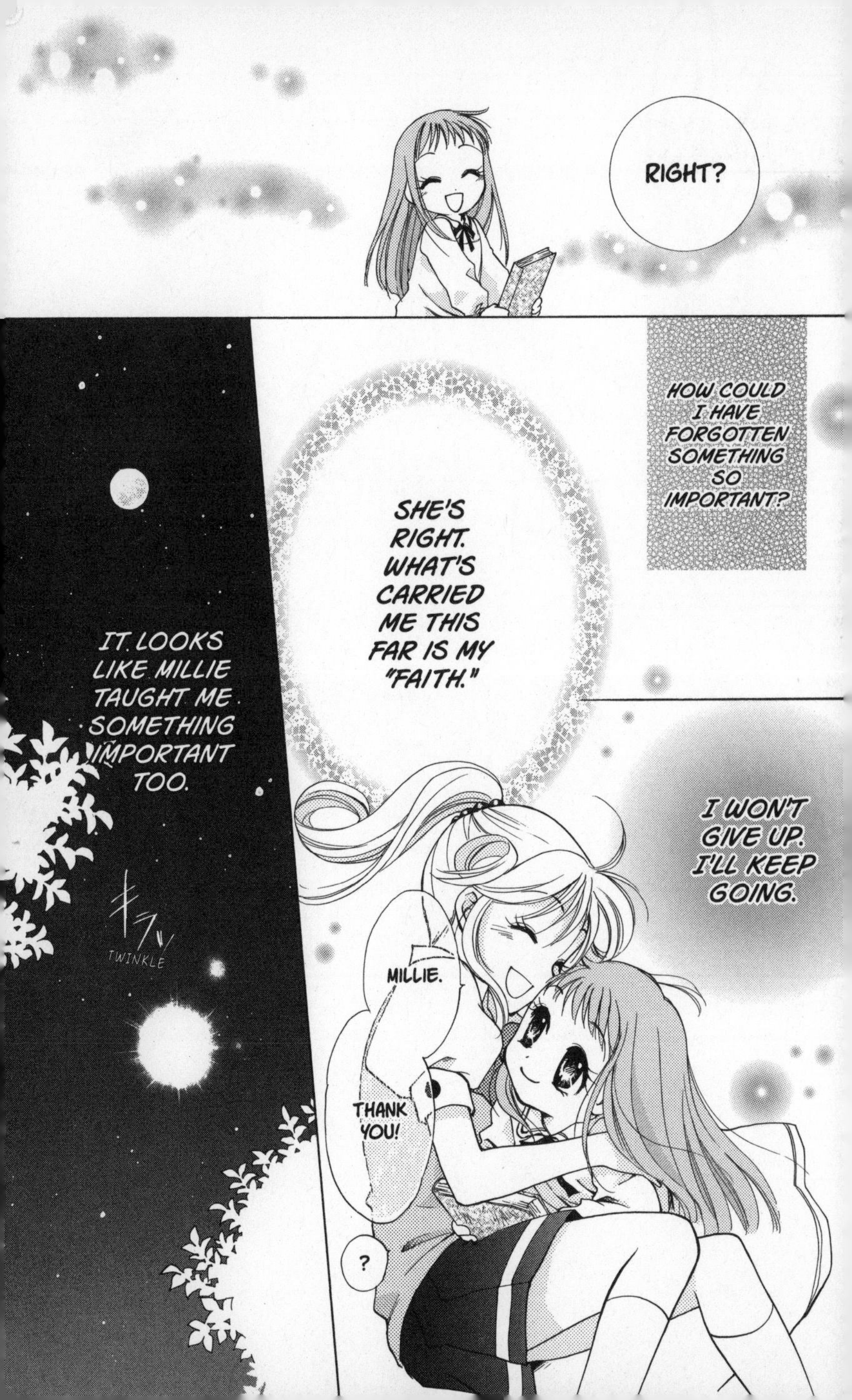
RIGHT?
HOW COULD I HAVE FORGOTTEN SOMETHING SO IMPORTANT?
SHE'S RIGHT. WHAT'S CARRIED ME THIS FAR IS MY "FAITH."
I WON'T GIVE UP. I'LL KEEP GOING.
MILLIE.
THANK YOU!
?
IT LOOKS LIKE MILLIE TAUGHT ME SOMETHING IMPORTANT TOO.
キラッ
TWINKLE

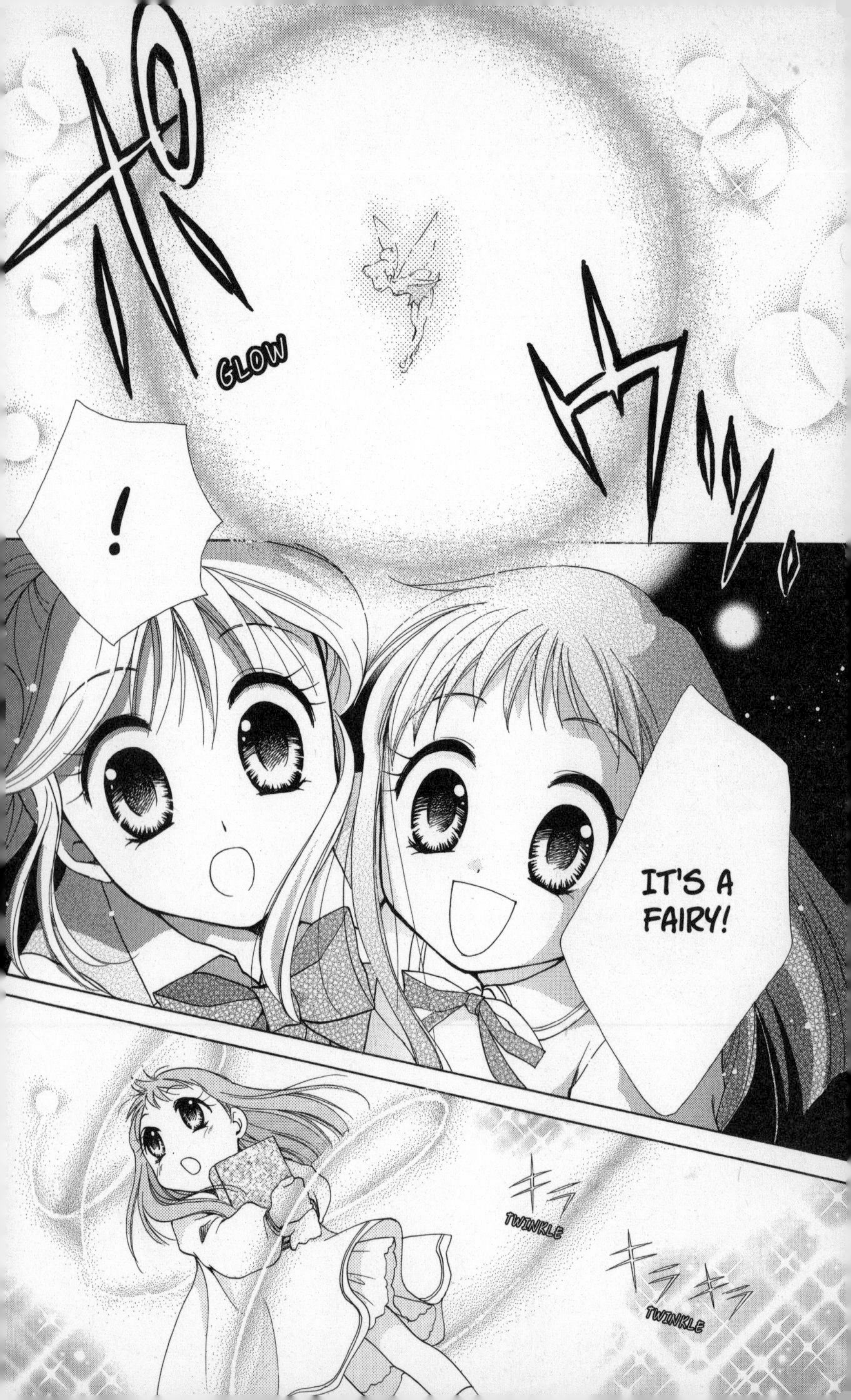
GLOW
!
IT'S A FAIRY!
TWINKLE
TWINKLE

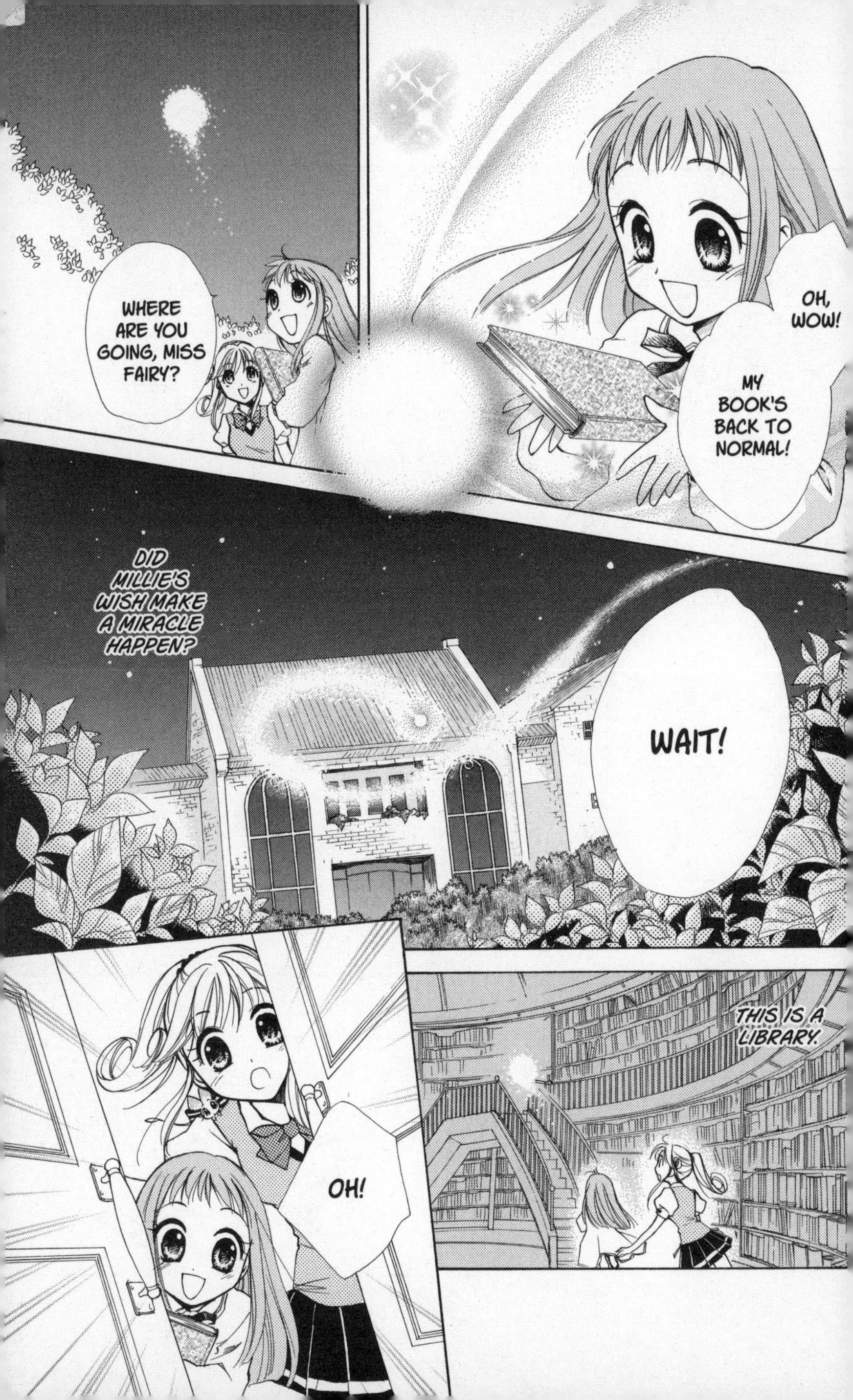
OH, WOW!
MY BOOK'S BACK TO NORMAL!
WHERE ARE YOU GOING, MISS FAIRY?
WAIT!
DID MILLIE'S WISH MAKE A MIRACLE HAPPEN?
THIS IS A LIBRARY.
OH!

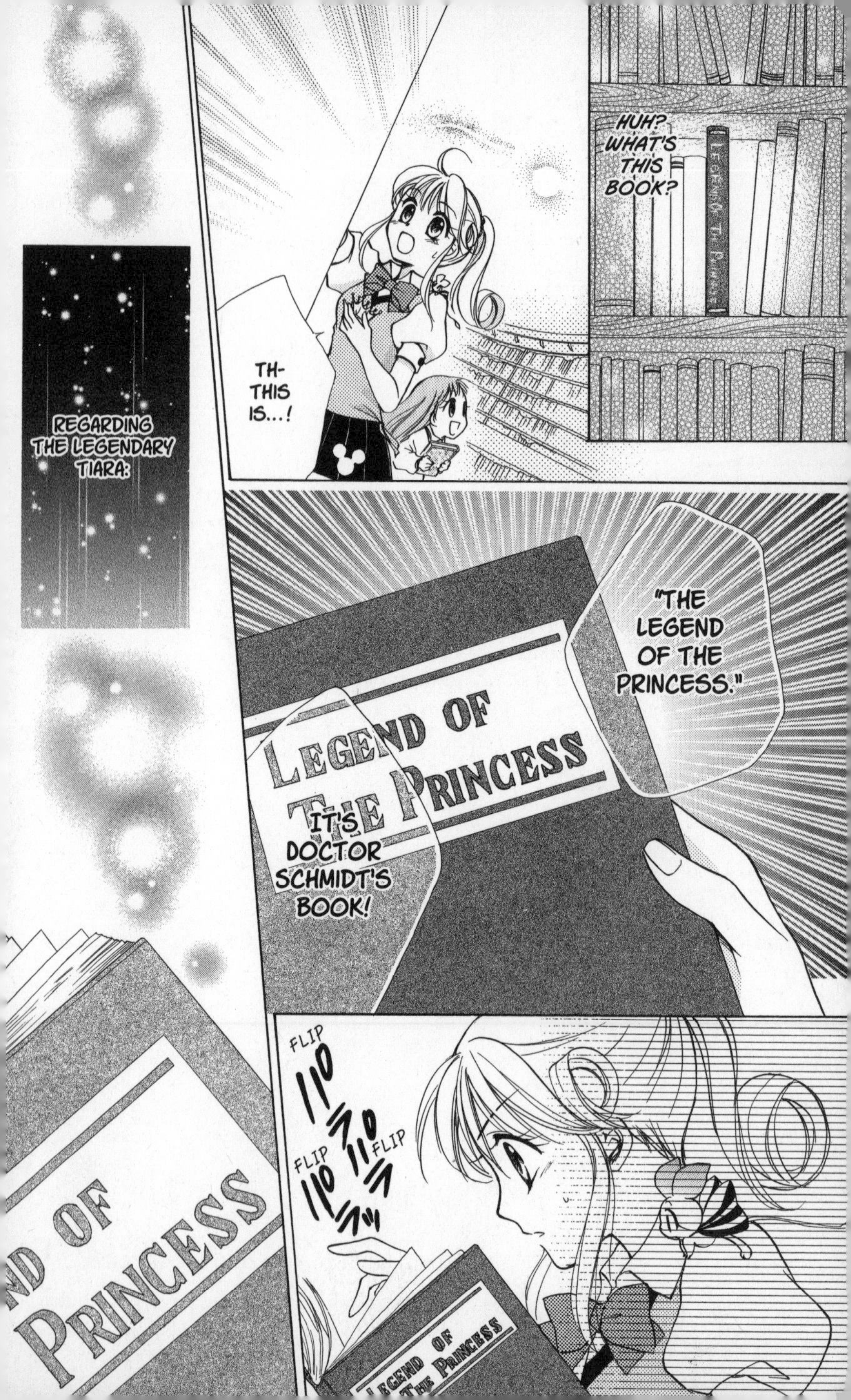
HUH? WHAT'S THIS BOOK?
TH-THIS IS...!
"THE LEGEND OF THE PRINCESS."
LEGEND OF THE PRINCESS
IT'S DOCTOR SCHMIDT'S BOOK!
FLIP
FLIP
FLIP
LEGEND OF THE PRINCESS
REGARDING THE LEGENDARY TIARA:

READ THIS WAY

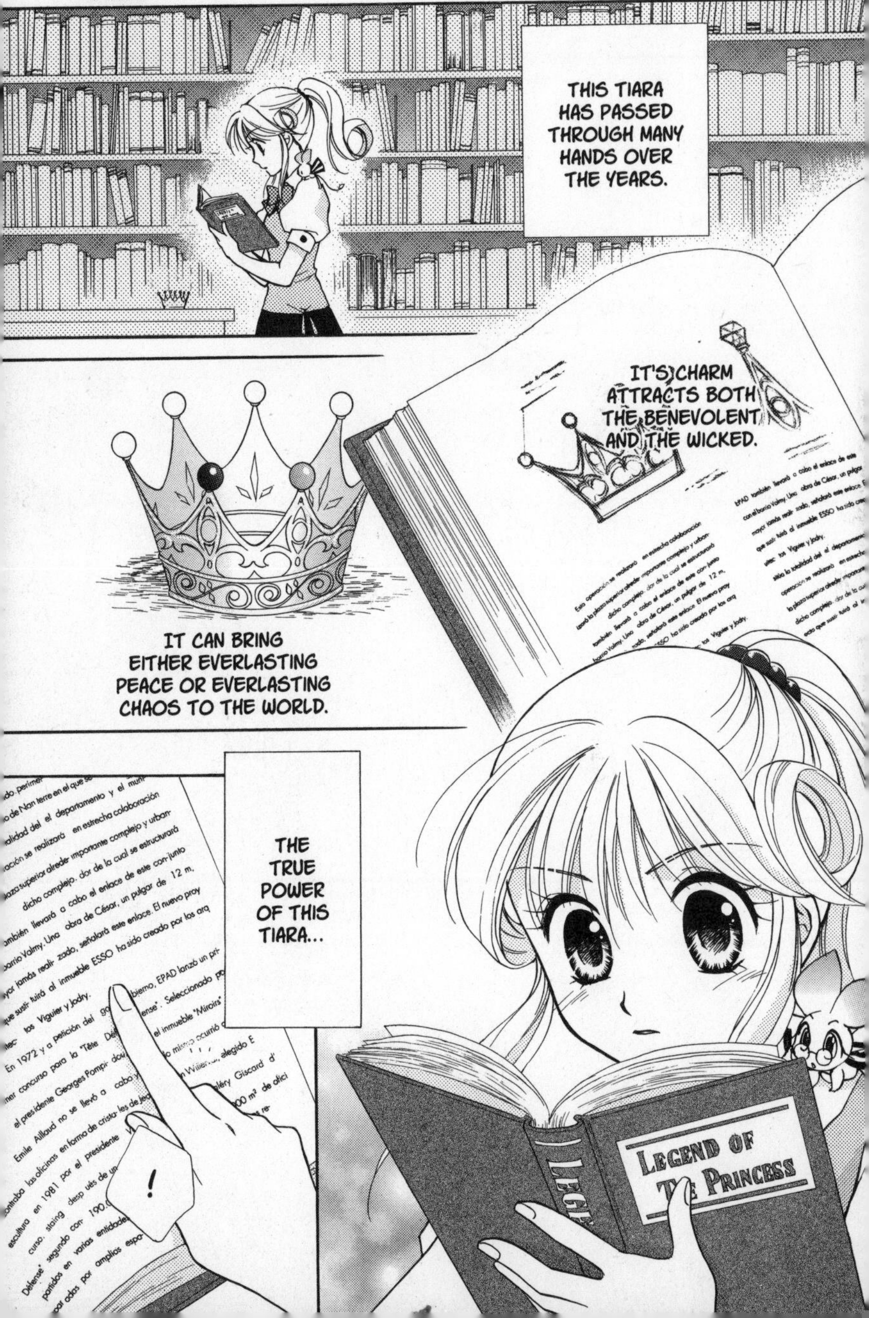
THIS TIARA HAS PASSED THROUGH MANY HANDS OVER THE YEARS.
IT'S CHARM ATTRACTS BOTH THE BENEVOLENT AND THE WICKED.
LEGEND OF THE PRINCESS
IT CAN BRING EITHER EVERLASTING PEACE OR EVERLASTING CHAOS TO THE WORLD.
THE TRUE POWER OF THIS TIARA...
!

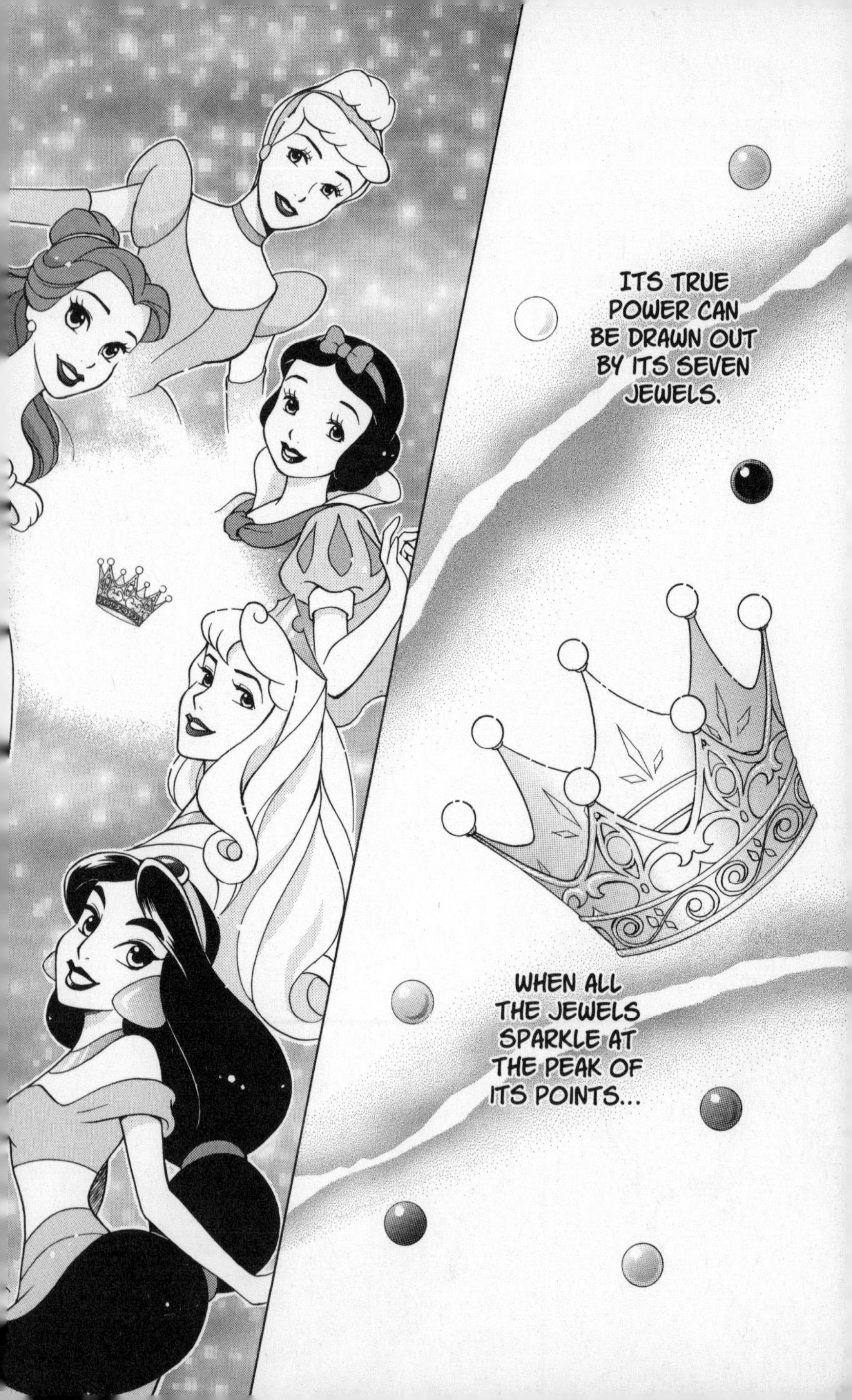
ITS TRUE POWER CAN BE DRAWN OUT BY ITS SEVEN JEWELS.
WHEN ALL THE JEWELS SPARKLE AT THE PEAK OF ITS POINTS...

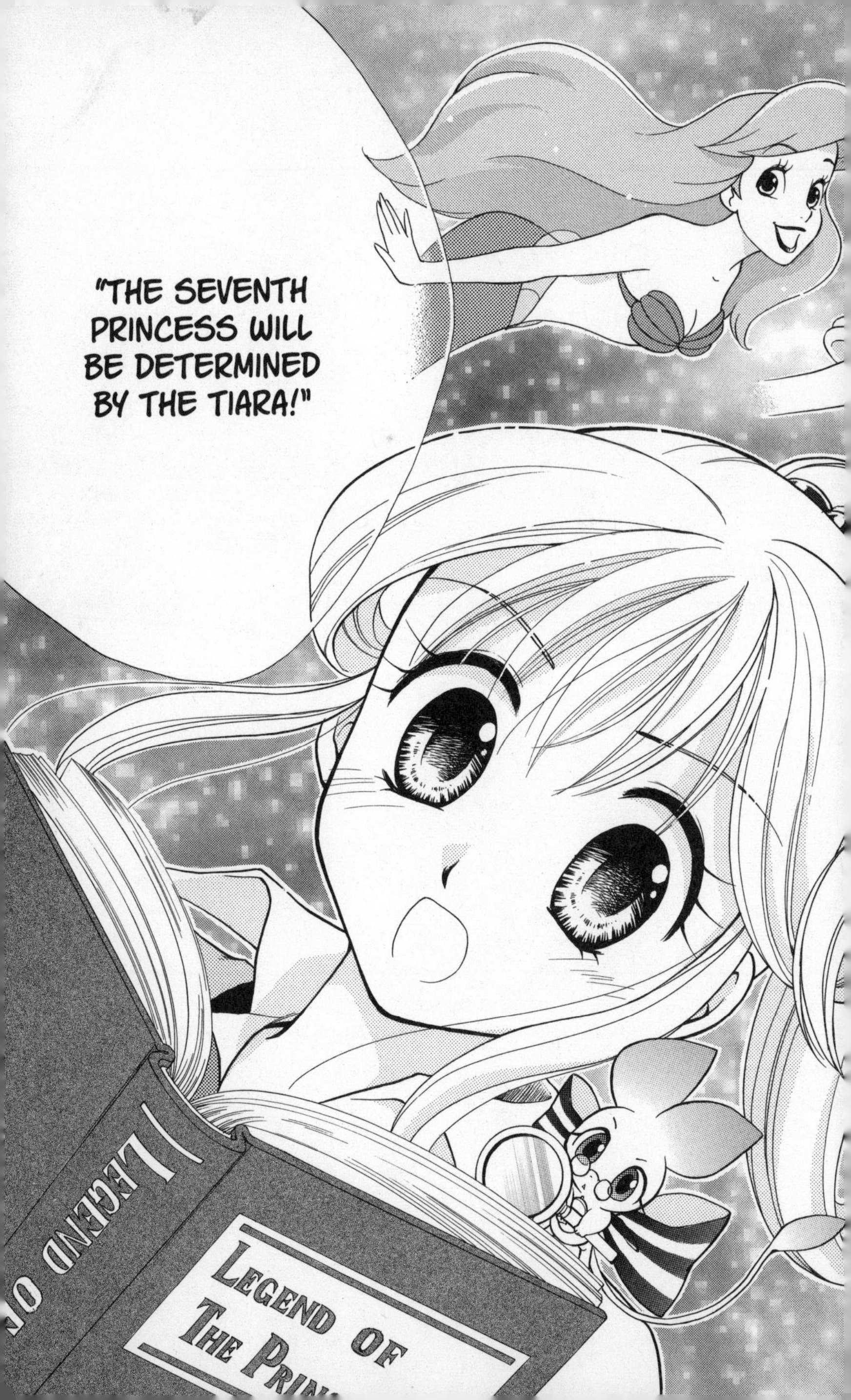
"THE SEVENTH PRINCESS WILL BE DETERMINED BY THE TIARA!"
LEGEND OF THE PRIN
LEGEND OF

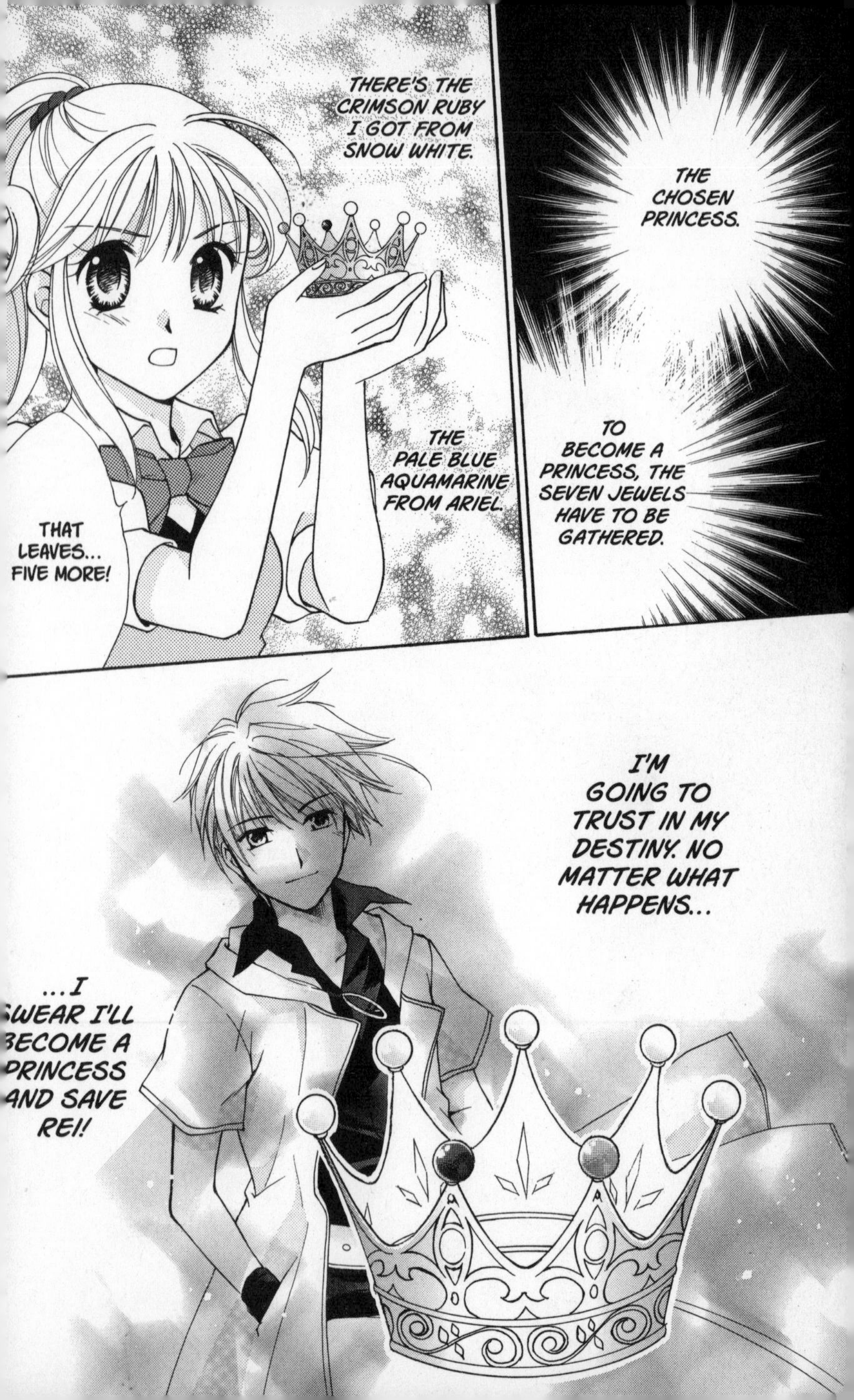

THE CHOSEN PRINCESS.
TO BECOME A PRINCESS, THE SEVEN JEWELS HAVE TO BE GATHERED.
THERE'S THE CRIMSON RUBY I GOT FROM SNOW WHITE.
THE PALE BLUE AQUAMARINE FROM ARIEL.
THAT LEAVES... FIVE MORE!
I'M GOING TO TRUST IN MY DESTINY. NO MATTER WHAT HAPPENS...
...I SWEAR I'LL BECOME A PRINCESS AND SAVE REI!

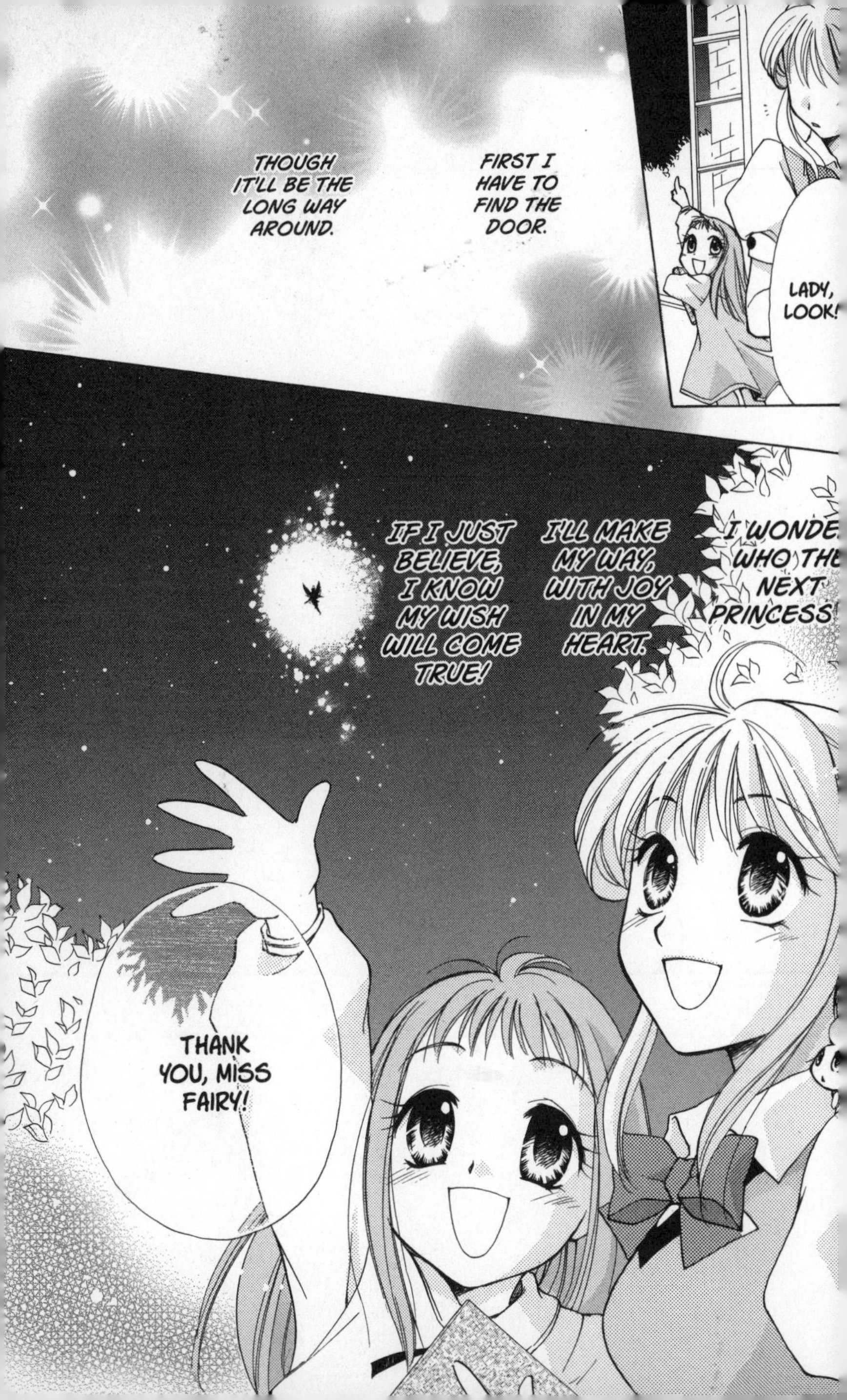
LADY, LOOK!
FIRST I HAVE TO FIND THE DOOR.
THOUGH IT'LL BE THE LONG WAY AROUND.
I WONDE WHO TH NEXT PRINCESS
I'LL MAKE MY WAY, WITH JOY IN MY HEART.
IF I JUST BELIEVE, I KNOW MY WISH WILL COME TRUE!
THANK YOU, MISS FAIRY!

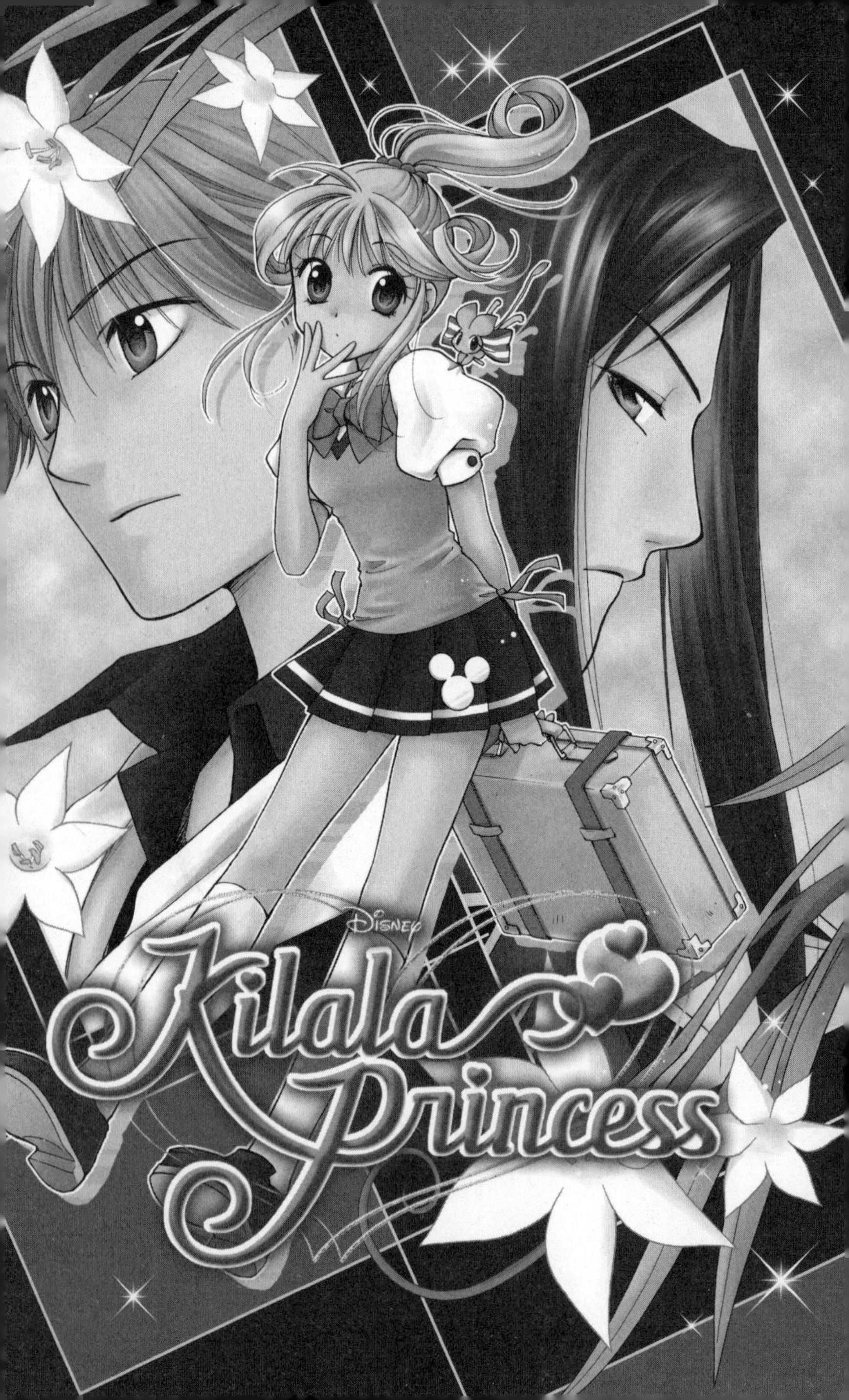
Disney
Kilala Princess

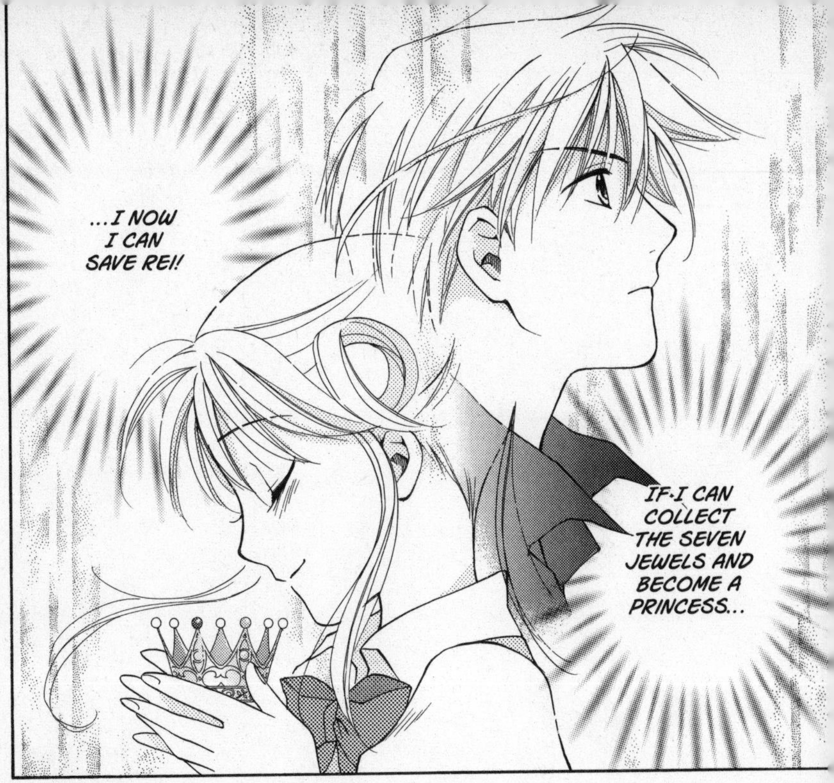
IF I CAN COLLECT THE SEVEN JEWELS AND BECOME A PRINCESS...
...I NOW I CAN SAVE REI!

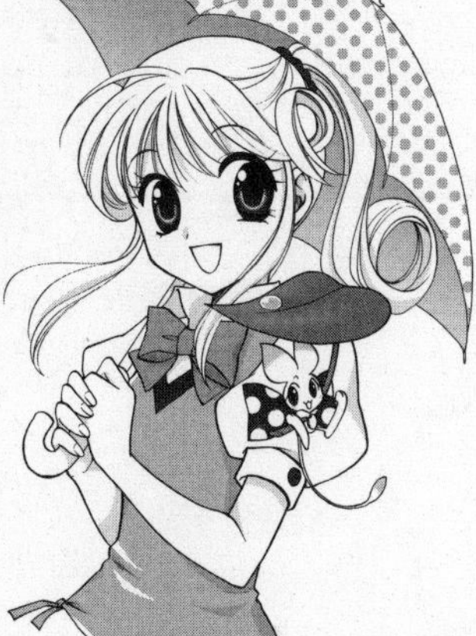

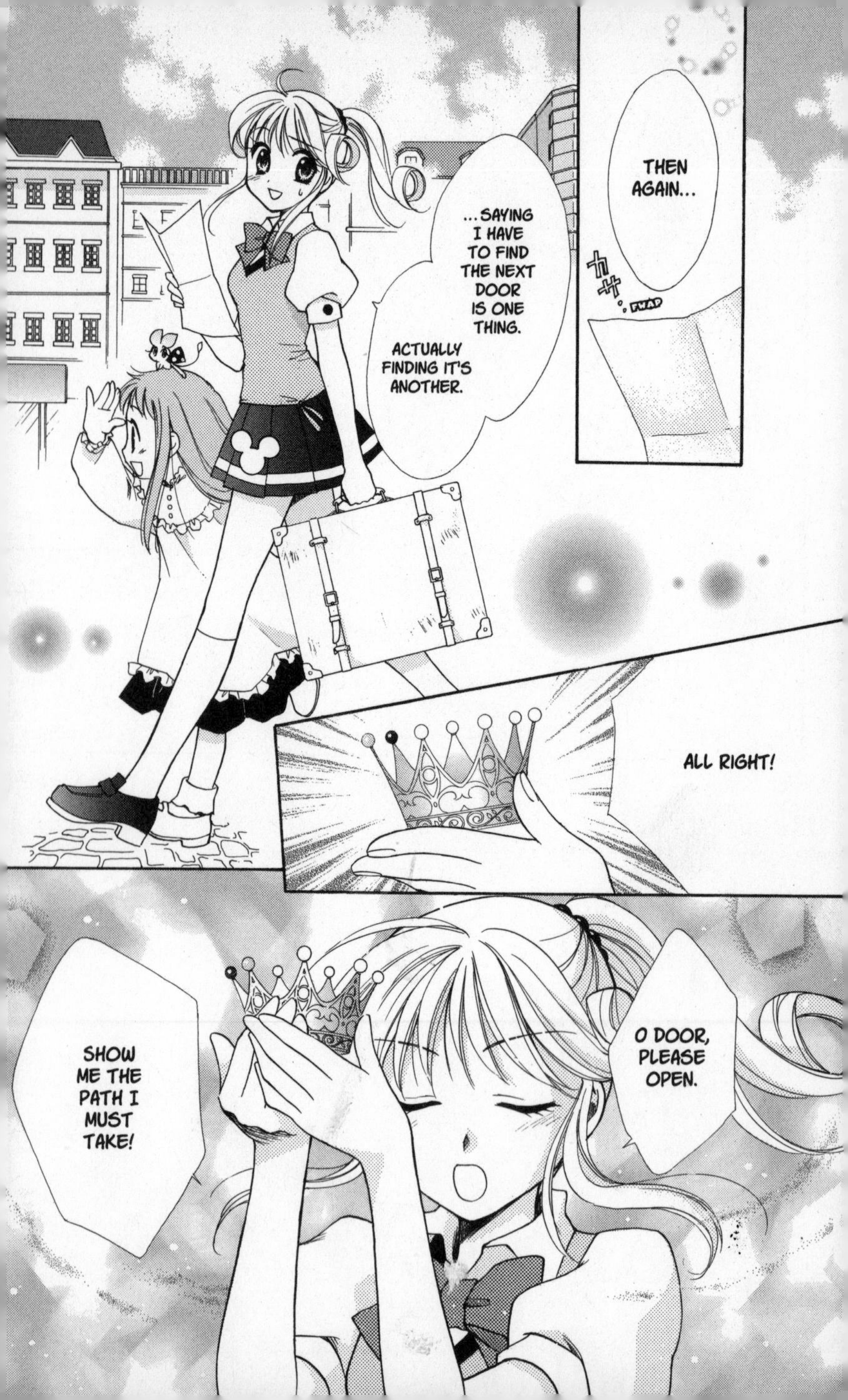
THEN AGAIN...
FWAP
...SAYING I HAVE TO FIND THE NEXT DOOR IS ONE THING.
ACTUALLY FINDING IT'S ANOTHER.
ALL RIGHT!
O DOOR, PLEASE OPEN.
SHOW ME THE PATH I MUST TAKE!

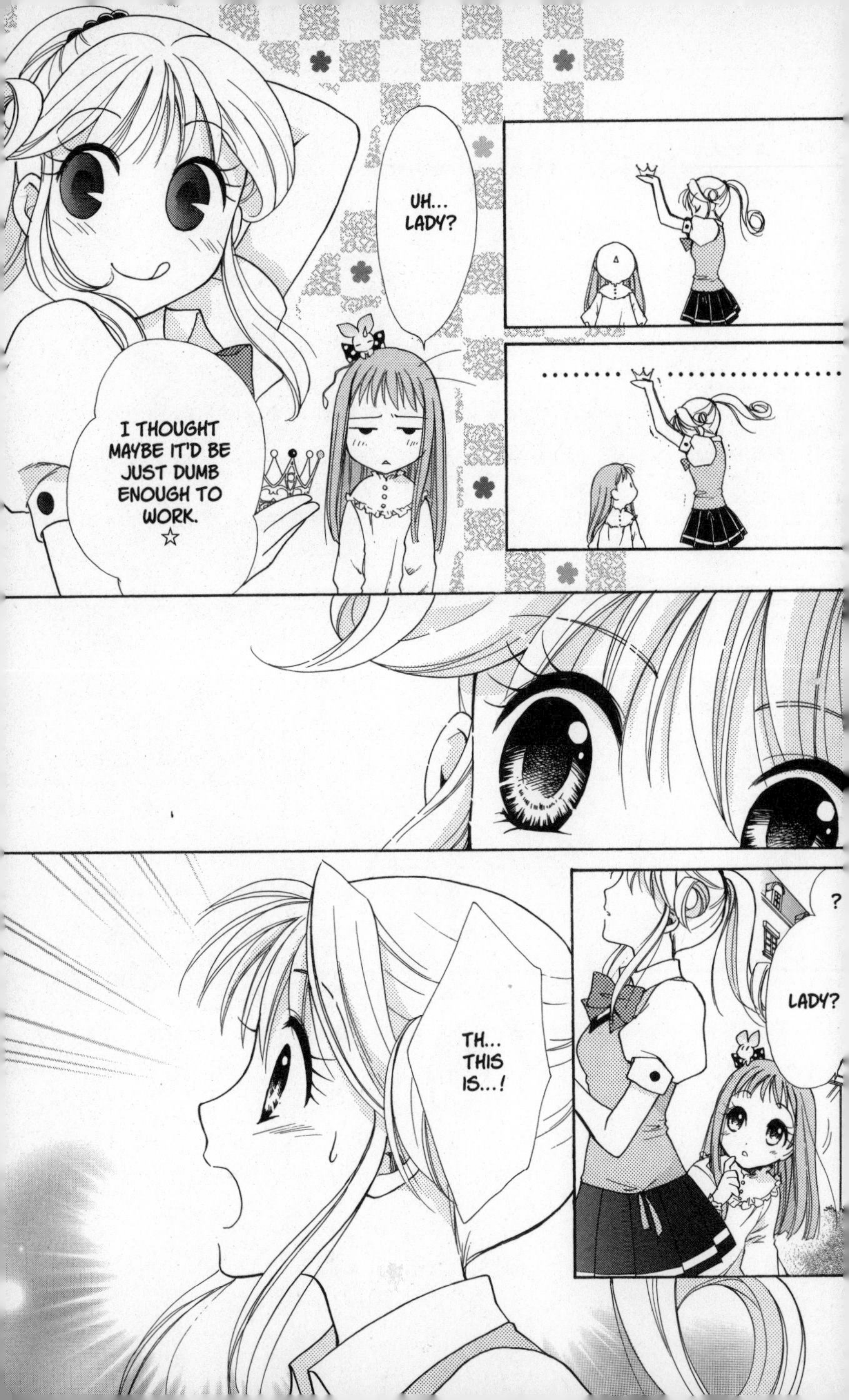

....
UH... LADY?
I THOUGHT MAYBE IT'D BE JUST DUMB ENOUGH TO WORK. ☆
? LADY?
TH... THIS IS...!

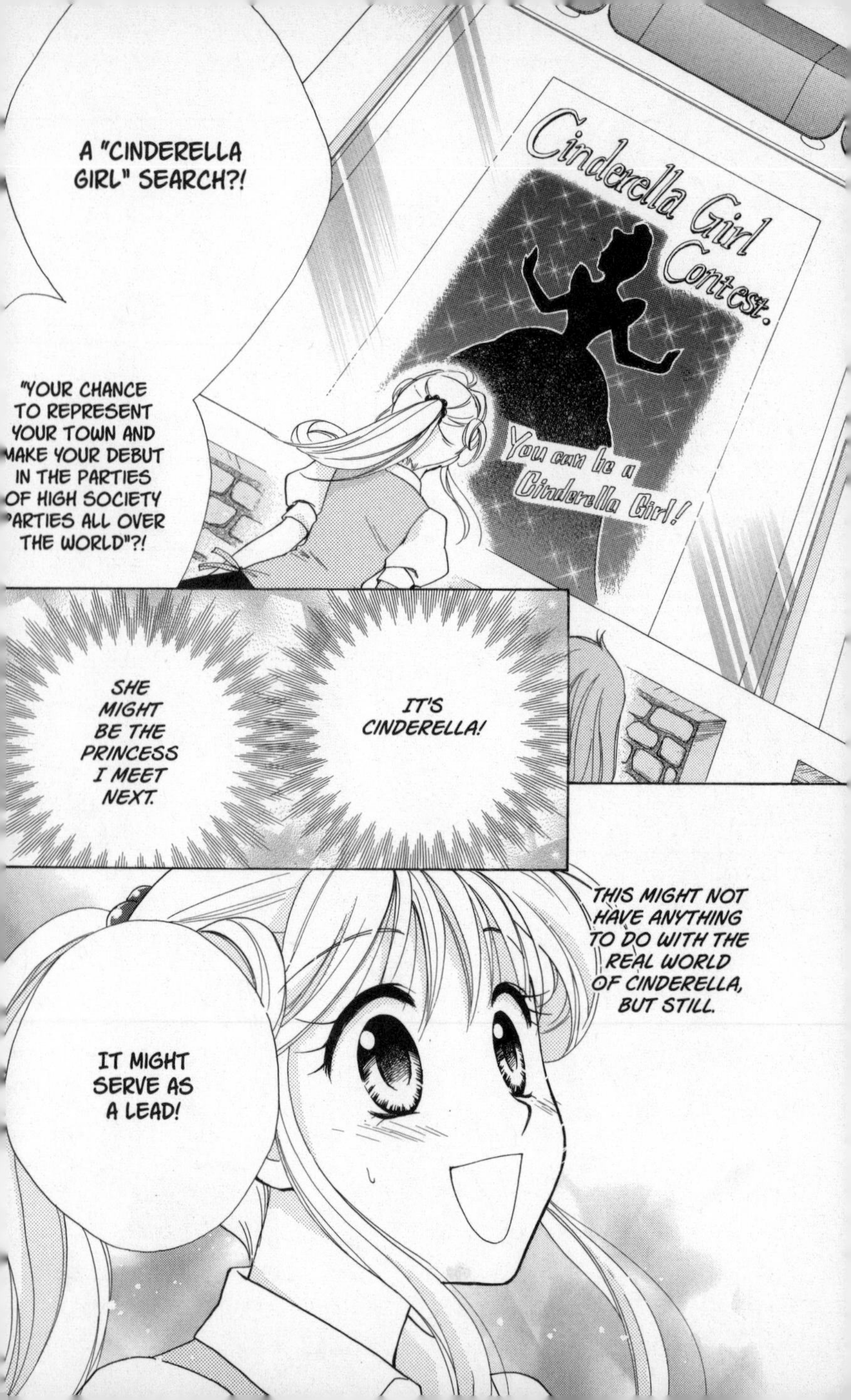

Cinderella Girl Contest.
You can be a Cinderella Girl!
A "CINDERELLA GIRL" SEARCH?!
"YOUR CHANCE TO REPRESENT YOUR TOWN AND MAKE YOUR DEBUT IN THE PARTIES OF HIGH SOCIETY PARTIES ALL OVER THE WORLD"?!
IT'S CINDERELLA!
SHE MIGHT BE THE PRINCESS I MEET NEXT.
THIS MIGHT NOT HAVE ANYTHING TO DO WITH THE REAL WORLD OF CINDERELLA, BUT STILL.
IT MIGHT SERVE AS A LEAD!

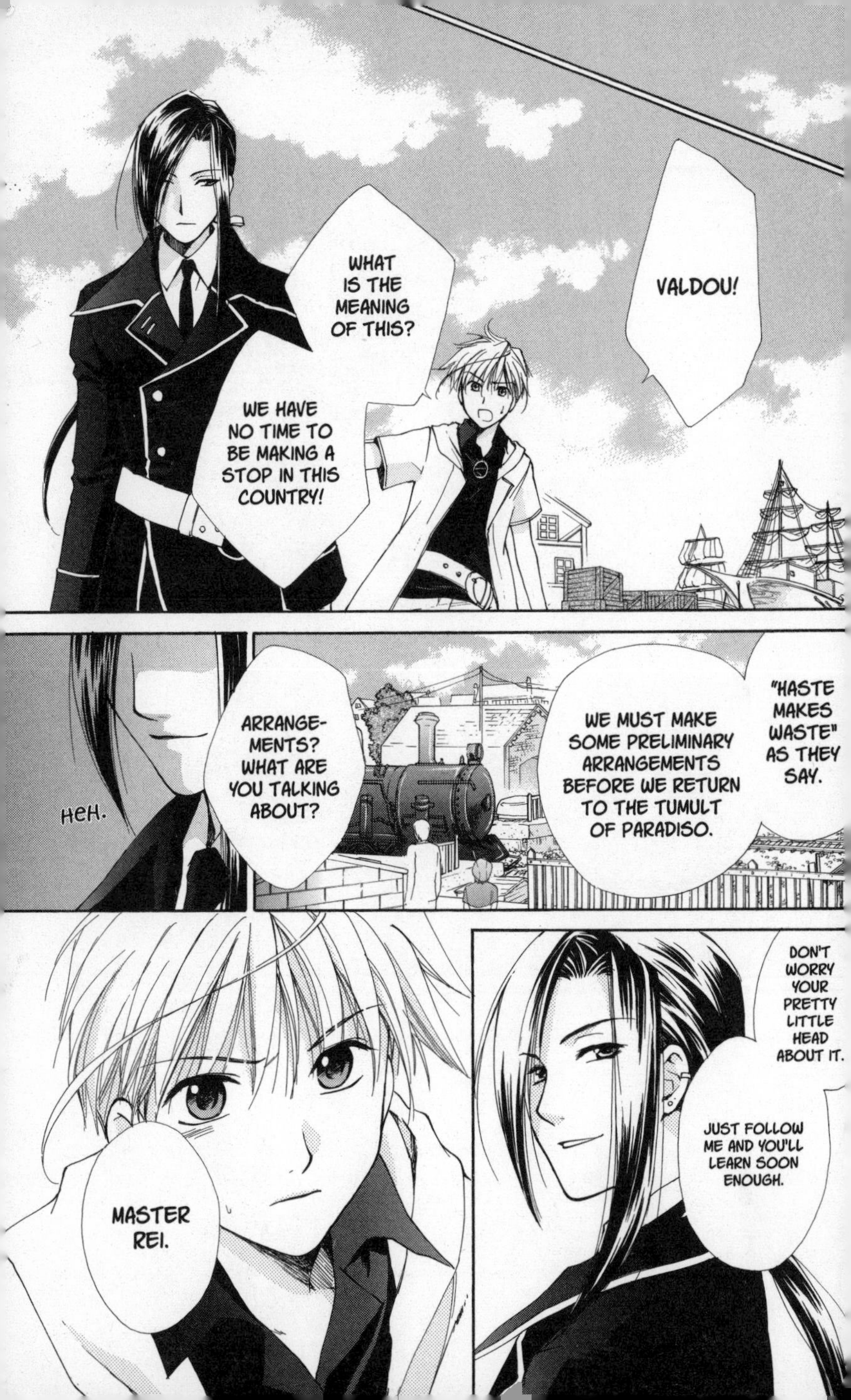
VALDOU!
WHAT IS THE MEANING OF THIS?
WE HAVE NO TIME TO BE MAKING A STOP IN THIS COUNTRY!
"HASTE MAKES WASTE" AS THEY SAY.
WE MUST MAKE SOME PRELIMINARY ARRANGEMENTS BEFORE WE RETURN TO THE TUMULT OF PARADISO.
ARRANGE-MENTS? WHAT ARE YOU TALKING ABOUT?
HEH.
DON'T WORRY YOUR PRETTY LITTLE HEAD ABOUT IT.
JUST FOLLOW ME AND YOU'LL LEARN SOON ENOUGH.
MASTER REI.

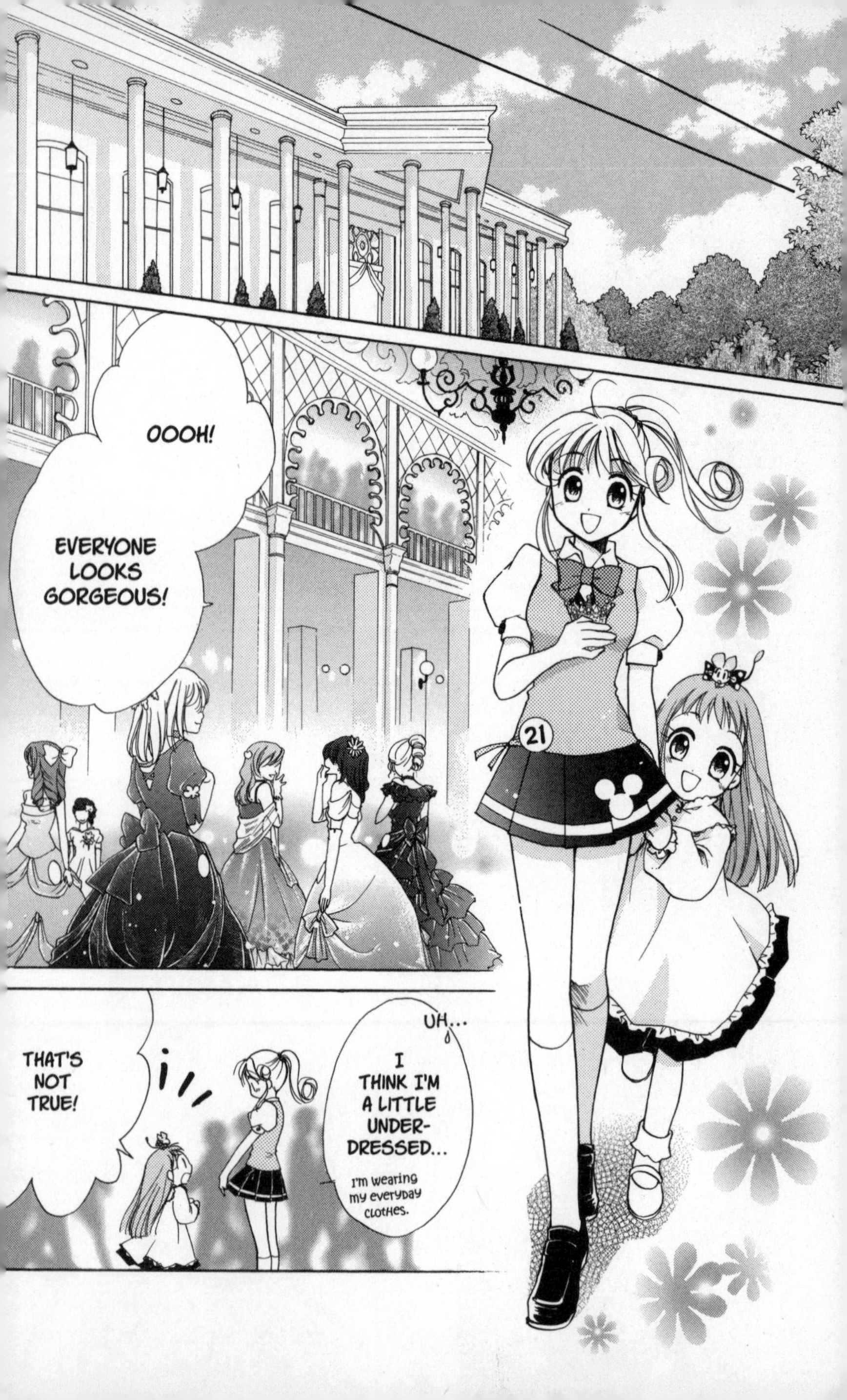
21
OOOH!
EVERYONE LOOKS GORGEOUS!
UH...
I THINK I'M A LITTLE UNDER-DRESSED...
I'm wearing my everyday clothes.
THAT'S NOT TRUE!

READ THIS WAY

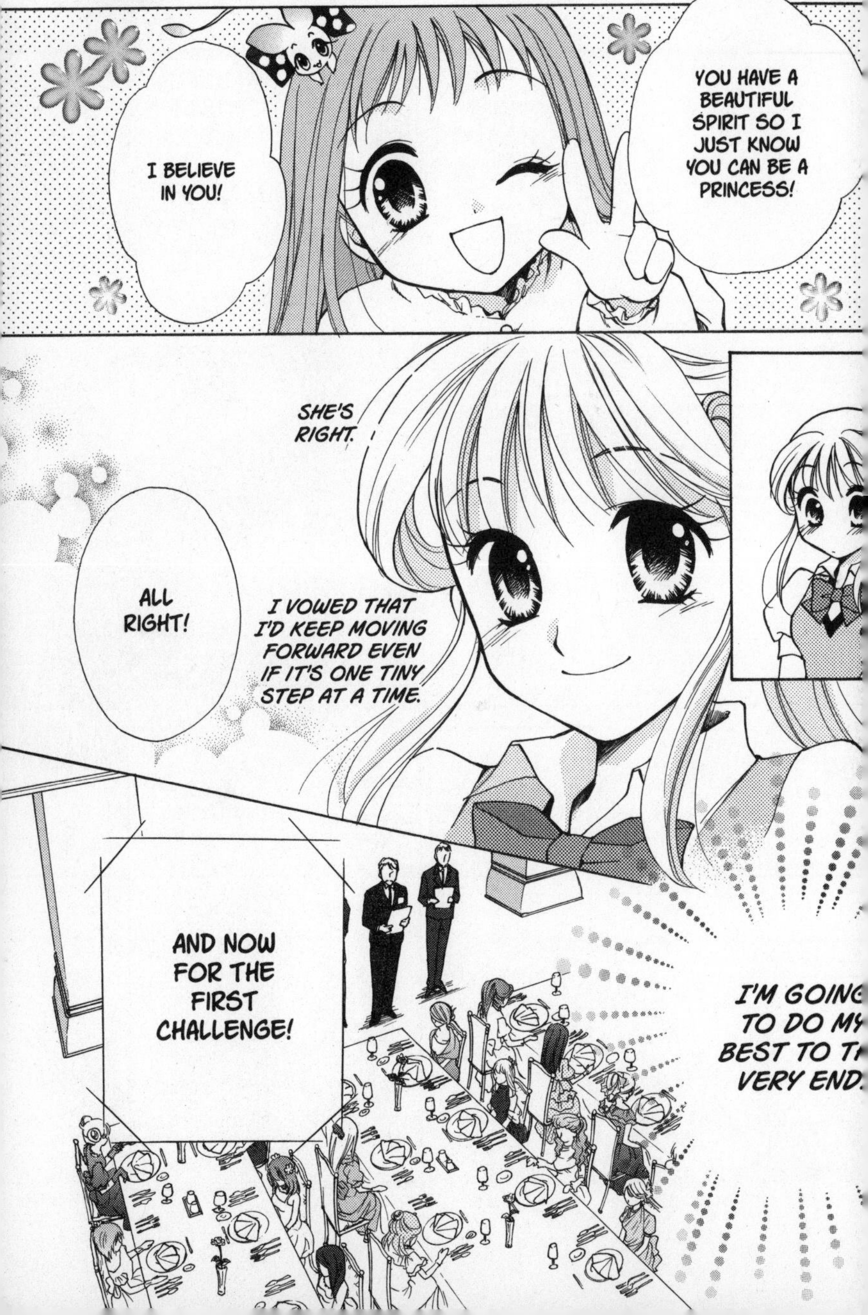
YOU HAVE A BEAUTIFUL SPIRIT SO I JUST KNOW YOU CAN BE A PRINCESS!
I BELIEVE IN YOU!
SHE'S RIGHT.
I VOWED THAT I'D KEEP MOVING FORWARD EVEN IF IT'S ONE TINY STEP AT A TIME.
ALL RIGHT!
I'M GOING TO DO MY BEST TO TH VERY END.
AND NOW FOR THE FIRST CHALLENGE!

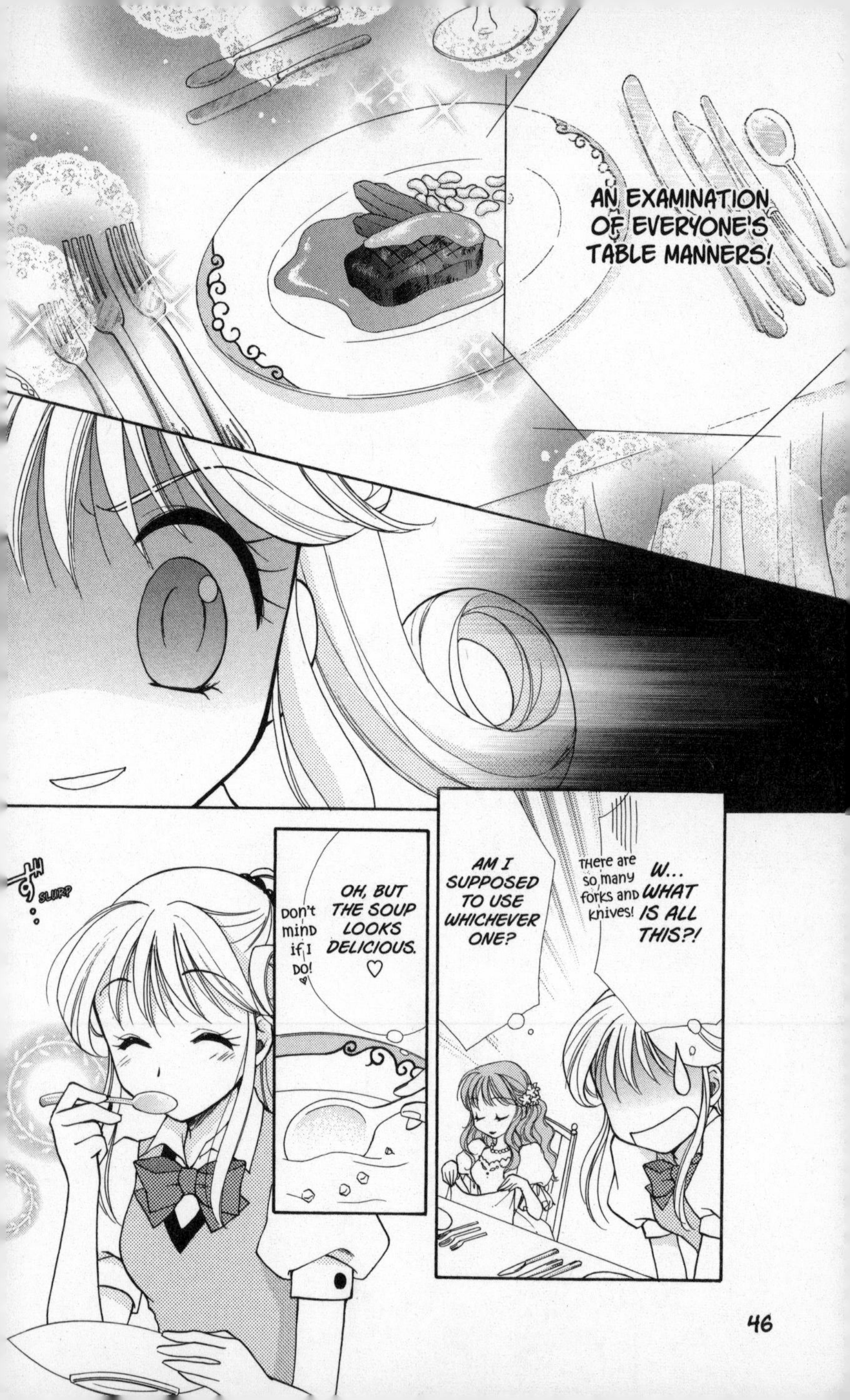
AN EXAMINATION OF EVERYONE'S TABLE MANNERS!
W... WHAT IS ALL THIS?!
There are so many forks and knives!
AM I SUPPOSED TO USE WHICHEVER ONE?
OH, BUT THE SOUP LOOKS DELICIOUS. ♡
Don't mind if I DO! ♡
SLURP

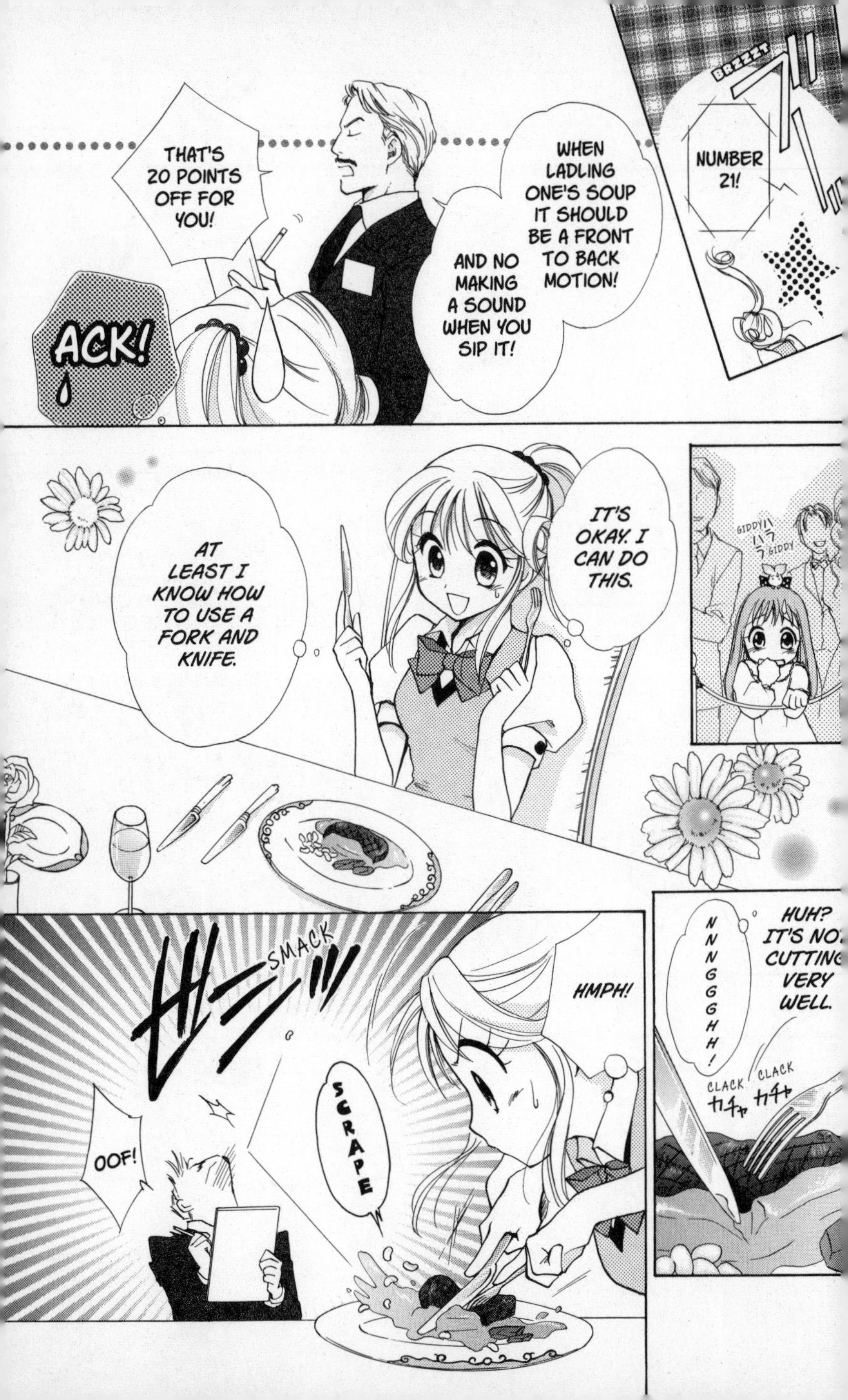

BRZZZT
NUMBER 21!
WHEN LADLING ONE'S SOUP IT SHOULD BE A FRONT TO BACK MOTION!
AND NO MAKING A SOUND WHEN YOU SIP IT!
THAT'S 20 POINTS OFF FOR YOU!
ACK!
GIDDY GIDDY
IT'S OKAY. I CAN DO THIS.
AT LEAST I KNOW HOW TO USE A FORK AND KNIFE.
HUH? IT'S NO CUTTIN VERY WELL.
NNNGGGHH!
CLACK CLACK
HMPH!
SMACK
SCRAPE
OOF!

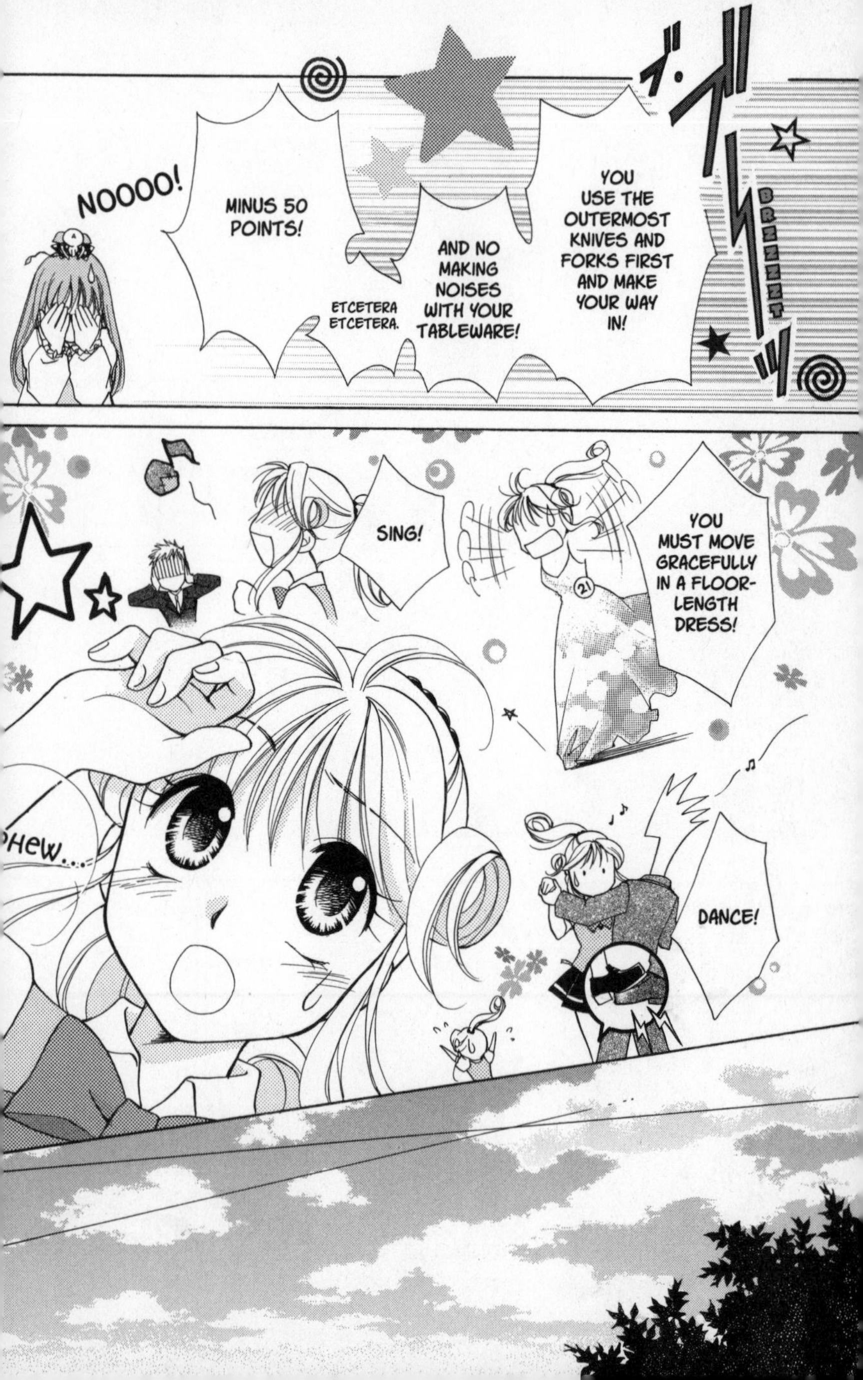
BRZZZT
YOU USE THE OUTERMOST KNIVES AND FORKS FIRST AND MAKE YOUR WAY IN!
AND NO MAKING NOISES WITH YOUR TABLEWARE!
ETCETERA ETCETERA.
MINUS 50 POINTS!
NOOOO!
YOU MUST MOVE GRACEFULLY IN A FLOOR-LENGTH DRESS!
SING!
DANCE!
PHEW......

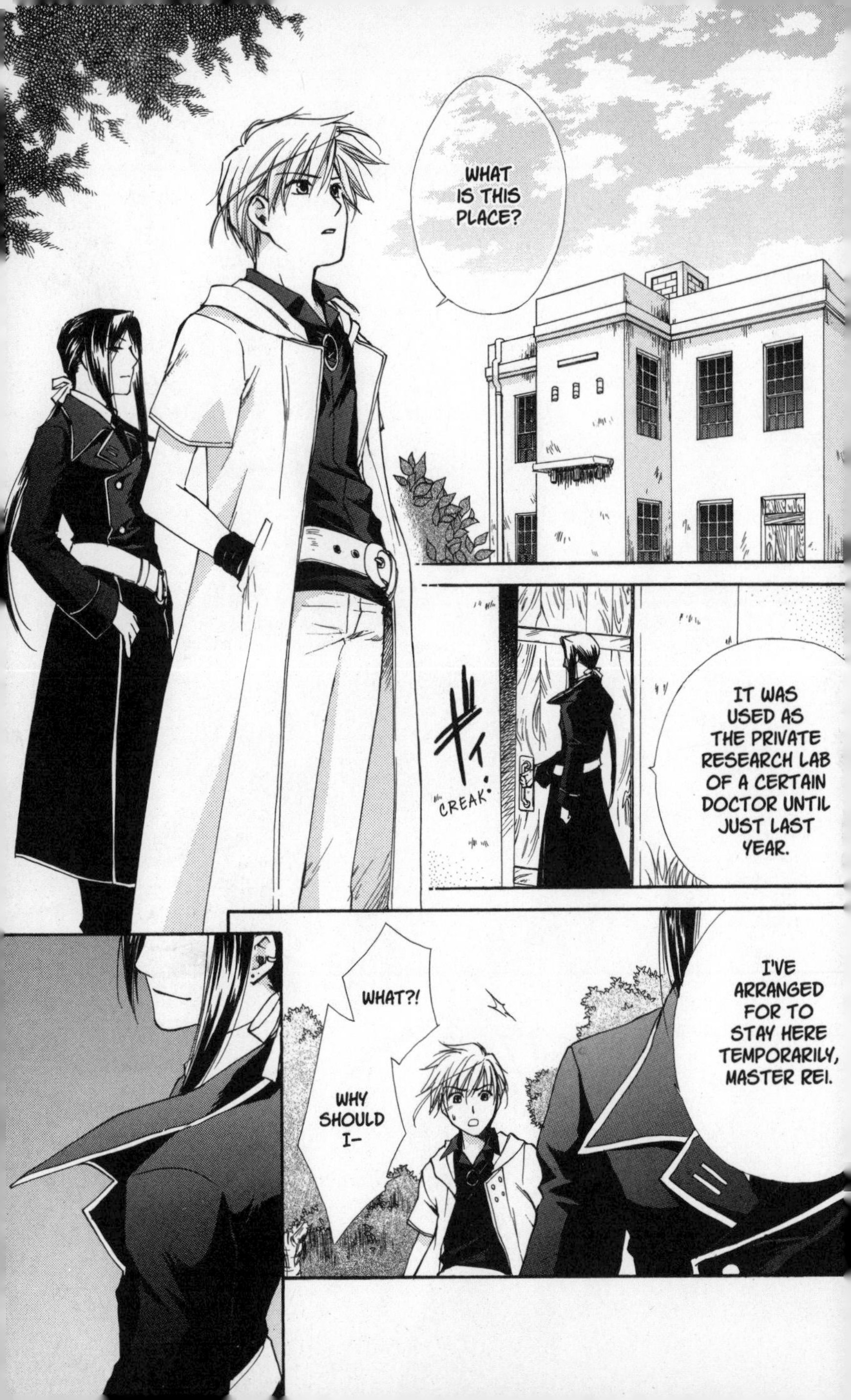
WHAT IS THIS PLACE?
IT WAS USED AS THE PRIVATE RESEARCH LAB OF A CERTAIN DOCTOR UNTIL JUST LAST YEAR.
CREAK
I'VE ARRANGED FOR TO STAY HERE TEMPORARILY, MASTER REI.
WHAT?!
WHY SHOULD I-

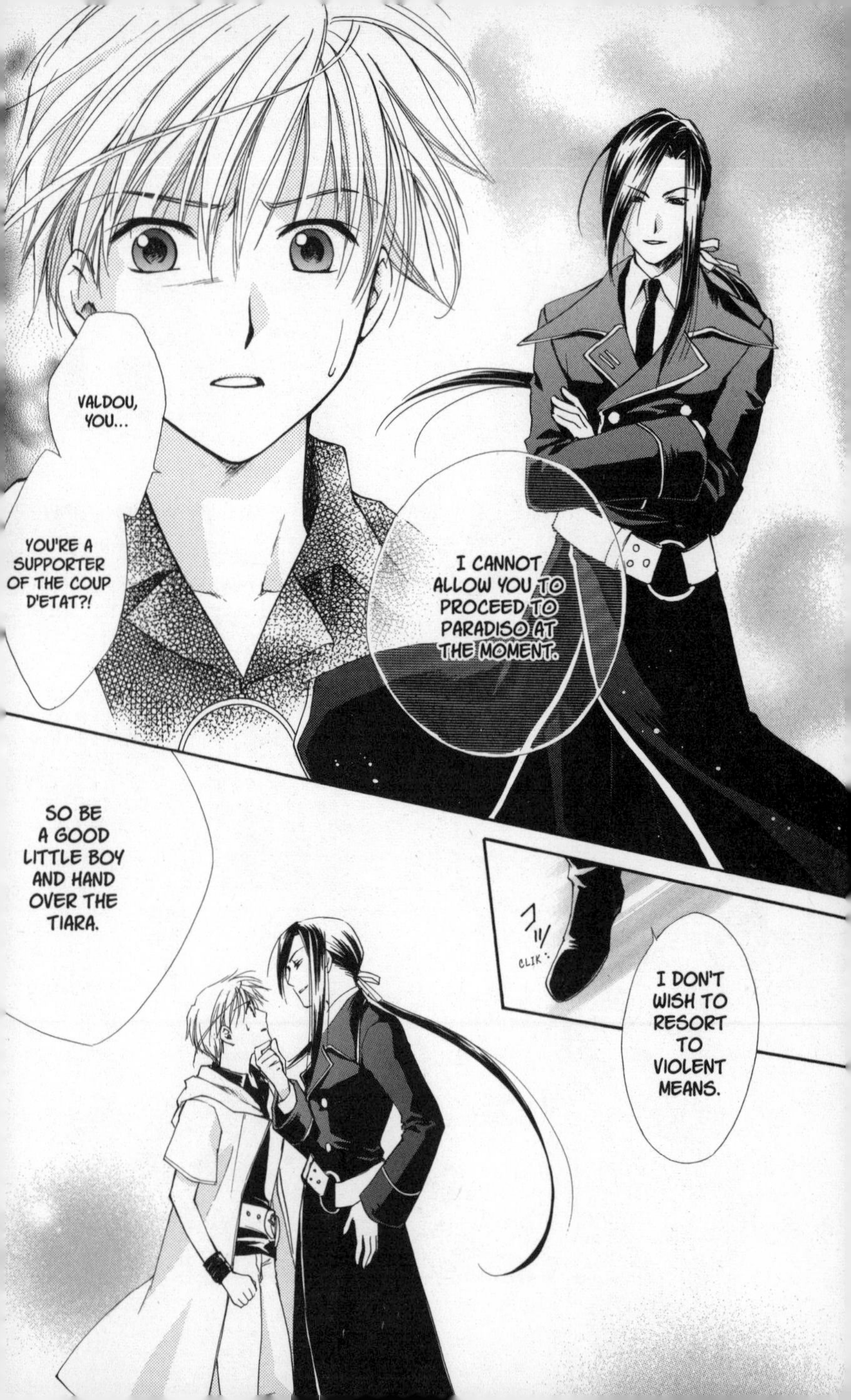
I CANNOT ALLOW YOU TO PROCEED TO PARADISO AT THE MOMENT.
VALDOU, YOU...
YOU'RE A SUPPORTER OF THE COUP D'ETAT?!
CLIK
I DON'T WISH TO RESORT TO VIOLENT MEANS.
SO BE A GOOD LITTLE BOY AND HAND OVER THE TIARA.

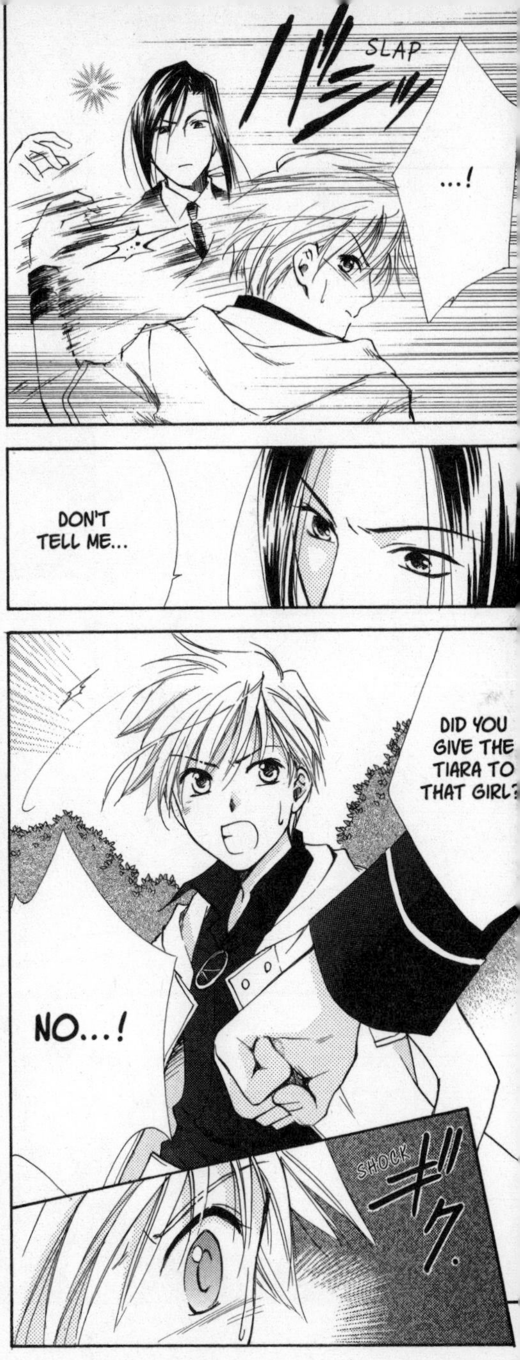
SLAP
バシッ
...!
DON'T TELL ME...
DID YOU GIVE THE TIARA TO THAT GIRL?
NO...!
SHOCK
ギク.

TIPPE HELPS OUT

2

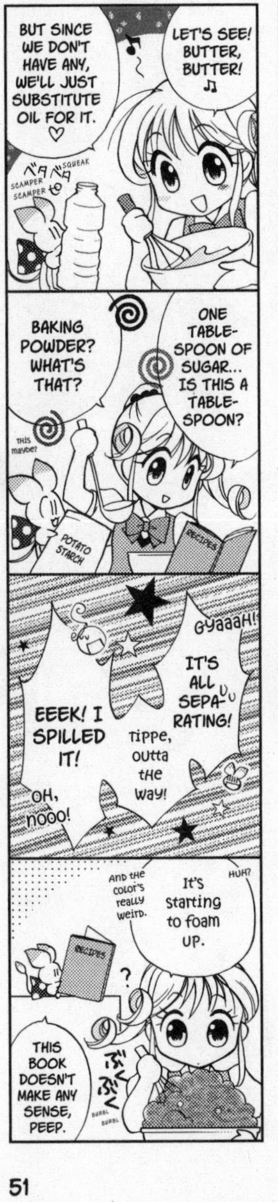
LET'S SEE! BUTTER, BUTTER! ♫
BUT SINCE WE DON'T HAVE ANY, WE'LL JUST SUBSTITUTE OIL FOR IT. ♡
SQUEAK
ベタベタ
SCAMPER SCAMPER
ONE TABLE-SPOON OF SUGAR... IS THIS A TABLE-SPOON?
BAKING POWDER? WHAT'S THAT?
THIS maybe?
POTATO STARCH
RECIPES
GYaaaH!
IT'S ALL SEPA-RATING!
Tippe, outta the way!
EEEK! I SPILLED IT!
OH, nooo!
HUH?
It's starting to foam up.
And the color's really weird.
RECIPES
?
THIS BOOK DOESN'T MAKE ANY SENSE, PEEP.
ぶくぶく
BURBL BURBL

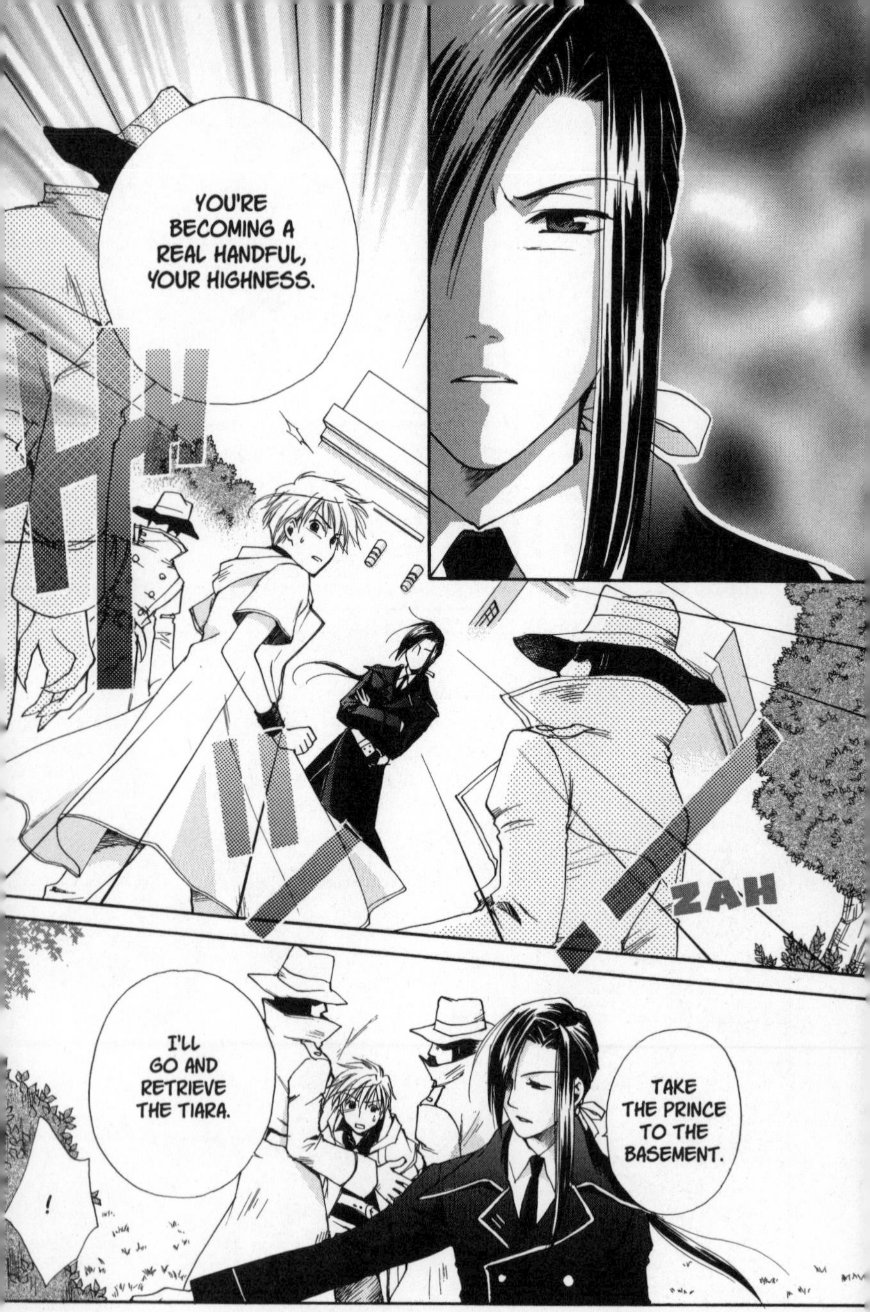

YOU'RE BECOMING A REAL HANDFUL, YOUR HIGHNESS.
ZAH
TAKE THE PRINCE TO THE BASEMENT.
I'LL GO AND RETRIEVE THE TIARA.
!

READ THIS WAY

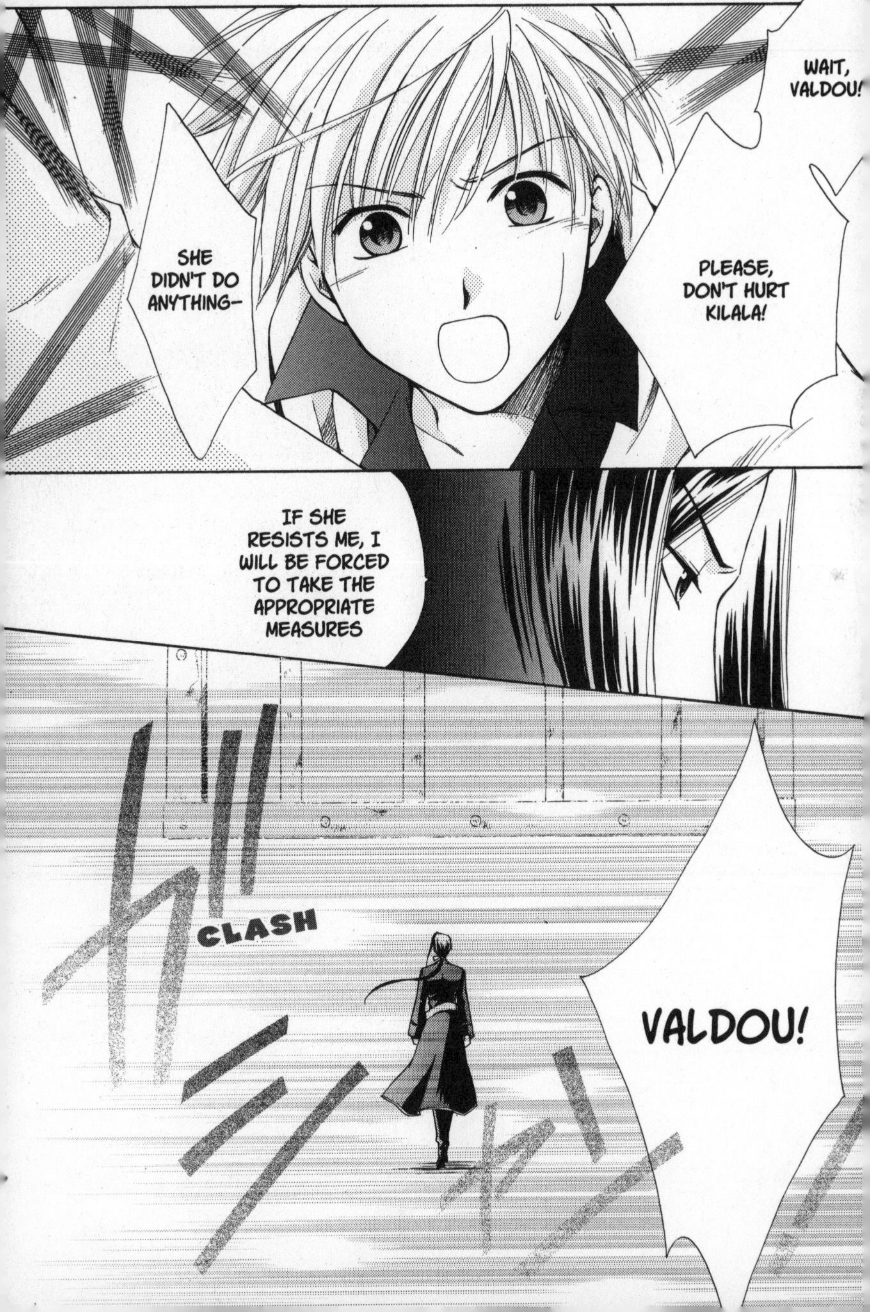
WAIT, VALDOU!
PLEASE, DON'T HURT KILALA!
SHE DIDN'T DO ANYTHING–
IF SHE RESISTS ME, I WILL BE FORCED TO TAKE THE APPROPRIATE MEASURES
VALDOU!
CLASH

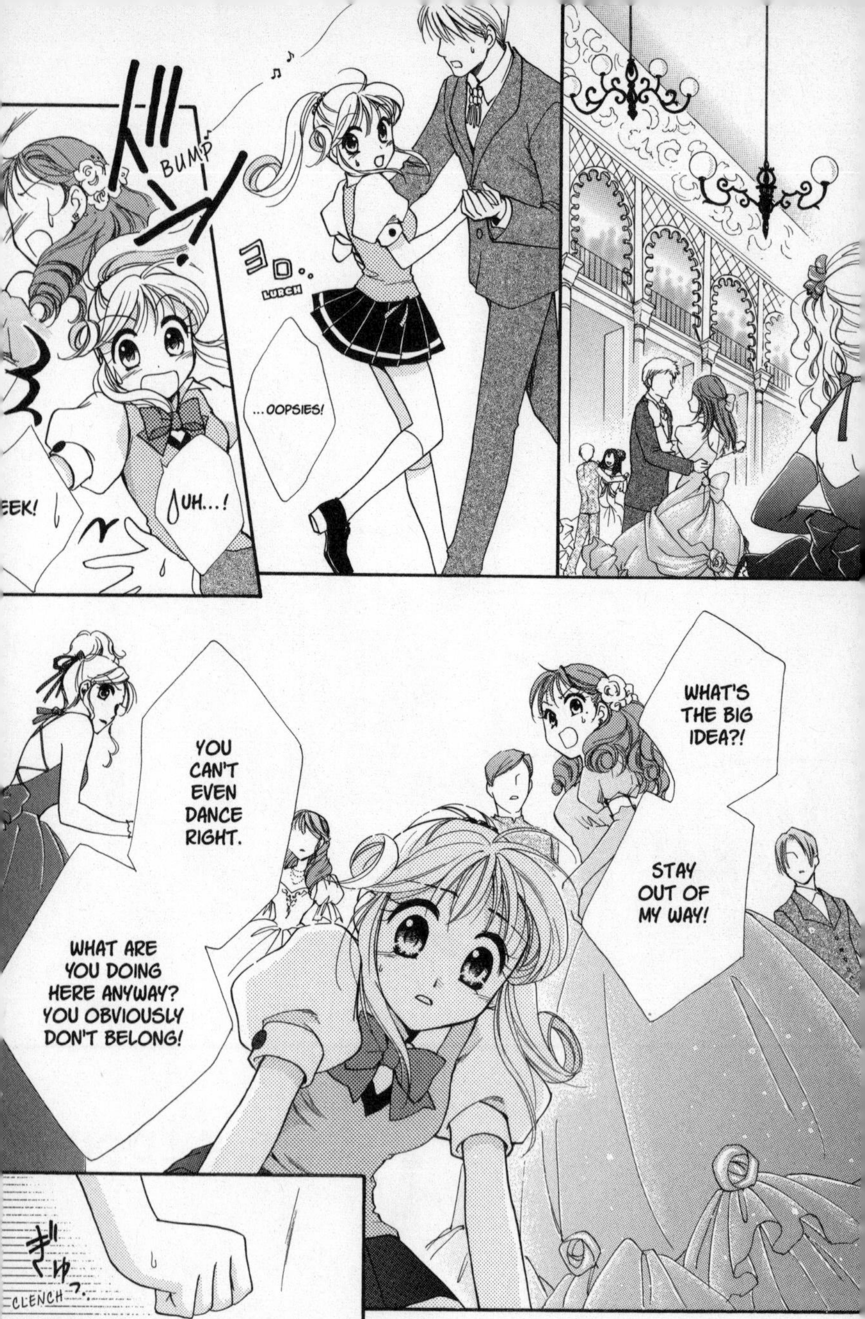
ヨロ..
LURCH
...OOPSIES!
BUMP
EEK!
UH...!
WHAT'S THE BIG IDEA?!
STAY OUT OF MY WAY!
YOU CAN'T EVEN DANCE RIGHT.
WHAT ARE YOU DOING HERE ANYWAY? YOU OBVIOUSLY DON'T BELONG!
ぎゅっ
CLENCH

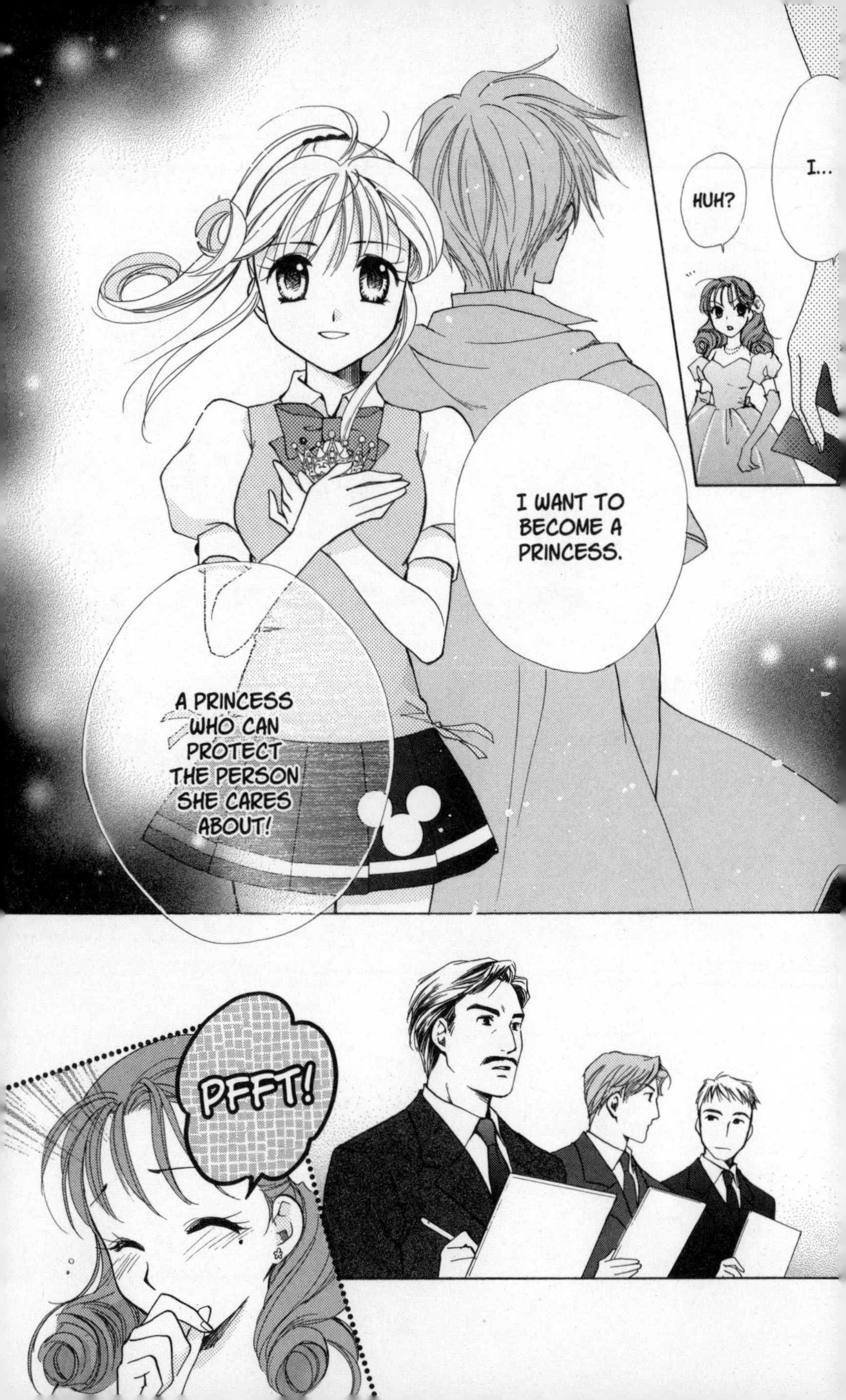
I...
HUH?
I WANT TO BECOME A PRINCESS.
A PRINCESS WHO CAN PROTECT THE PERSON SHE CARES ABOUT!
PFFT!

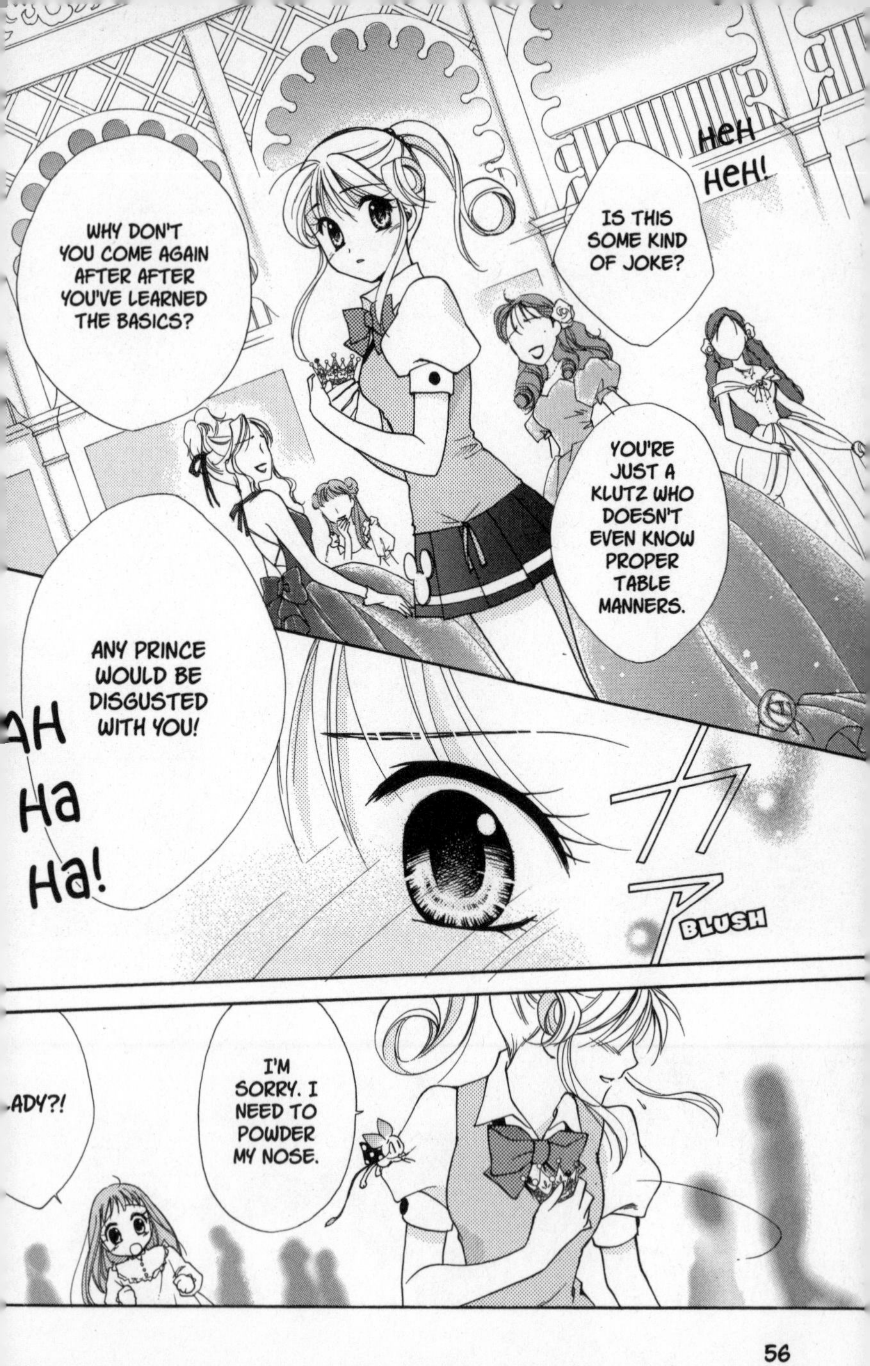
HEH HEH!
IS THIS SOME KIND OF JOKE?
YOU'RE JUST A KLUTZ WHO DOESN'T EVEN KNOW PROPER TABLE MANNERS.
WHY DON'T YOU COME AGAIN AFTER AFTER YOU'VE LEARNED THE BASICS?
ANY PRINCE WOULD BE DISGUSTED WITH YOU!
AH HA HA!
BLUSH
I'M SORRY. I NEED TO POWDER MY NOSE.
ADY?!

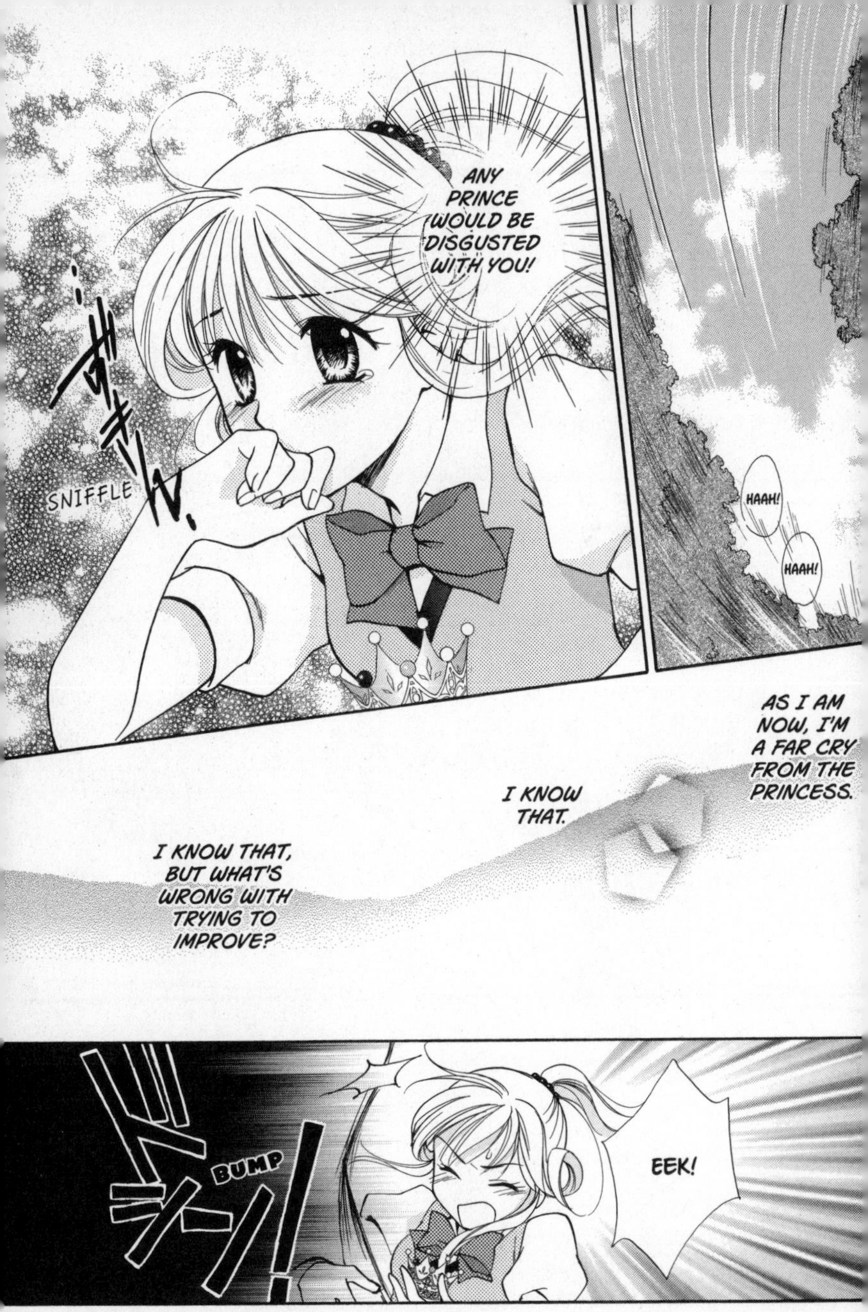
HAAH!
HAAH!
ANY PRINCE WOULD BE DISGUSTED WITH YOU!
SNIFFLE
AS I AM NOW, I'M A FAR CRY FROM THE PRINCESS.
I KNOW THAT.
I KNOW THAT, BUT WHAT'S WRONG WITH TRYING TO IMPROVE?
EEK!
BUMP

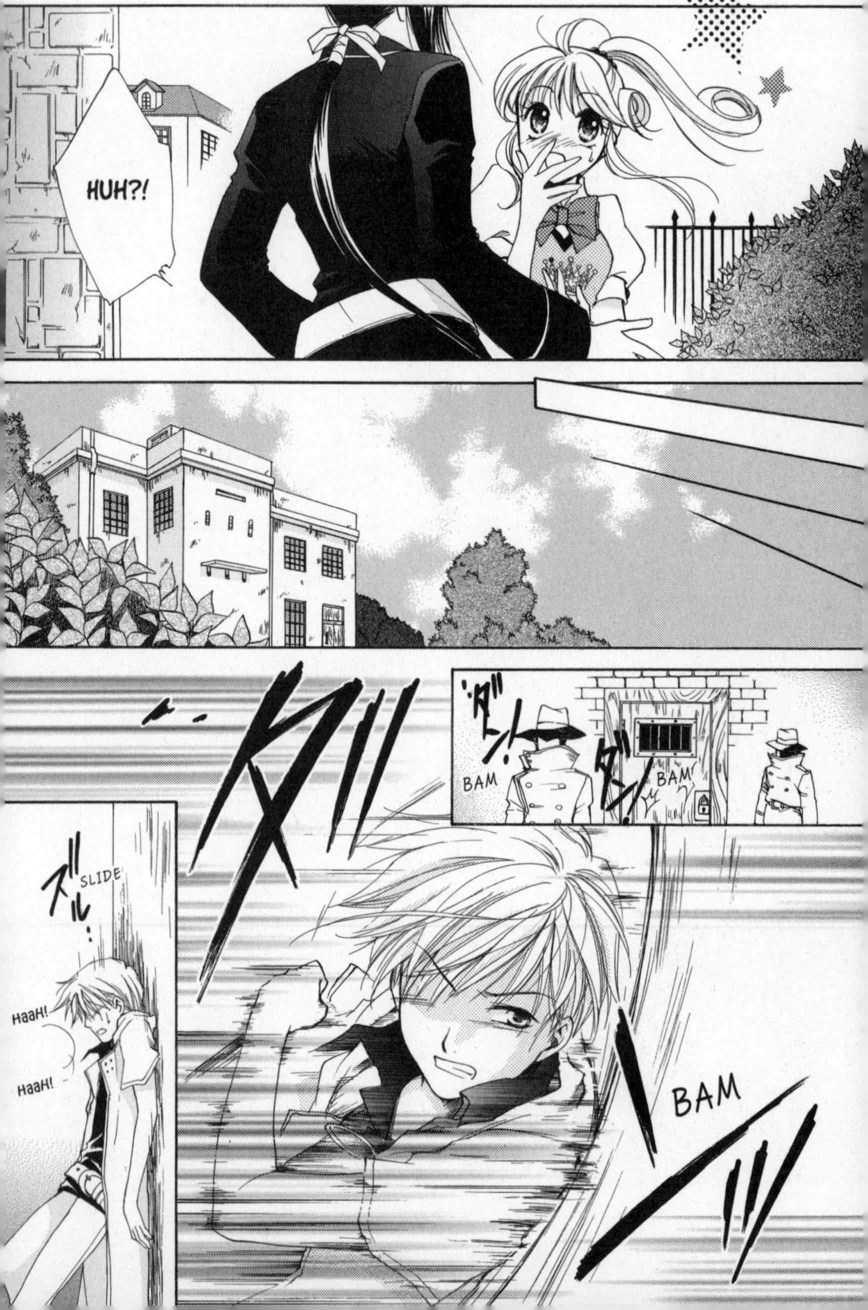
HUH?!
ダン!
BAM
ダン!
BAM
ダン
BAM
ズル
SLIDE
HaaH!
HaaH!

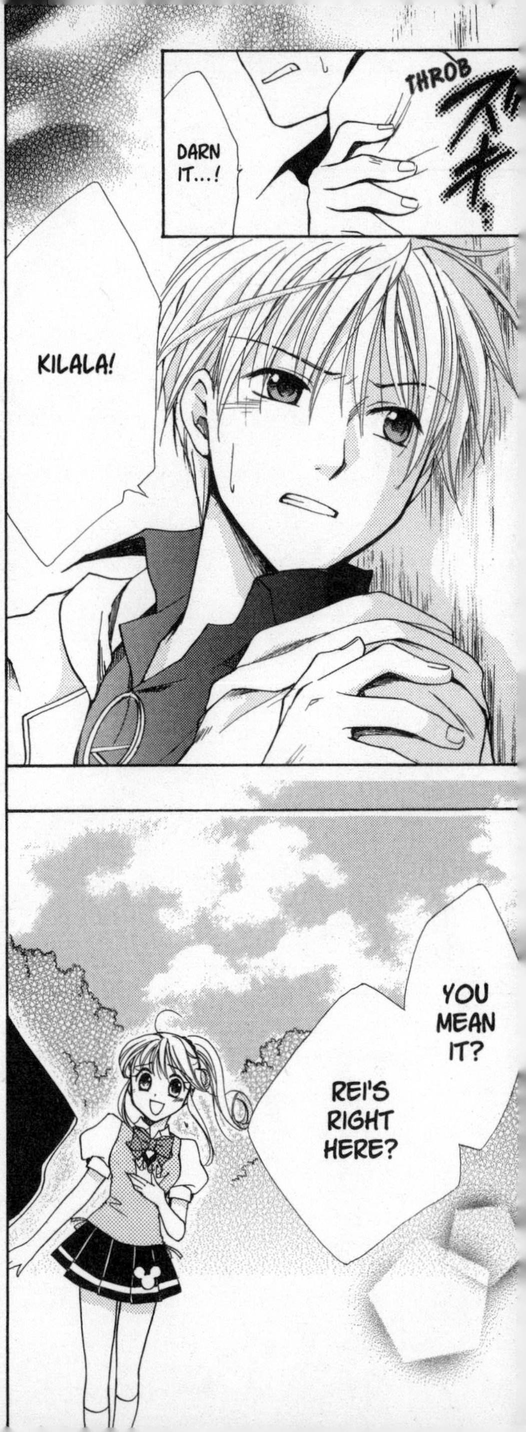
THROB
DARN IT...!
KILALA!
YOU MEAN IT?
REI'S RIGHT HERE?

TIPPE HELPS OUT 3

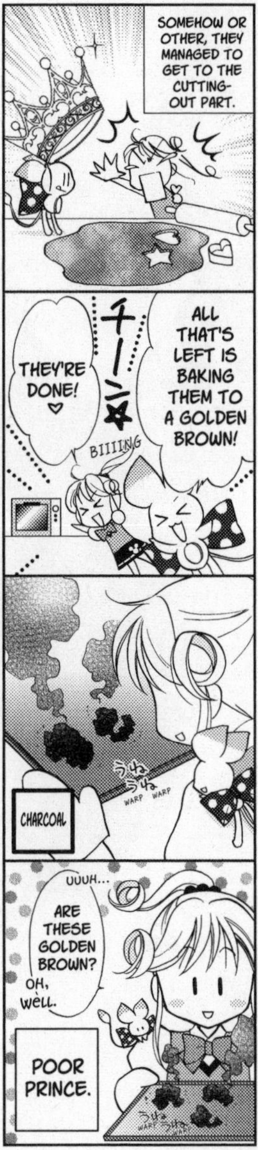
SOMEHOW OR OTHER, THEY MANAGED TO GET TO THE CUTTING-OUT PART.
ALL THAT'S LEFT IS BAKING THEM TO A GOLDEN BROWN!
BIIIING
THEY'RE DONE! ♡
CHARCOAL
WARP WARP
UUUH...
ARE THESE GOLDEN BROWN?
OH, WELL.
POOR PRINCE.

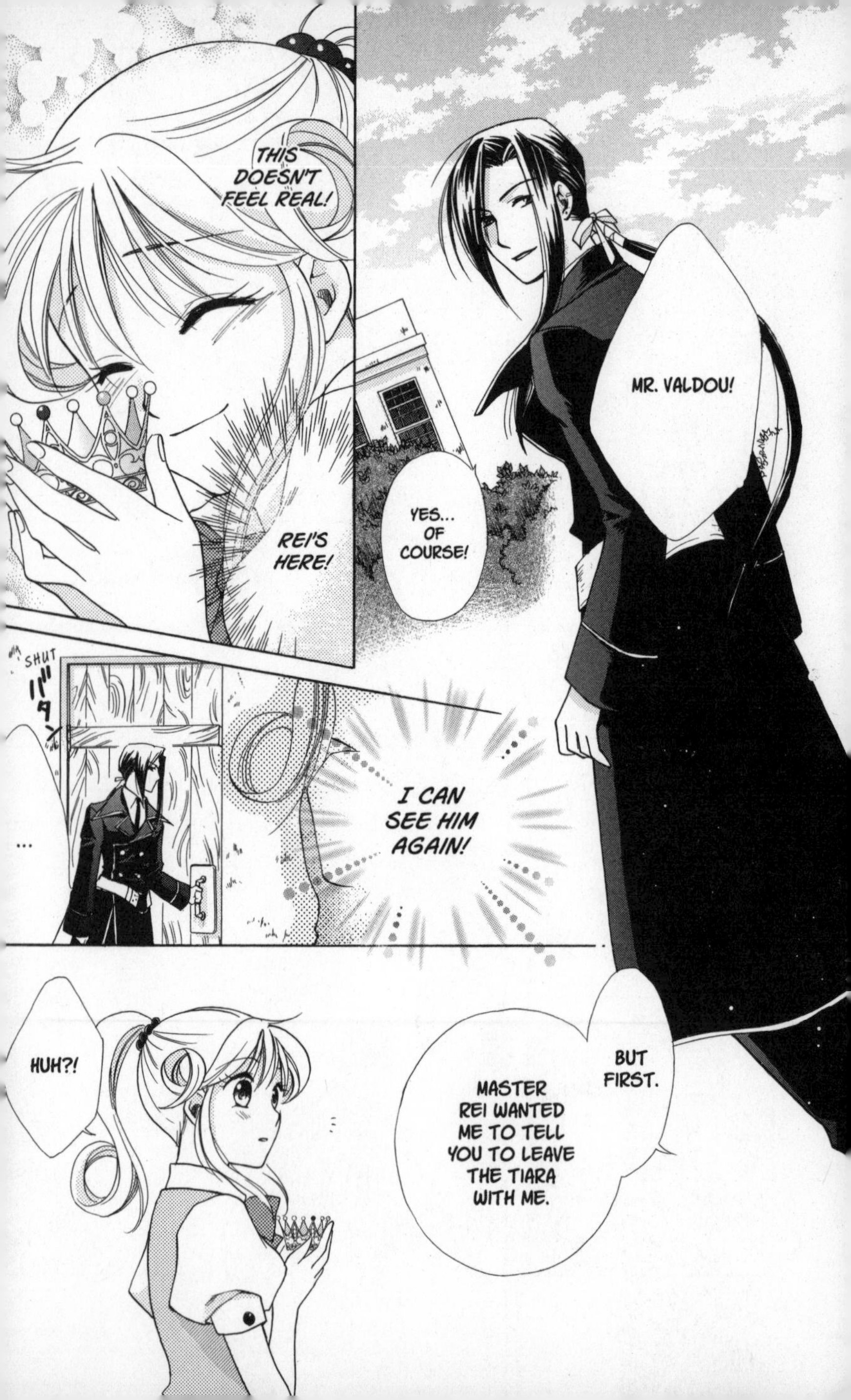

MR. VALDOU!
YES... OF COURSE!
THIS DOESN'T FEEL REAL!
REI'S HERE!
I CAN SEE HIM AGAIN!
バタン SHUT
...
BUT FIRST.
MASTER REI WANTED ME TO TELL YOU TO LEAVE THE TIARA WITH ME.
HUH?!

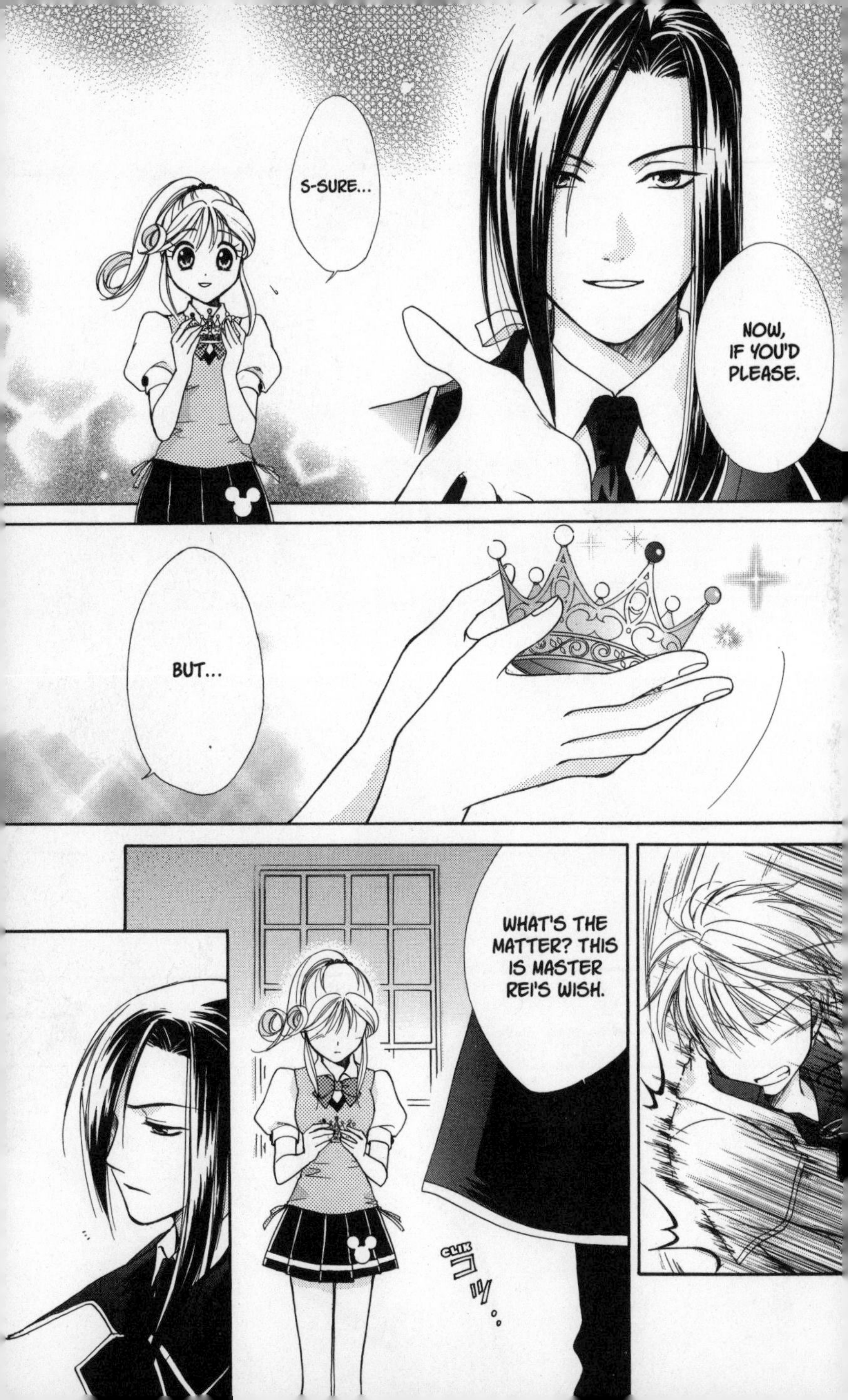
NOW, IF YOU'D PLEASE.
S-SURE...
BUT...
WHAT'S THE MATTER? THIS IS MASTER REI'S WISH.
CLIK

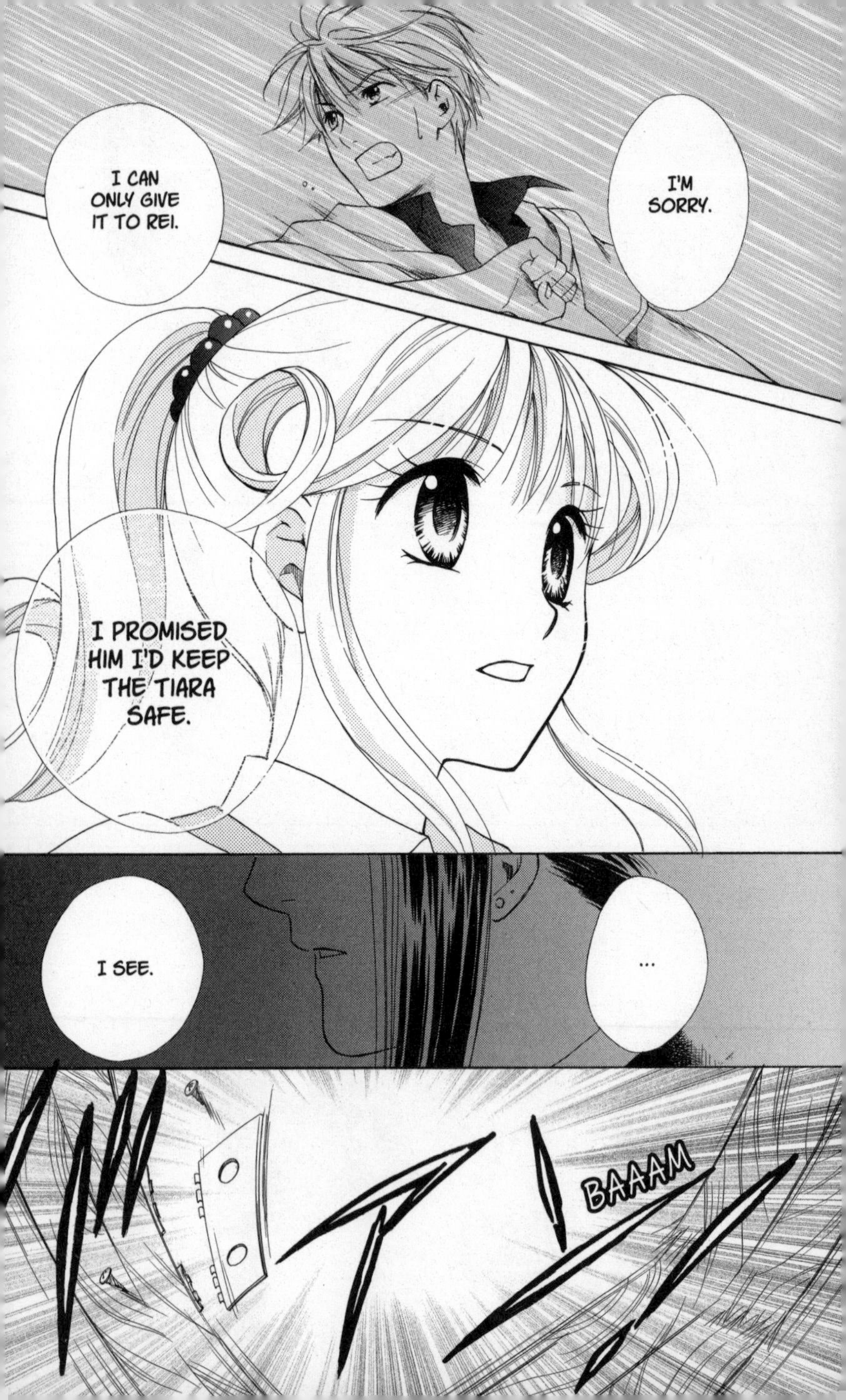
I'M SORRY.
I CAN ONLY GIVE IT TO REI.
I PROMISED HIM I'D KEEP THE TIARA SAFE.
...
I SEE.
BAAAM

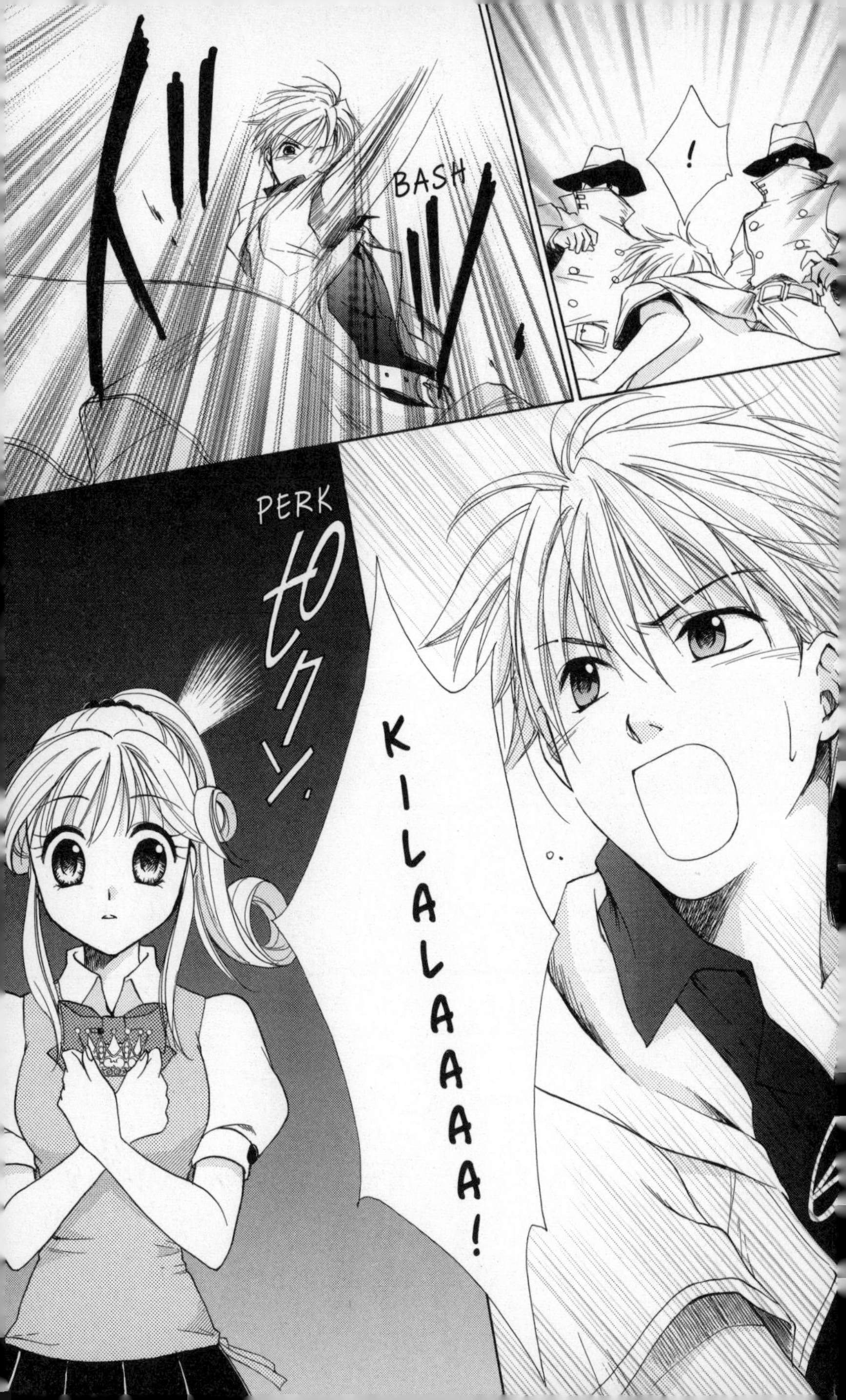
!
BASH
KILLAAAA!
PERK

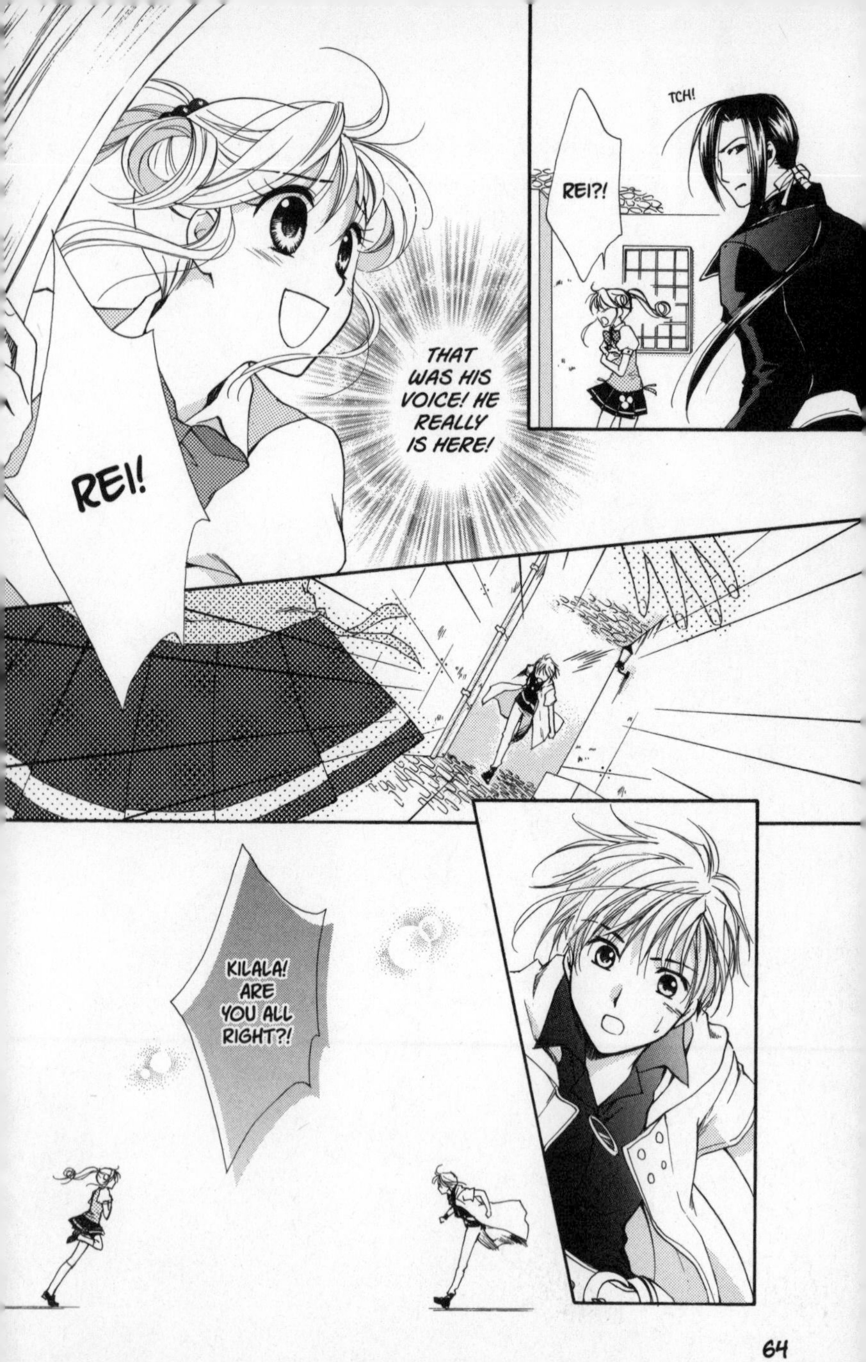
TCH!
REI?!
THAT WAS HIS VOICE! HE REALLY IS HERE!
REI!
KILALA! ARE YOU ALL RIGHT?!

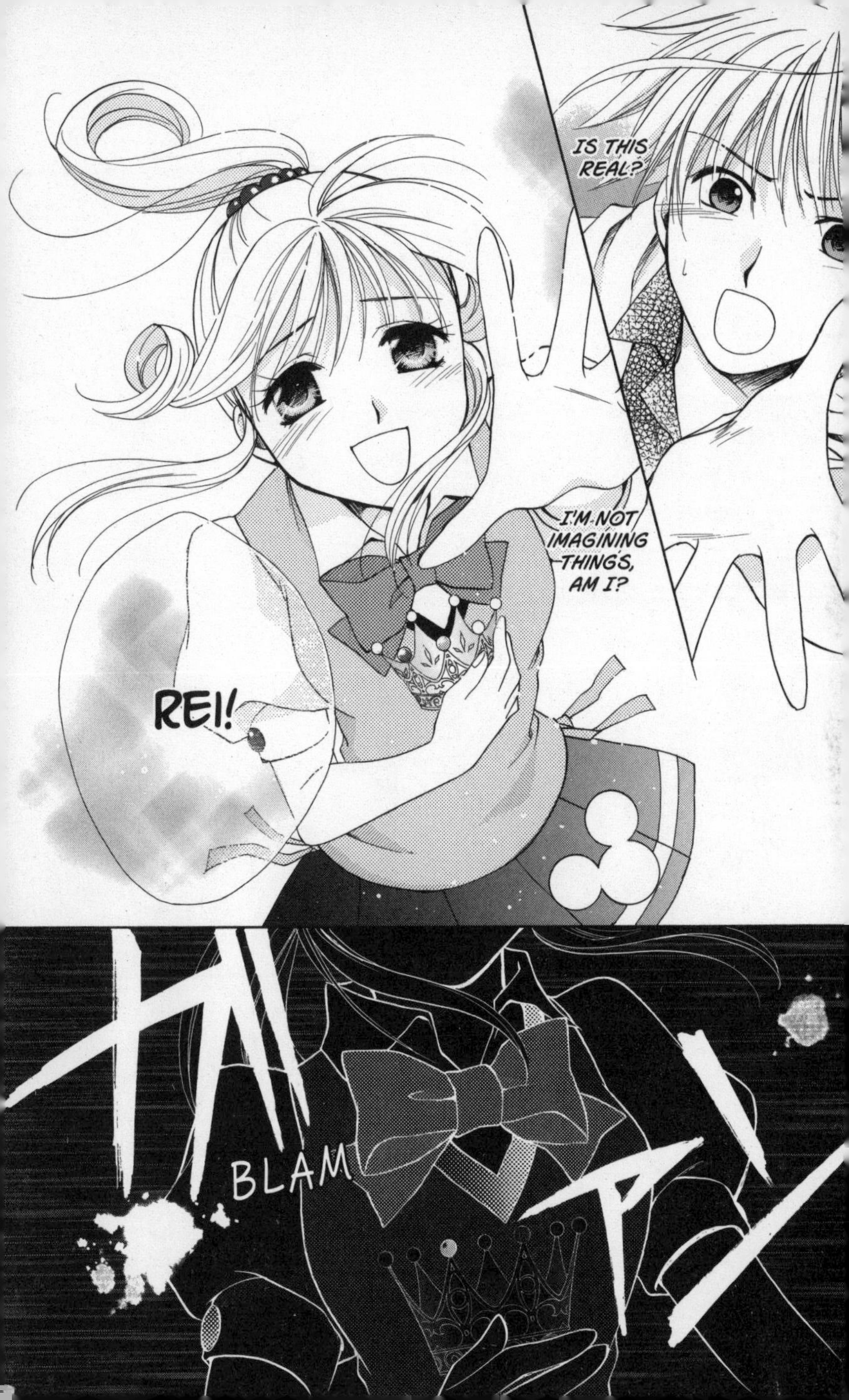
IS THIS REAL?
I'M NOT IMAGINING THINGS, AM I?
REI!
BLAM

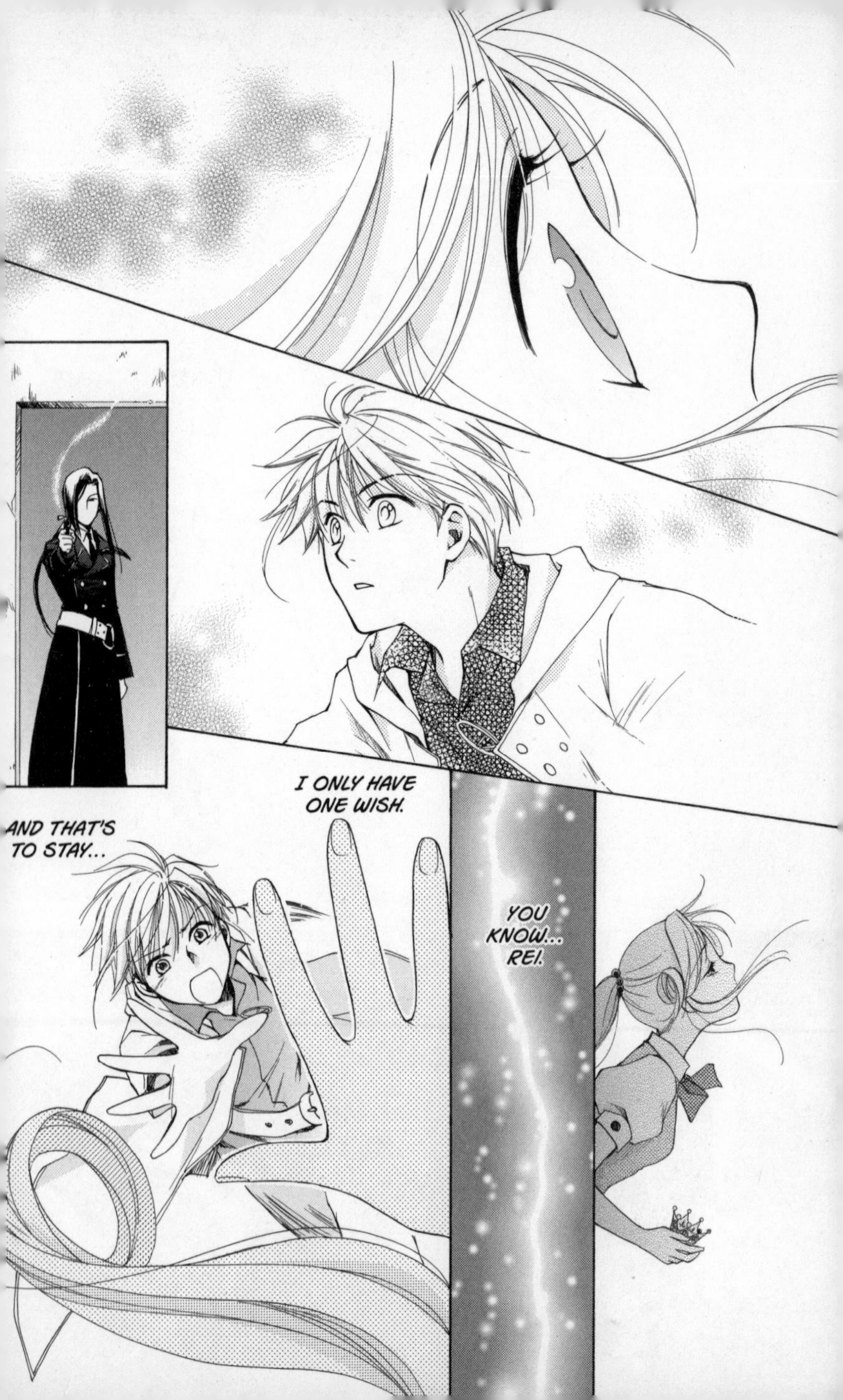
YOU KNOW... REI.
I ONLY HAVE ONE WISH.
AND THAT'S TO STAY...

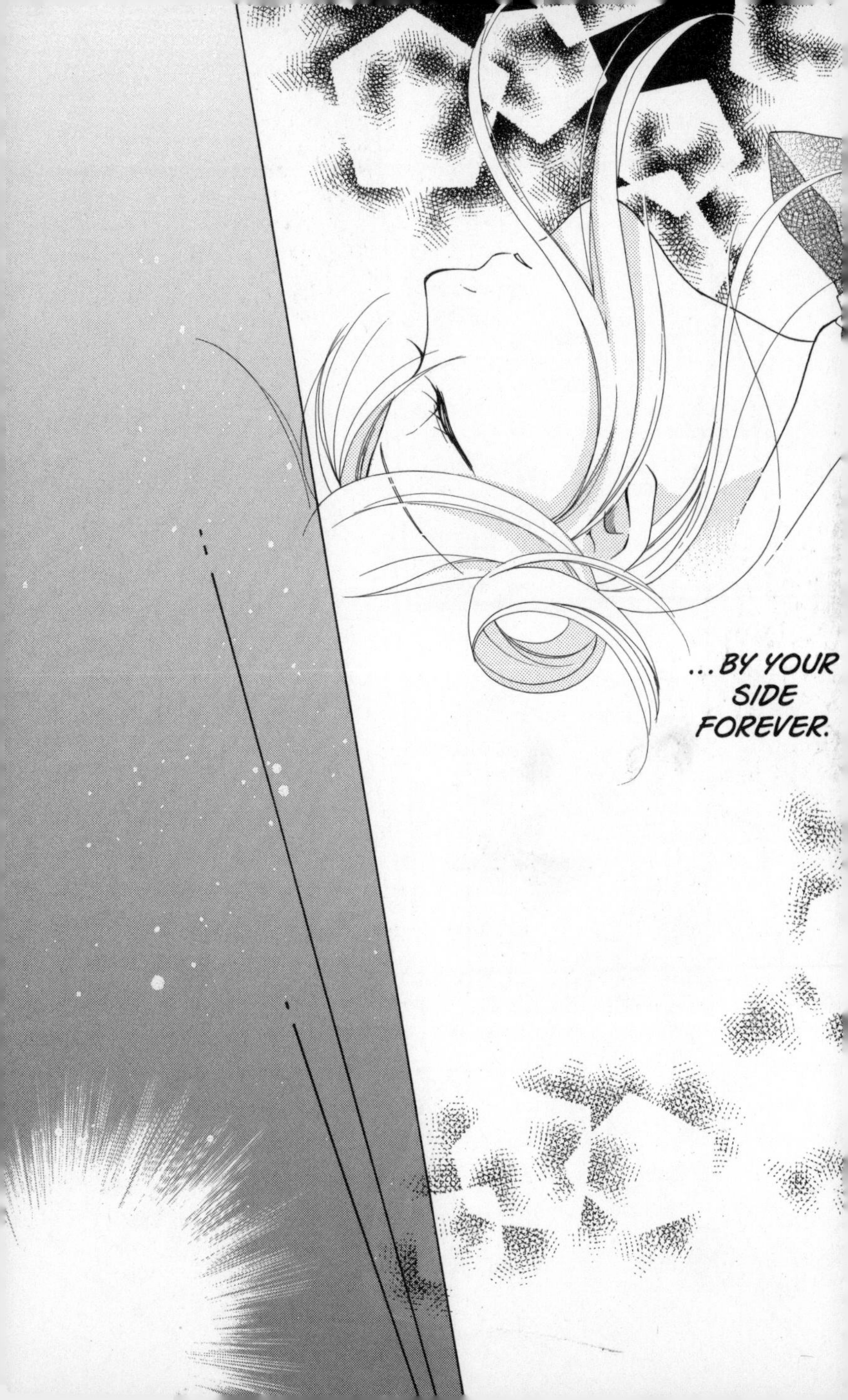
...BY YOUR SIDE FOREVER.

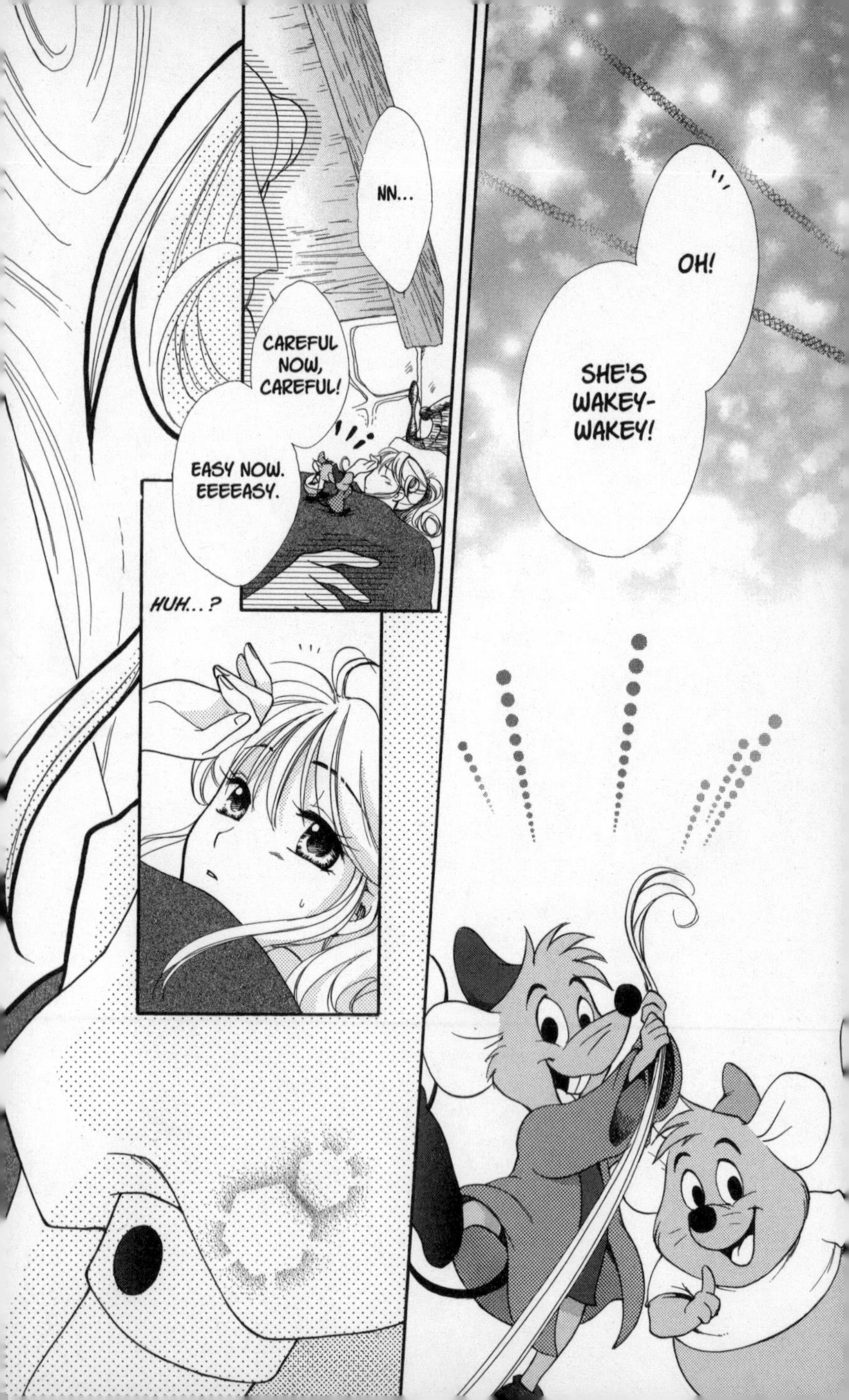
OH!
SHE'S WAKEY-WAKEY!
NN...
CAREFUL NOW, CAREFUL!
EASY NOW. EEEEASY.
HUH...?

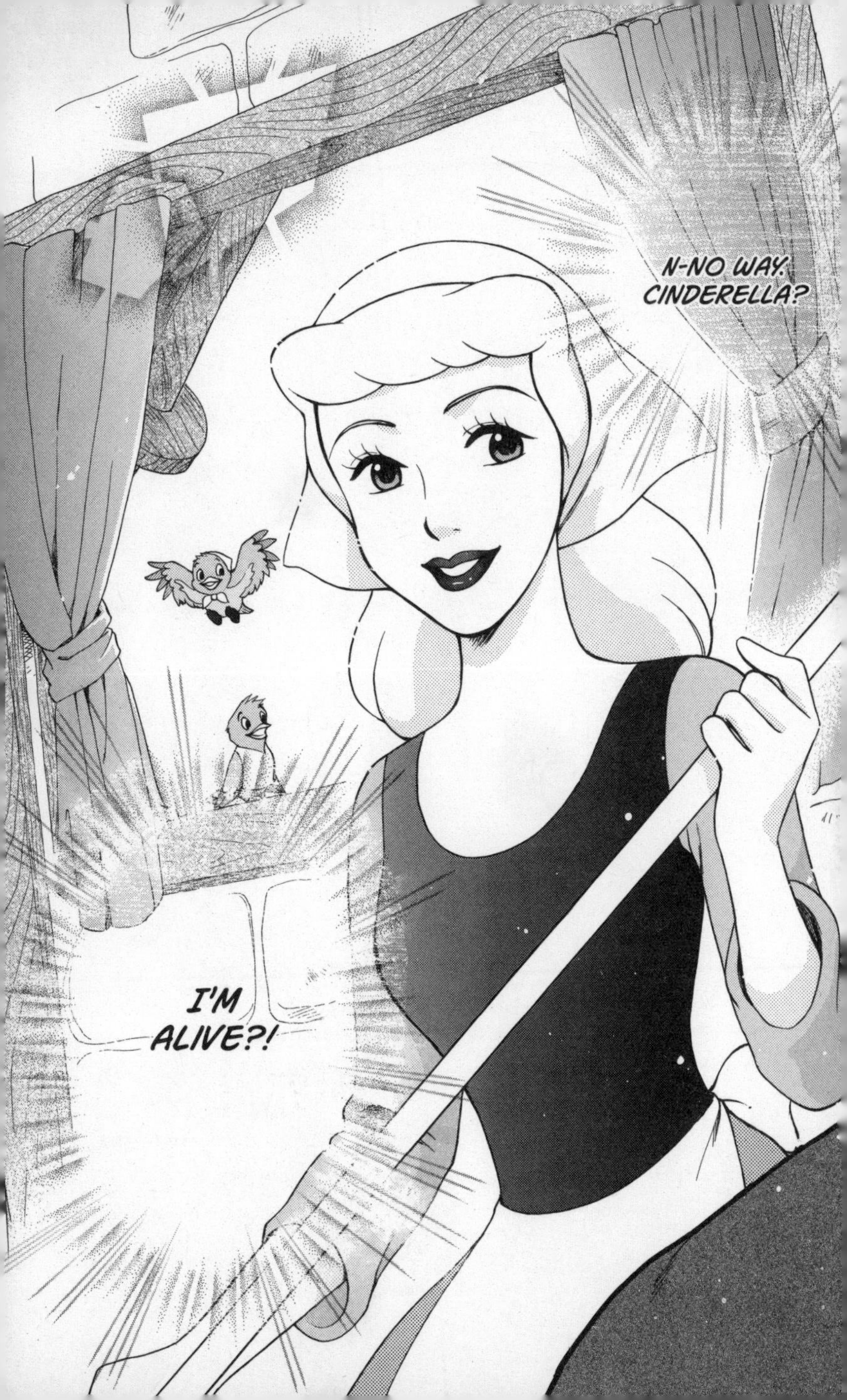
N-NO WAY. CINDERELLA?
I'M ALIVE?!

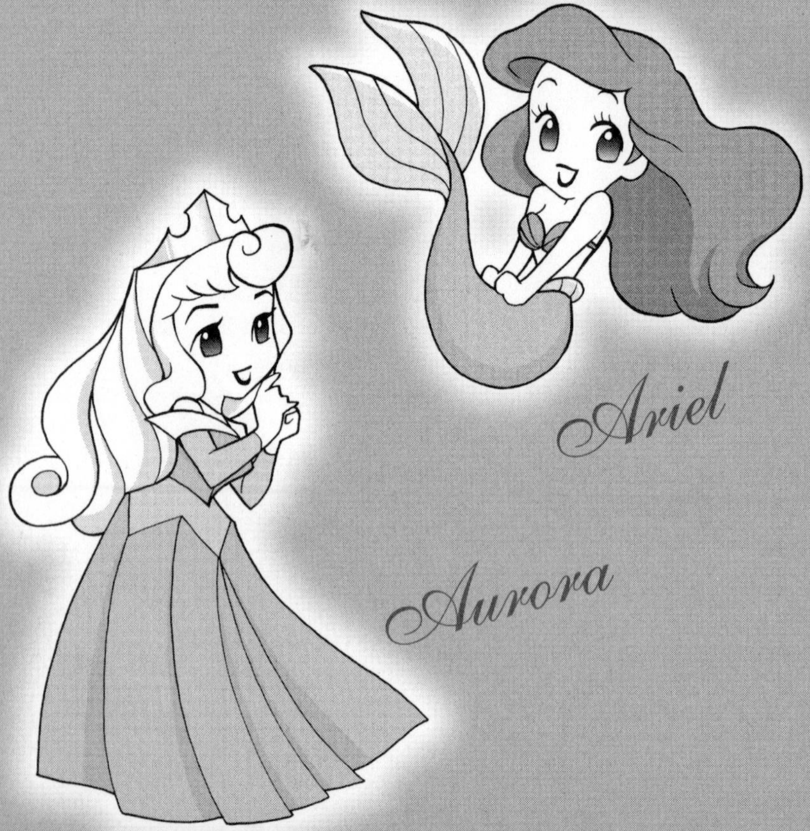
Ariel
Aurora

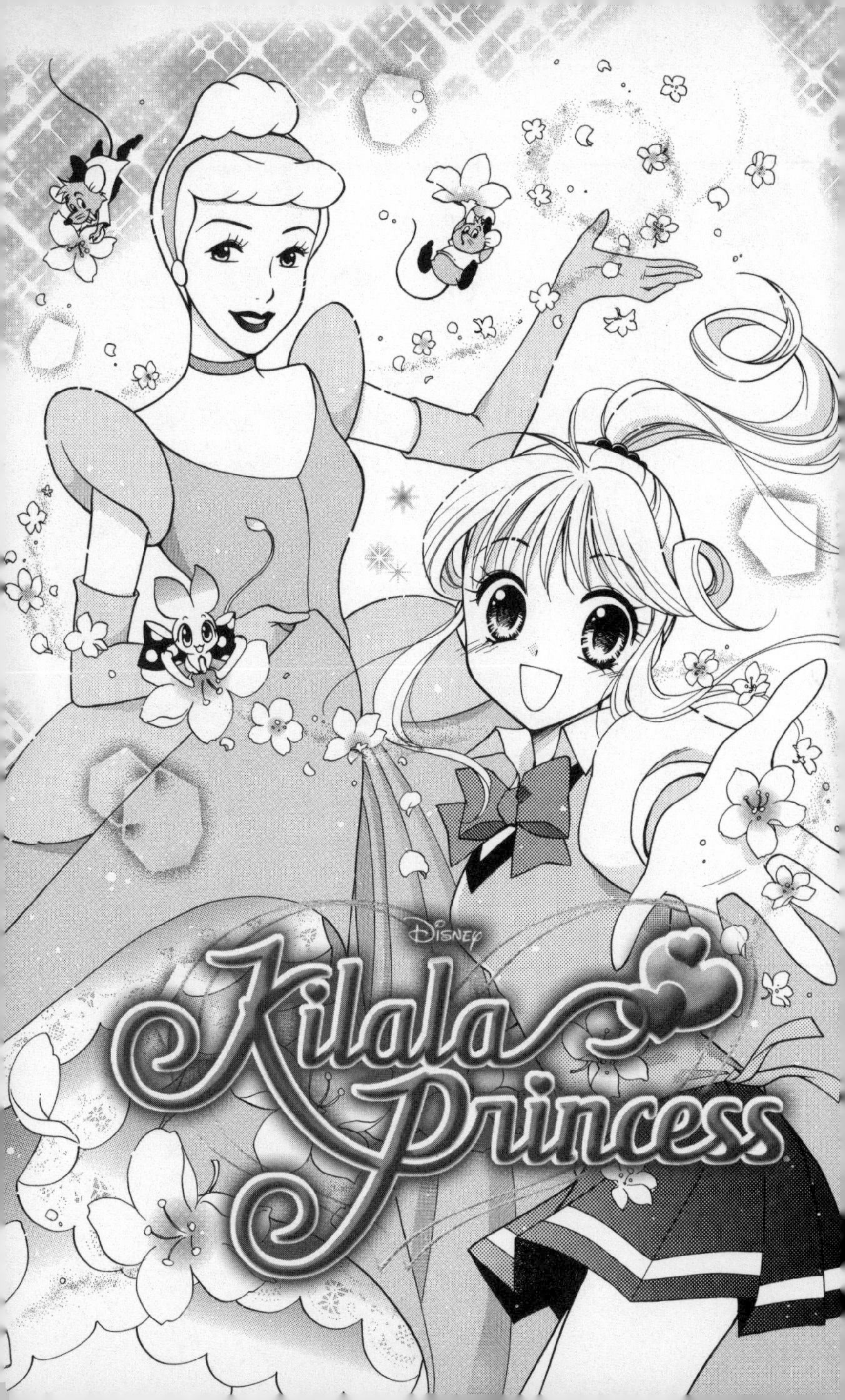
Disney
Kilala Princess

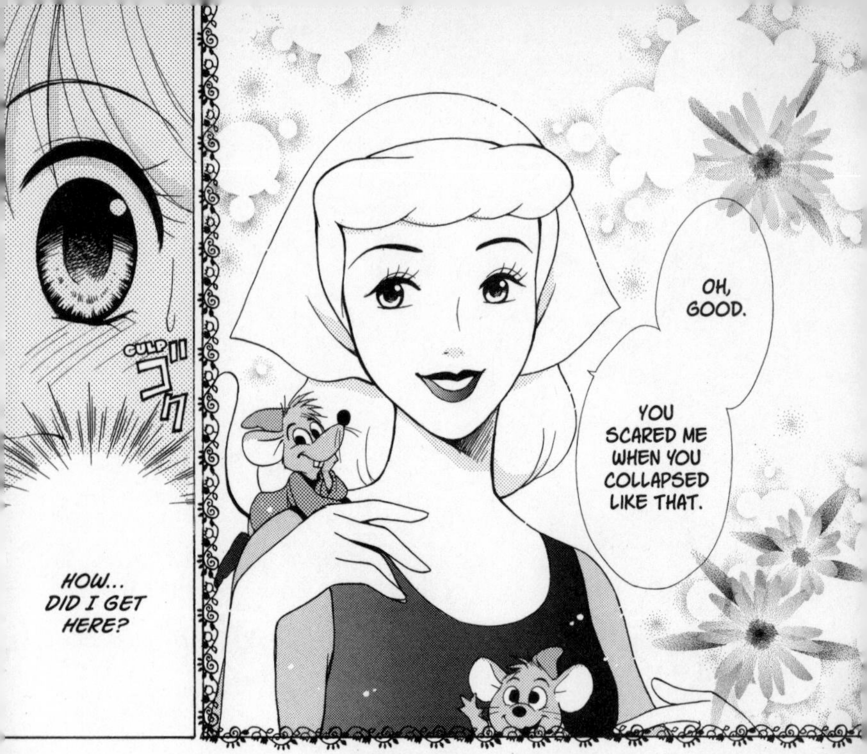
OH, GOOD.
YOU SCARED ME WHEN YOU COLLAPSED LIKE THAT.
GULP!!
ゴク
HOW... DID I GET HERE?

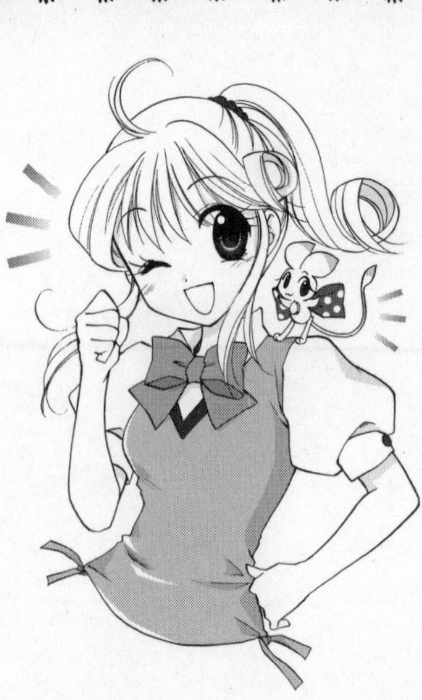

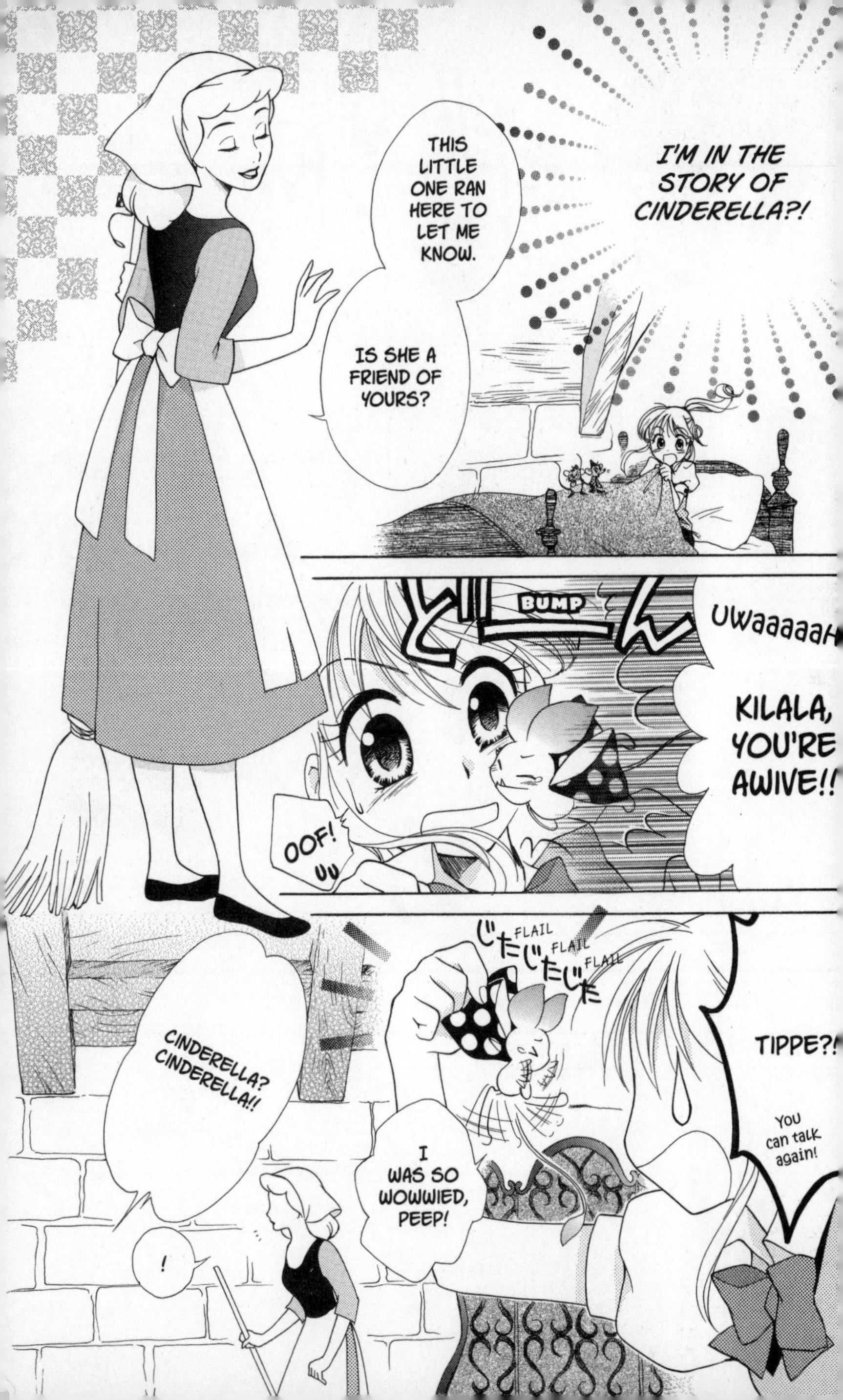

I'M IN THE STORY OF CINDERELLA?!
THIS LITTLE ONE RAN HERE TO LET ME KNOW.
IS SHE A FRIEND OF YOURS?
BUMP
UWaaaaaH
KILALA, YOU'RE AWIVE!!
OOF! UU
じたじたじた
FLAIL FLAIL FLAIL
TIPPE?!
You can talk again!
I WAS SO WOWWIED, PEEP!
CINDERELLA? CINDERELLA!!
!

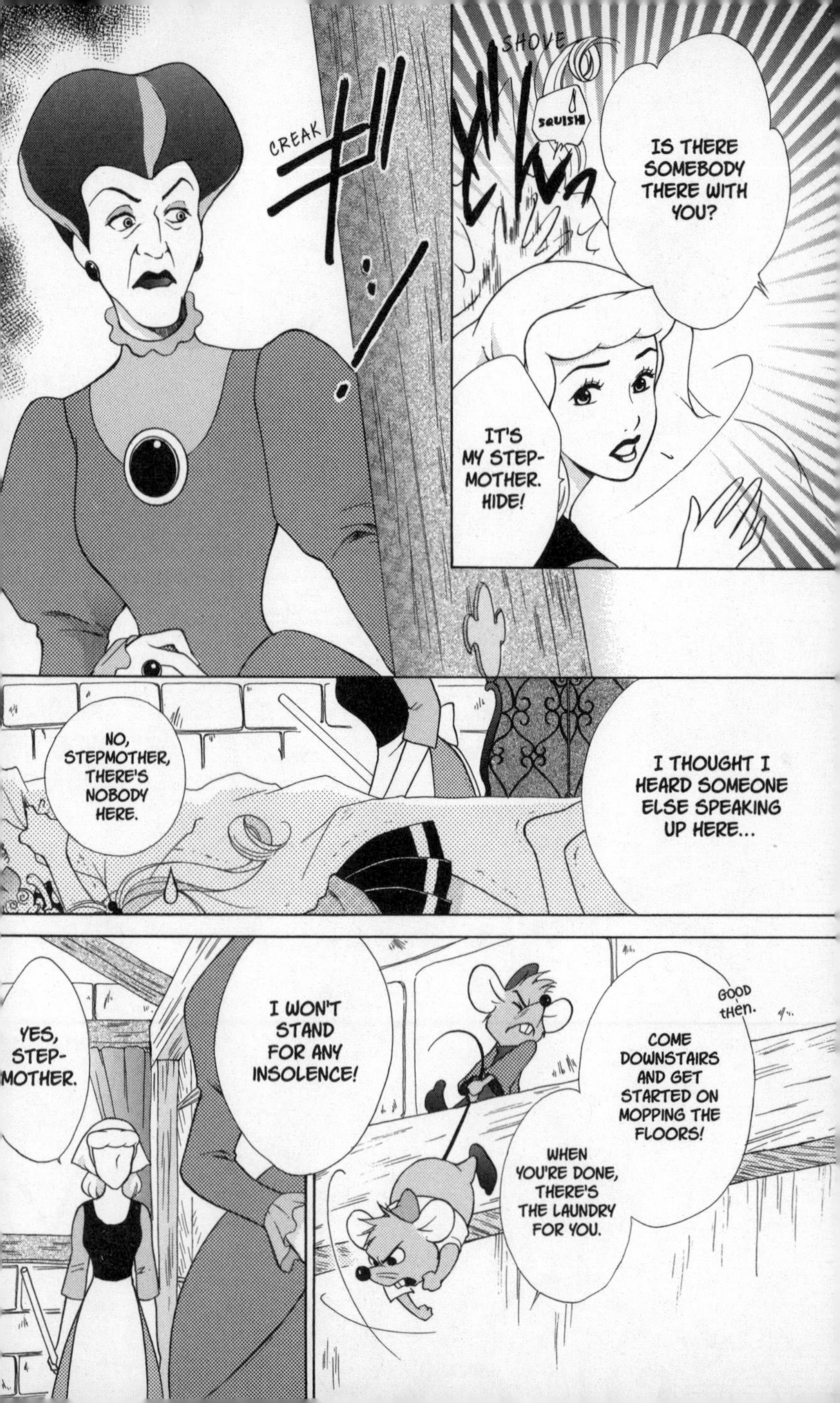
SHOVE
SQUISH
IS THERE SOMEBODY THERE WITH YOU?
IT'S MY STEP-MOTHER. HIDE!
CREAK
I THOUGHT I HEARD SOMEONE ELSE SPEAKING UP HERE...
NO, STEPMOTHER, THERE'S NOBODY HERE.
GOOD THEN.
COME DOWNSTAIRS AND GET STARTED ON MOPPING THE FLOORS!
WHEN YOU'RE DONE, THERE'S THE LAUNDRY FOR YOU.
I WON'T STAND FOR ANY INSOLENCE!
YES, STEP-MOTHER.

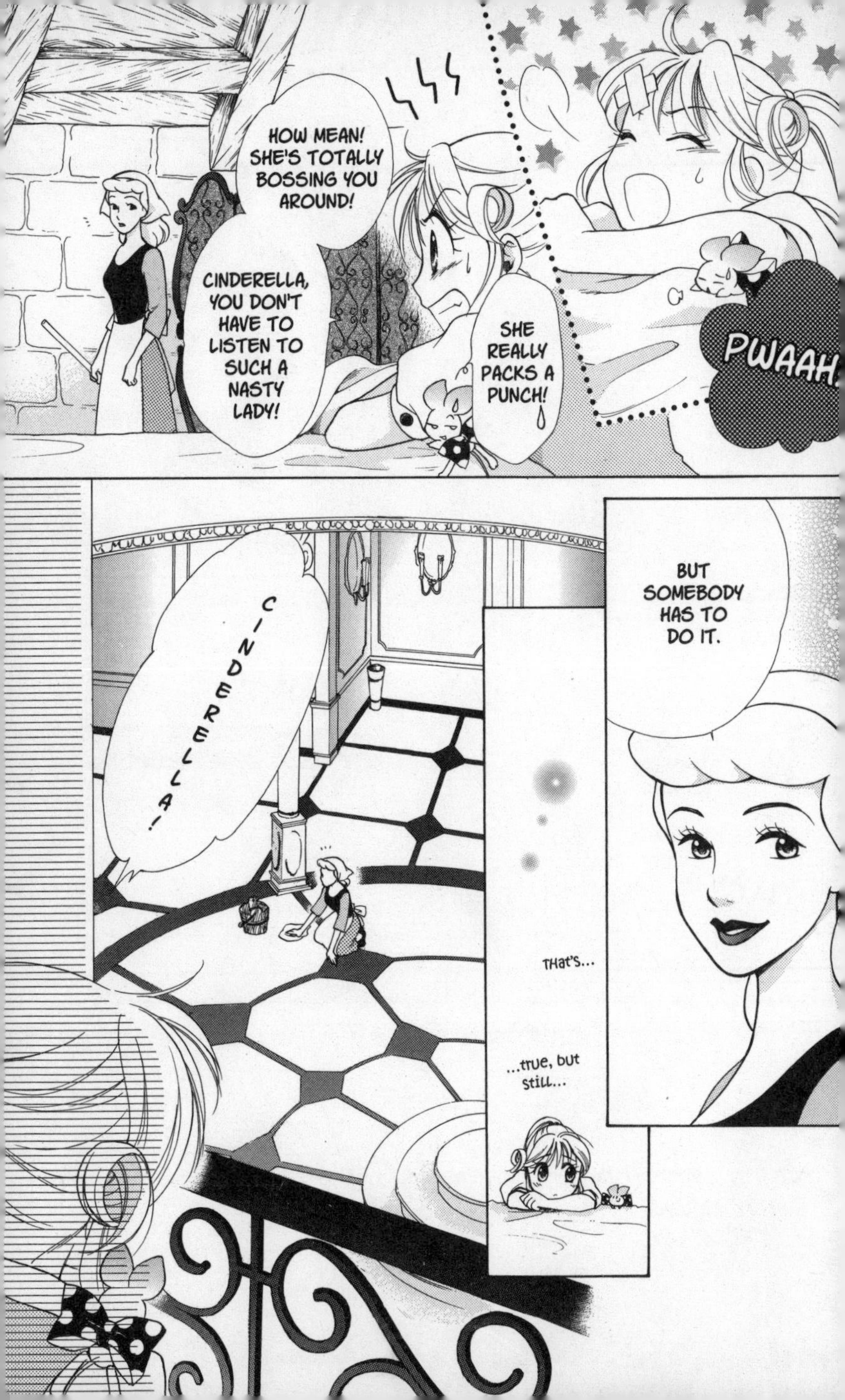
PWAAH
SHE REALLY PACKS A PUNCH!
HOW MEAN! SHE'S TOTALLY BOSSING YOU AROUND!
CINDERELLA, YOU DON'T HAVE TO LISTEN TO SUCH A NASTY LADY!
BUT SOMEBODY HAS TO DO IT.
That's...
...true, but still...
CINDERELLA!

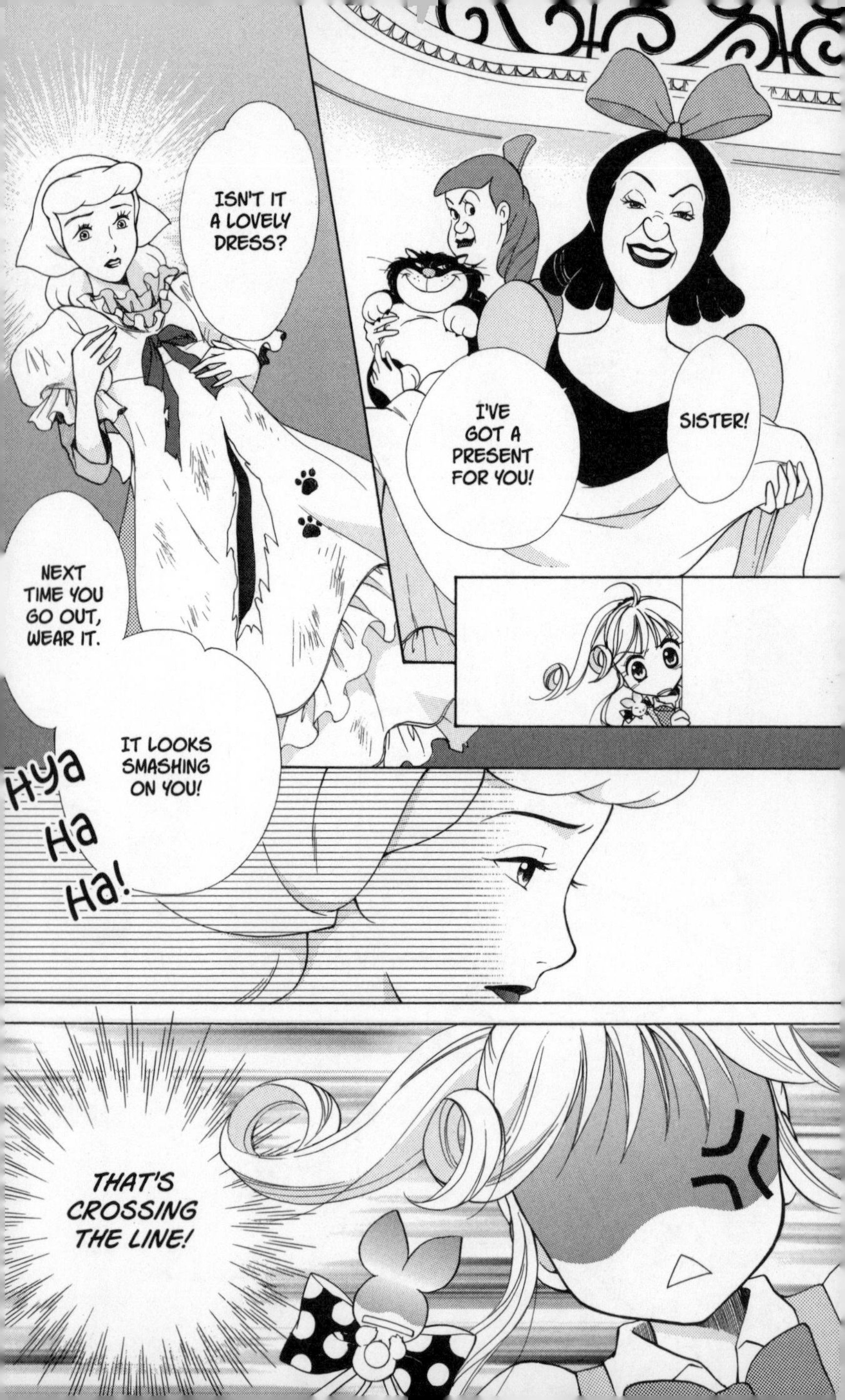
SISTER!
I'VE GOT A PRESENT FOR YOU!
ISN'T IT A LOVELY DRESS?
NEXT TIME YOU GO OUT, WEAR IT.
IT LOOKS SMASHING ON YOU!
Hya Ha Ha!
THAT'S CROSSING THE LINE!

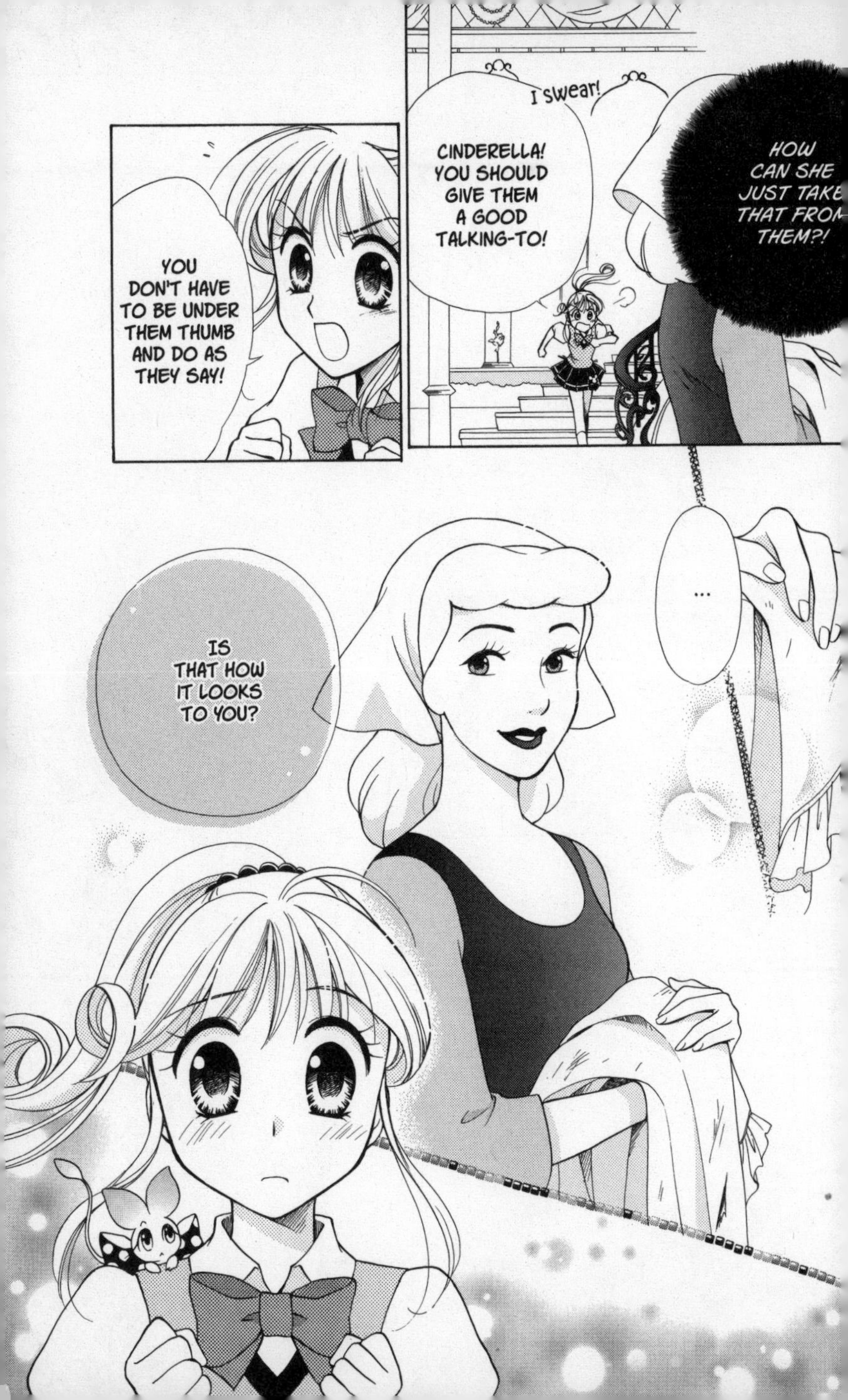
HOW CAN SHE JUST TAKE THAT FROM THEM?!
I swear!
CINDERELLA! YOU SHOULD GIVE THEM A GOOD TALKING-TO!
YOU DON'T HAVE TO BE UNDER THEM THUMB AND DO AS THEY SAY!
...
IS THAT HOW IT LOOKS TO YOU?

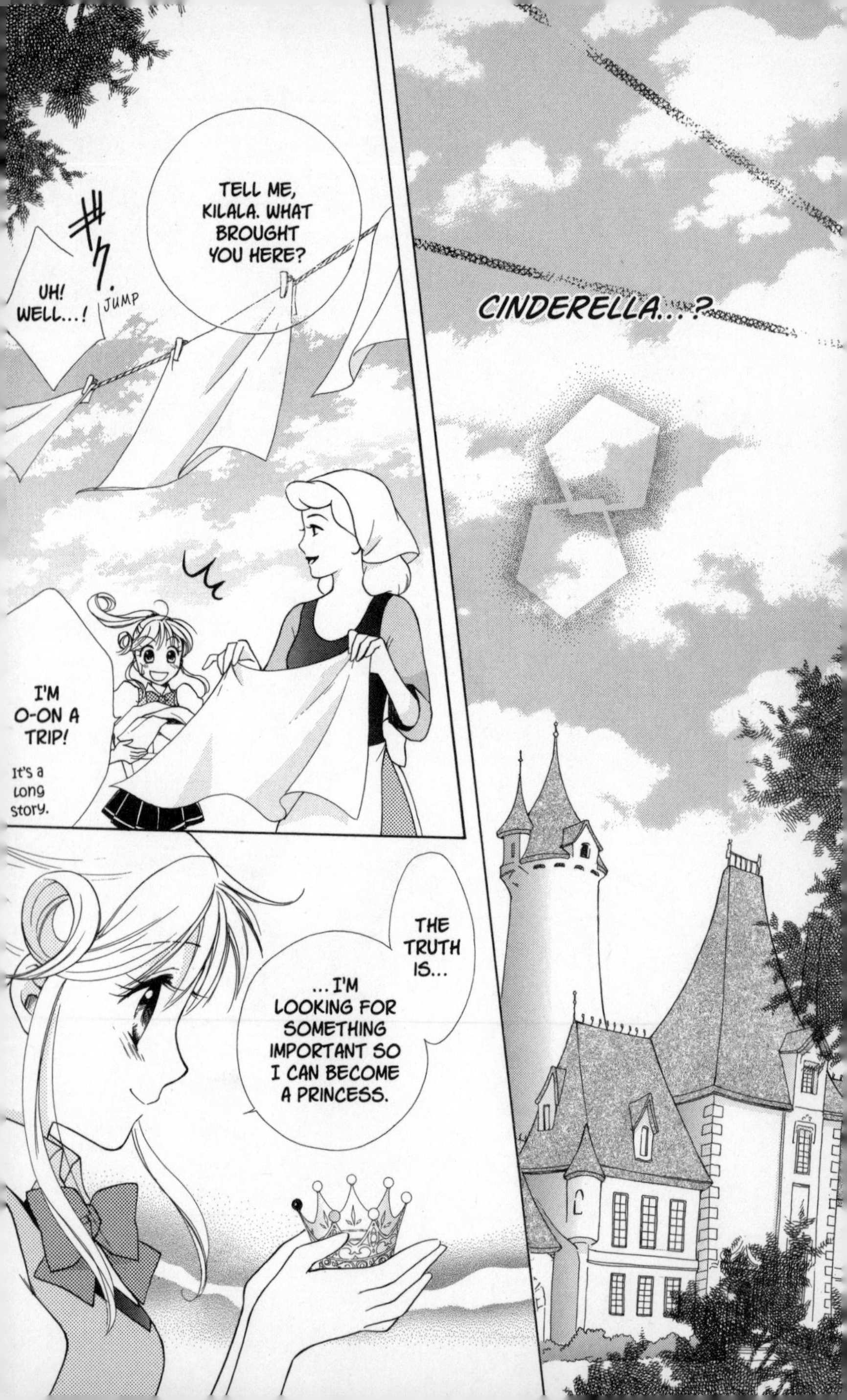
CINDERELLA...?
TELL ME, KILALA. WHAT BROUGHT YOU HERE?
ギク.
JUMP
UH! WELL...!
I'M O-ON A TRIP!
It's a long story.
THE TRUTH IS...
...I'M LOOKING FOR SOMETHING IMPORTANT SO I CAN BECOME A PRINCESS.

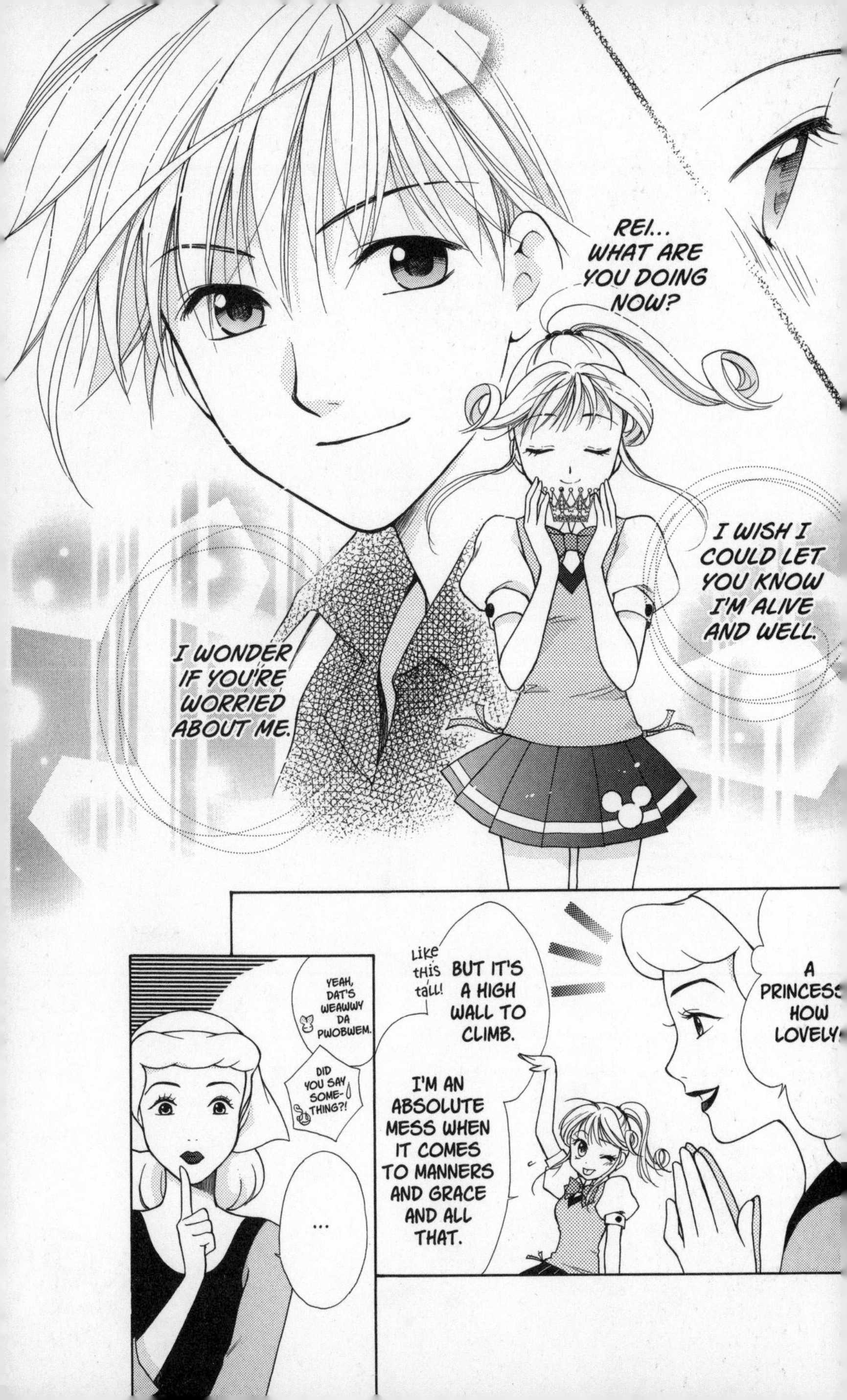
REI... WHAT ARE YOU DOING NOW?
I WISH I COULD LET YOU KNOW I'M ALIVE AND WELL.
I WONDER IF YOU'RE WORRIED ABOUT ME.
A PRINCESS HOW LOVELY
BUT IT'S A HIGH WALL TO CLIMB.
Like this tall!
I'M AN ABSOLUTE MESS WHEN IT COMES TO MANNERS AND GRACE AND ALL THAT.
YEAH, DAT'S WEAWWY DA PWOBWEM.
DID YOU SAY SOME-THING?!
...

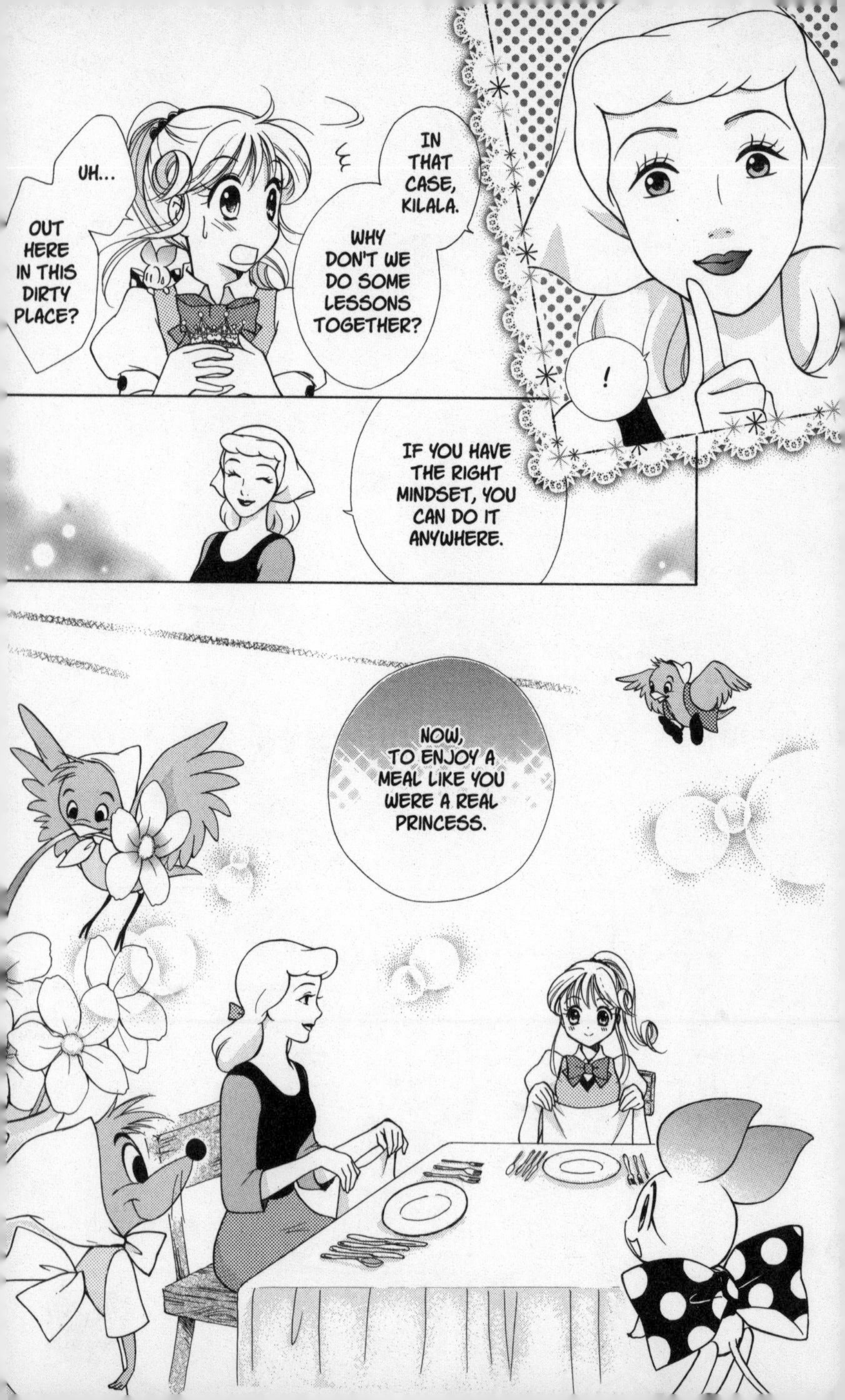
!
IN THAT CASE, KILALA.
WHY DON'T WE DO SOME LESSONS TOGETHER?
UH...
OUT HERE IN THIS DIRTY PLACE?
IF YOU HAVE THE RIGHT MINDSET, YOU CAN DO IT ANYWHERE.
NOW, TO ENJOY A MEAL LIKE YOU WERE A REAL PRINCESS.

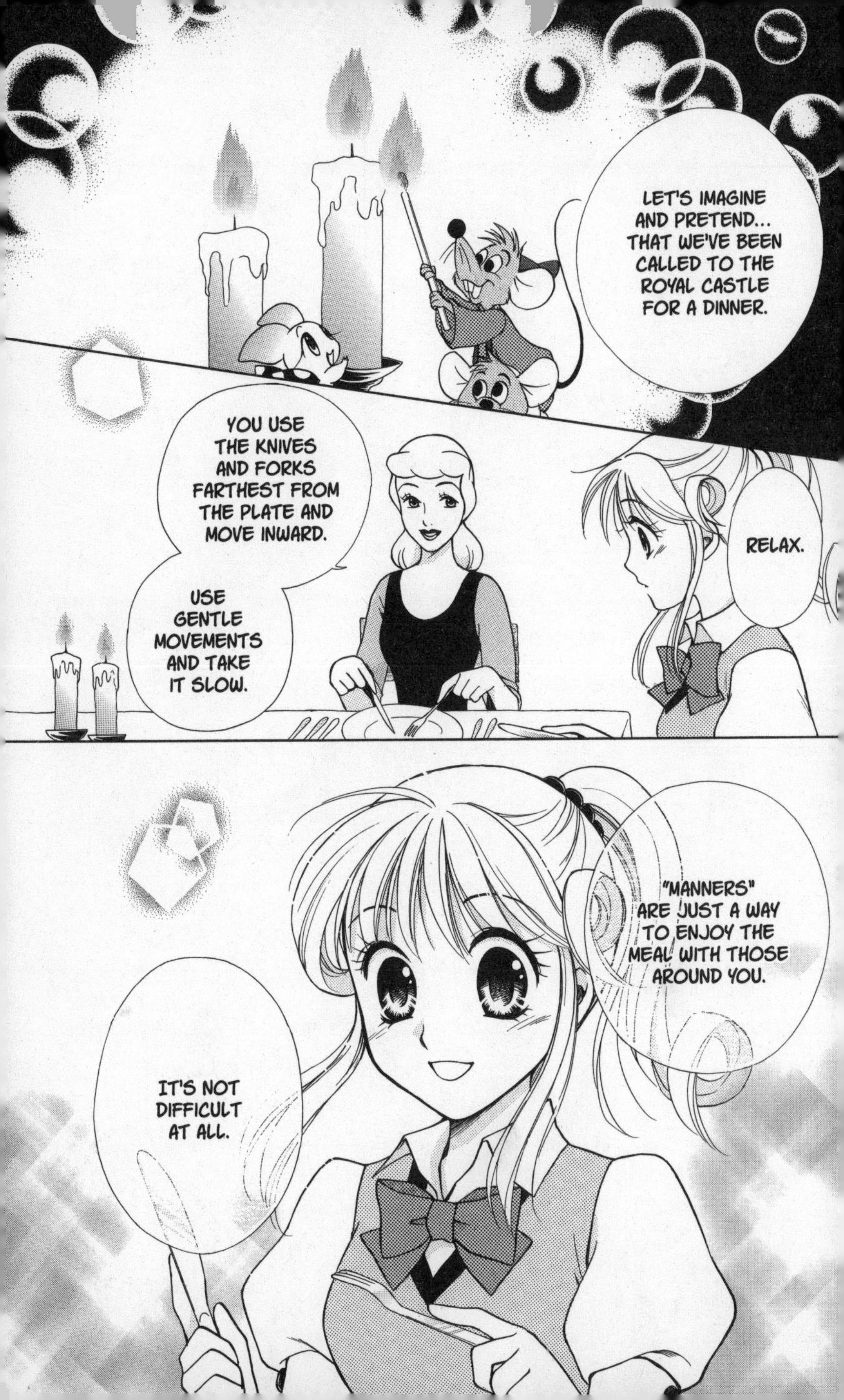
LET'S IMAGINE AND PRETEND... THAT WE'VE BEEN CALLED TO THE ROYAL CASTLE FOR A DINNER.
RELAX.
YOU USE THE KNIVES AND FORKS FARTHEST FROM THE PLATE AND MOVE INWARD.
USE GENTLE MOVEMENTS AND TAKE IT SLOW.
"MANNERS" ARE JUST A WAY TO ENJOY THE MEAL WITH THOSE AROUND YOU.
IT'S NOT DIFFICULT AT ALL.

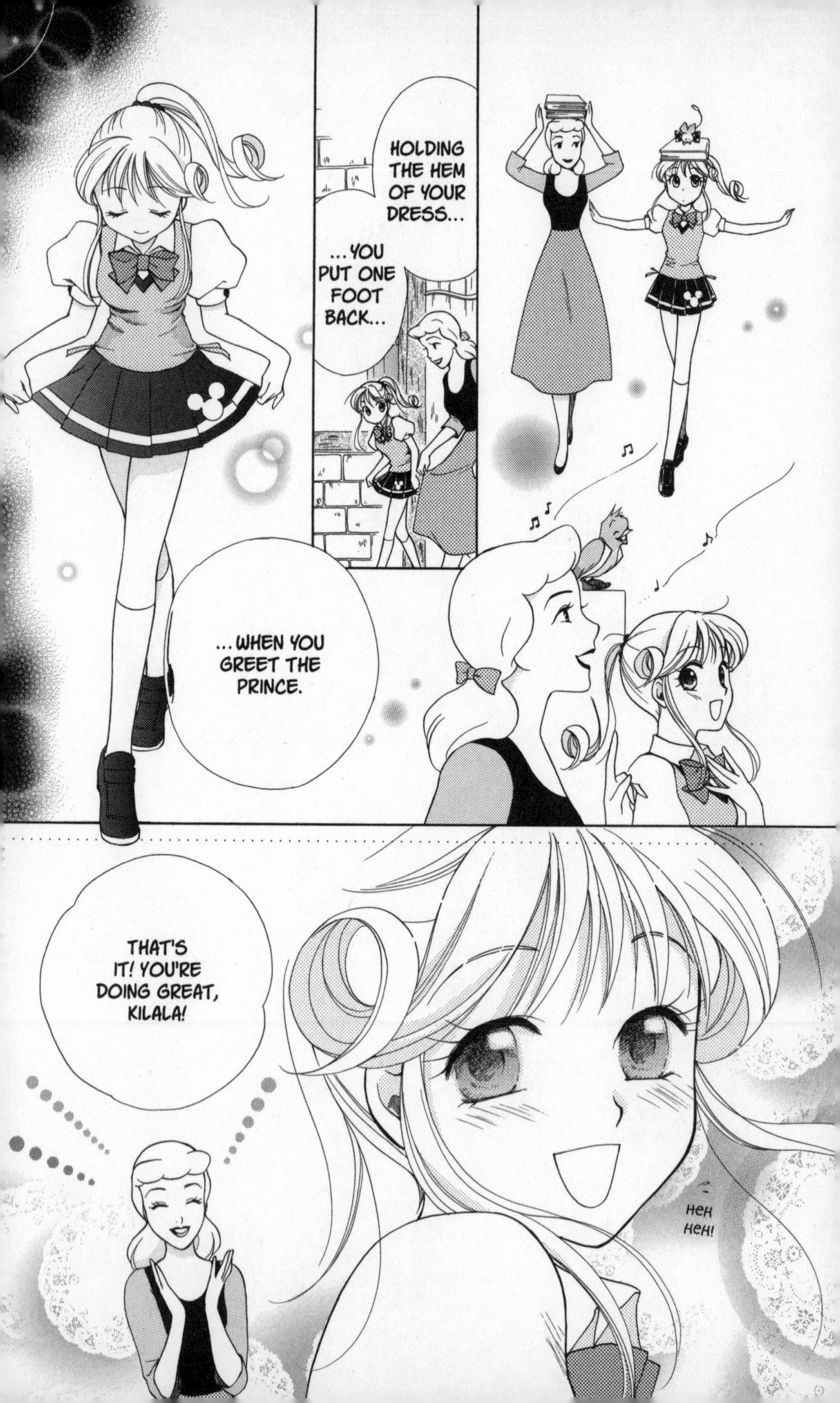
HOLDING THE HEM OF YOUR DRESS...
...YOU PUT ONE FOOT BACK...
...WHEN YOU GREET THE PRINCE.
THAT'S IT! YOU'RE DOING GREAT, KILALA!
HEH HEH!

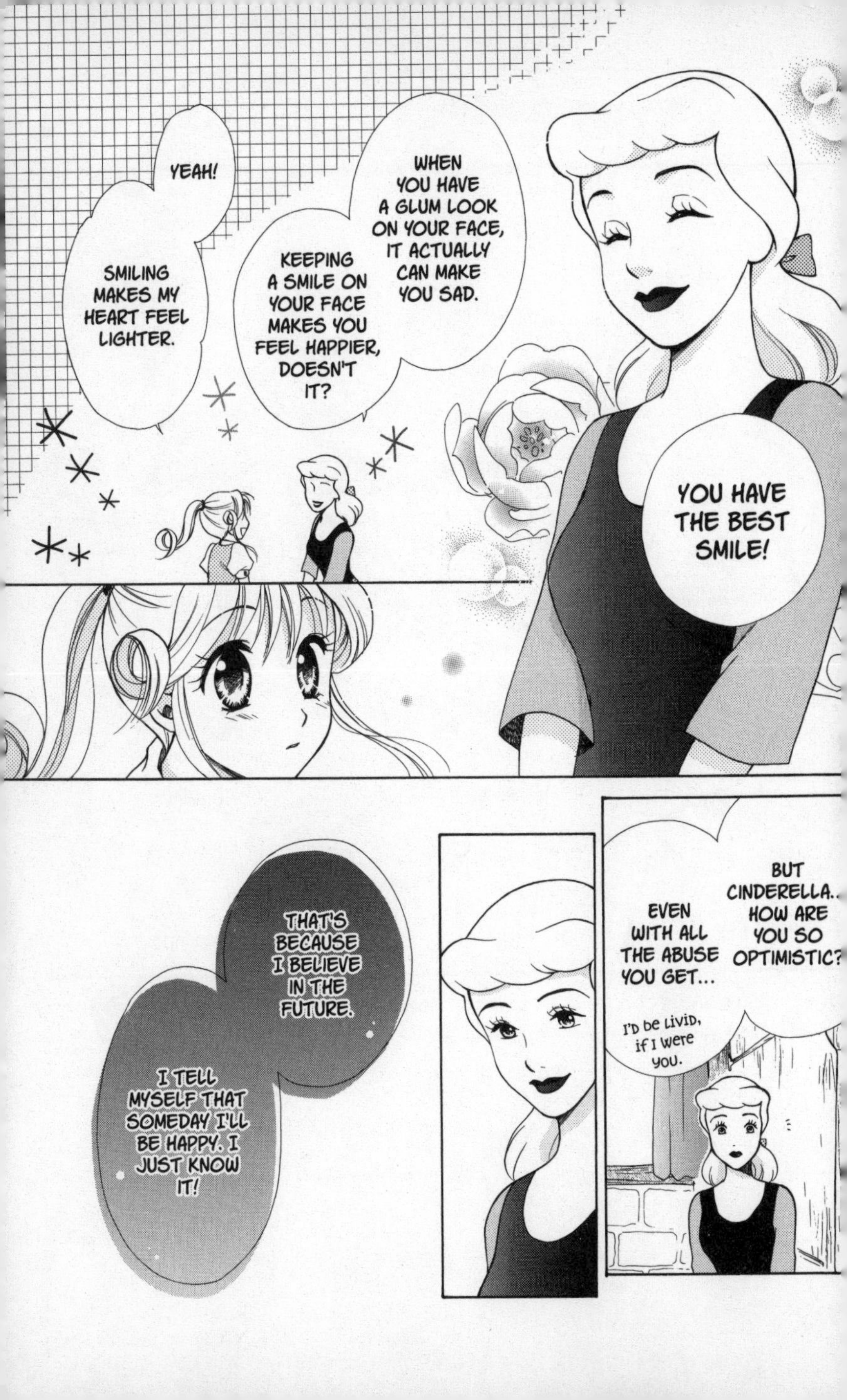
WHEN YOU HAVE A GLUM LOOK ON YOUR FACE, IT ACTUALLY CAN MAKE YOU SAD.
KEEPING A SMILE ON YOUR FACE MAKES YOU FEEL HAPPIER, DOESN'T IT?
YEAH!
SMILING MAKES MY HEART FEEL LIGHTER.
YOU HAVE THE BEST SMILE!
BUT CINDERELLA... HOW ARE YOU SO OPTIMISTIC?
EVEN WITH ALL THE ABUSE YOU GET...
I'D be Livid, if I Were you.
THAT'S BECAUSE I BELIEVE IN THE FUTURE.
I TELL MYSELF THAT SOMEDAY I'LL BE HAPPY. I JUST KNOW IT!

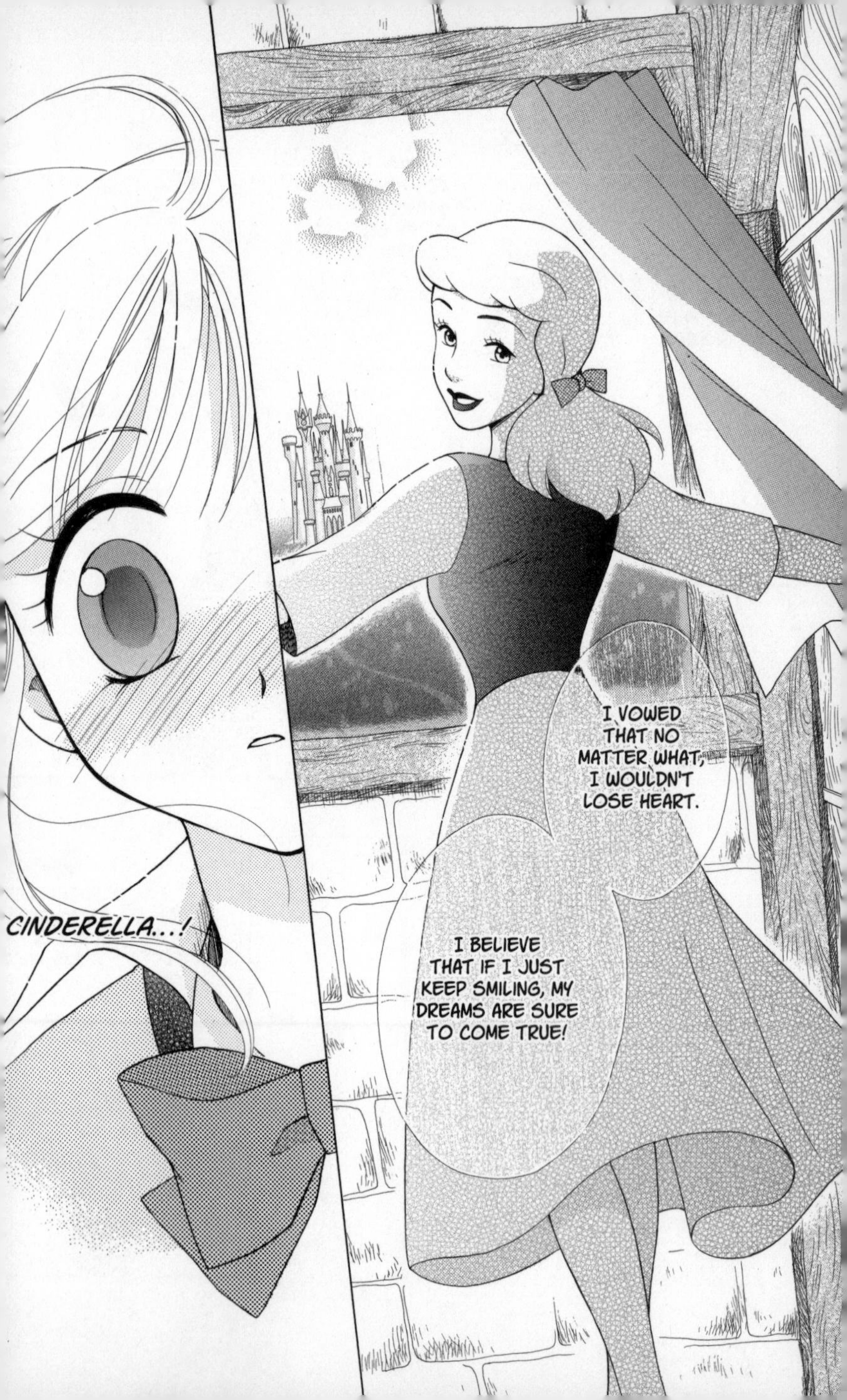
I VOWED THAT NO MATTER WHAT, I WOULDN'T LOSE HEART.
I BELIEVE THAT IF I JUST KEEP SMILING, MY DREAMS ARE SURE TO COME TRUE!
CINDERELLA...!

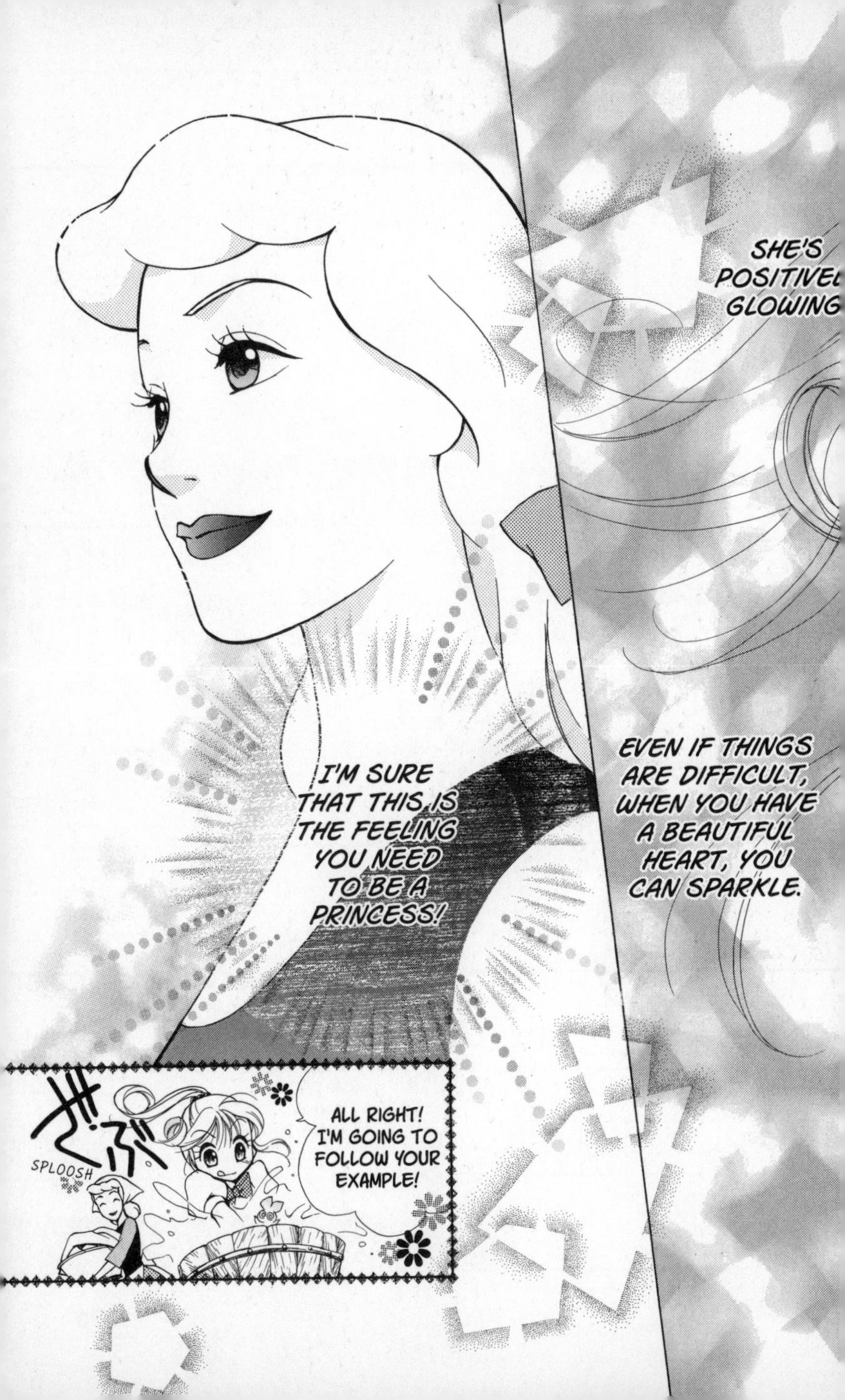
SHE'S POSITIVEL GLOWING
EVEN IF THINGS ARE DIFFICULT, WHEN YOU HAVE A BEAUTIFUL HEART, YOU CAN SPARKLE.
I'M SURE THAT THIS IS THE FEELING YOU NEED TO BE A PRINCESS!
ALL RIGHT! I'M GOING TO FOLLOW YOUR EXAMPLE!
SPLOOSH

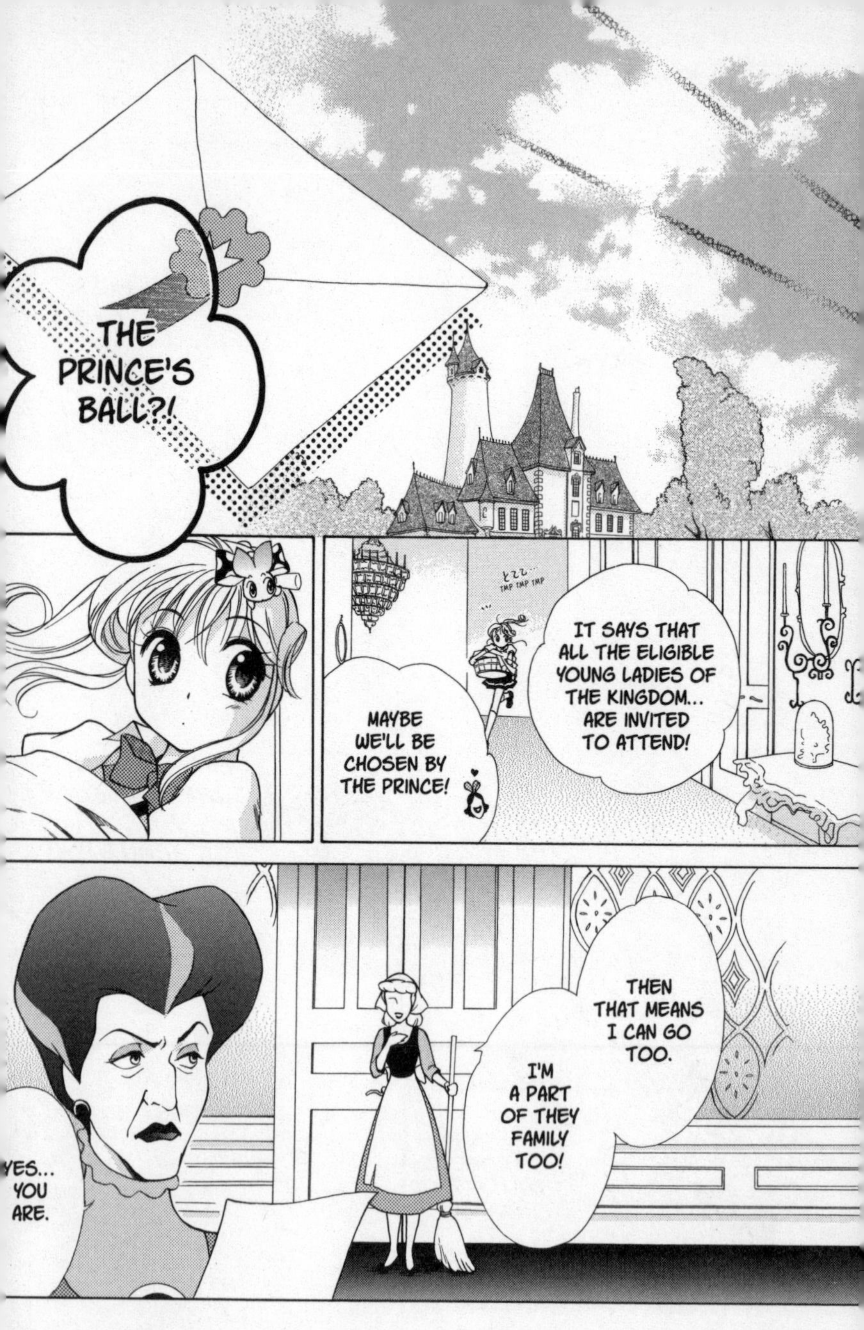
THE PRINCE'S BALL?!
TMP TMP TMP
IT SAYS THAT ALL THE ELIGIBLE YOUNG LADIES OF THE KINGDOM... ARE INVITED TO ATTEND!
MAYBE WE'LL BE CHOSEN BY THE PRINCE!
THEN THAT MEANS I CAN GO TOO.
I'M A PART OF THEY FAMILY TOO!
YES... YOU ARE.

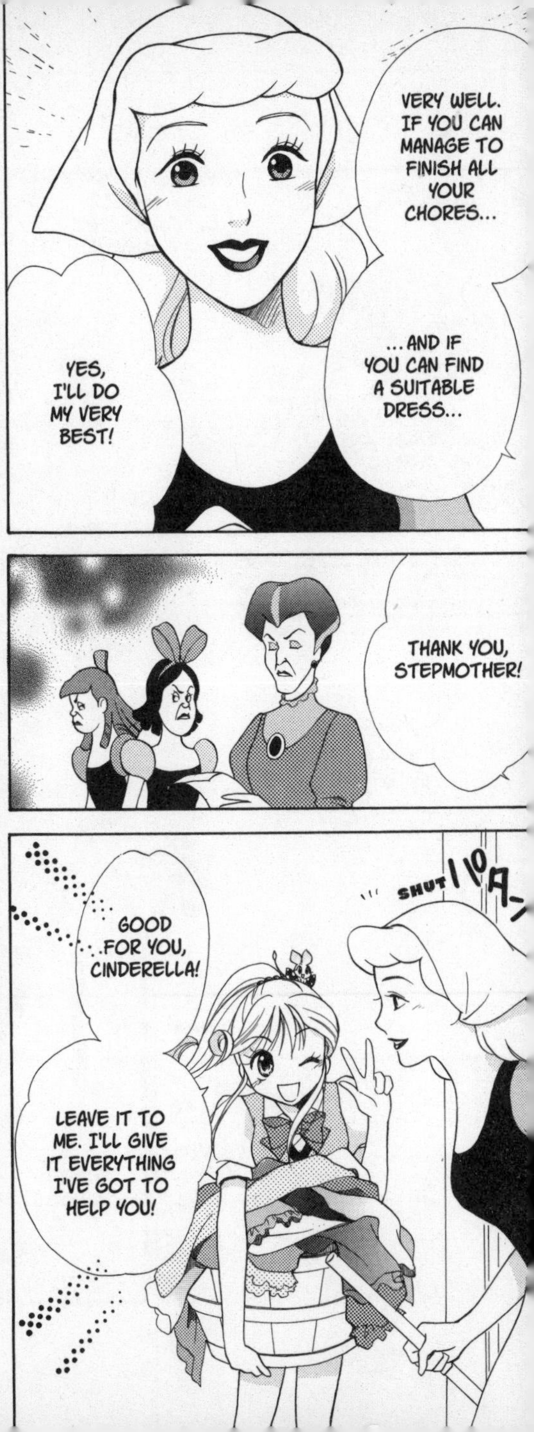
VERY WELL. IF YOU CAN MANAGE TO FINISH ALL YOUR CHORES...
...AND IF YOU CAN FIND A SUITABLE DRESS...
YES, I'LL DO MY VERY BEST!
THANK YOU, STEPMOTHER!
SHUT
GOOD FOR YOU, CINDERELLA!
LEAVE IT TO ME. I'LL GIVE IT EVERYTHING I'VE GOT TO HELP YOU!

TIPPE HELPS OUT

4

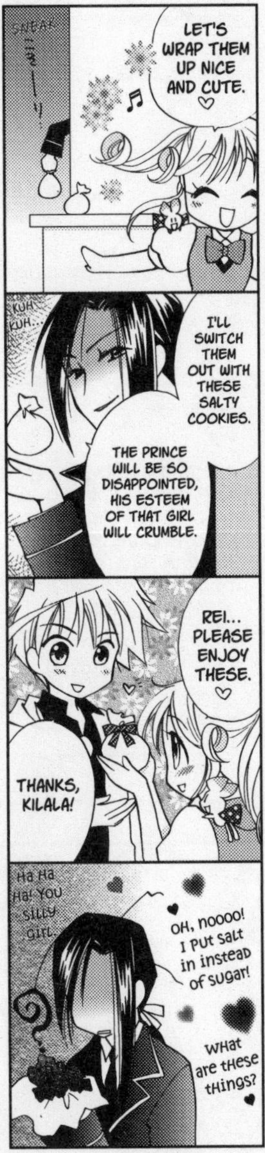
SNEAK
LET'S WRAP THEM UP NICE AND CUTE. ♡
KUH KUH...
I'LL SWITCH THEM OUT WITH THESE SALTY COOKIES.
THE PRINCE WILL BE SO DISAPPOINTED, HIS ESTEEM OF THAT GIRL WILL CRUMBLE.
REI... PLEASE ENJOY THESE. ♡
THANKS, KILALA!
OH, noooo! I Put salt in instead of sugar!
WHat are these things? ♥
Ha Ha Ha! You silly girl...

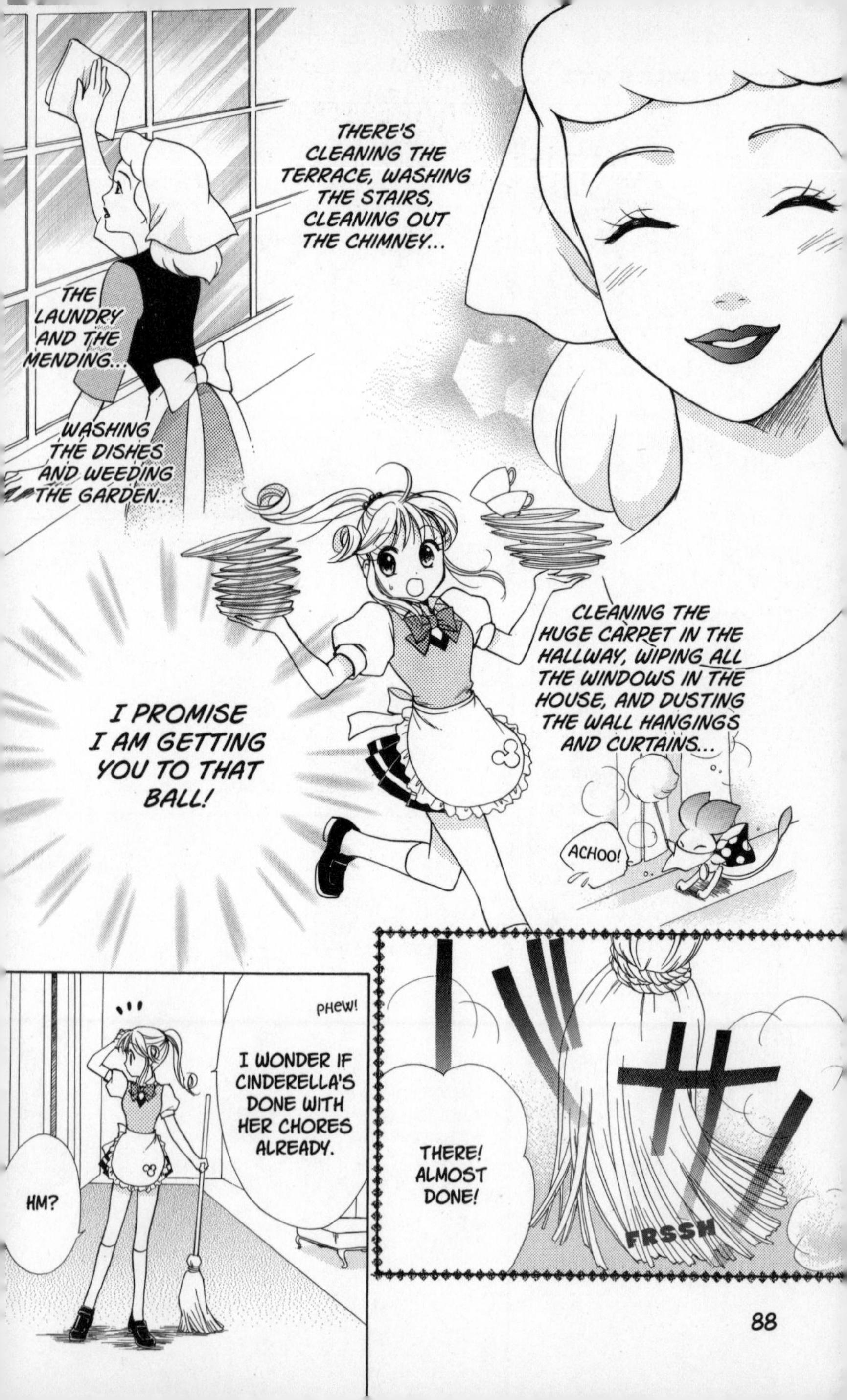
THERE'S CLEANING THE TERRACE, WASHING THE STAIRS, CLEANING OUT THE CHIMNEY...
THE LAUNDRY AND THE MENDING...
WASHING THE DISHES AND WEEDING THE GARDEN...
CLEANING THE HUGE CARPET IN THE HALLWAY, WIPING ALL THE WINDOWS IN THE HOUSE, AND DUSTING THE WALL HANGINGS AND CURTAINS...
ACHOO!
I PROMISE I AM GETTING YOU TO THAT BALL!
THERE! ALMOST DONE!
FRSSH
PHEW!
I WONDER IF CINDERELLA'S DONE WITH HER CHORES ALREADY.
HM?

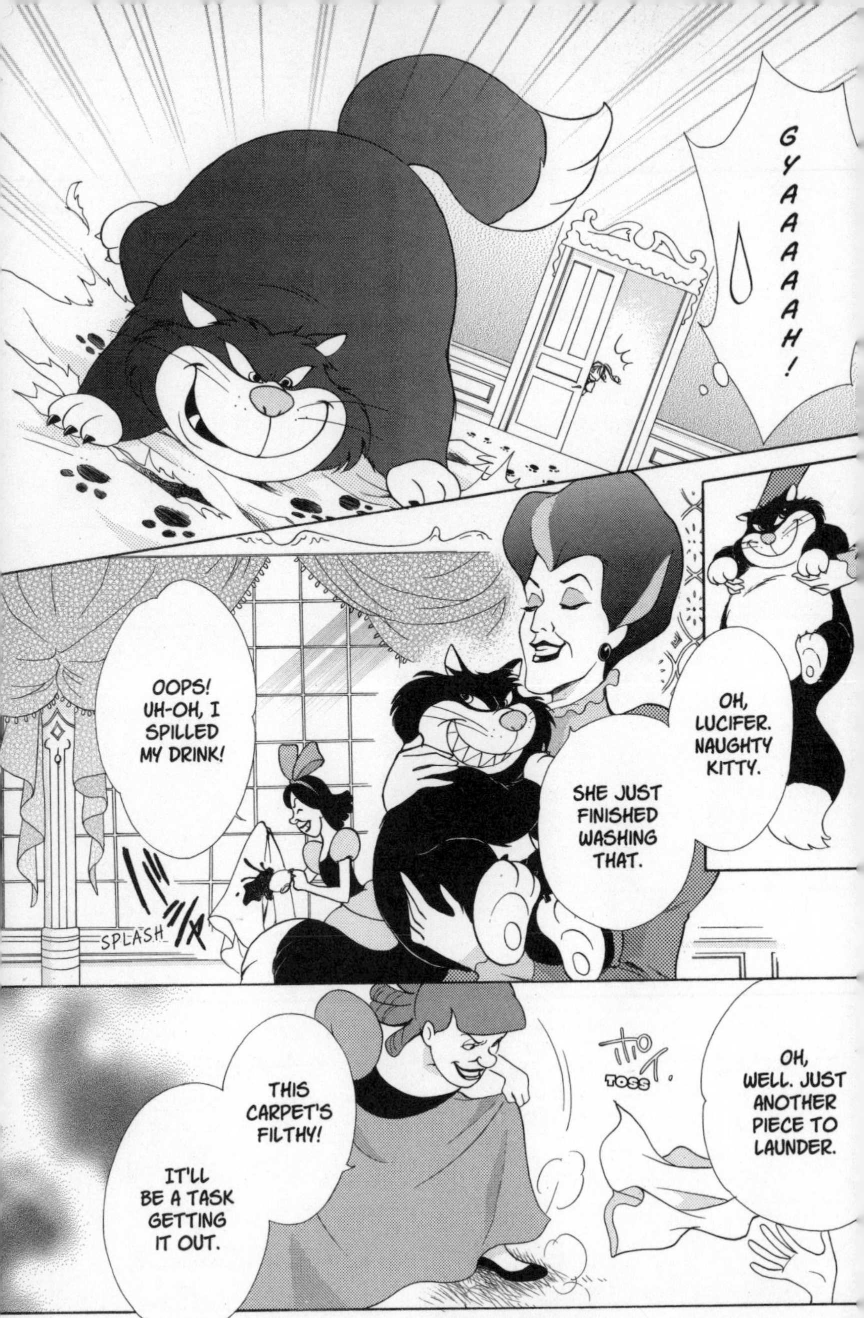
GYAAAAAH!
OH, LUCIFER. NAUGHTY KITTY.
SHE JUST FINISHED WASHING THAT.
OOPS! UH-OH, I SPILLED MY DRINK!
SPLASH
OH, WELL. JUST ANOTHER PIECE TO LAUNDER.
TOSS
THIS CARPET'S FILTHY!
IT'LL BE A TASK GETTING IT OUT.

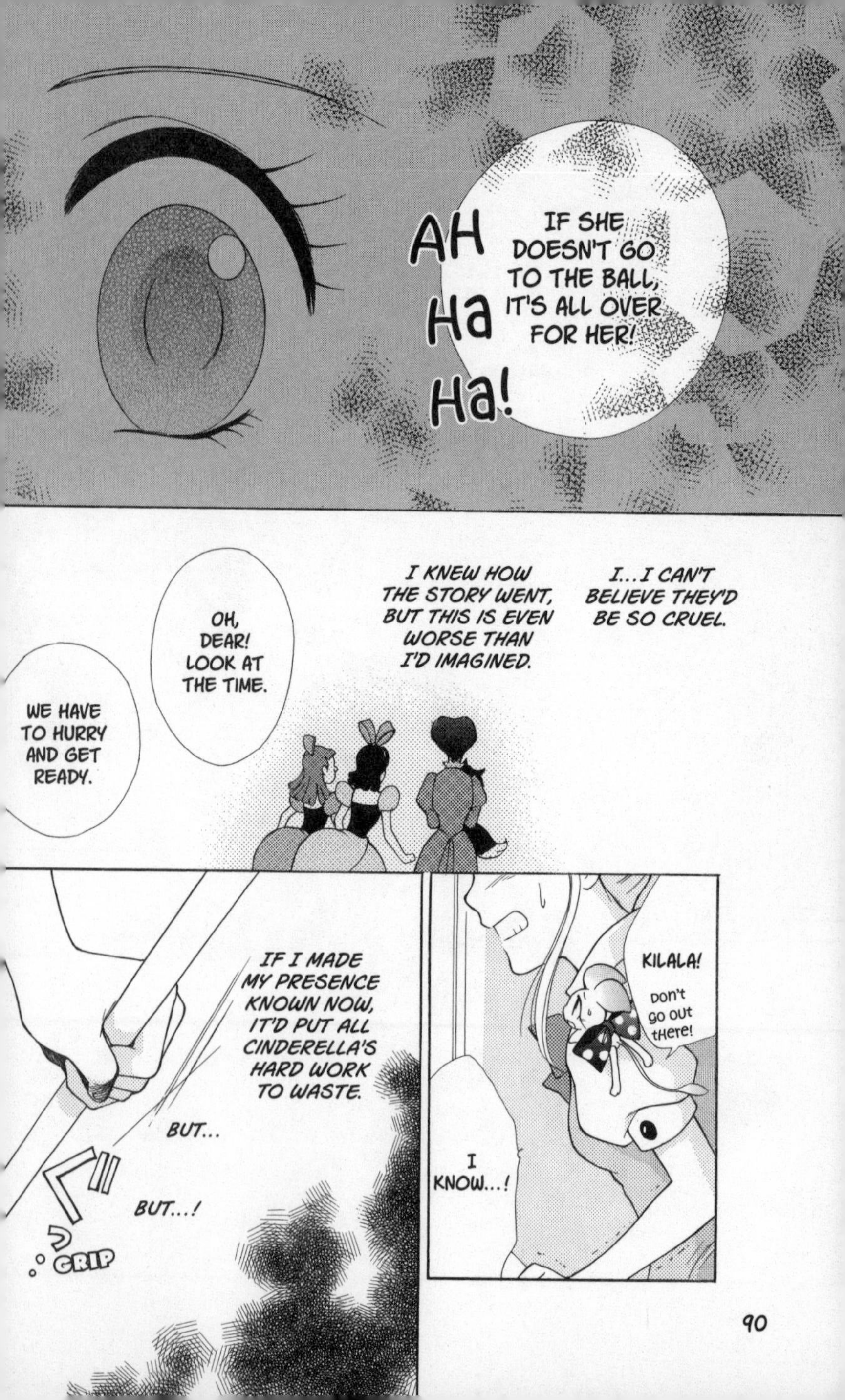
IF SHE DOESN'T GO TO THE BALL, IT'S ALL OVER FOR HER!
AH Ha Ha!
I...I CAN'T BELIEVE THEY'D BE SO CRUEL.
I KNEW HOW THE STORY WENT, BUT THIS IS EVEN WORSE THAN I'D IMAGINED.
OH, DEAR! LOOK AT THE TIME.
WE HAVE TO HURRY AND GET READY.
KILALA!
Don't go out there!
I KNOW...!
IF I MADE MY PRESENCE KNOWN NOW, IT'D PUT ALL CINDERELLA'S HARD WORK TO WASTE.
BUT...
BUT...!
GRIP

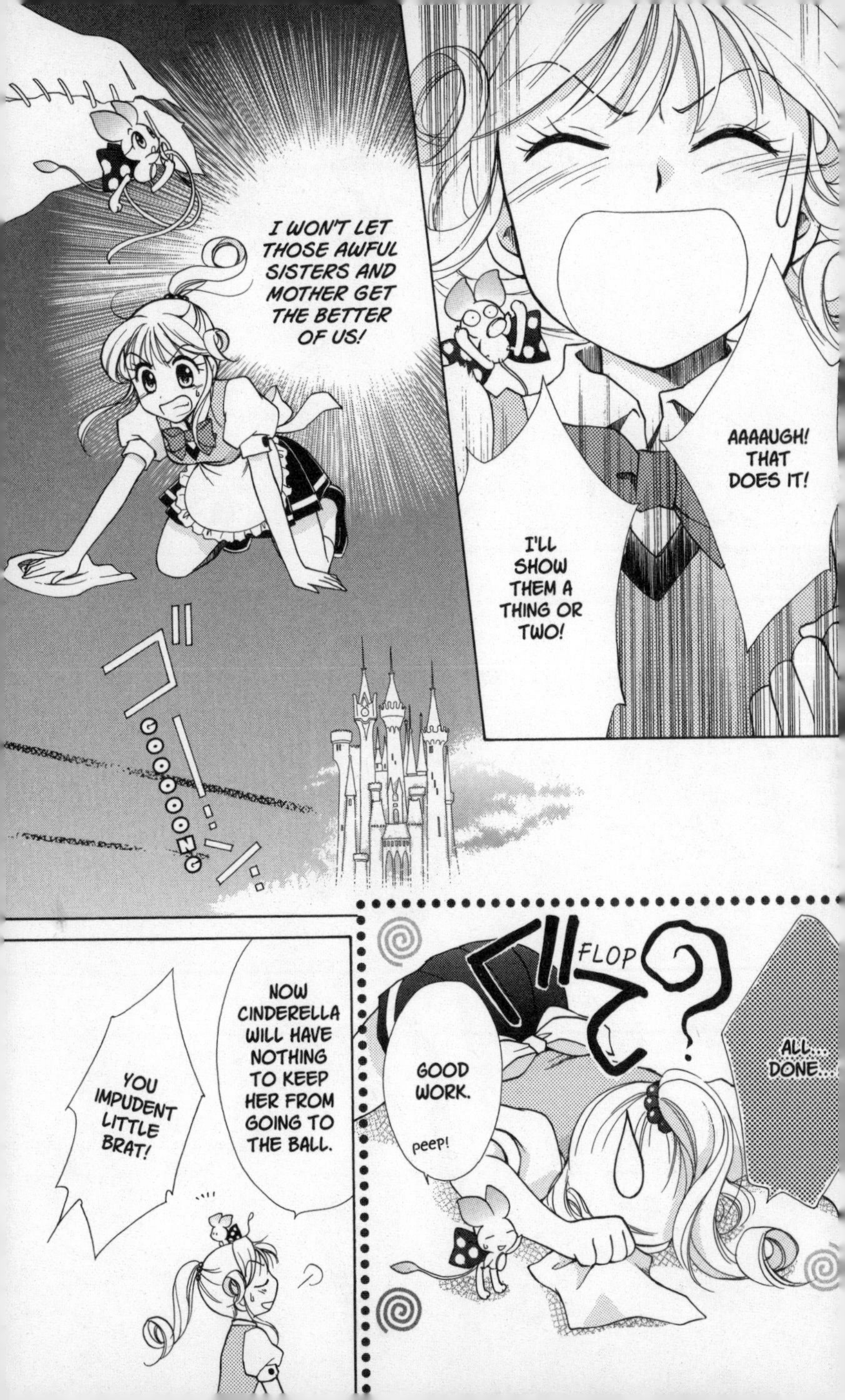

AAAAUGH! THAT DOES IT!
I'LL SHOW THEM A THING OR TWO!
I WON'T LET THOSE AWFUL SISTERS AND MOTHER GET THE BETTER OF US!
GOOOOOONG
ALL... DONE...
FLOP
GOOD WORK.
peep!
NOW CINDERELLA WILL HAVE NOTHING TO KEEP HER FROM GOING TO THE BALL.
YOU IMPUDENT LITTLE BRAT!

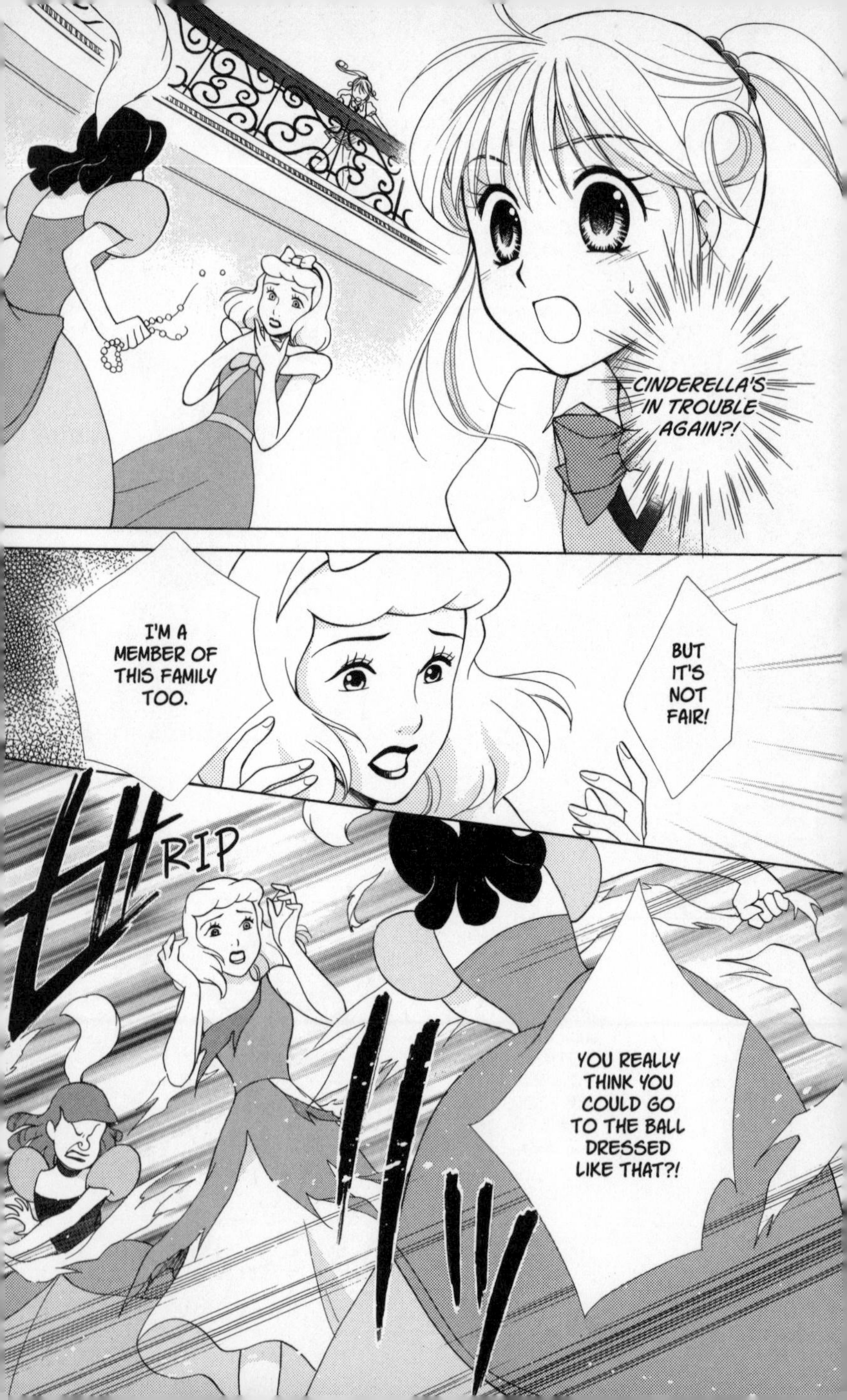
CINDERELLA'S IN TROUBLE AGAIN?!
BUT IT'S NOT FAIR!
I'M A MEMBER OF THIS FAMILY TOO.
YOU REALLY THINK YOU COULD GO TO THE BALL DRESSED LIKE THAT?!
RIP

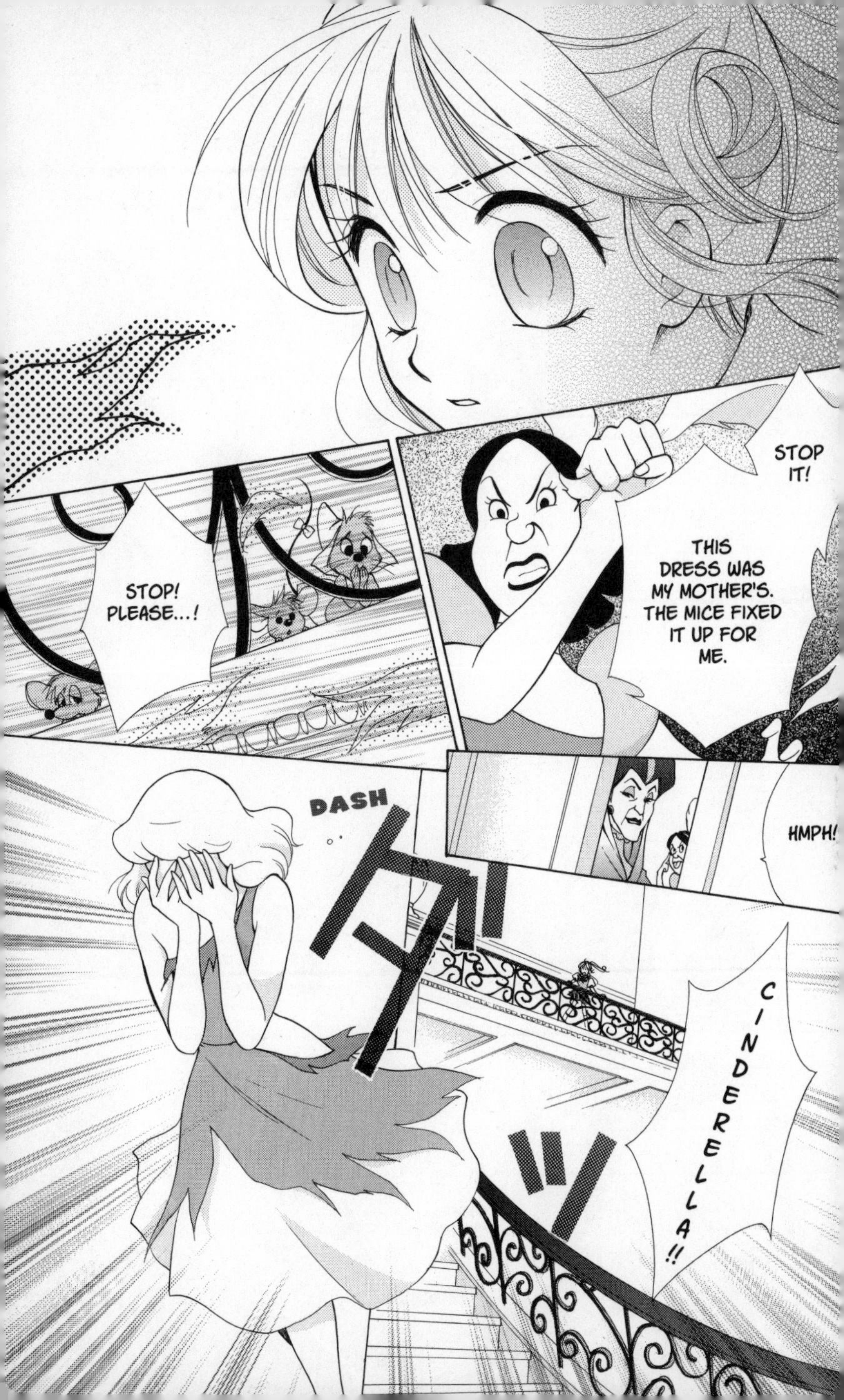
STOP IT!
THIS DRESS WAS MY MOTHER'S. THE MICE FIXED IT UP FOR ME.
STOP! PLEASE...!
HMPH!
CINDERELLA!!
DASH

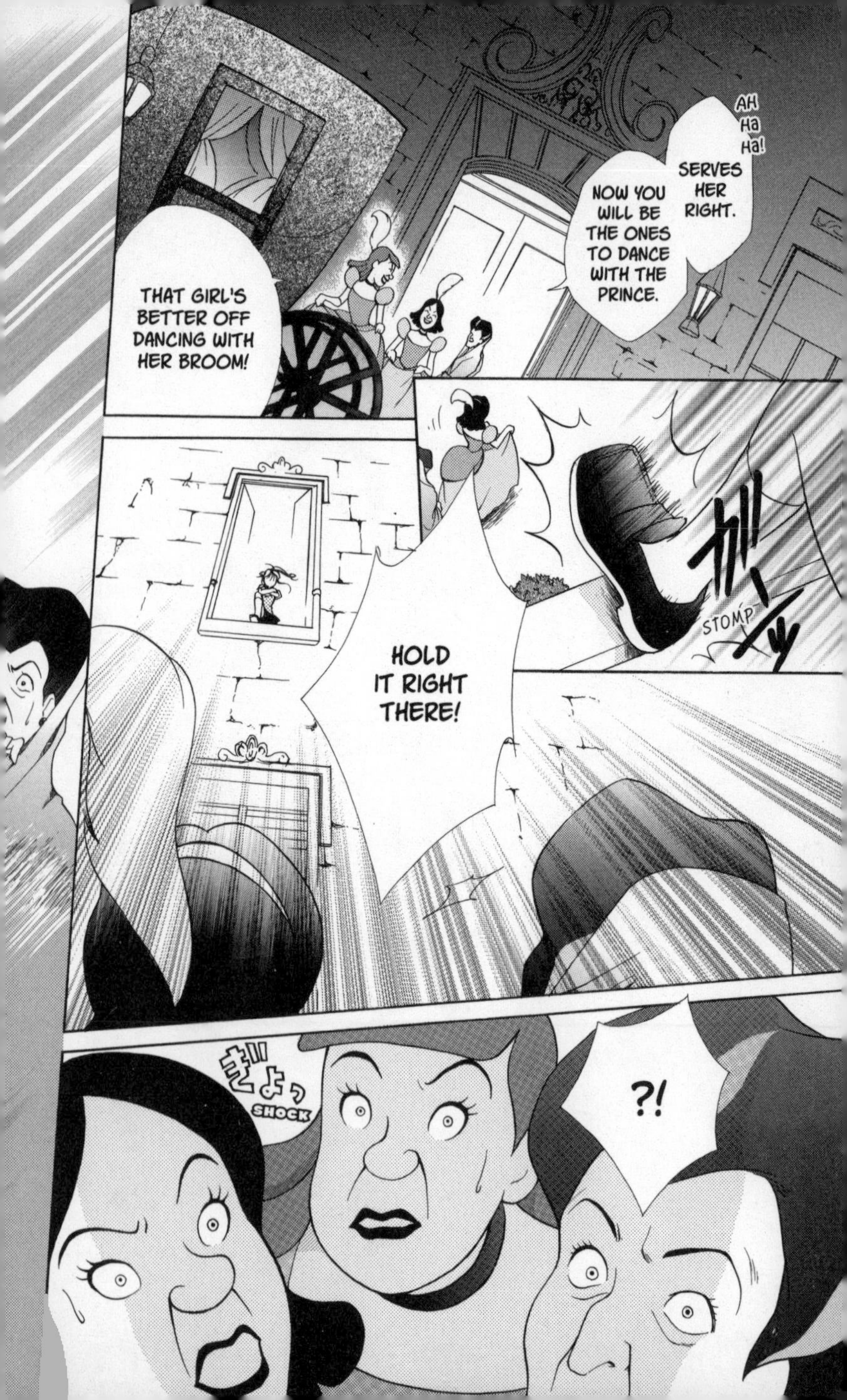
AH Ha Ha!
SERVES HER RIGHT.
NOW YOU WILL BE THE ONES TO DANCE WITH THE PRINCE.
THAT GIRL'S BETTER OFF DANCING WITH HER BROOM!
STOMP
HOLD IT RIGHT THERE!
?!
ぎょっ
SHOCK

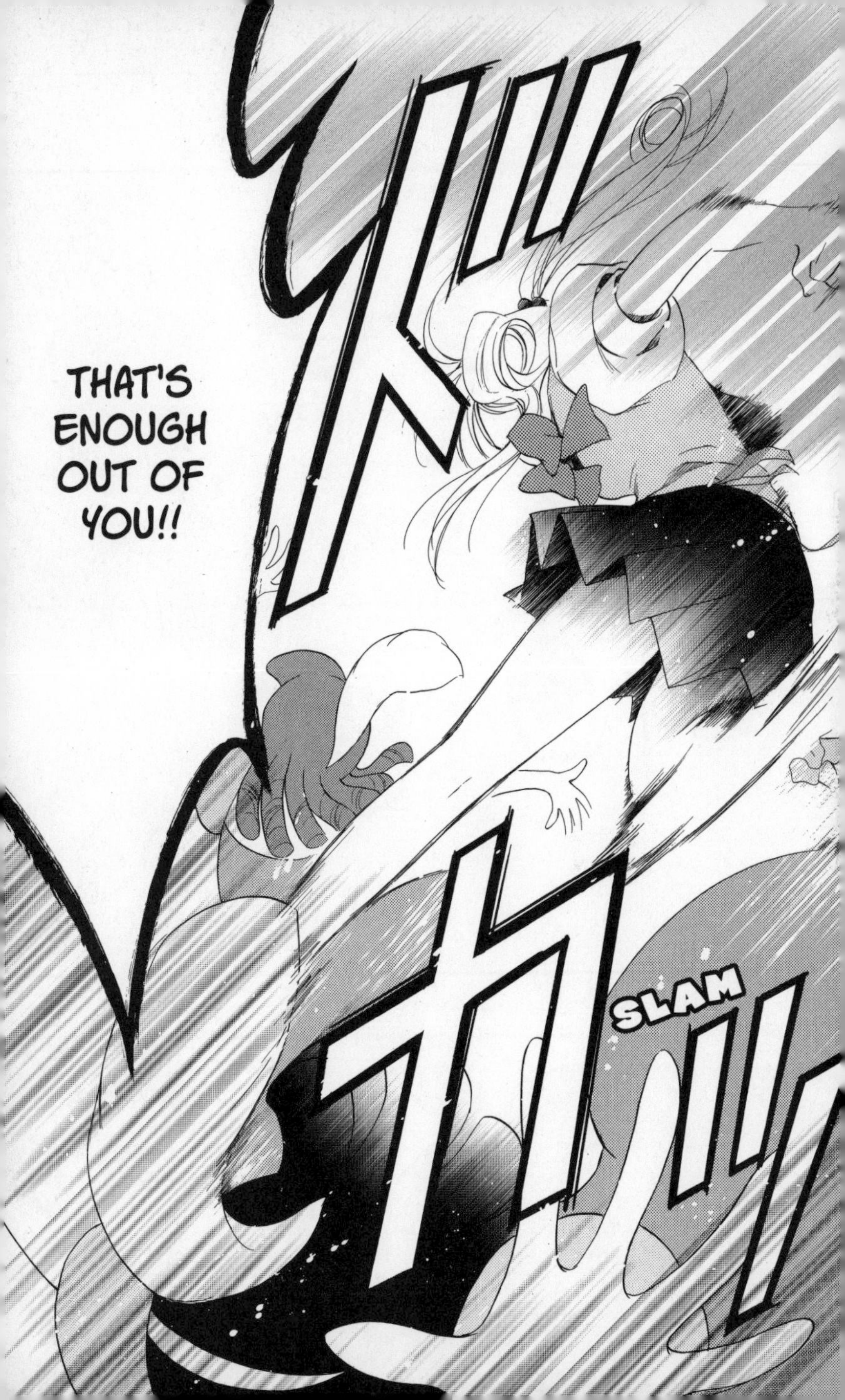
THAT'S ENOUGH OUT OF YOU!!
SLAM

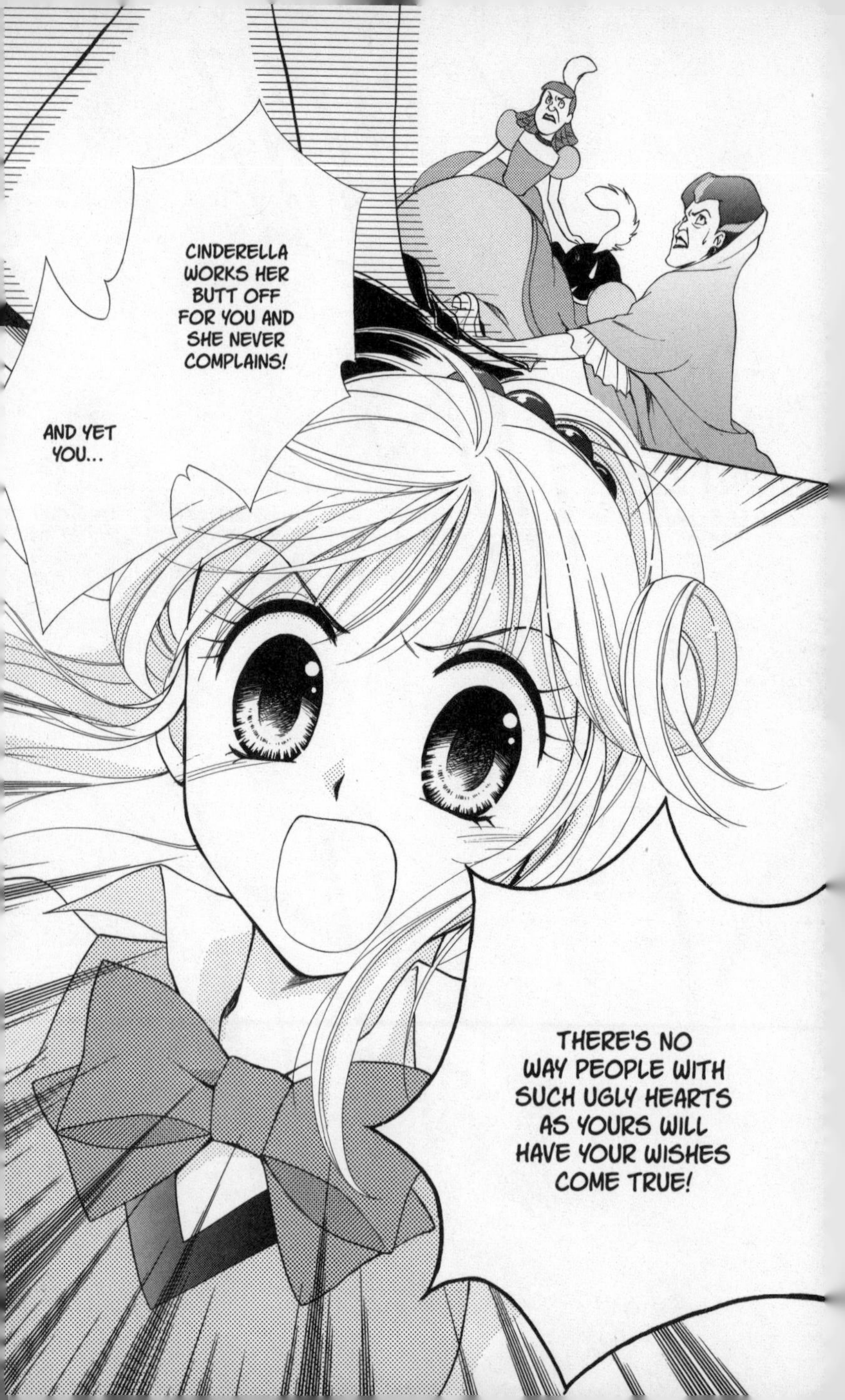
CINDERELLA WORKS HER BUTT OFF FOR YOU AND SHE NEVER COMPLAINS!
AND YET YOU...
THERE'S NO WAY PEOPLE WITH SUCH UGLY HEARTS AS YOURS WILL HAVE YOUR WISHES COME TRUE!

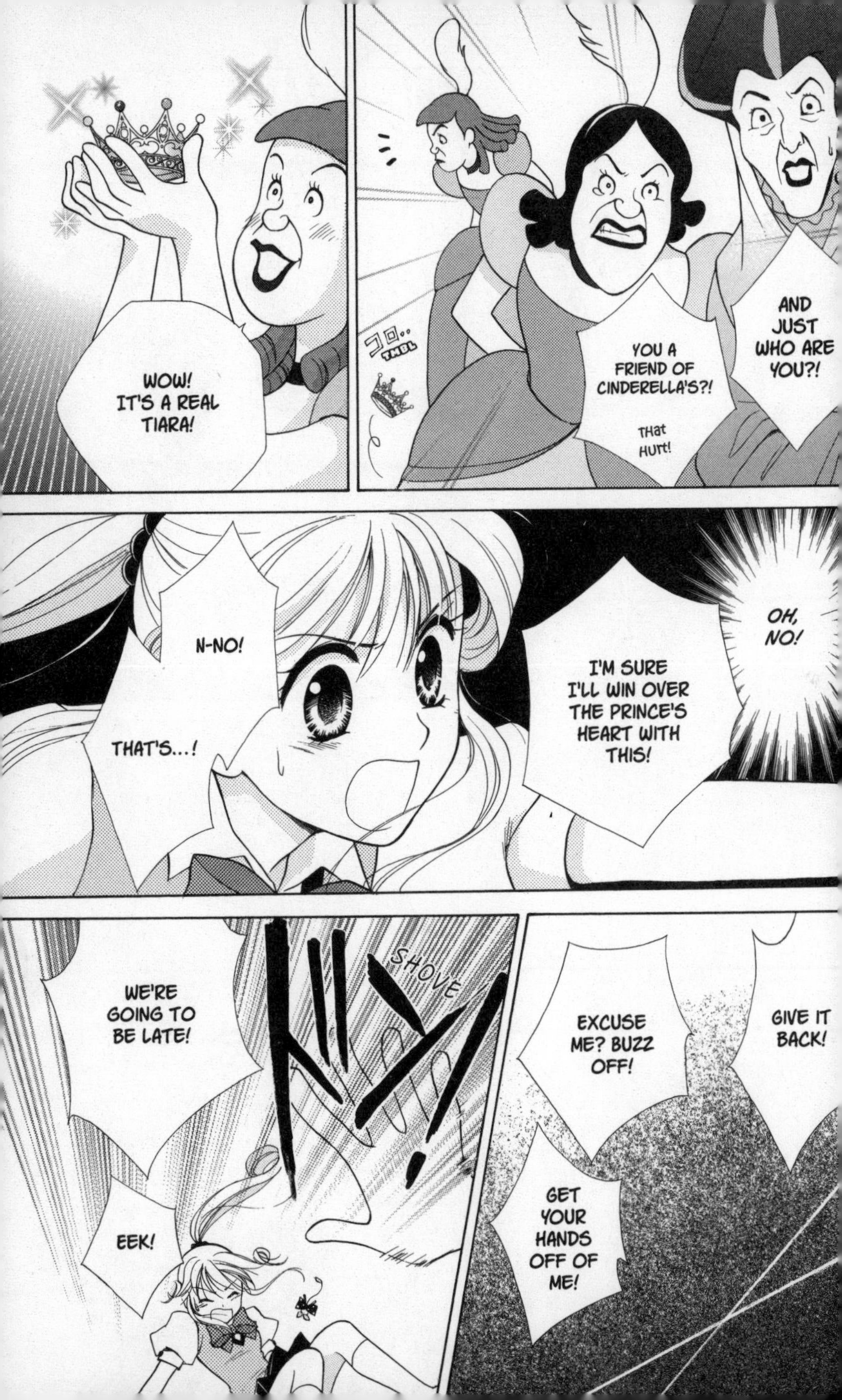

AND JUST WHO ARE YOU?!
YOU A FRIEND OF CINDERELLA'S?!
That Hurt!
コロ..
TMBL
WOW! IT'S A REAL TIARA!
OH, NO!
I'M SURE I'LL WIN OVER THE PRINCE'S HEART WITH THIS!
N-NO!
THAT'S...!
GIVE IT BACK!
EXCUSE ME? BUZZ OFF!
GET YOUR HANDS OFF OF ME!
WE'RE GOING TO BE LATE!
SHOVE
EEK!

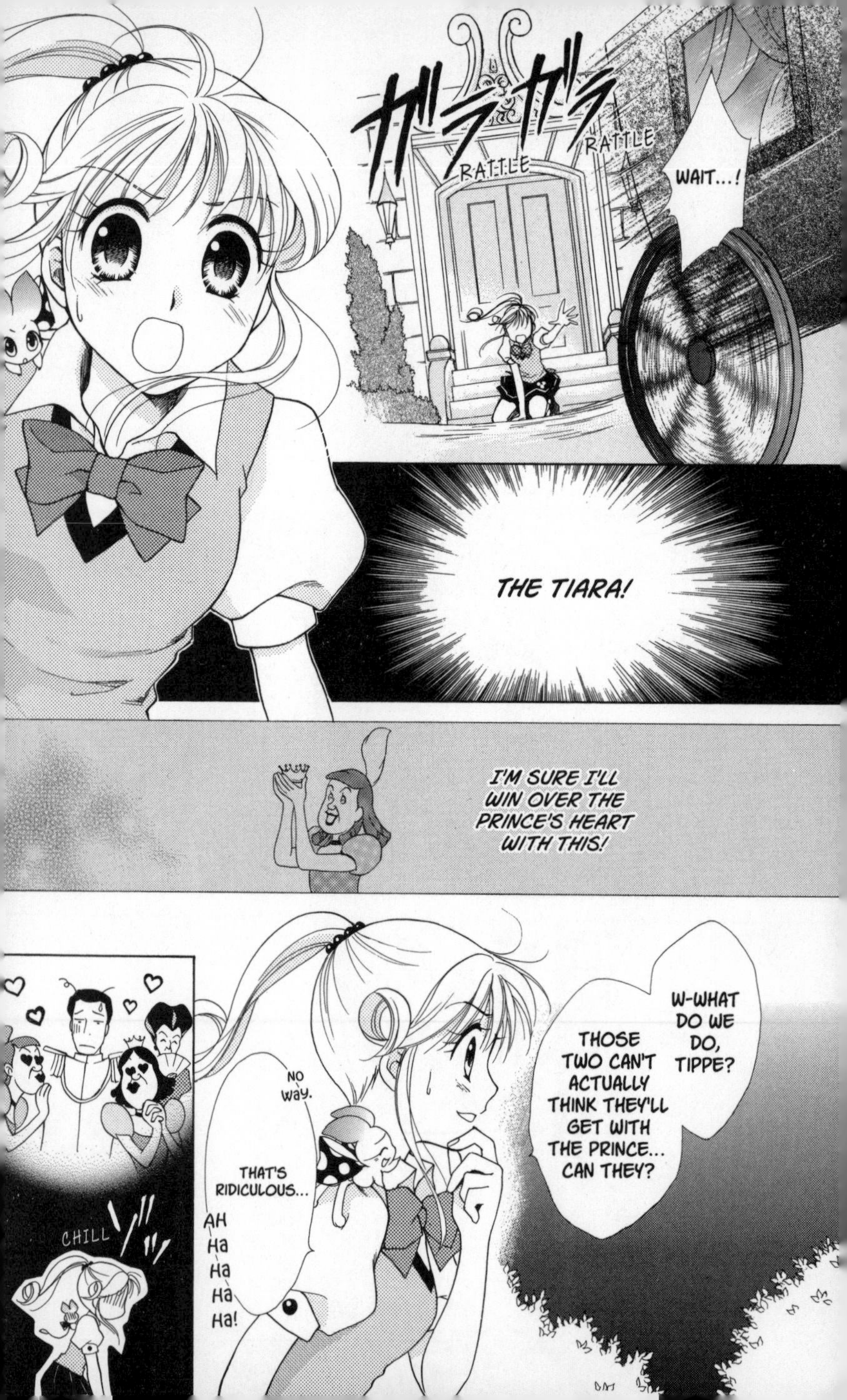

ガラガラ
RATTLE RATTLE
WAIT...!
THE TIARA!
I'M SURE I'LL WIN OVER THE PRINCE'S HEART WITH THIS!
W-WHAT DO WE DO, TIPPE?
THOSE TWO CAN'T ACTUALLY THINK THEY'LL GET WITH THE PRINCE... CAN THEY?
NO WAY.
THAT'S RIDICULOUS...
AH HA HA HA HA!
CHILL

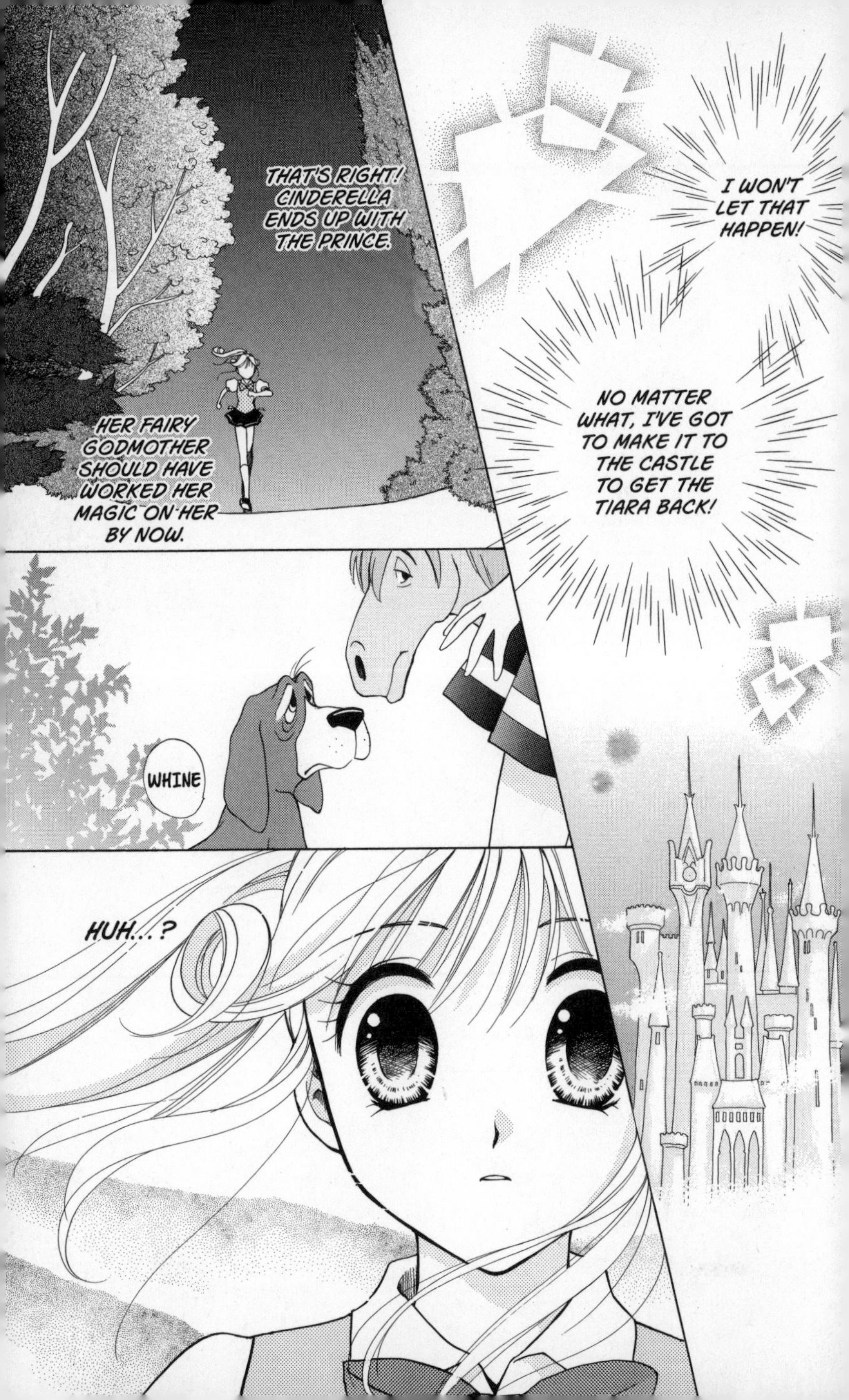
I WON'T LET THAT HAPPEN!
NO MATTER WHAT, I'VE GOT TO MAKE IT TO THE CASTLE TO GET THE TIARA BACK!
THAT'S RIGHT! CINDERELLA ENDS UP WITH THE PRINCE.
HER FAIRY GODMOTHER SHOULD HAVE WORKED HER MAGIC ON HER BY NOW.
WHINE
HUH...?

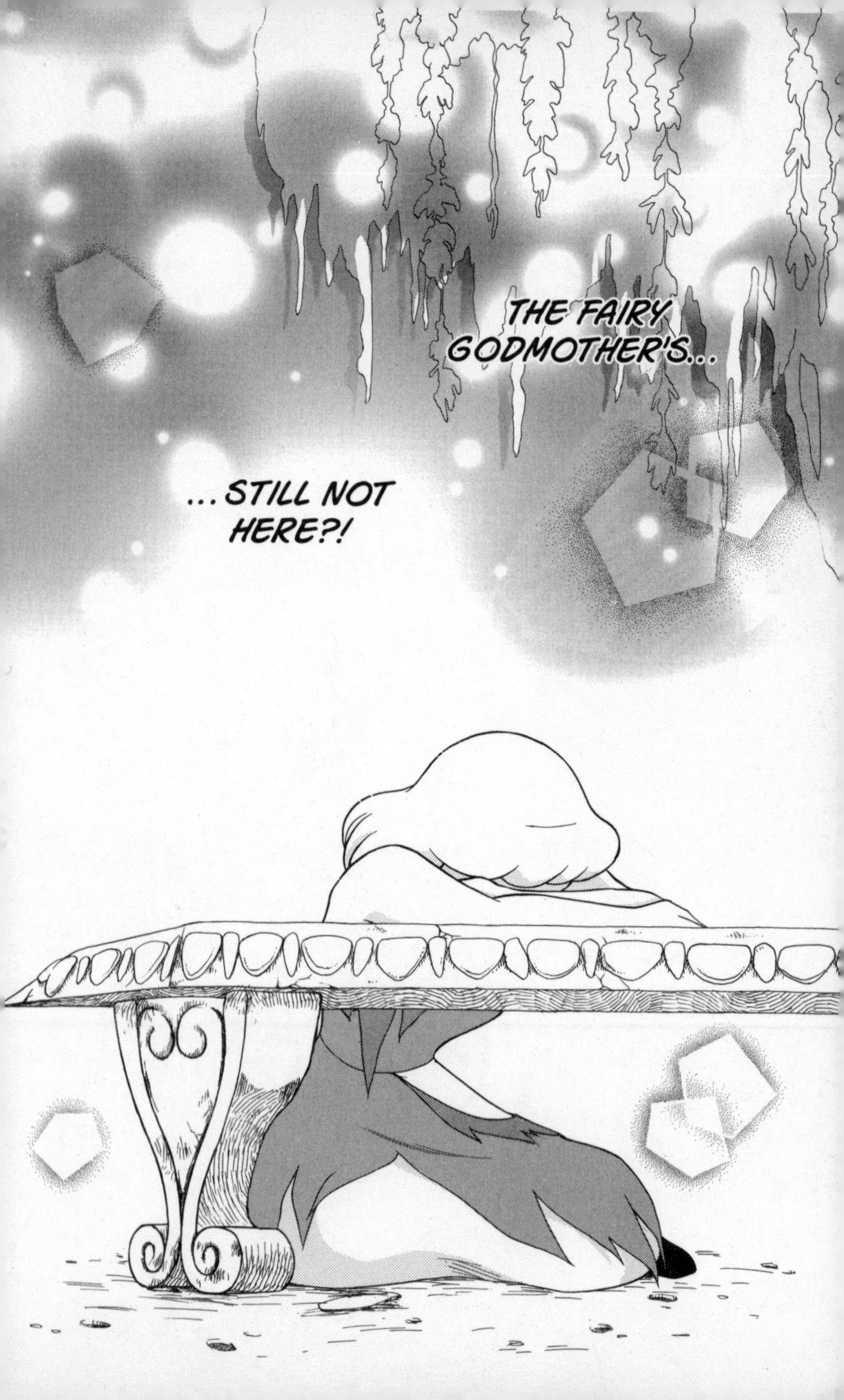
THE FAIRY GODMOTHER'S...
...STILL NOT HERE?!

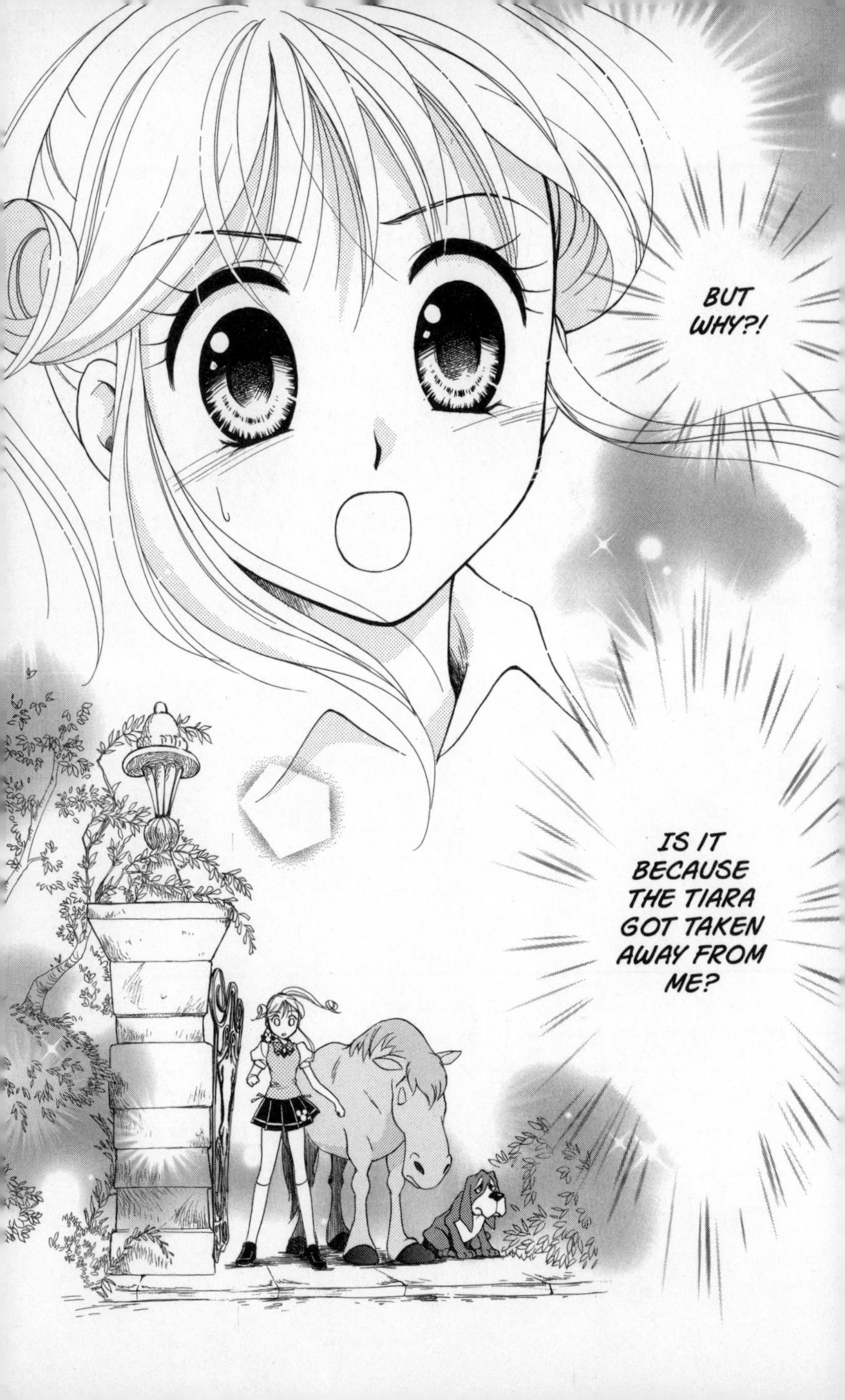
BUT WHY?!
IS IT BECAUSE THE TIARA GOT TAKEN AWAY FROM ME?

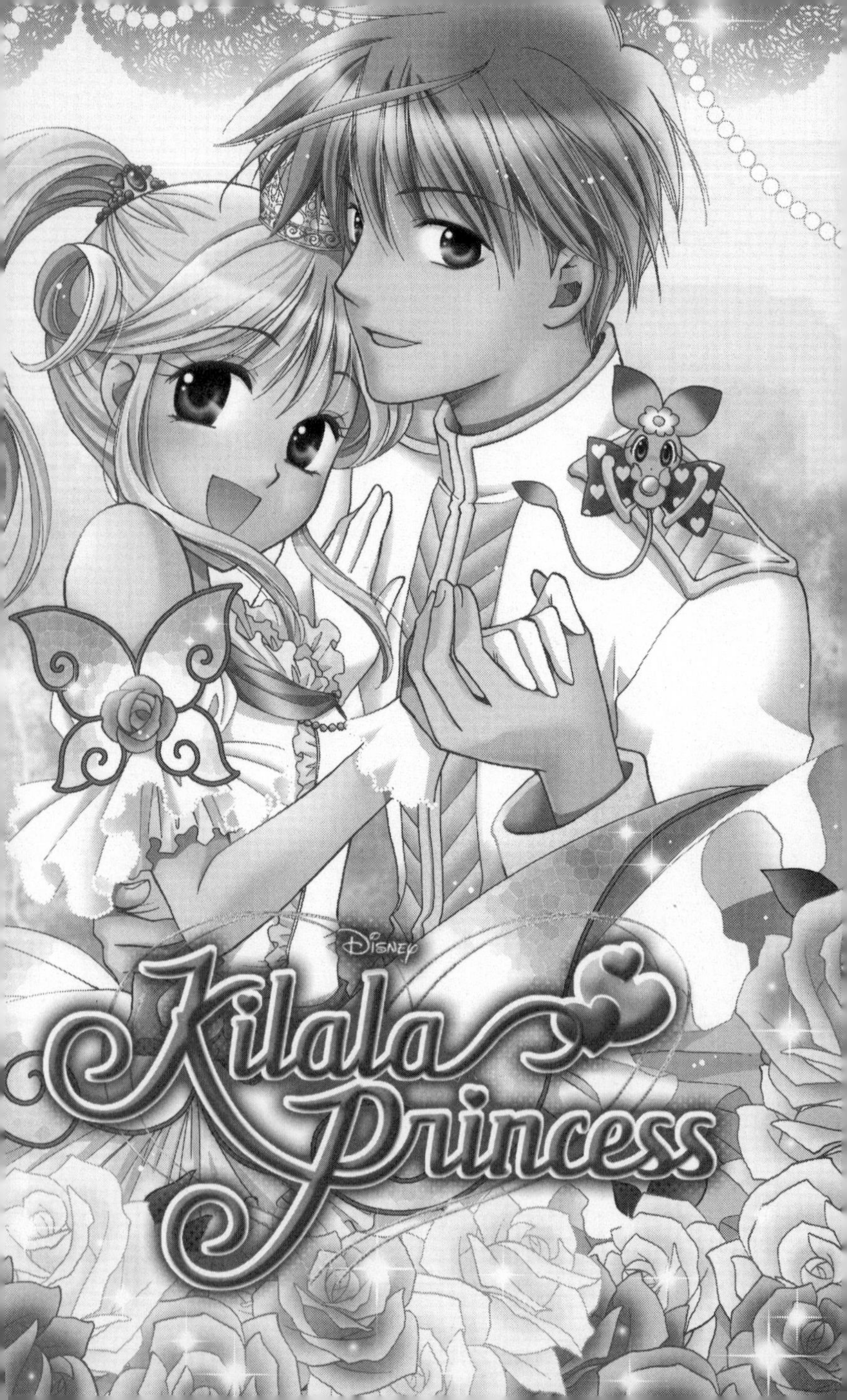
Disney
Kilala Princess

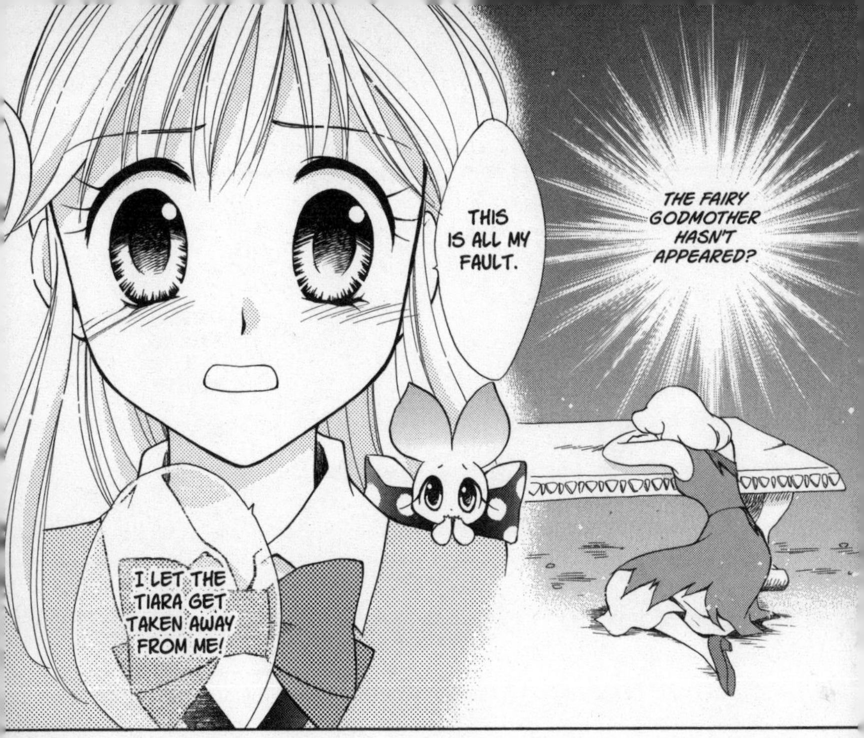
THE FAIRY GODMOTHER HASN'T APPEARED?
THIS IS ALL MY FAULT.
I LET THE TIARA GET TAKEN AWAY FROM ME!

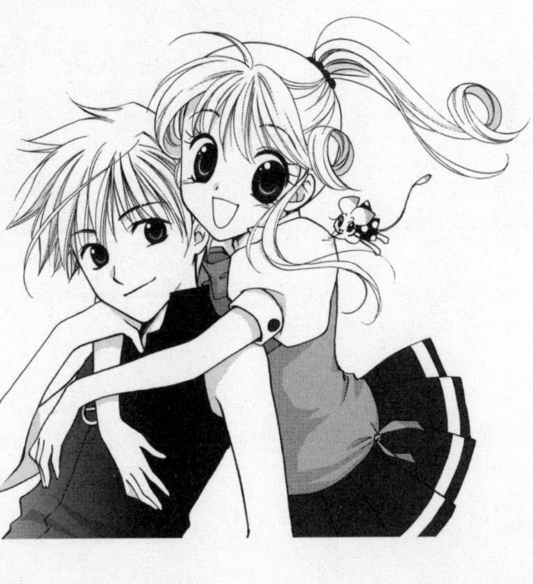

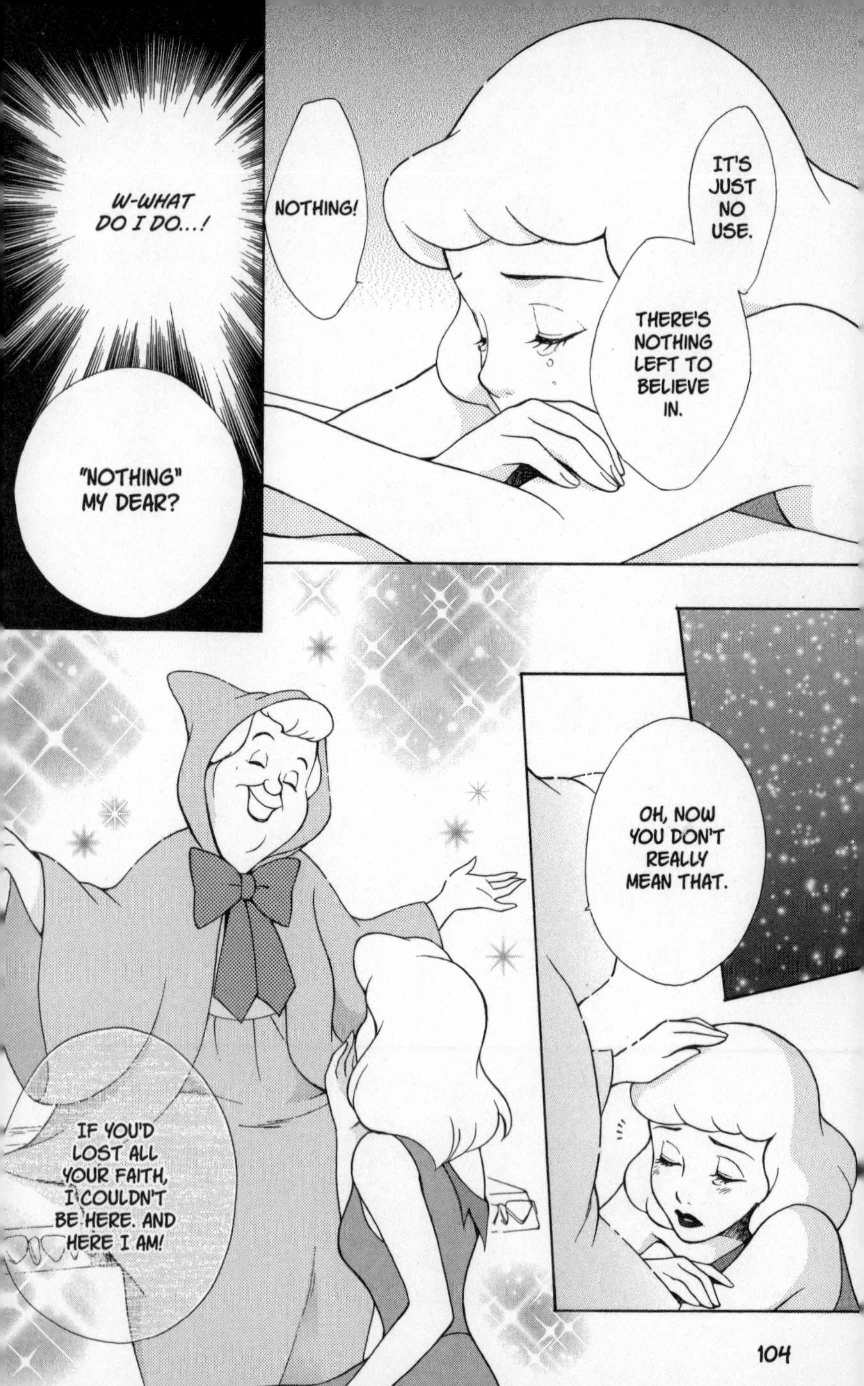
IT'S JUST NO USE.
THERE'S NOTHING LEFT TO BELIEVE IN.
NOTHING!
W-WHAT DO I DO...!
"NOTHING" MY DEAR?
OH, NOW YOU DON'T REALLY MEAN THAT.
IF YOU'D LOST ALL YOUR FAITH, I COULDN'T BE HERE. AND HERE I AM!

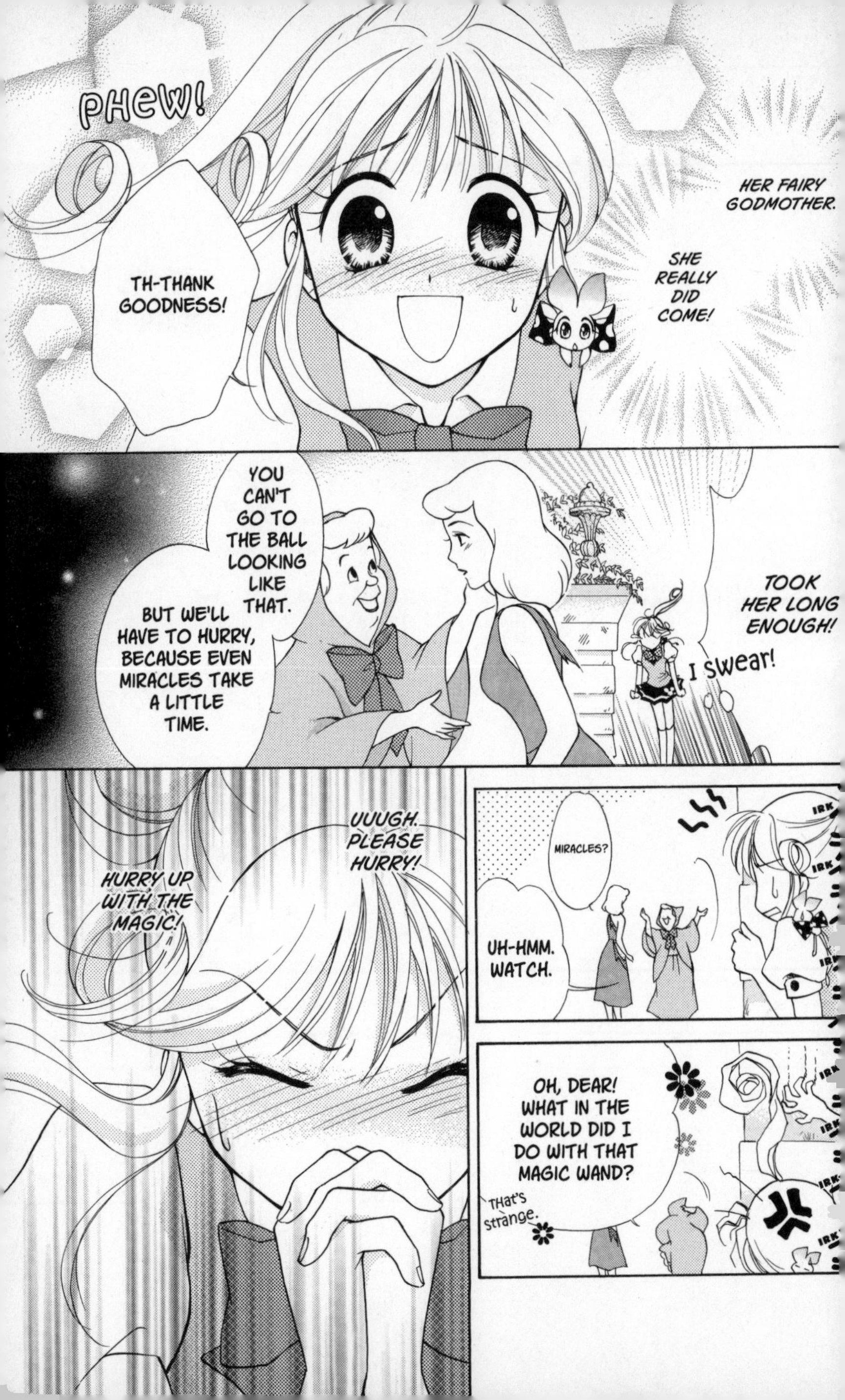
HER FAIRY GODMOTHER.
SHE REALLY DID COME!
PHEW!
TH-THANK GOODNESS!
TOOK HER LONG ENOUGH!
I swear!
YOU CAN'T GO TO THE BALL LOOKING LIKE THAT.
BUT WE'LL HAVE TO HURRY, BECAUSE EVEN MIRACLES TAKE A LITTLE TIME.
IRK
MIRACLES?
UH-HMM. WATCH.
IRK
OH, DEAR! WHAT IN THE WORLD DID I DO WITH THAT MAGIC WAND?
That's strange.
UUUGH. PLEASE HURRY!
HURRY UP WITH THE MAGIC!

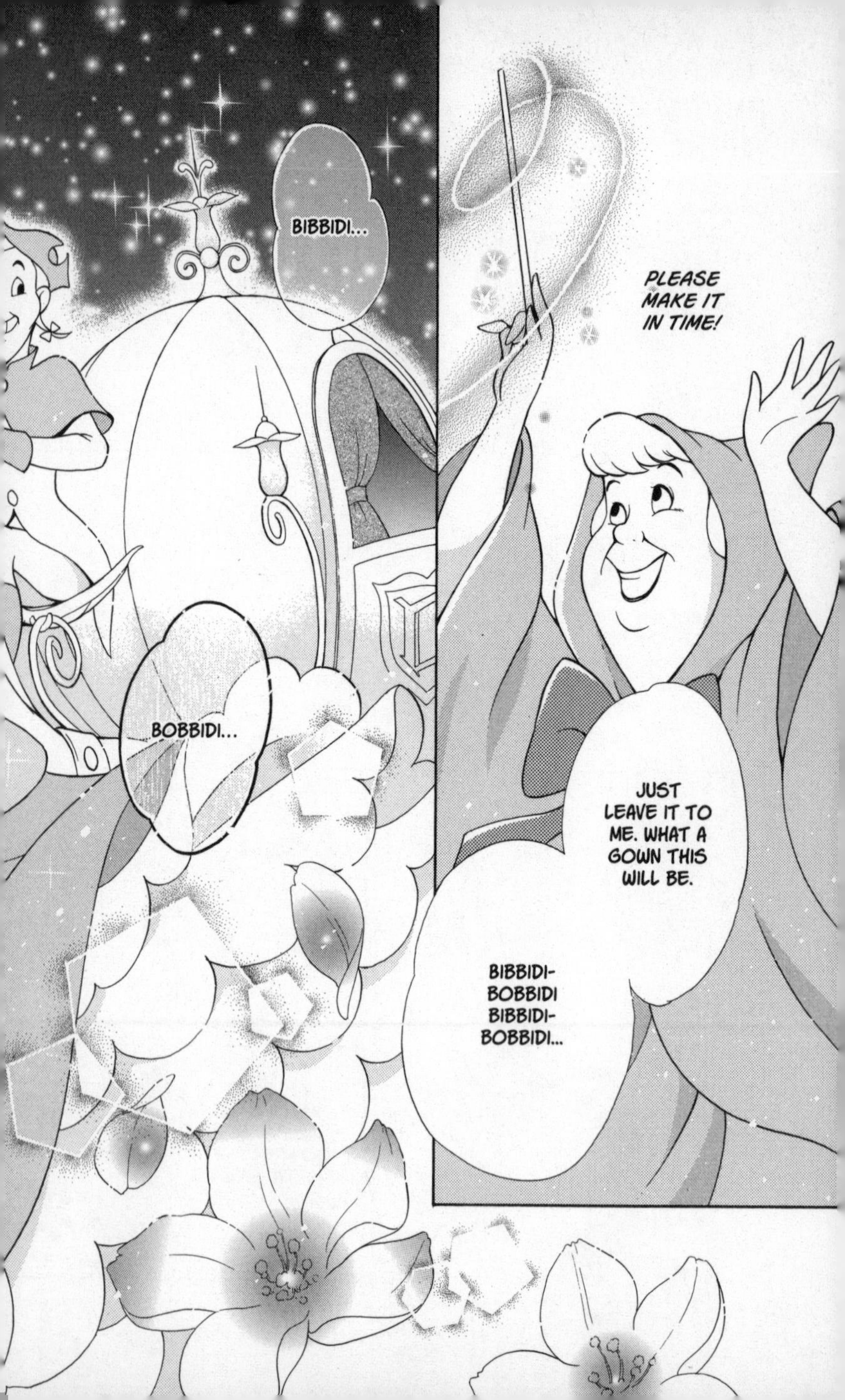
PLEASE MAKE IT IN TIME!
JUST LEAVE IT TO ME. WHAT A GOWN THIS WILL BE.
BIBBIDI-BOBBIDI BIBBIDI-BOBBIDI...
BIBBIDI...
BOBBIDI...

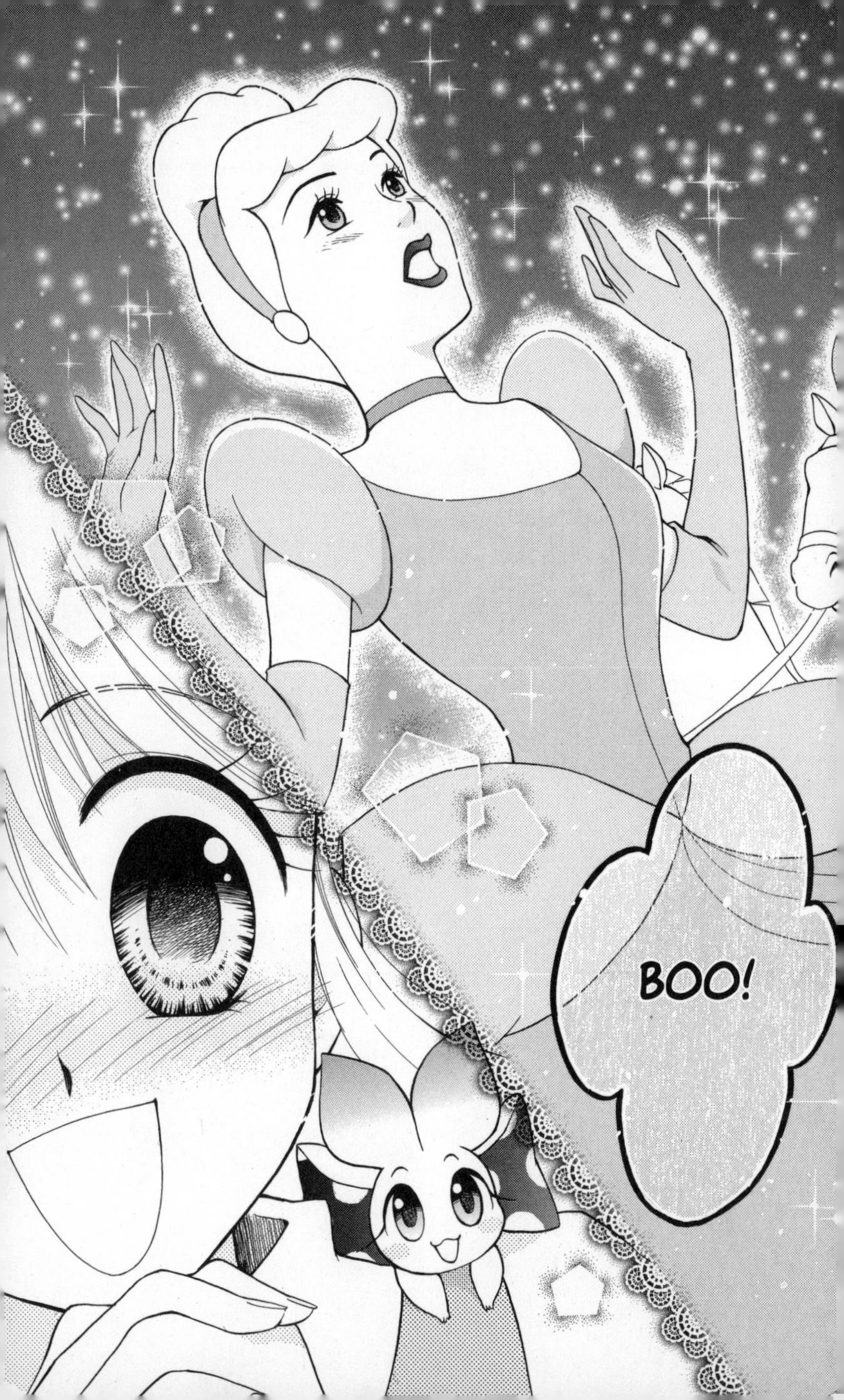
BOO!

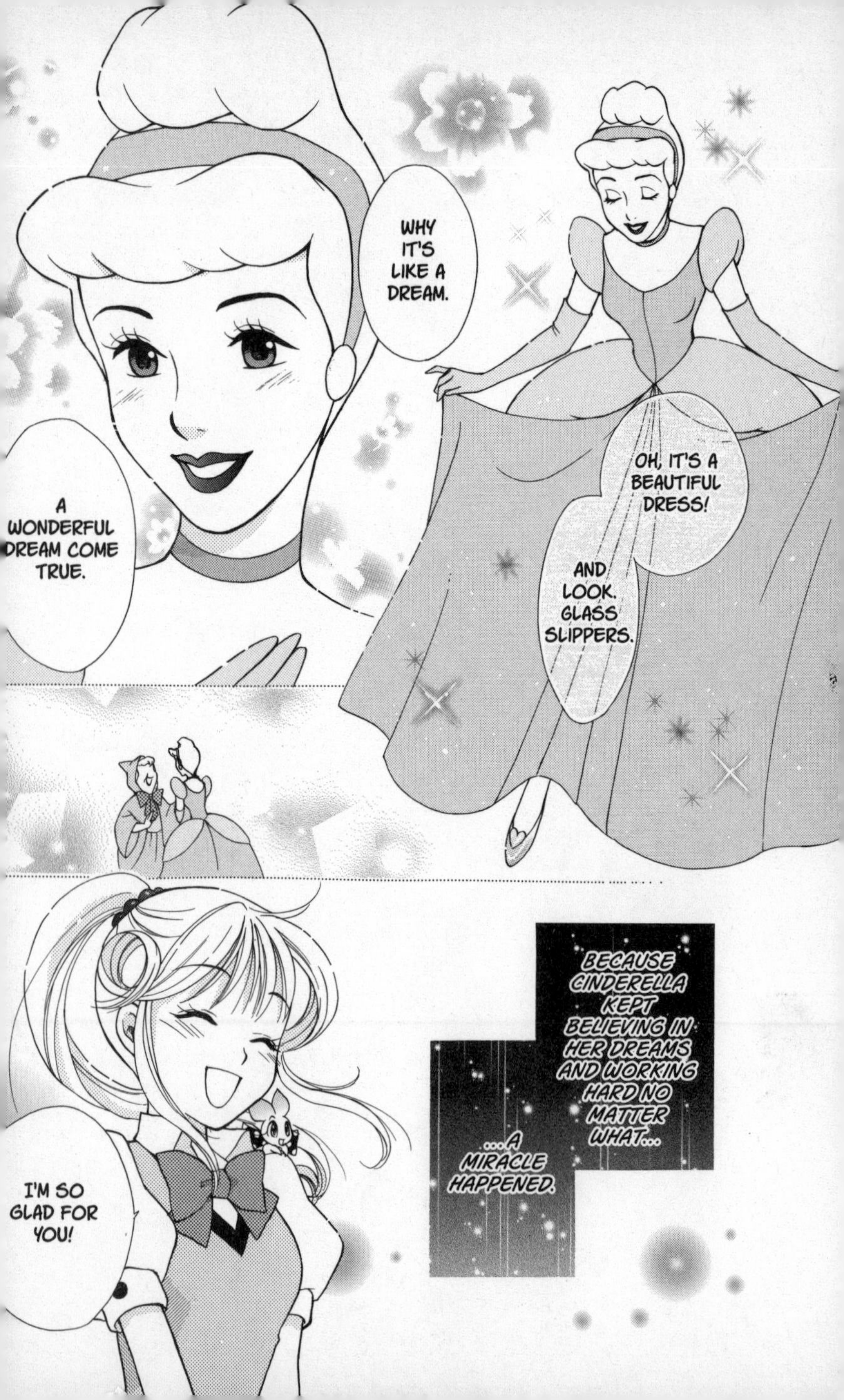
OH, IT'S A BEAUTIFUL DRESS!
AND LOOK. GLASS SLIPPERS.
WHY IT'S LIKE A DREAM.
A WONDERFUL DREAM COME TRUE.
BECAUSE CINDERELLA KEPT BELIEVING IN HER DREAMS AND WORKING HARD NO MATTER WHAT...
...A MIRACLE HAPPENED.
I'M SO GLAD FOR YOU!

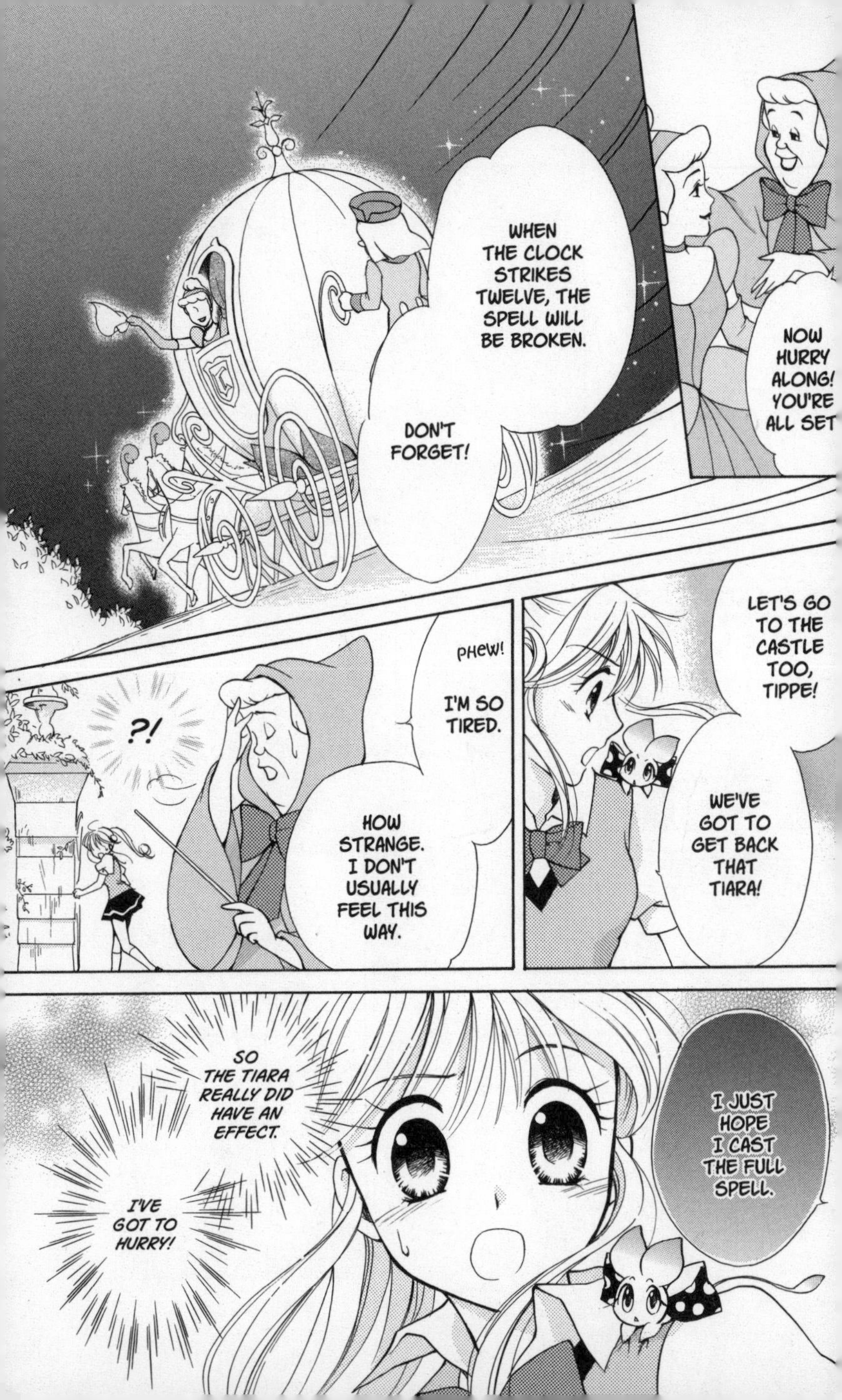
NOW HURRY ALONG! YOU'RE ALL SET
WHEN THE CLOCK STRIKES TWELVE, THE SPELL WILL BE BROKEN.
DON'T FORGET!
LET'S GO TO THE CASTLE TOO, TIPPE!
WE'VE GOT TO GET BACK THAT TIARA!
PHEW!
I'M SO TIRED.
HOW STRANGE. I DON'T USUALLY FEEL THIS WAY.
?!
I JUST HOPE I CAST THE FULL SPELL.
SO THE TIARA REALLY DID HAVE AN EFFECT.
I'VE GOT TO HURRY!

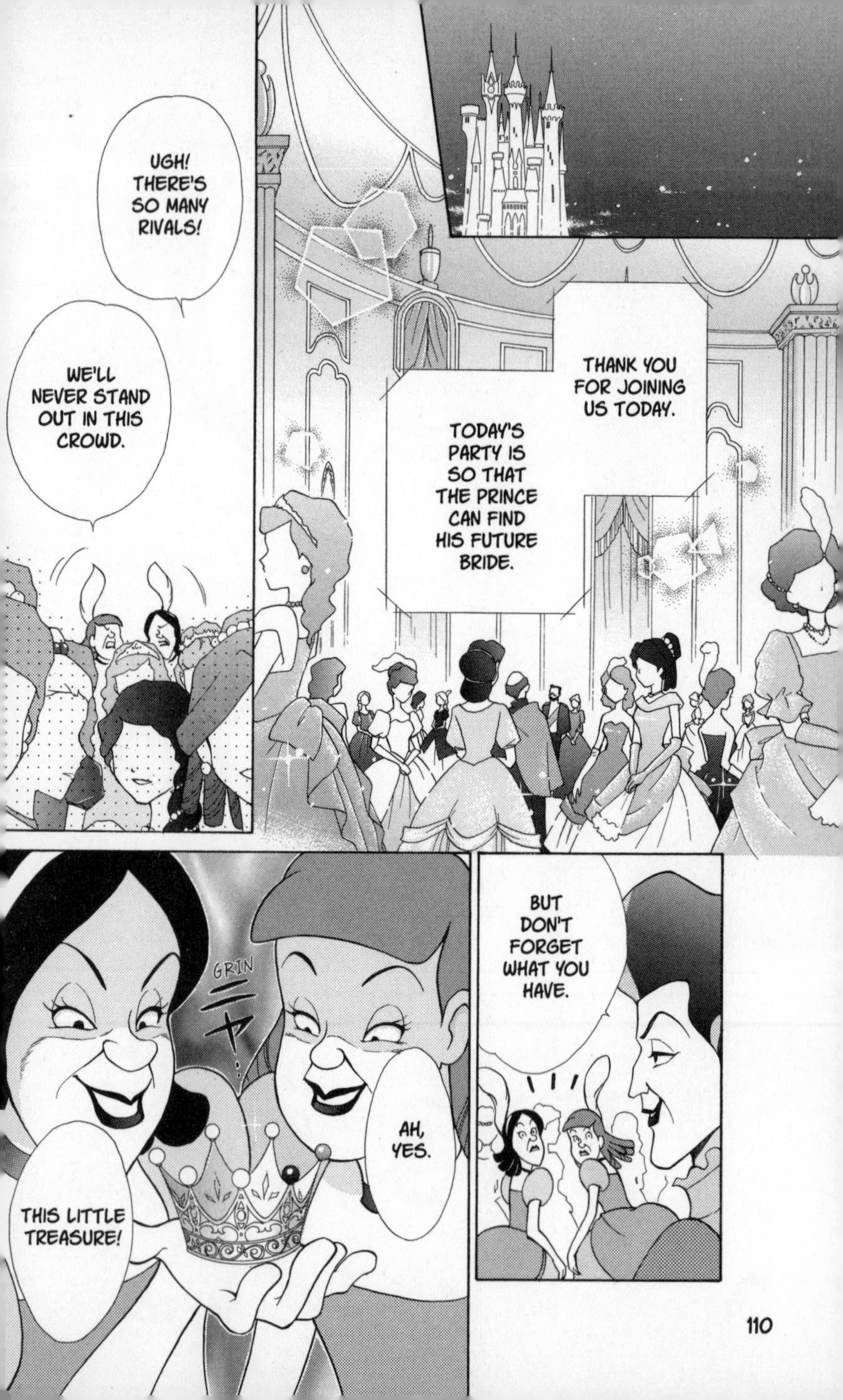
THANK YOU FOR JOINING US TODAY.
TODAY'S PARTY IS SO THAT THE PRINCE CAN FIND HIS FUTURE BRIDE.
UGH! THERE'S SO MANY RIVALS!
WE'LL NEVER STAND OUT IN THIS CROWD.
BUT DON'T FORGET WHAT YOU HAVE.
GRIN
ニヤ
AH, YES.
THIS LITTLE TREASURE!

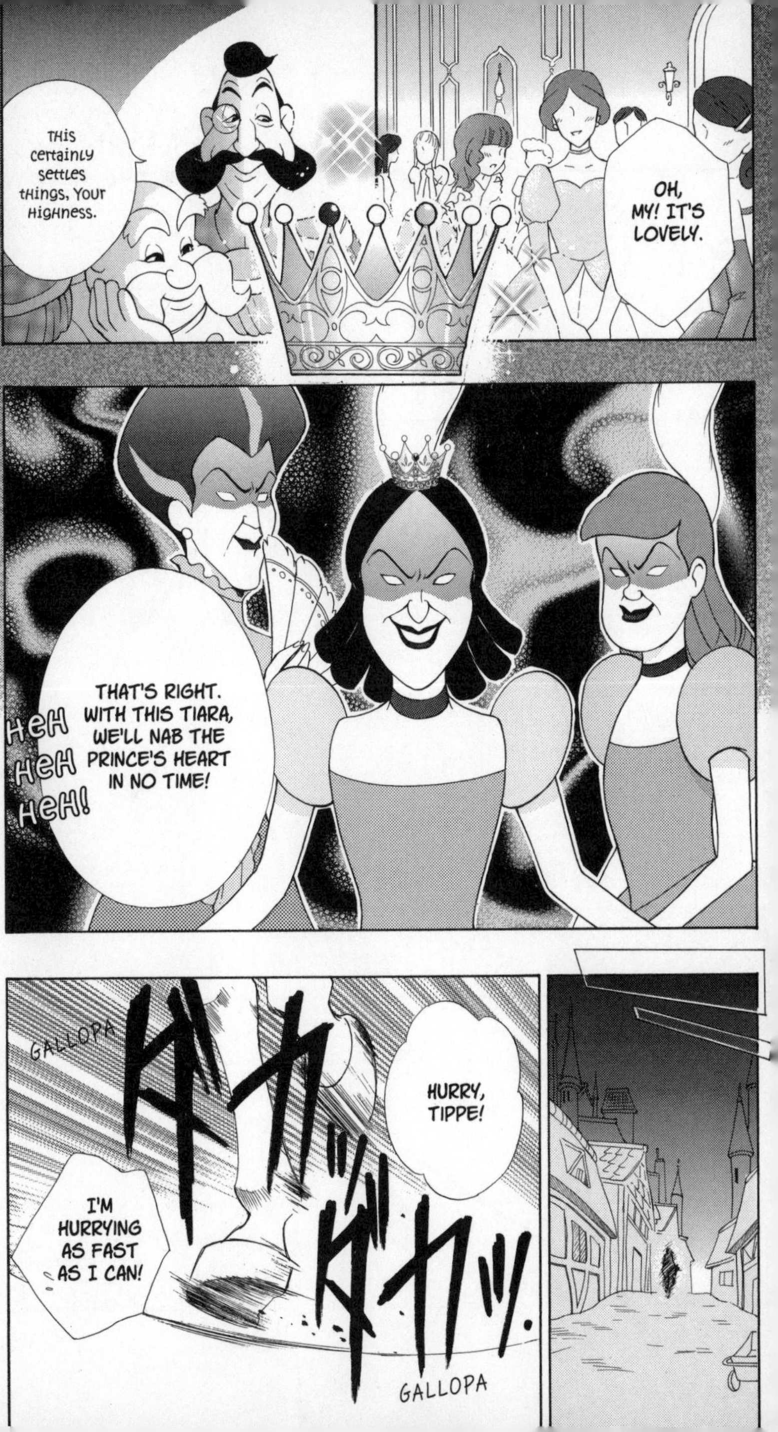
OH, MY! IT'S LOVELY.
THIS certainly settles things, Your Highness.
THAT'S RIGHT. WITH THIS TIARA, WE'LL NAB THE PRINCE'S HEART IN NO TIME!
HEH HEH HEH!
HURRY, TIPPE!
GALLOPA
I'M HURRYING AS FAST AS I CAN!
GALLOPA

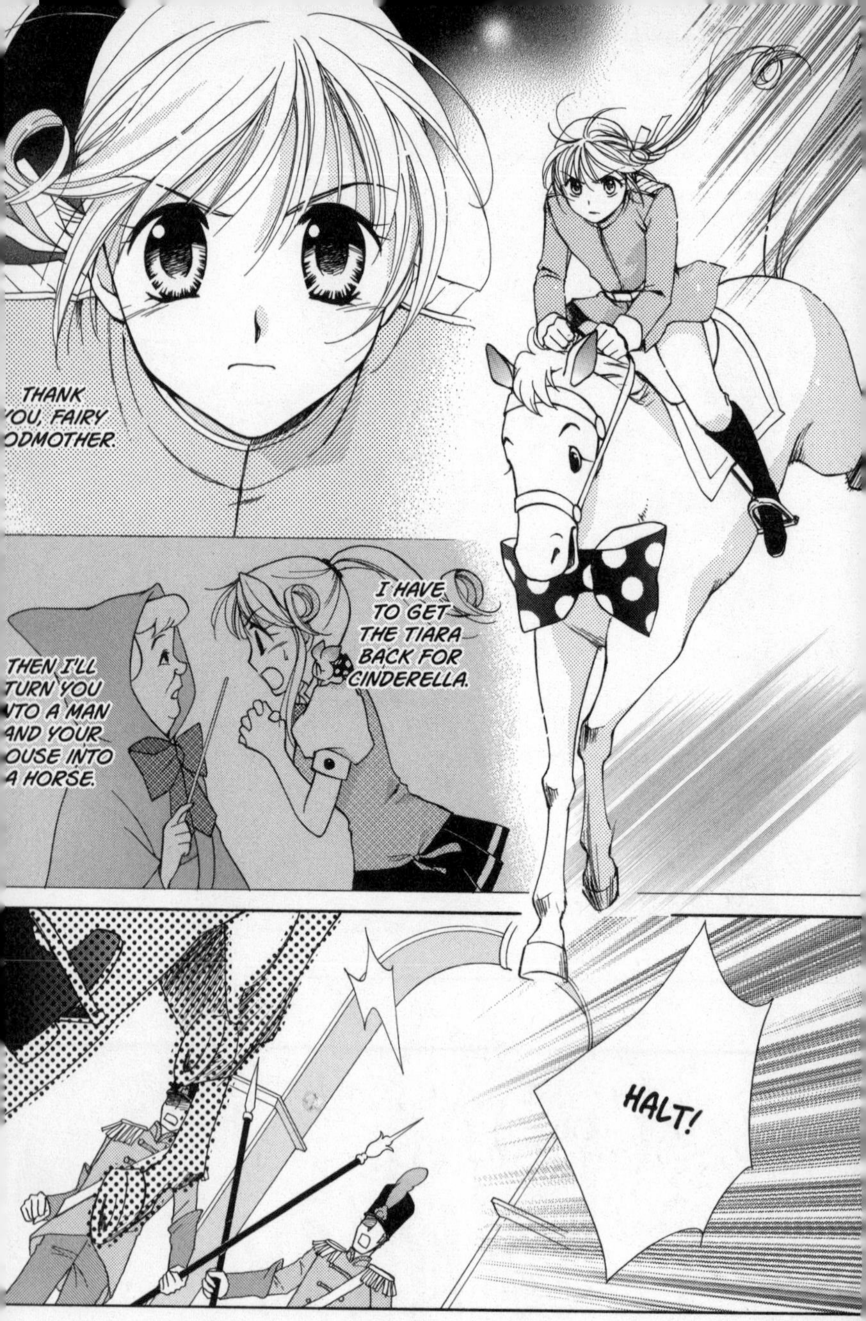
THANK YOU, FAIRY ODMOTHER.
I HAVE TO GET THE TIARA BACK FOR CINDERELLA.
THEN I'LL TURN YOU NTO A MAN AND YOUR OUSE INTO A HORSE.
HALT!

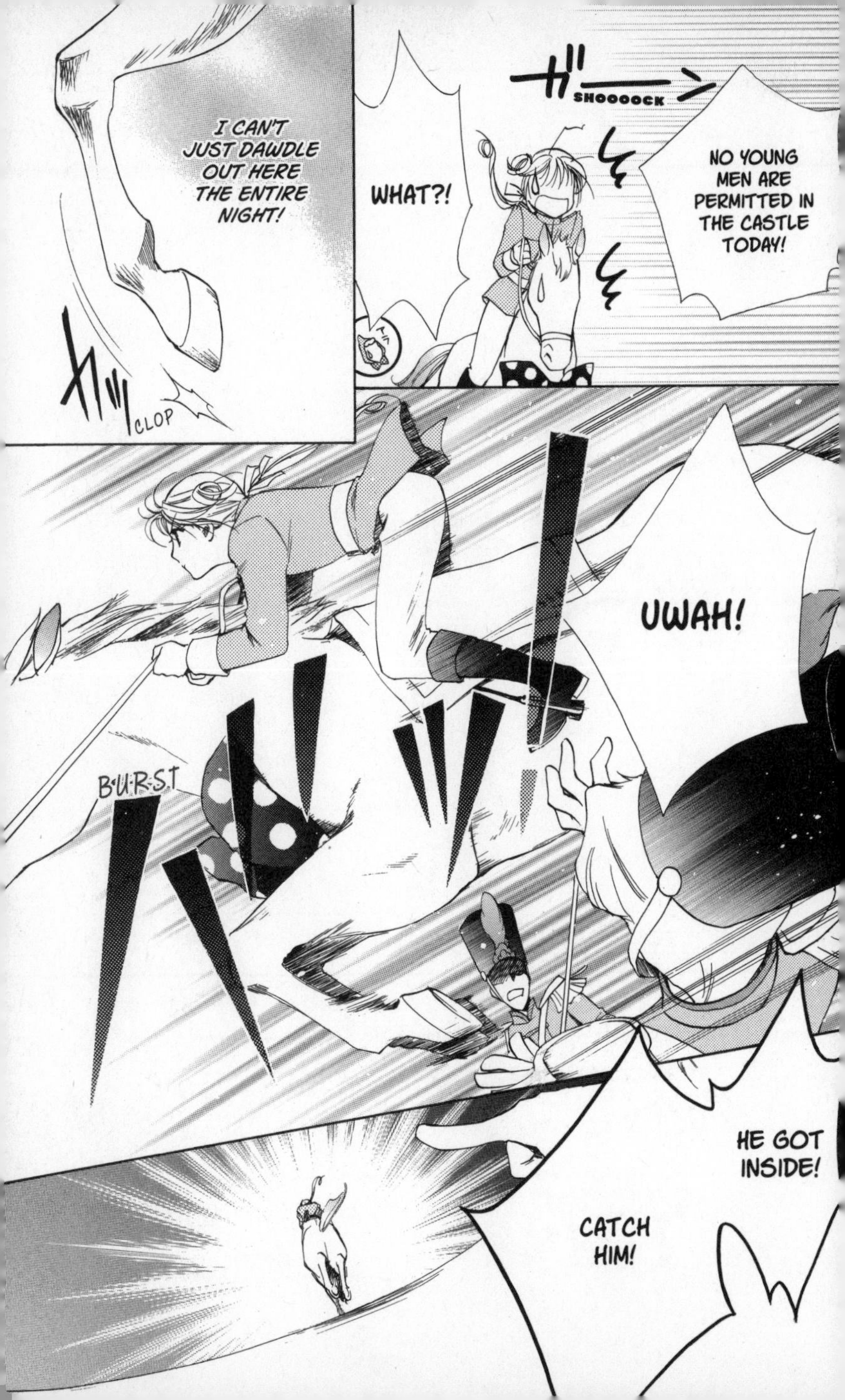
SHOOOOCK
NO YOUNG MEN ARE PERMITTED IN THE CASTLE TODAY!
WHAT?!
I CAN'T JUST DAWDLE OUT HERE THE ENTIRE NIGHT!
CLOP
UWAH!
B·U·R·S·T
HE GOT INSIDE!
CATCH HIM!

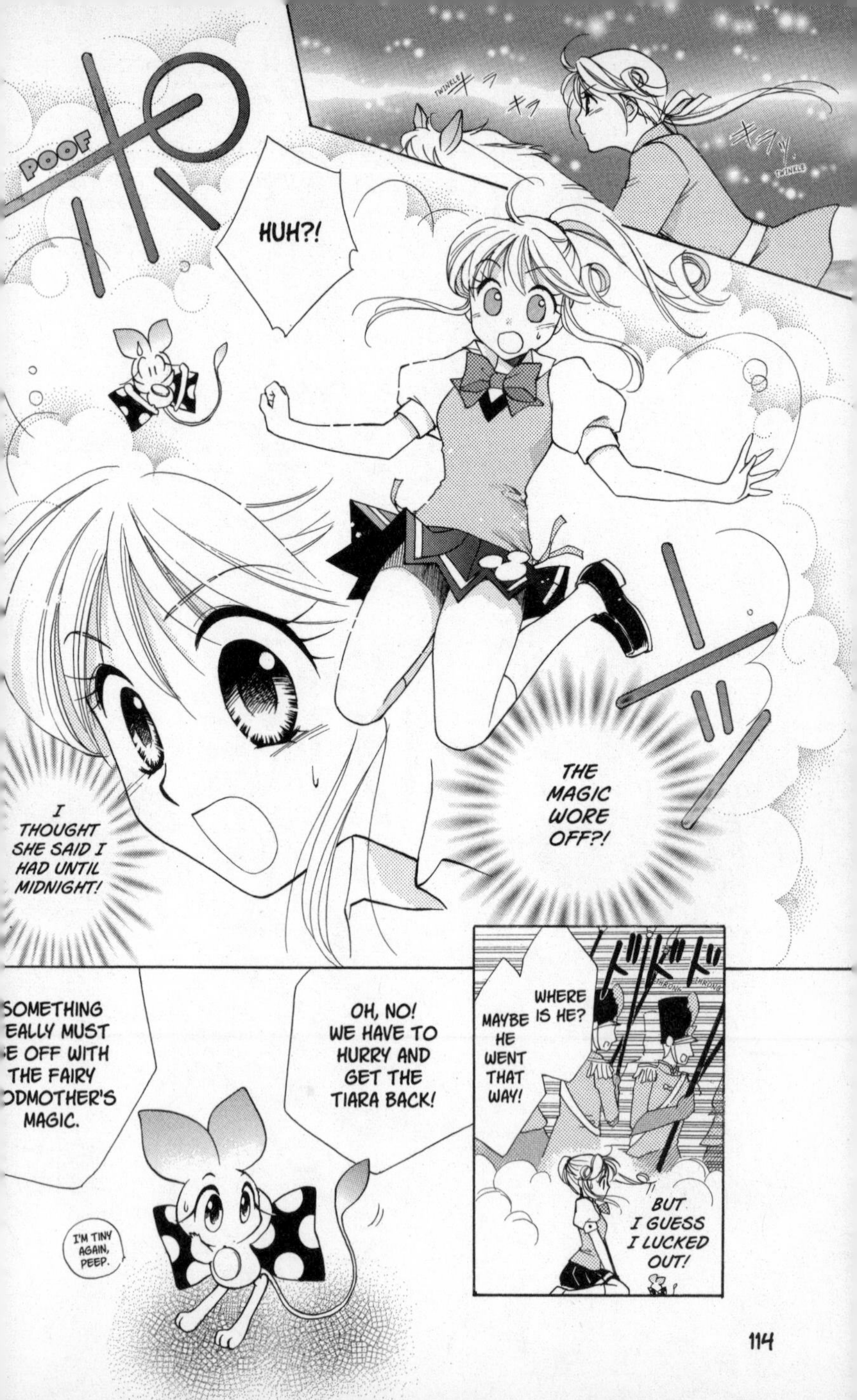
TWINKLE
TWINKLE
POOF
HUH?!
THE MAGIC WORE OFF?!
I THOUGHT SHE SAID I HAD UNTIL MIDNIGHT!
THRONG
THRONG
WHERE IS HE?
MAYBE HE WENT THAT WAY!
BUT I GUESS I LUCKED OUT!
OH, NO! WE HAVE TO HURRY AND GET THE TIARA BACK!
SOMETHING EALLY MUST E OFF WITH THE FAIRY ODMOTHER'S MAGIC.
I'M TINY AGAIN, PEEP.

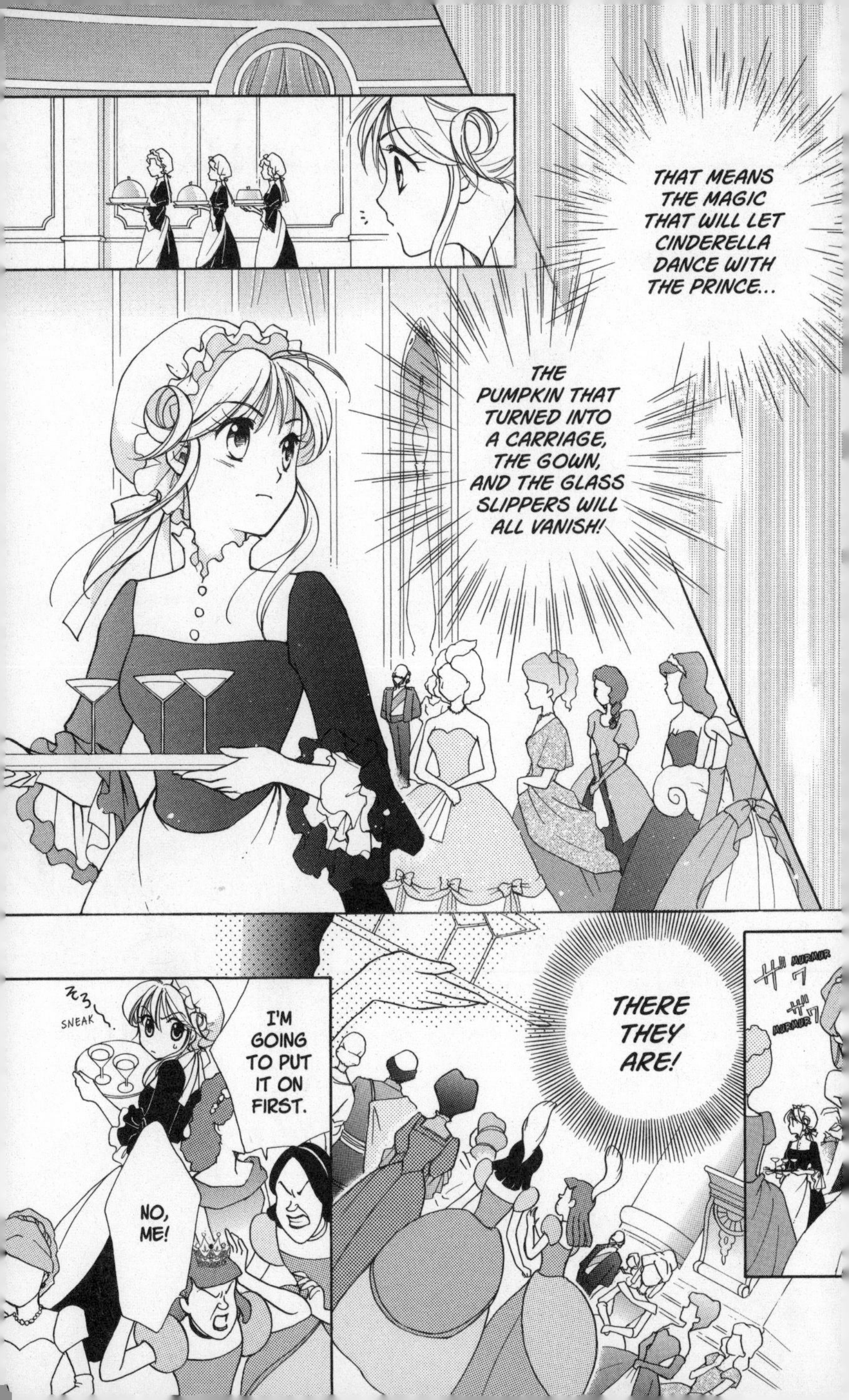
THAT MEANS THE MAGIC THAT WILL LET CINDERELLA DANCE WITH THE PRINCE...
THE PUMPKIN THAT TURNED INTO A CARRIAGE, THE GOWN, AND THE GLASS SLIPPERS WILL ALL VANISH!
MURMUR
MURMUR
THERE THEY ARE!
SNEAK
I'M GOING TO PUT IT ON FIRST.
NO, ME!

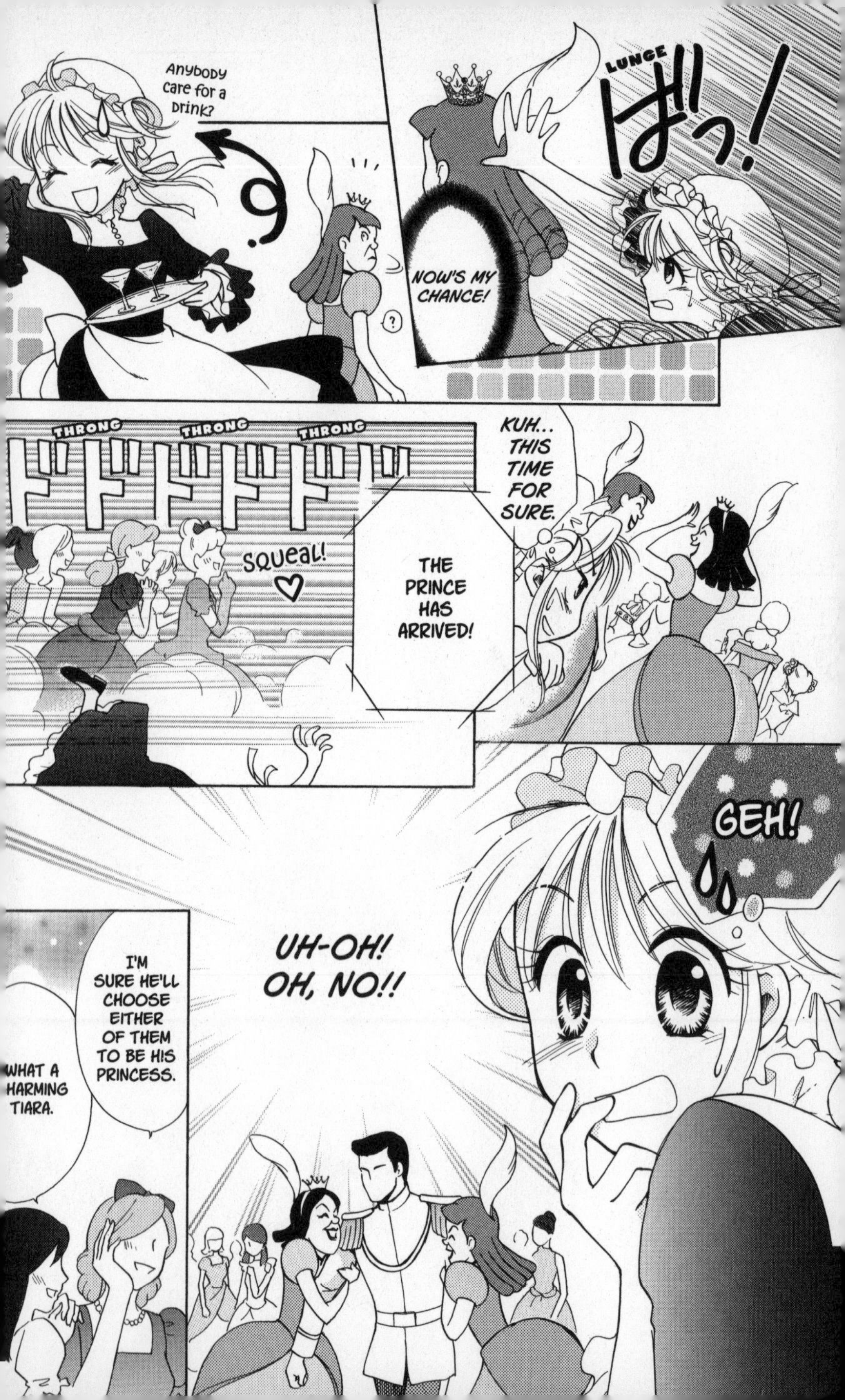

LUNGE
ばっ!
NOW'S MY CHANCE!
Anybody care for a drink?
KUH... THIS TIME FOR SURE.
THE PRINCE HAS ARRIVED!
THRONG THRONG THRONG
ドドドドドドッ
SQUEAL!
GEH!
UH-OH! OH, NO!!
I'M SURE HE'LL CHOOSE EITHER OF THEM TO BE HIS PRINCESS.
WHAT A HARMING TIARA.

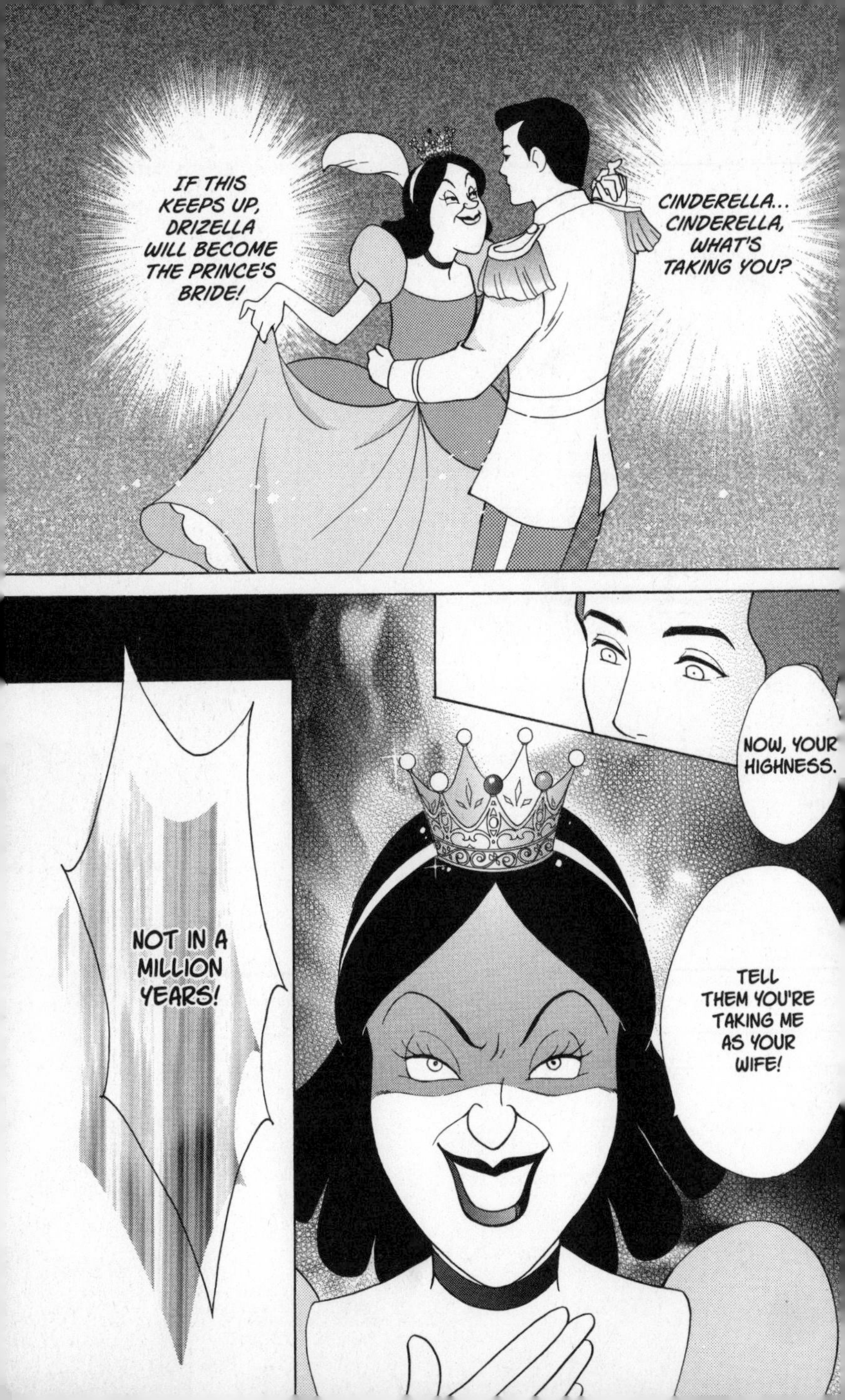
CINDERELLA... CINDERELLA, WHAT'S TAKING YOU?
IF THIS KEEPS UP, DRIZELLA WILL BECOME THE PRINCE'S BRIDE!
NOW, YOUR HIGHNESS.
TELL THEM YOU'RE TAKING ME AS YOUR WIFE!
NOT IN A MILLION YEARS!

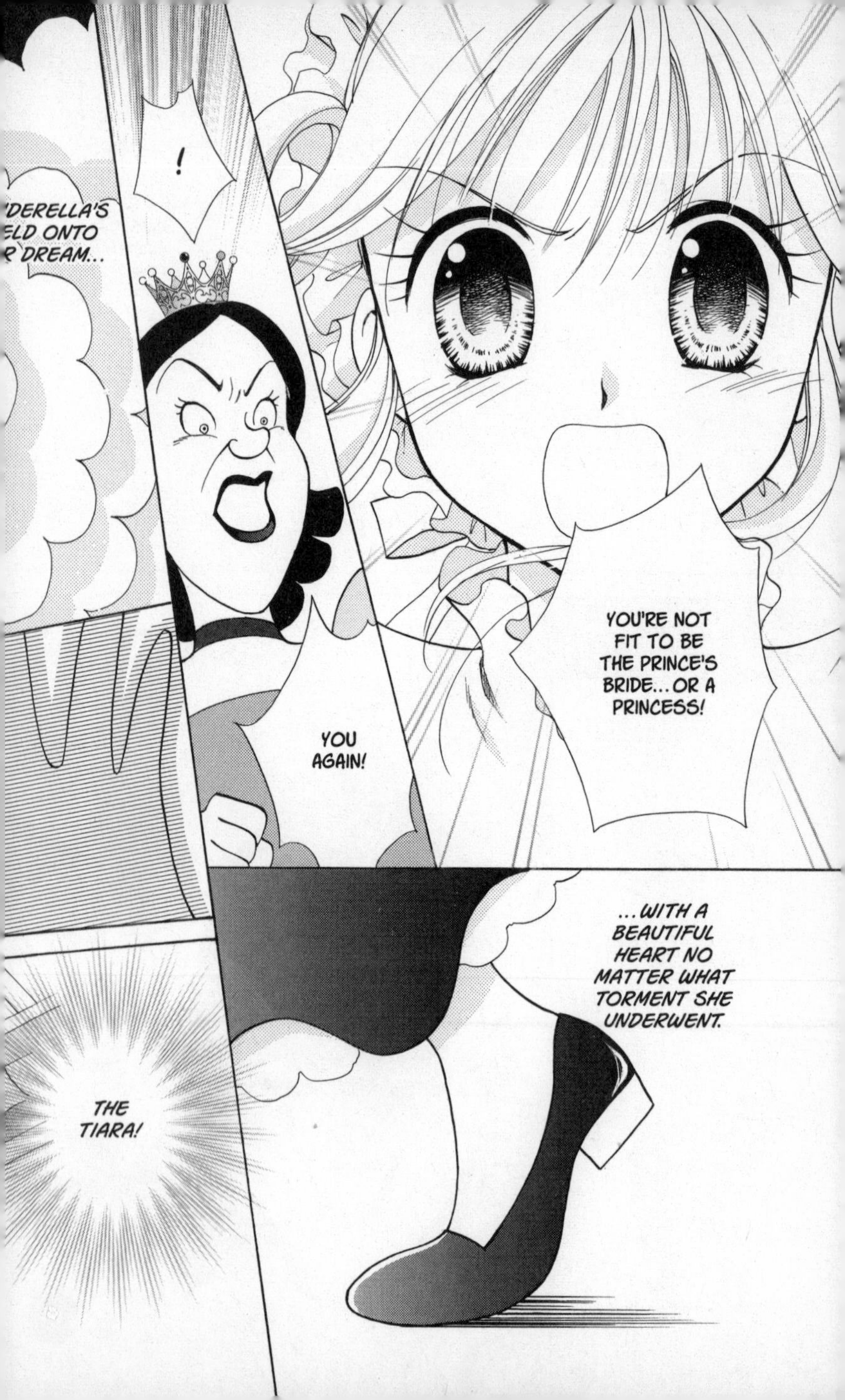
YOU'RE NOT FIT TO BE THE PRINCE'S BRIDE...OR A PRINCESS!
!
YOU AGAIN!
DERELLA'S ELD ONTO R DREAM...
...WITH A BEAUTIFUL HEART NO MATTER WHAT TORMENT SHE UNDERWENT.
THE TIARA!

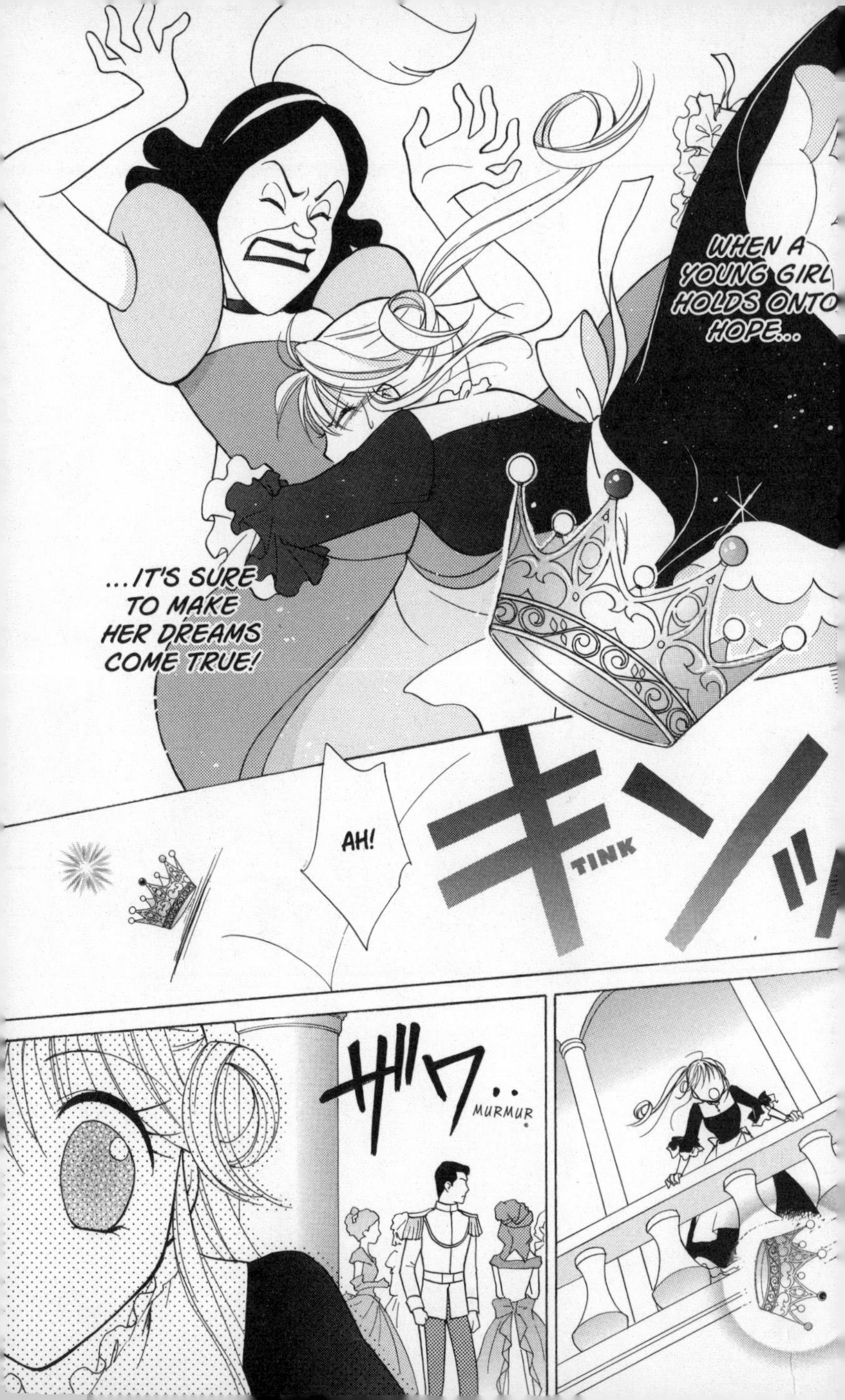
WHEN A YOUNG GIRL HOLDS ONTO HOPE...
...IT'S SURE TO MAKE HER DREAMS COME TRUE!
TINK
AH!
ザワ..
MURMUR

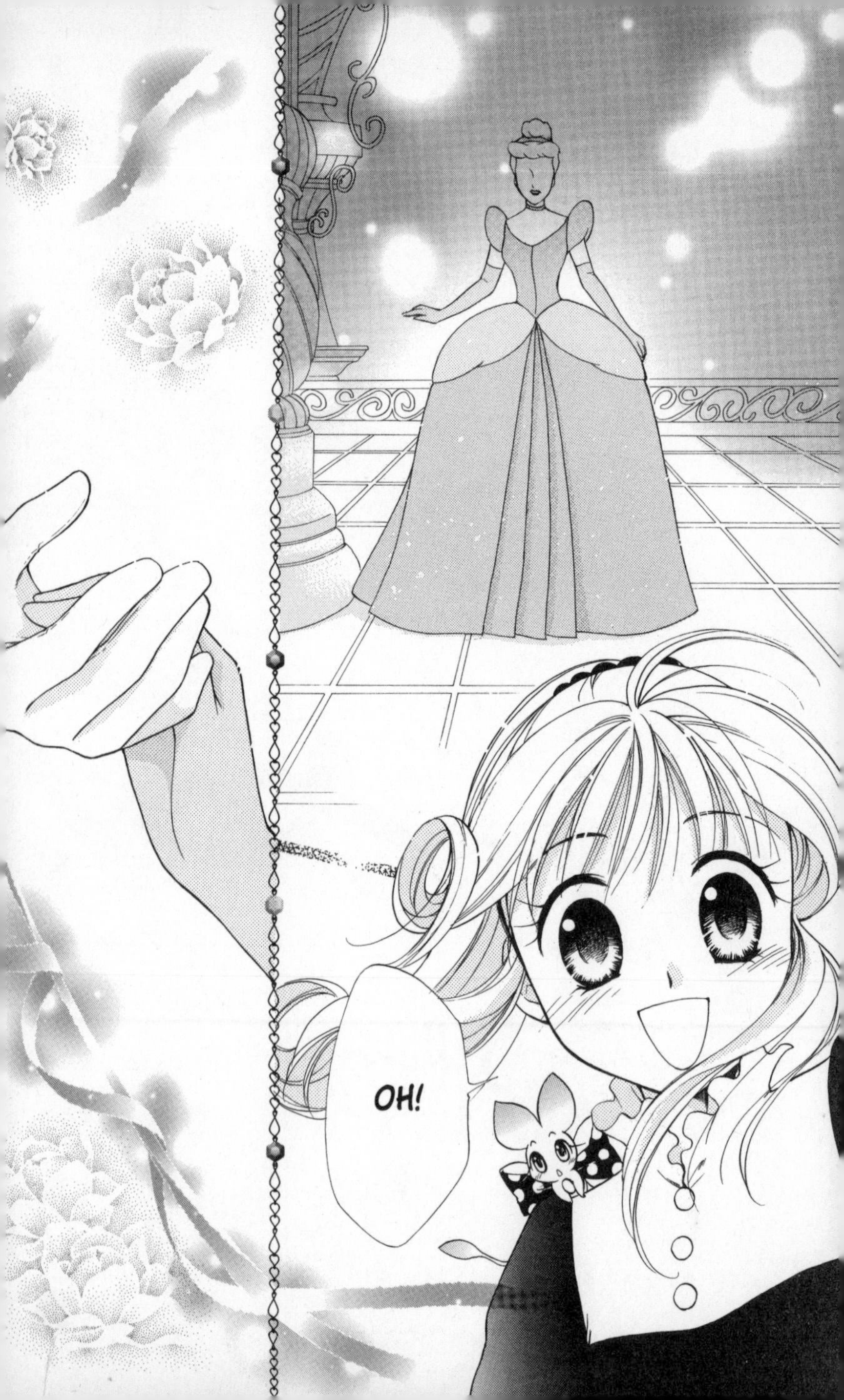
OH!

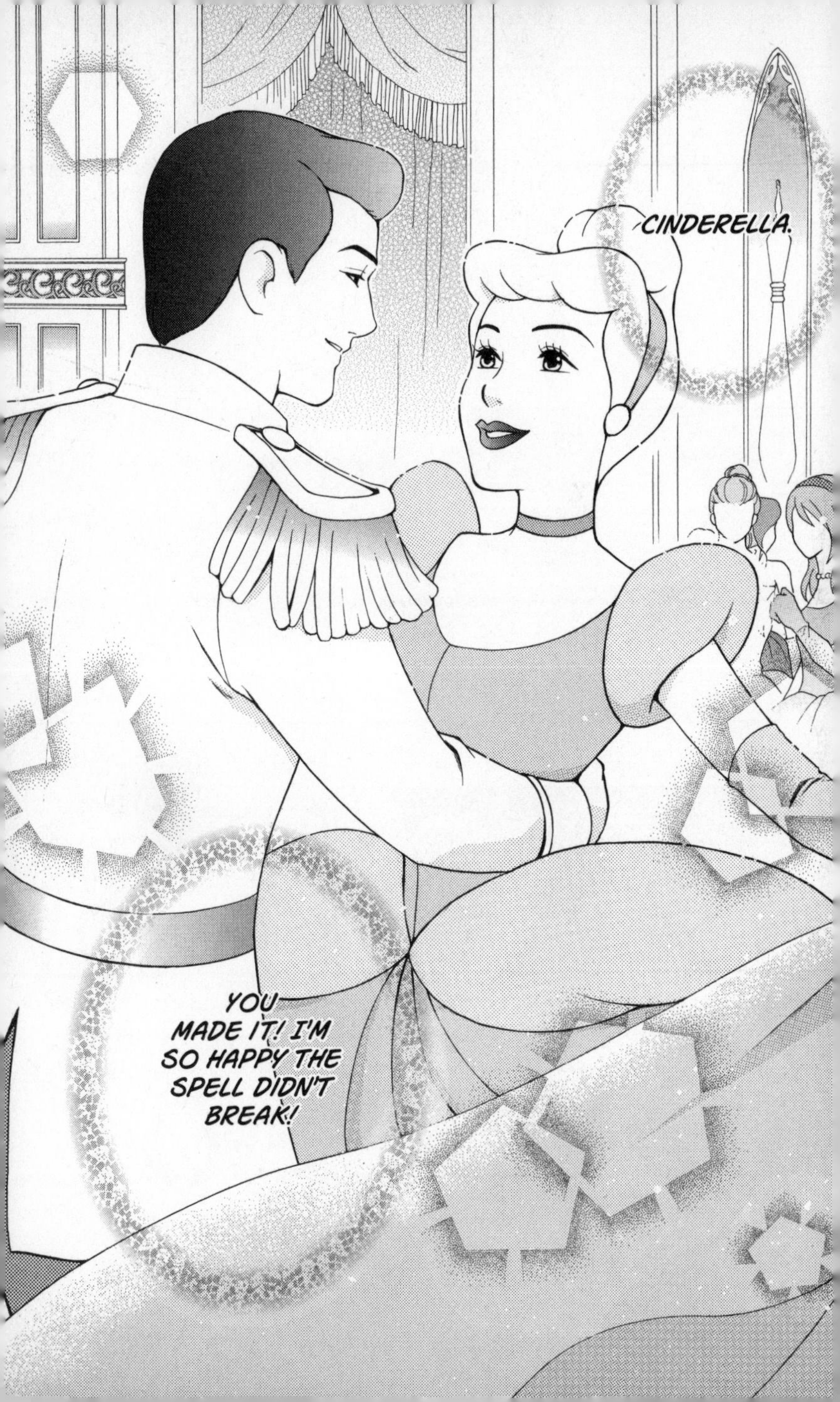
CINDERELLA.
YOU MADE IT! I'M SO HAPPY THE SPELL DIDN'T BREAK!

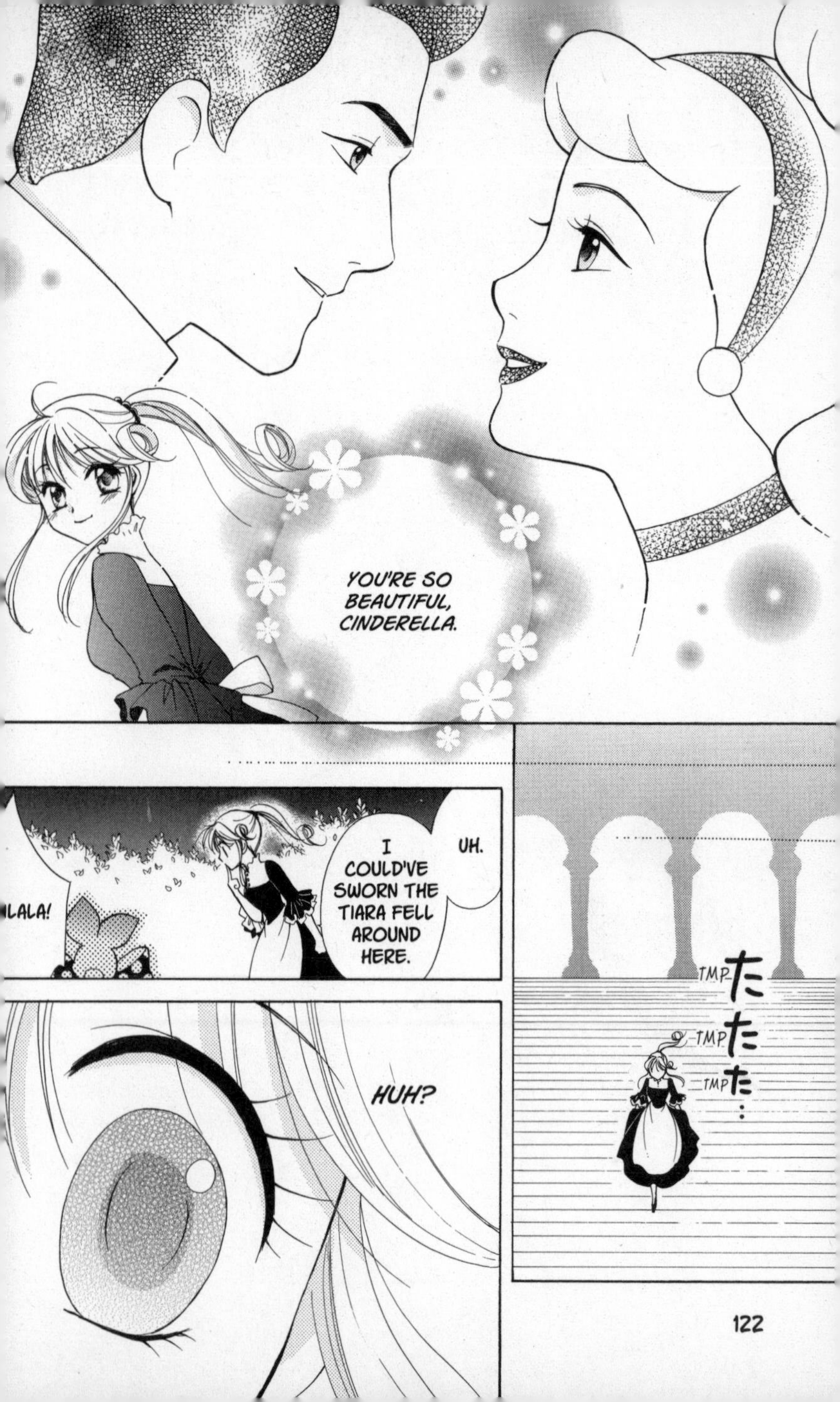
YOU'RE SO BEAUTIFUL, CINDERELLA.
TMP た
TMP た
TMP た
UH.
I COULD'VE SWORN THE TIARA FELL AROUND HERE.
LALA!
HUH?

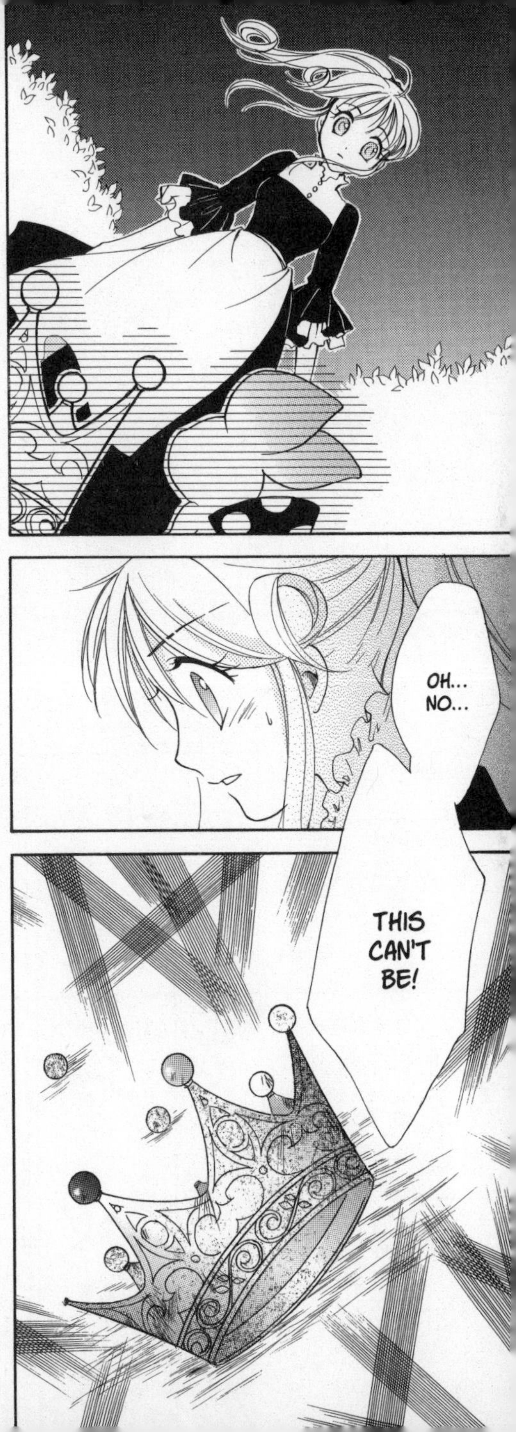
OH... NO...
THIS CAN'T BE!

Nao Kodaka

1

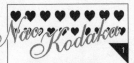

HELLO THIS IS NAO KODAKA. WE'VE PLUNGED ON INTO VOLUME 3 OF "KILALA PRINCESS".

I MADE A MINOR CHANGE TO KILALA'S HAIRSTYLE STARTING IN THIS VOLUME. ☆
WHEN OUR EDITOR SUGGESTED WE GIVE KILALA A BIT OF A MAKEOVER I DID AWAY WITH THE PONYTAIL AND EXPERIMENTED WITH GIVING HER A SHORTER BOB AMONG OTHER STYLES.
LIKE THIS ↓

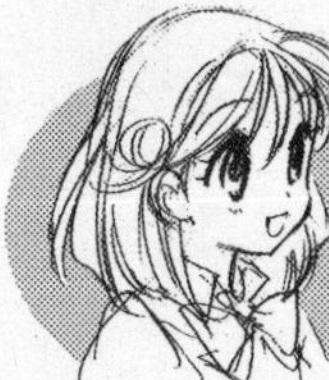

WHOA, WHO ARE YOU?

IN THE END, INSTEAD OF COMPLETELY CHANGING HER LOOK, I JUST GENERALLY TONED THE VOLUME DOWN ON IT SO THAT IT HAS A LIGHTER FEEL TO IT (LOL).

AS FOR THE PLOT OF THE STORY, IT'S REALLY RAMPED UP IN INTENSITY! VALDOU IS NOW AS BLACK ON THE INSIDE AS HE IS ON THE OUTSIDE. AND WE TOOK A BIT OF A DETOUR BEFORE MEETING THE NEXT PRINCESS. WE ONLY GOT TO SEE A SILHOUETTE OF THE "MISS FAIRY" THAT SHOWED UP, BUT OF COURSE WE ALL KNOW WHO SHE WAS... ♡♡

GOOOONG

ゴーン

GOOOONG

ゴーン

GOOOONG

THE BELLS TOLLING MIDNIGHT.

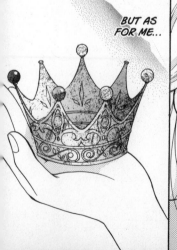

BUT AS FOR ME...

SHE'LL BE ALL RIGHT NOW.

CINDERELLA WILL FIND HER HAPPINESS.

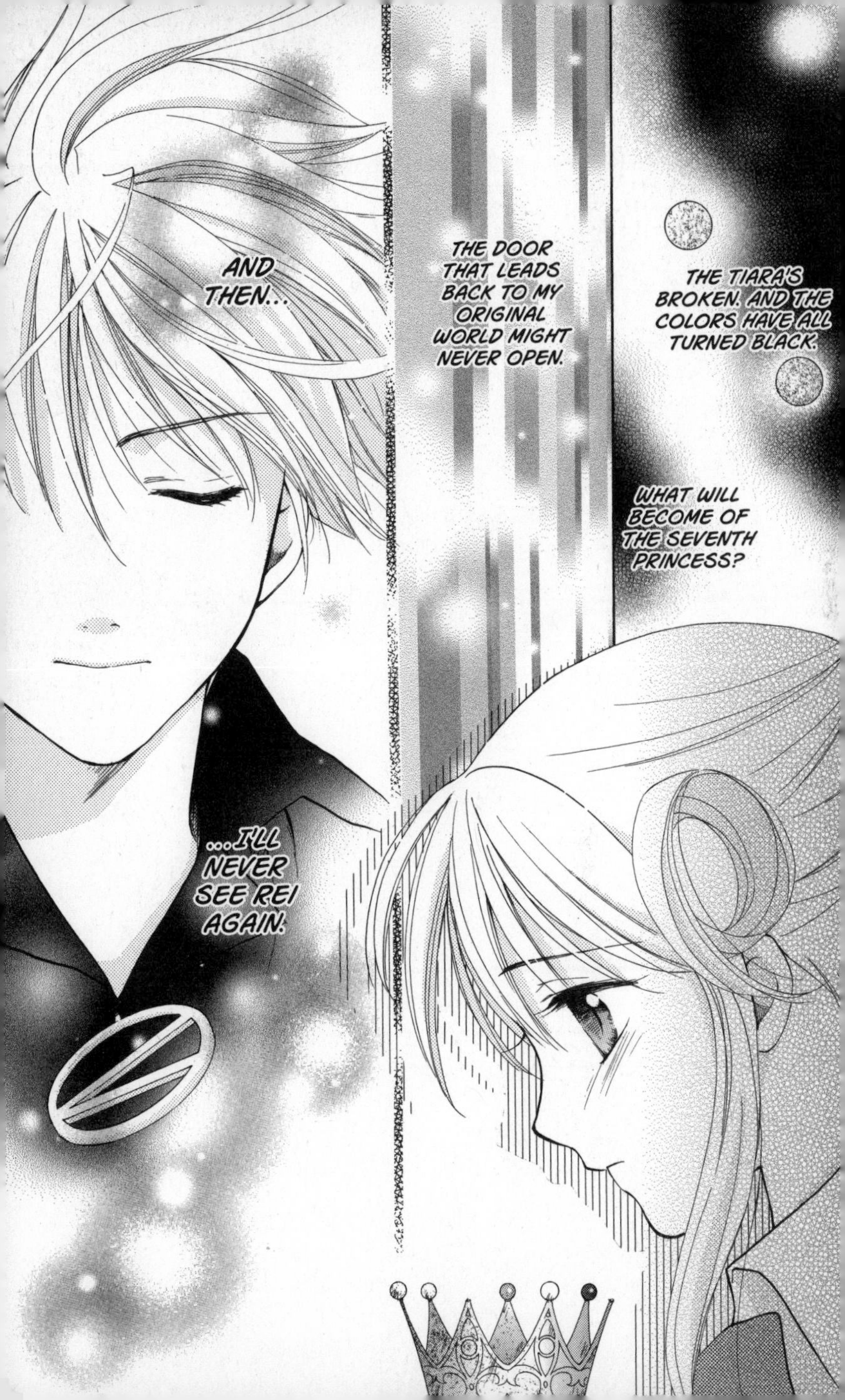
THE TIARA'S BROKEN. AND THE COLORS HAVE ALL TURNED BLACK.
WHAT WILL BECOME OF THE SEVENTH PRINCESS?
THE DOOR THAT LEADS BACK TO MY ORIGINAL WORLD MIGHT NEVER OPEN.
AND THEN...
...I'LL NEVER SEE REI AGAIN.

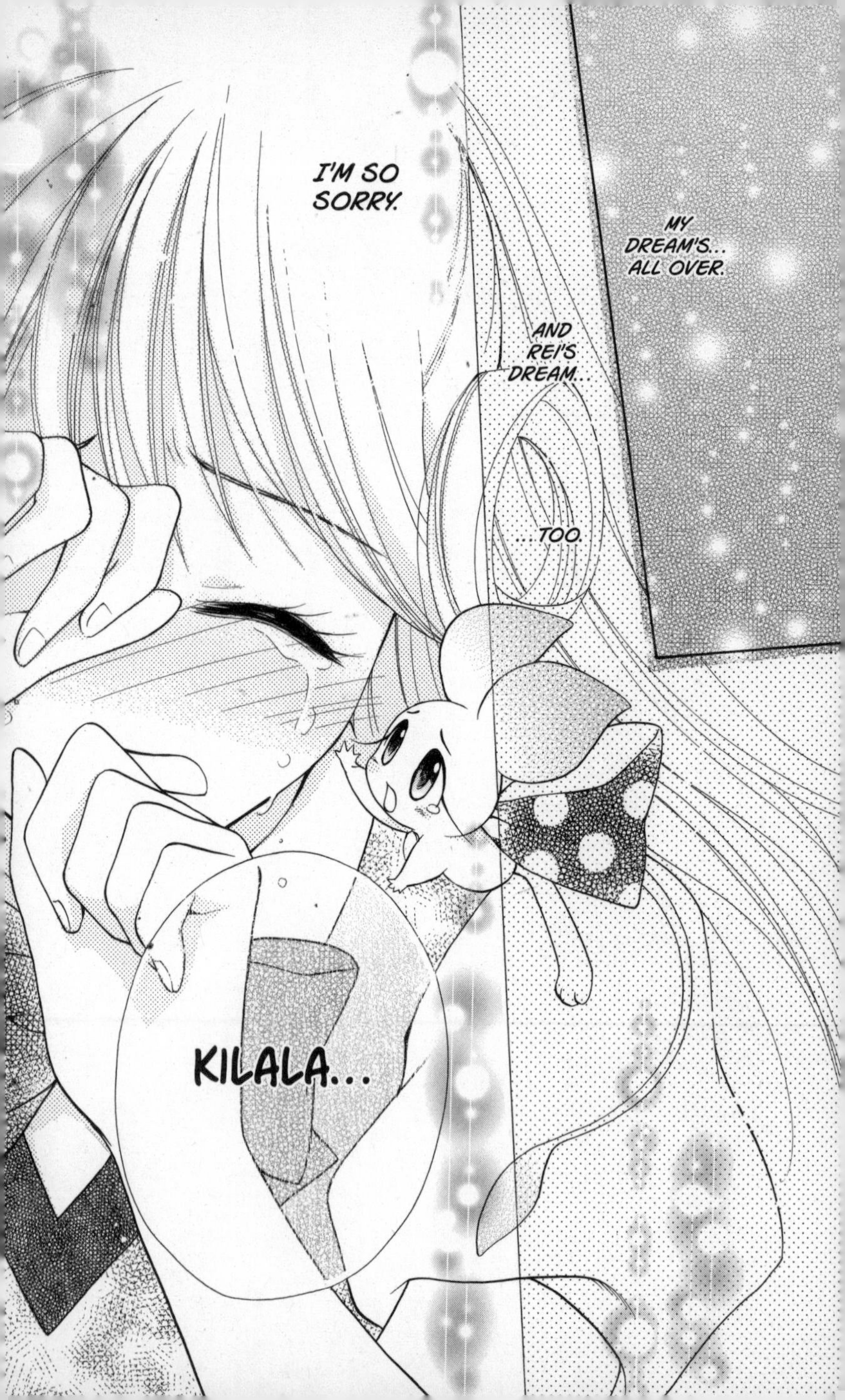
MY DREAM'S... ALL OVER.
AND REI'S DREAM...
...TOO.
I'M SO SORRY.
KILALA...

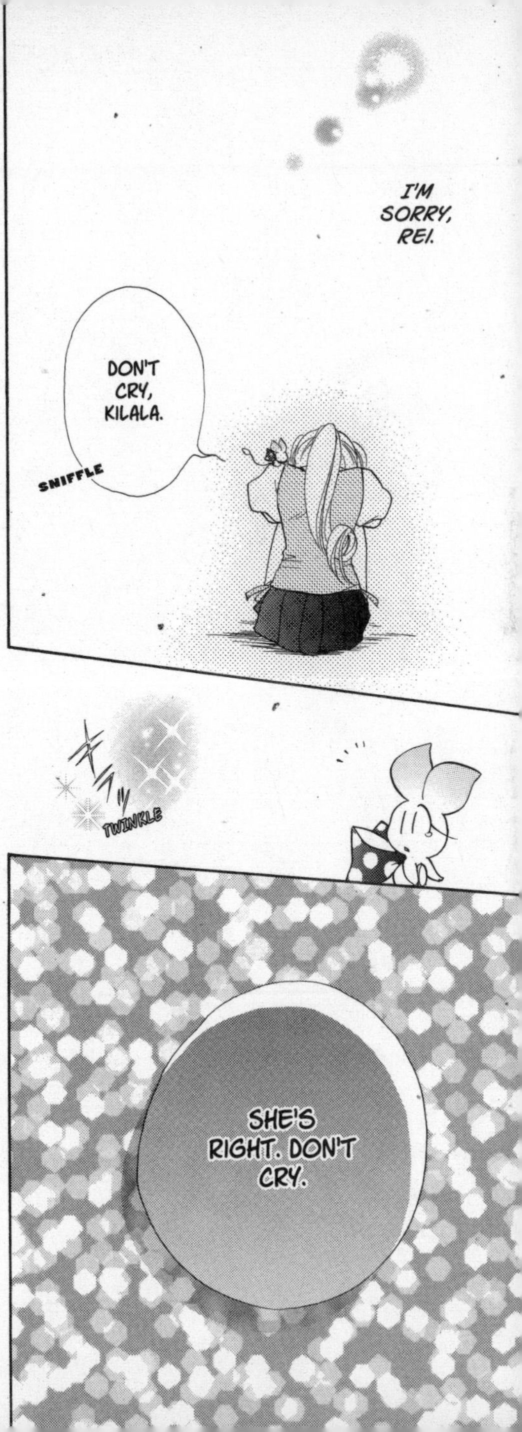
I'M SORRY, REI.
DON'T CRY, KILALA.
SNIFFLE
TWINKLE
SHE'S RIGHT. DON'T CRY.

Nao Kodaka 2

THE THIRD PRINCESS IS CINDERELLA. ♥ SHE REALLY HAS A GREAT PERSONALITY (LOL). SHE'S POSITIVE AND A KIND-HEARTED GIRL THROUGH AND THROUGH. BUT IN THIS ARC, I SHOULD MENTION THAT SHE REALLY IS MORE LIKE A SIDE CHARACTER! (LOL) WITH ALL THE TONES THE STEPMOTHER AND STEPSISTERS USE, I COULD HEAR MY ASSISTANTS WAILING ALL THE TIME OVER IT... D'OH! UNLIKE THE BAD GUYS THAT WE'VE SEEN SO FAR, THESE THREE ARE ORDINARY HUMANS WHO DON'T USE MAGIC. BUT MAYBE THAT'S WHAT MAKES THEM ALL THE SCARIER AND UGLIER.

HALFWAY THROUGH THIS VOLUME, WE REACHED THE ONE-YEAR ANNIVERSARY OF THE KILALA SERIALIZATION. HOW TIME FLIES~ WE'VE ONLY BEEN ABLE TO GET THIS FAR THANKS TO ALL OF YOU WHO SUPPORT US. THANK YOU SO MUCH! AND TO THE GODDESSES WHO KEEP UP WITH OUR CRAZY SCHEDULE: YUKI-CHAN, MEG-TAN, HINO-CHAN, AND JUN-JUN. TO OUR FRIENDLY AND SUPPORTIVE EDITORIAL DEPARTMENT, THE EDITORS WITH DISNEY, TANAKA-SENSEI, MY BIG, WONDERFUL SISTER AND ALL OF YOU WHO HAVE READ THIS FAR: I HAVE THE HIGHEST APPRECIATION FOR YOU.

THE STORY STILL HAS A WAY TO GO. SO I HOPE YOU'LL SUPPORT US HEREAFTER AS WELL! SEE YOU AGAIN IN VOLUME 4! ♥ ♥

♥♥♥♥♥♥♥♥♥♥

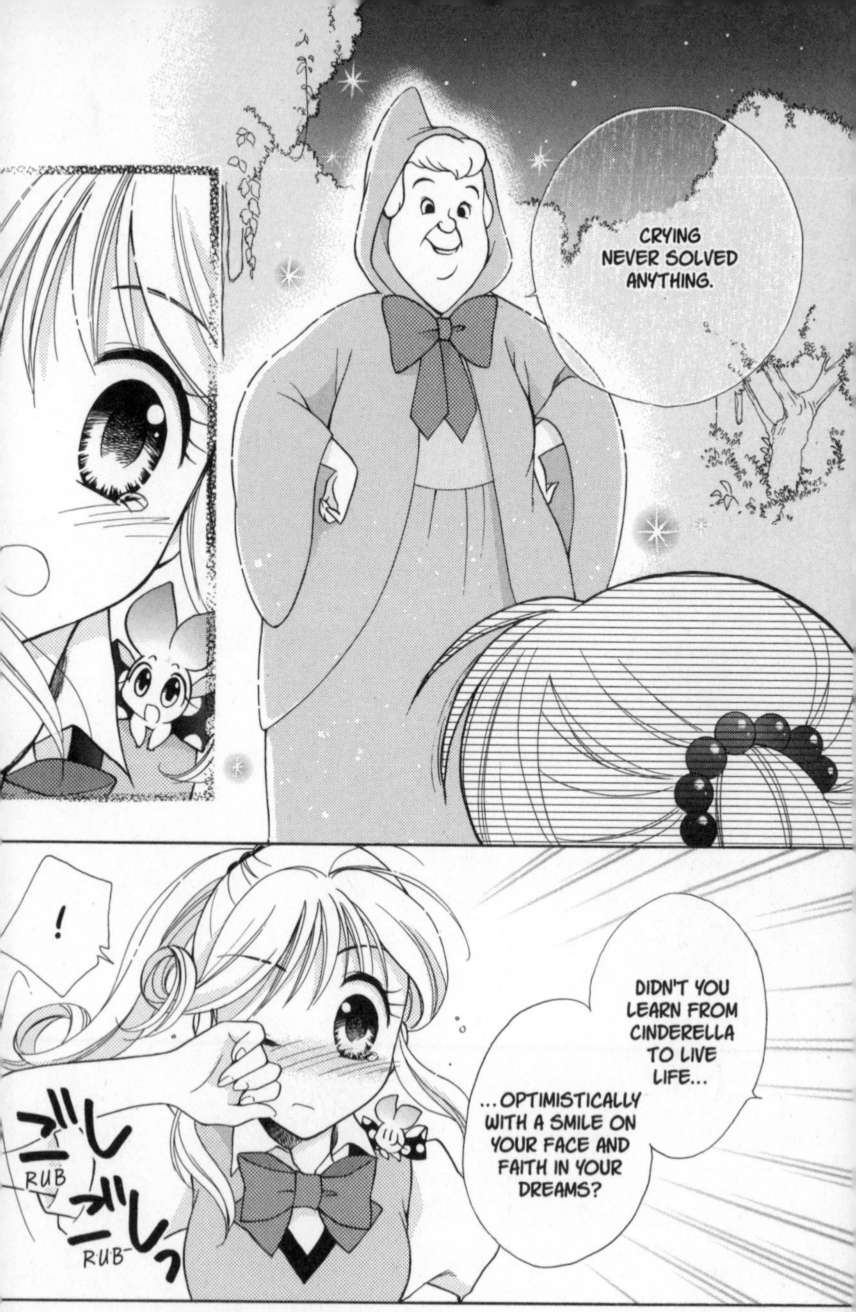
CRYING NEVER SOLVED ANYTHING.
DIDN'T YOU LEARN FROM CINDERELLA TO LIVE LIFE...
...OPTIMISTICALLY WITH A SMILE ON YOUR FACE AND FAITH IN YOUR DREAMS?
!
RUB
RUB

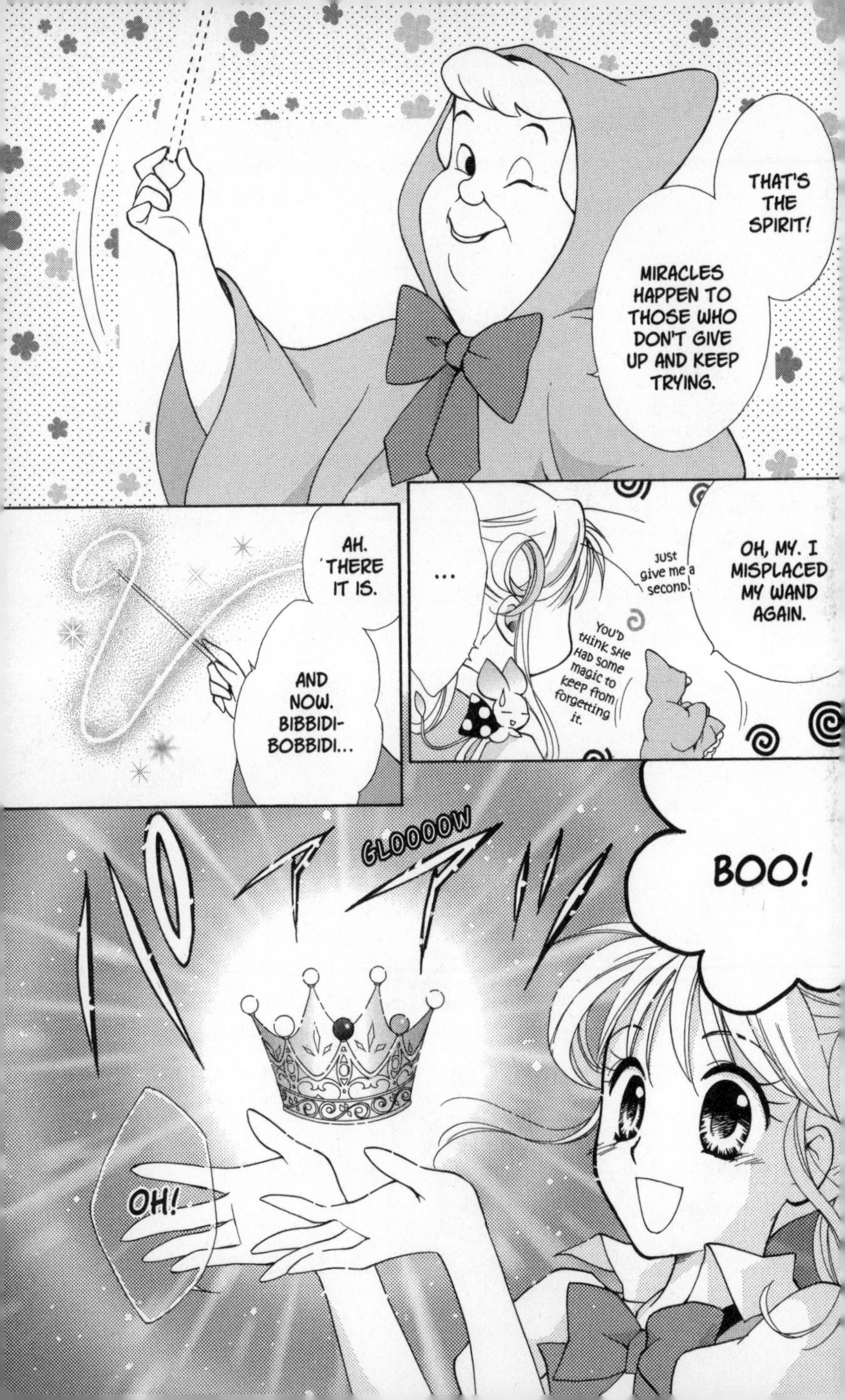
THAT'S THE SPIRIT!
MIRACLES HAPPEN TO THOSE WHO DON'T GIVE UP AND KEEP TRYING.
OH, MY. I MISPLACED MY WAND AGAIN.
JUST give me a second!
YOU'D think SHE HAD some magic to keep from forgetting it.
...
AH. THERE IT IS.
AND NOW. BIBBIDI-BOBBIDI...
BOO!
GLOOOOW
OH!

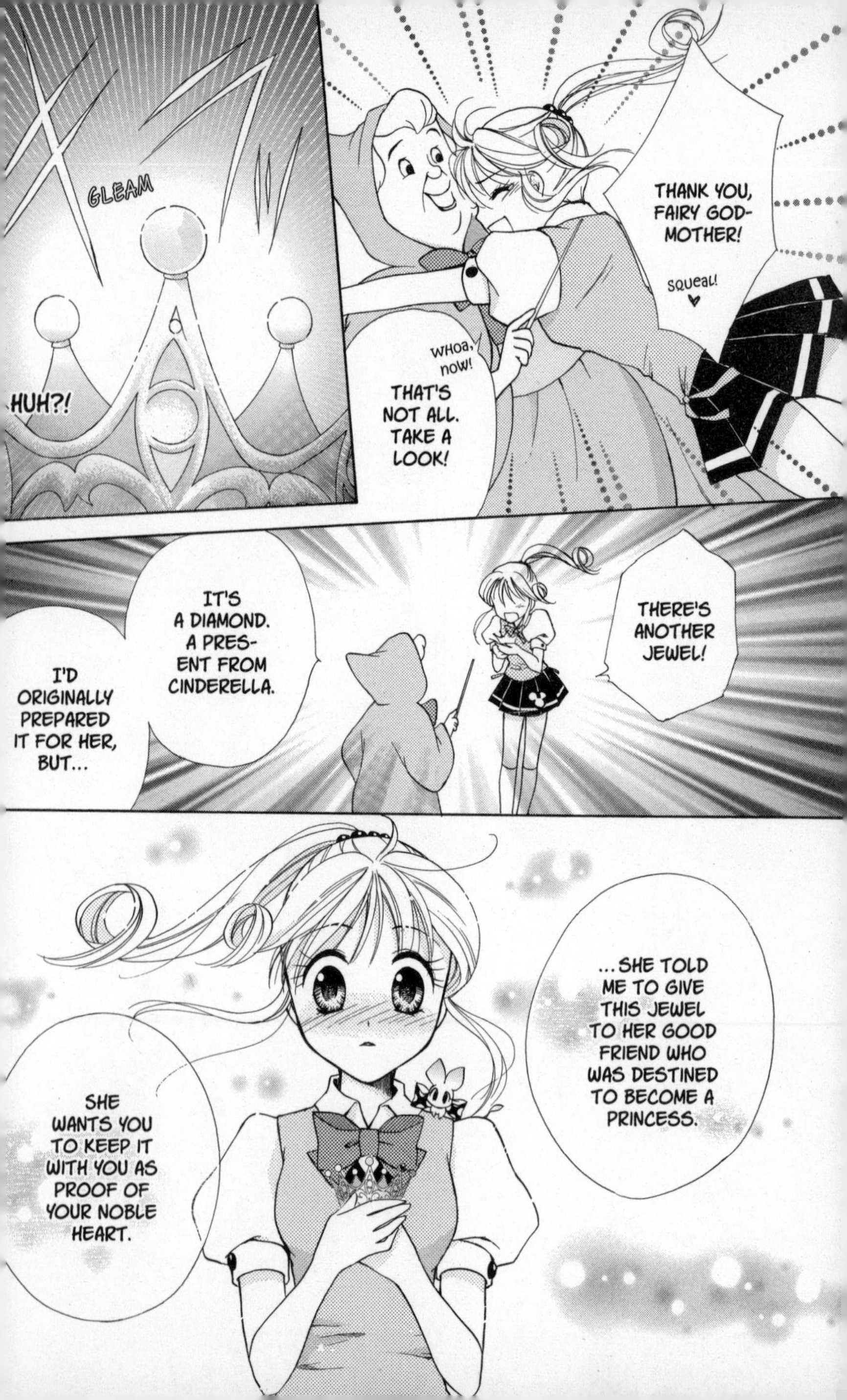
THANK YOU, FAIRY GOD-MOTHER!
SQUEAL! ♥
WHOA, NOW!
THAT'S NOT ALL. TAKE A LOOK!
GLEAM
HUH?!
THERE'S ANOTHER JEWEL!
IT'S A DIAMOND. A PRESENT FROM CINDERELLA.
I'D ORIGINALLY PREPARED IT FOR HER, BUT...
...SHE TOLD ME TO GIVE THIS JEWEL TO HER GOOD FRIEND WHO WAS DESTINED TO BECOME A PRINCESS.
SHE WANTS YOU TO KEEP IT WITH YOU AS PROOF OF YOUR NOBLE HEART.

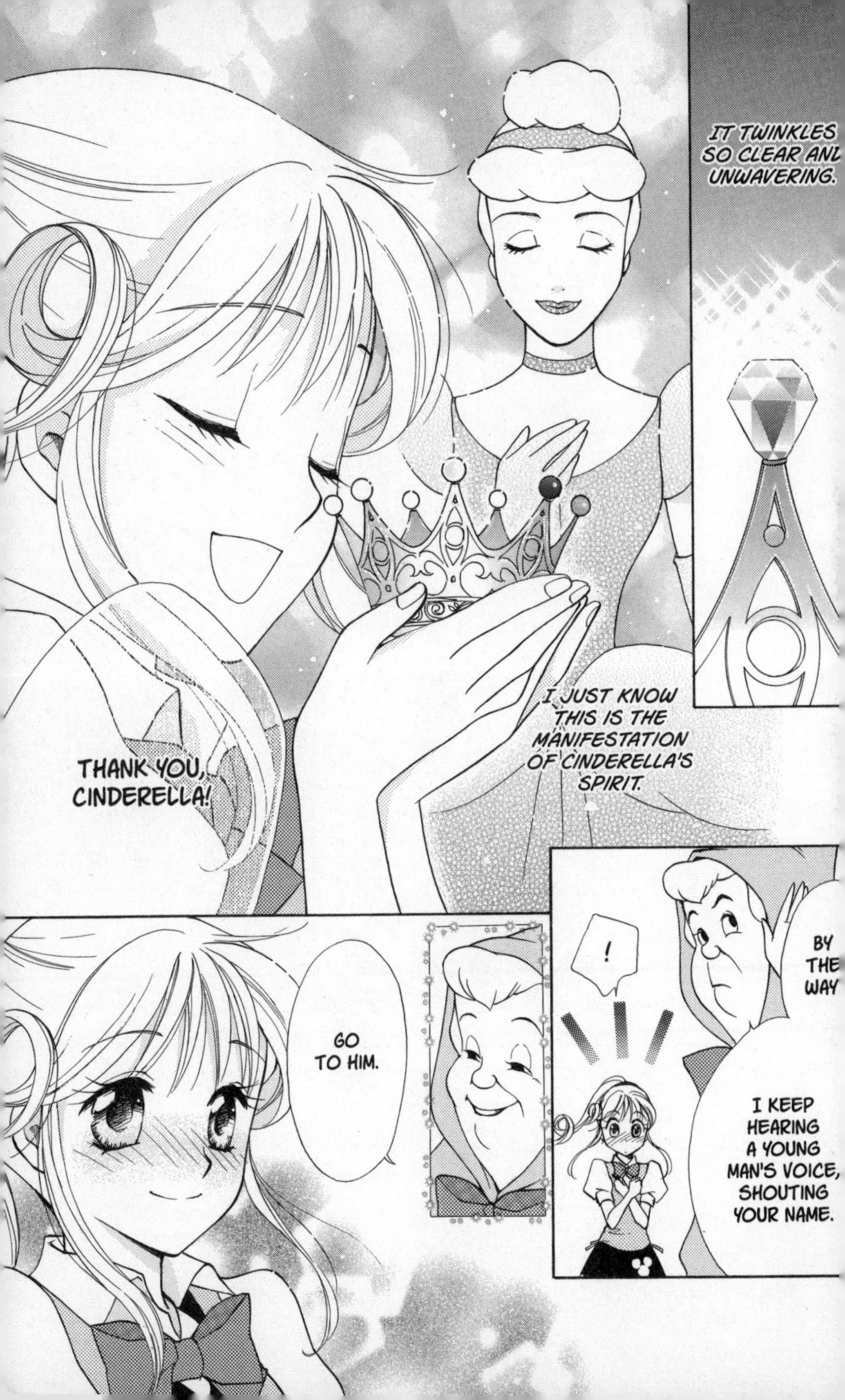
IT TWINKLES SO CLEAR AND UNWAVERING.
I JUST KNOW THIS IS THE MANIFESTATION OF CINDERELLA'S SPIRIT.
THANK YOU, CINDERELLA!
BY THE WAY
!
I KEEP HEARING A YOUNG MAN'S VOICE, SHOUTING YOUR NAME.
GO TO HIM.

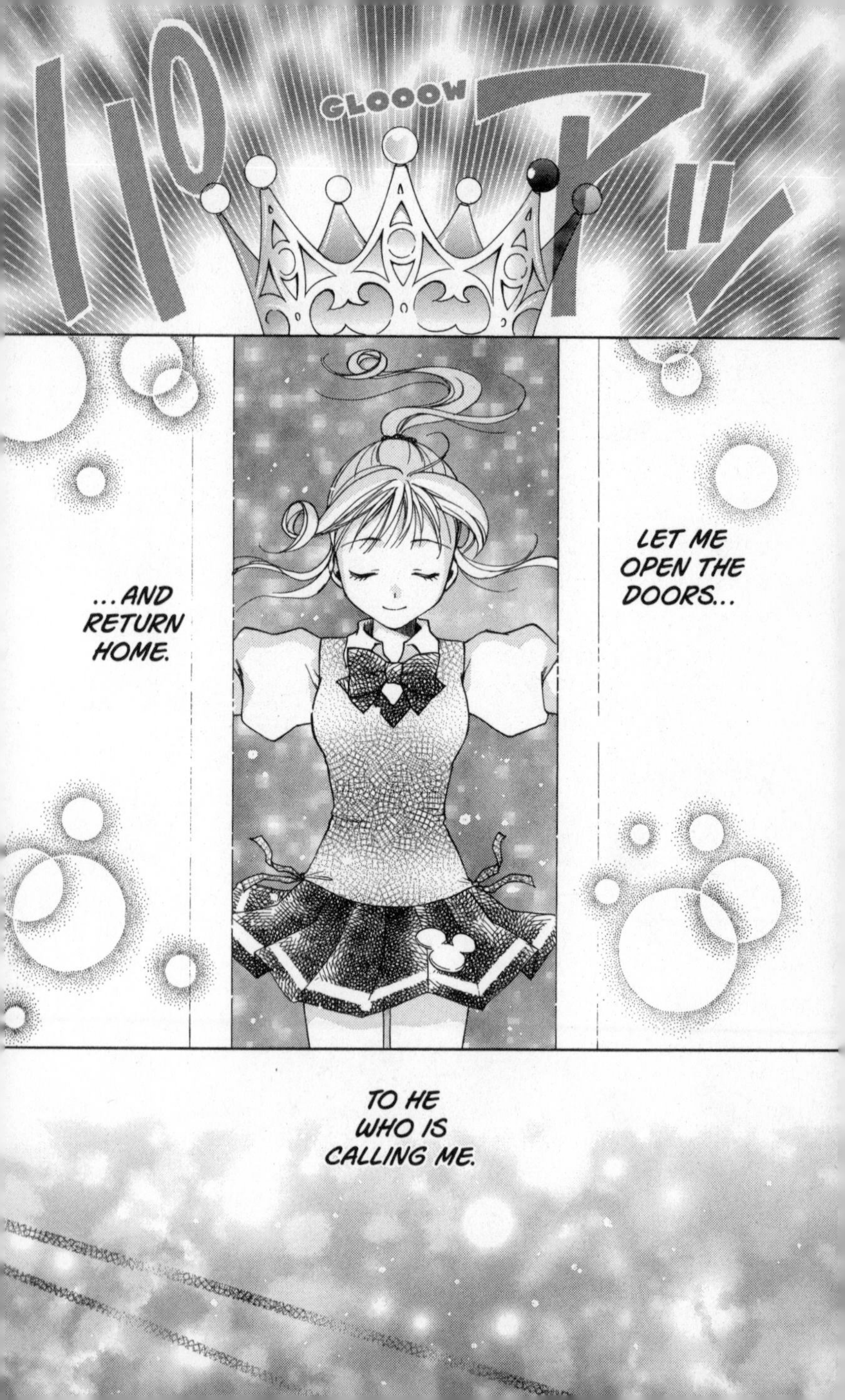
GLOOOW
LET ME OPEN THE DOORS...
...AND RETURN HOME.
TO HE WHO IS CALLING ME.

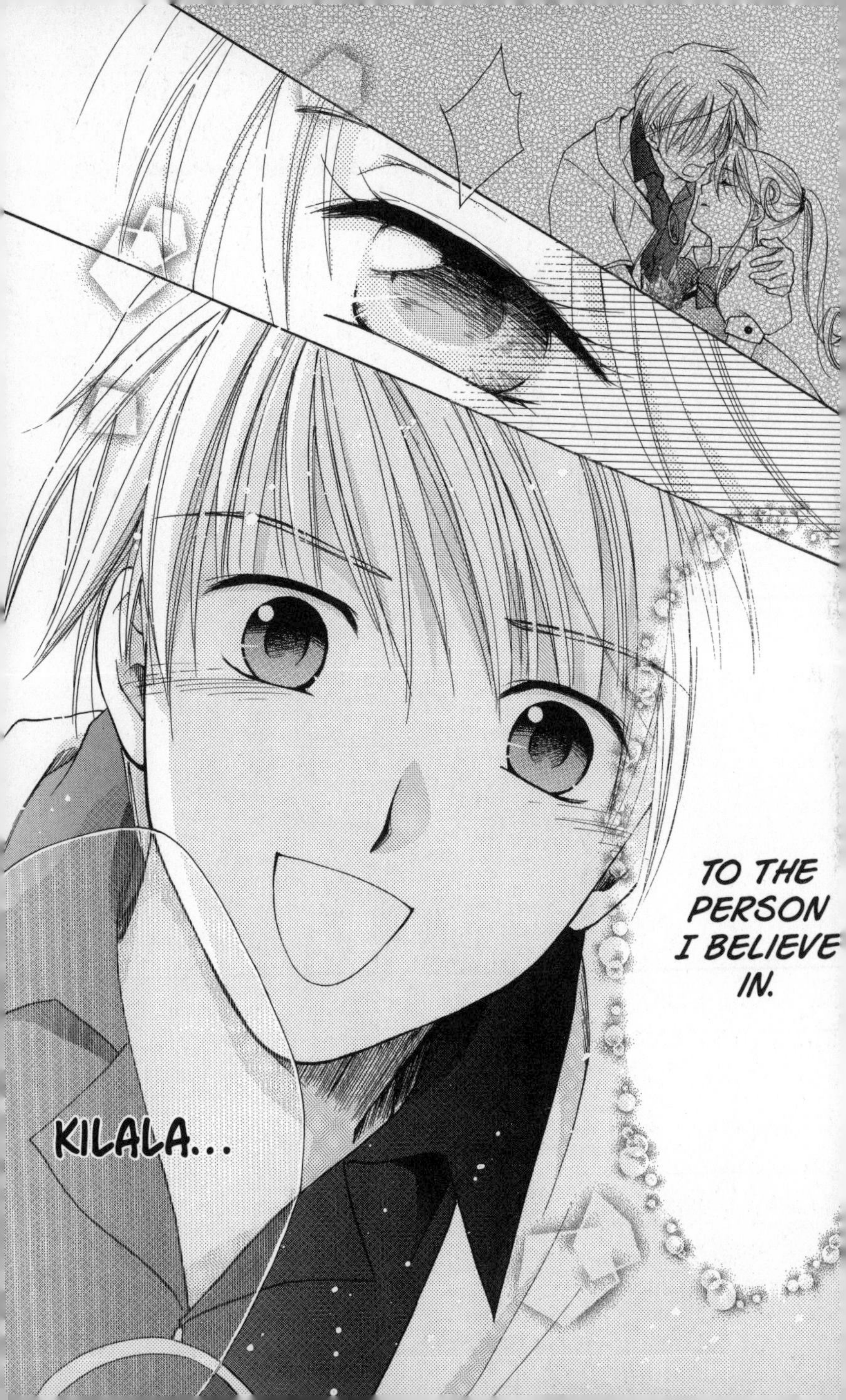
TO THE PERSON I BELIEVE IN.
KILALA...

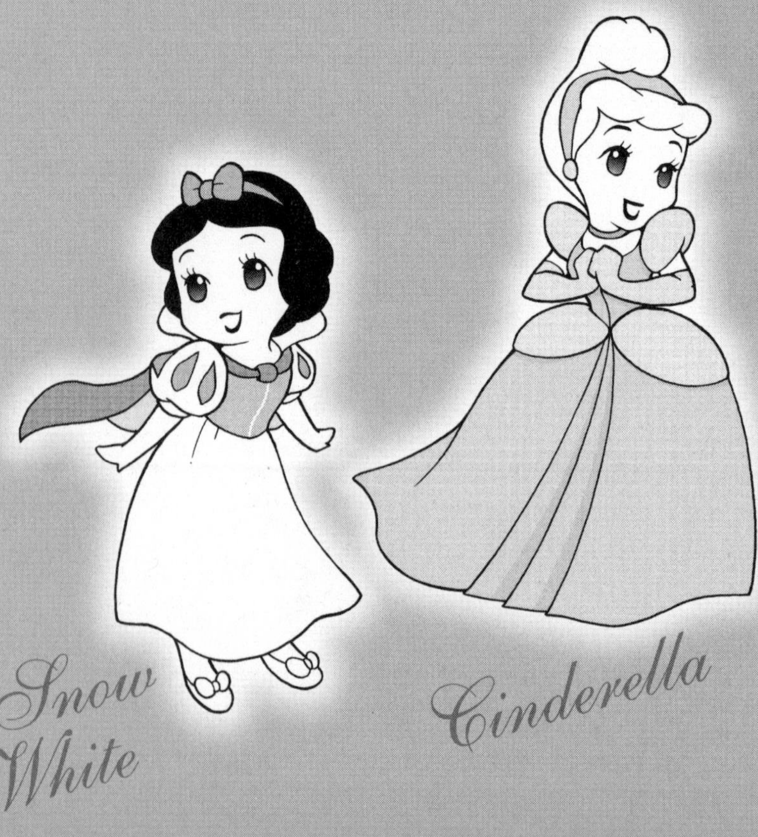
Snow White
Cinderella

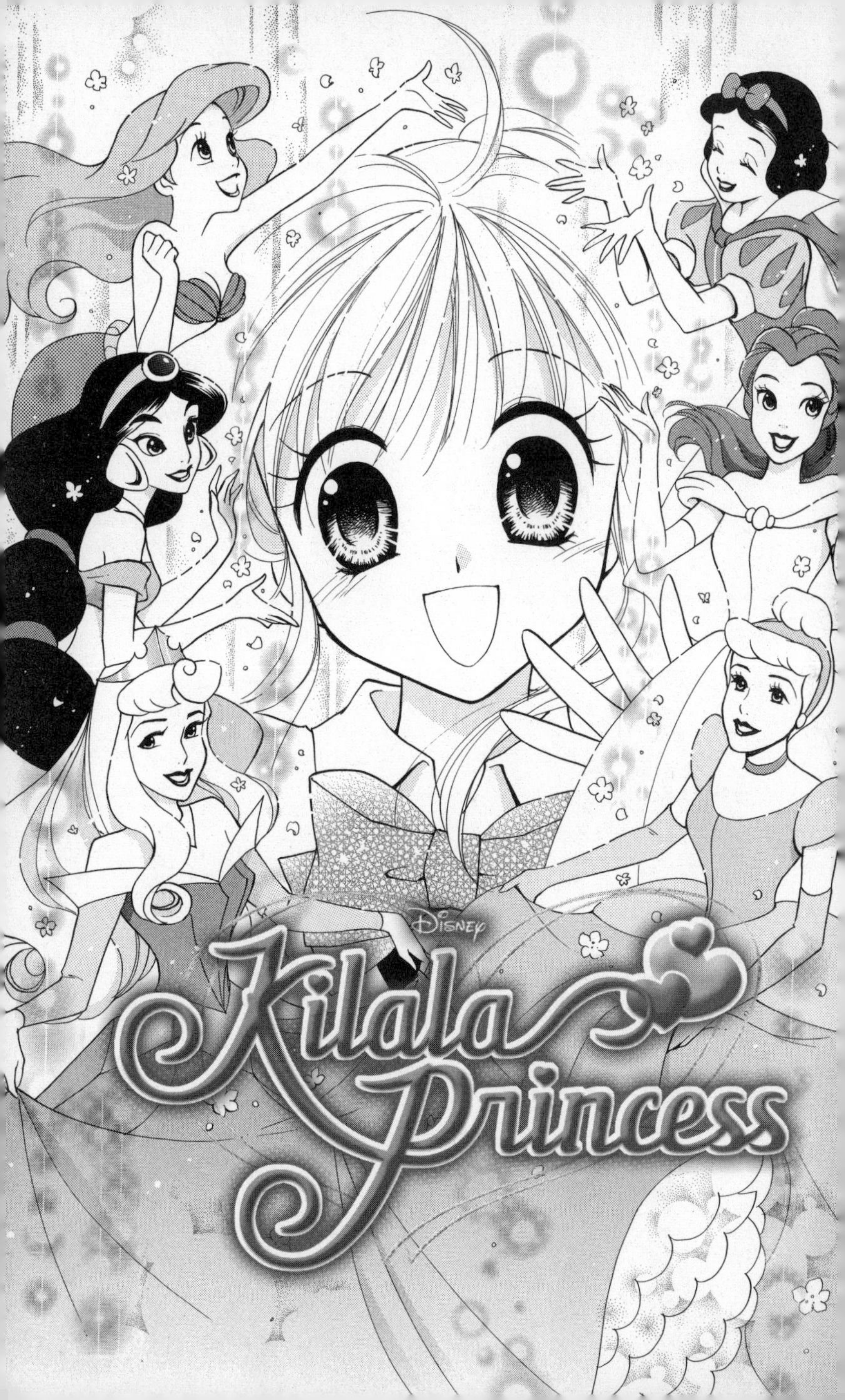
Disney
Kilala Princess

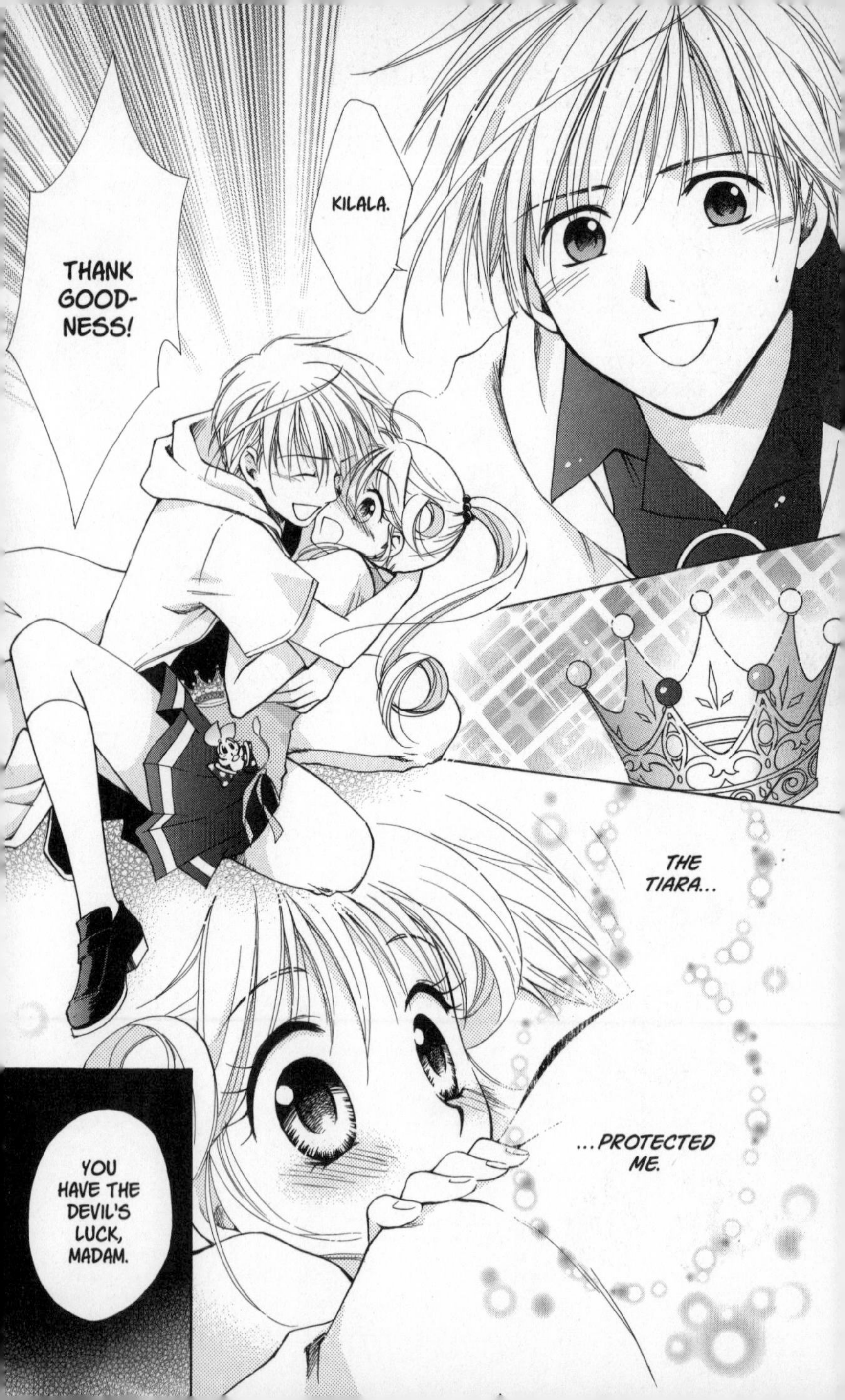
KILALA.
THANK GOODNESS!
THE TIARA...
...PROTECTED ME.
YOU HAVE THE DEVIL'S LUCK, MADAM.

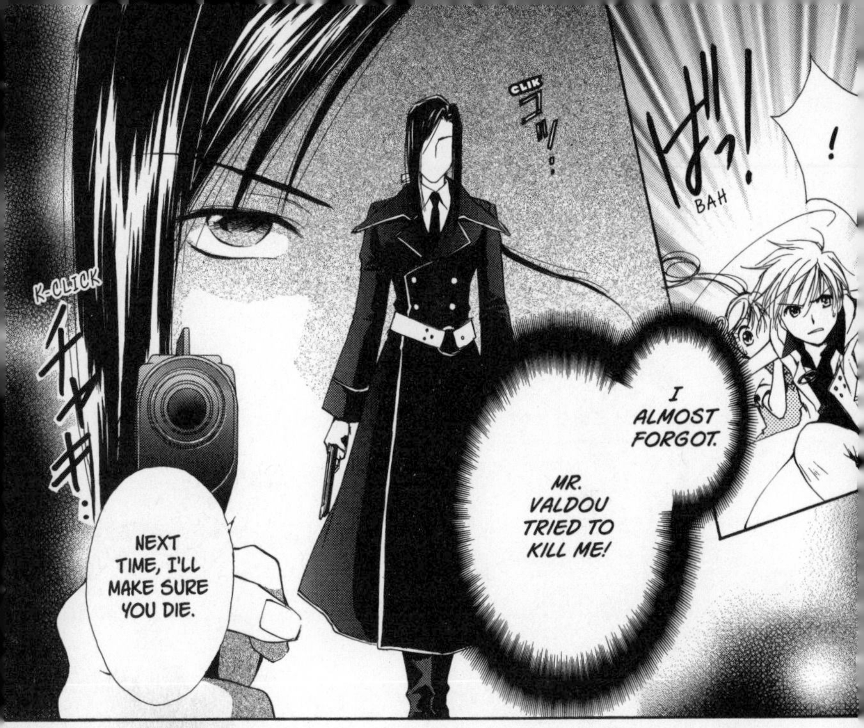
ばっ!
BAH
!
I ALMOST FORGOT.
MR. VALDOU TRIED TO KILL ME!
CLIK
K-CLICK
NEXT TIME, I'LL MAKE SURE YOU DIE.

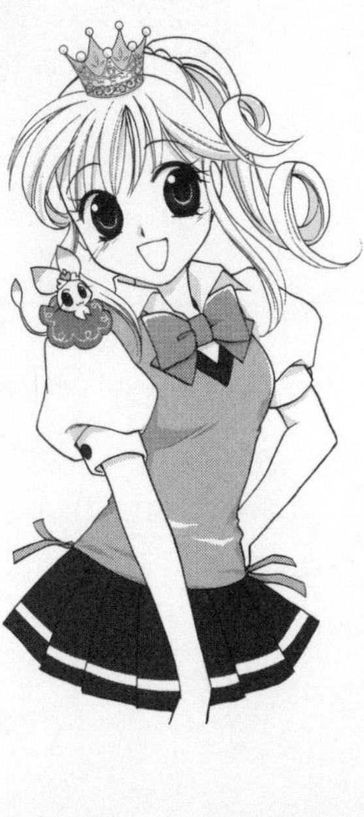

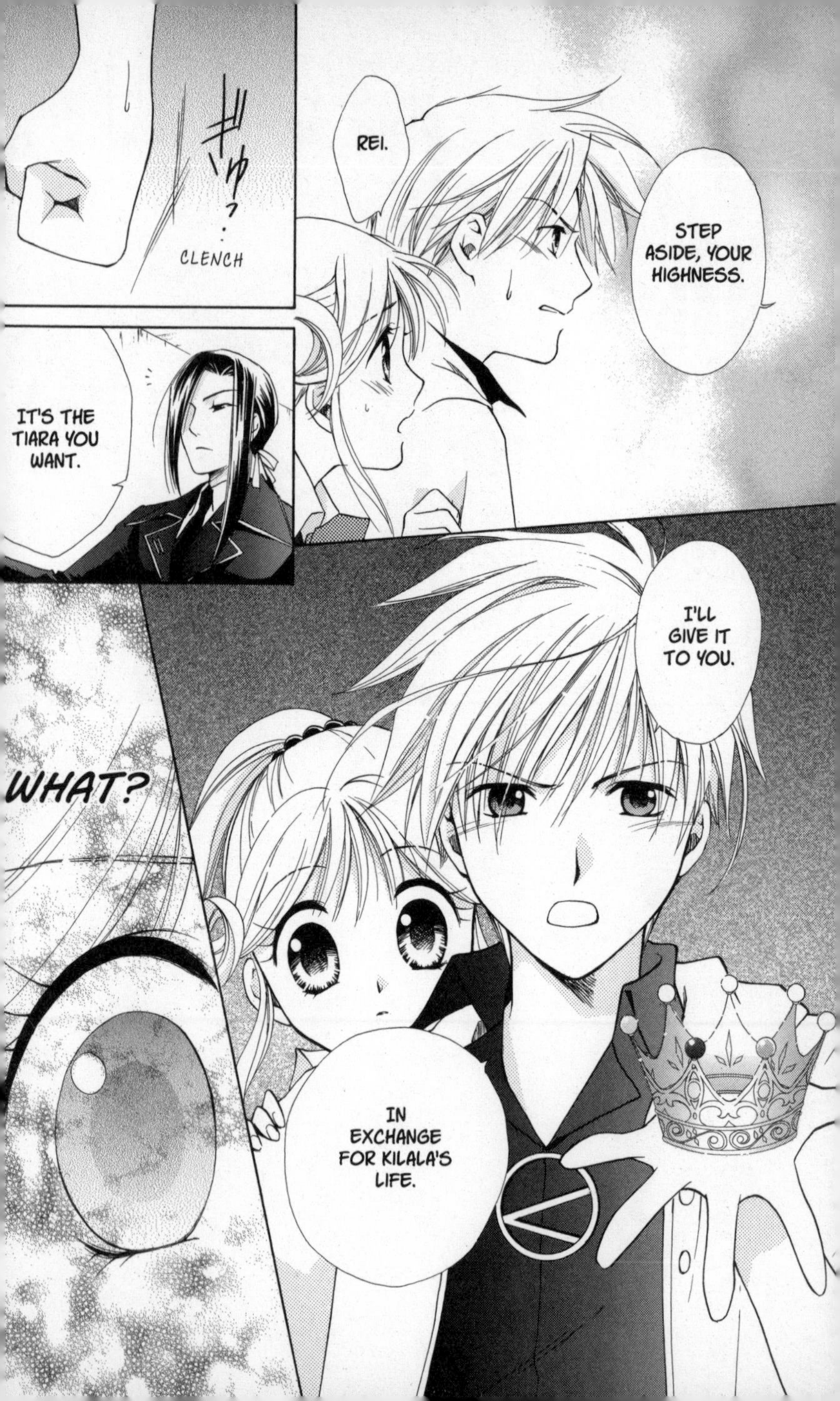
REI.
STEP ASIDE, YOUR HIGHNESS.
ぎゅっ
CLENCH
IT'S THE TIARA YOU WANT.
I'LL GIVE IT TO YOU.
IN EXCHANGE FOR KILALA'S LIFE.
WHAT?

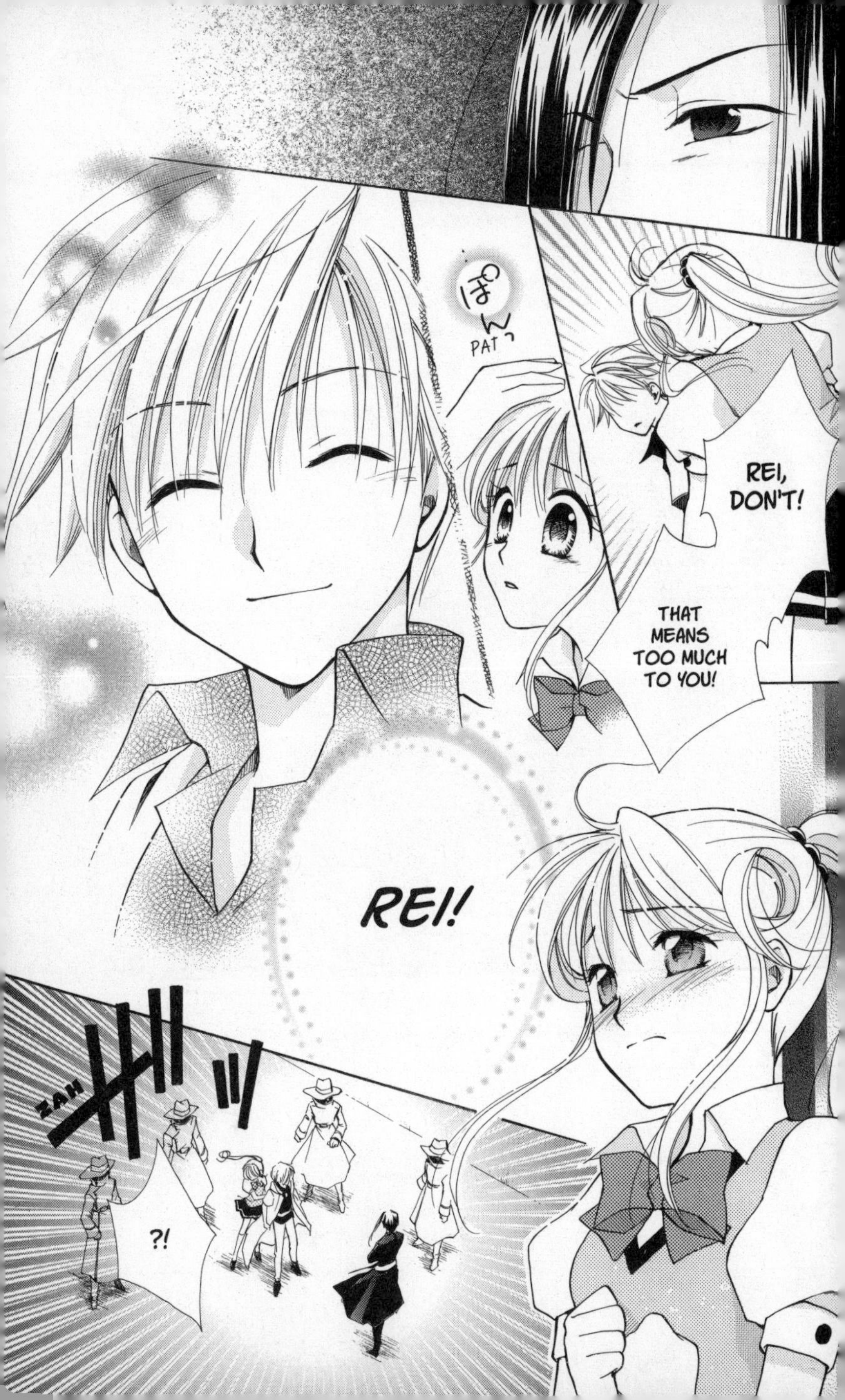
REI, DON'T!
THAT MEANS TOO MUCH TO YOU!
ぽん
PAT
REI!
ZAH
?!

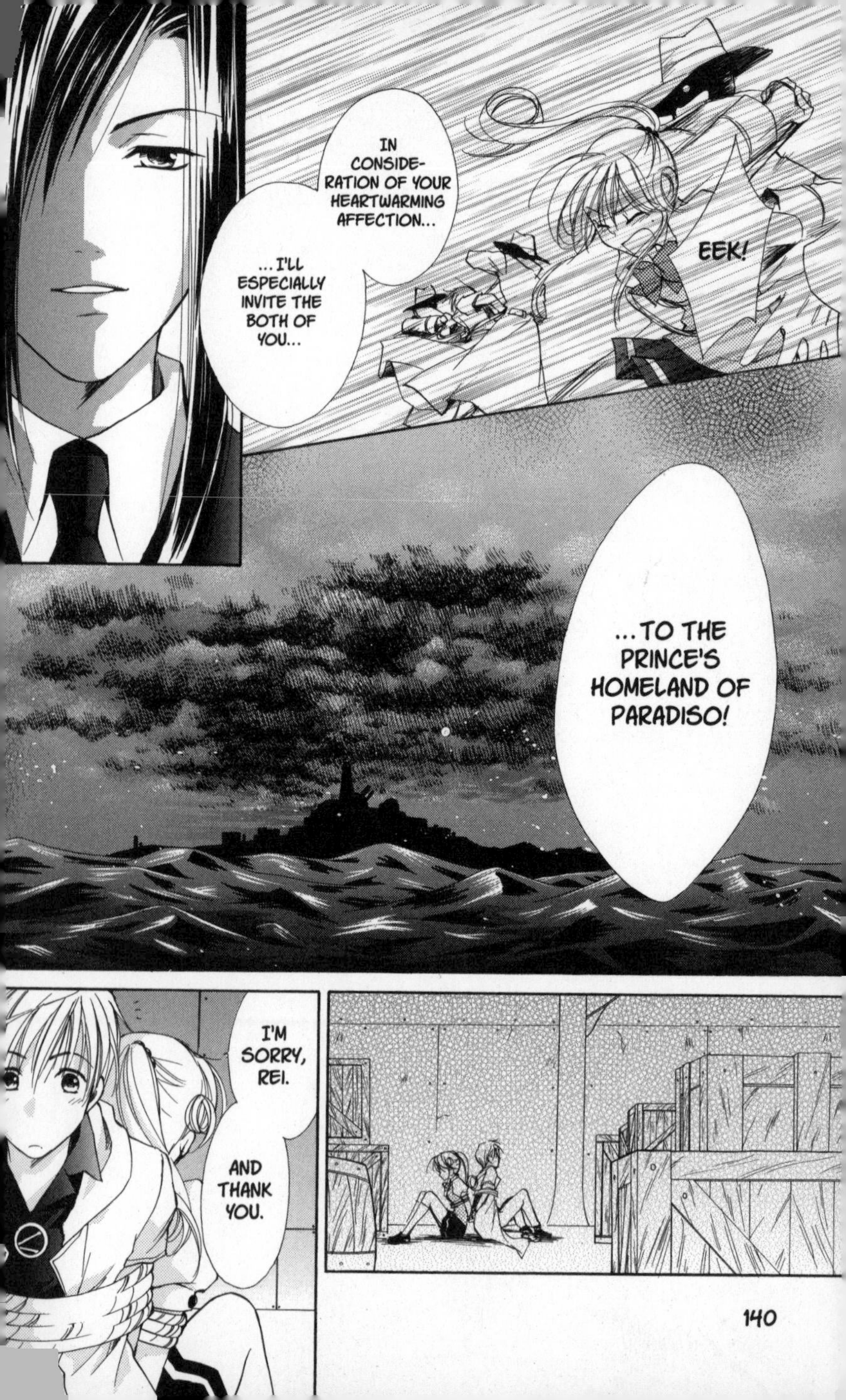
IN CONSIDERATION OF YOUR HEARTWARMING AFFECTION...
EEK!
...I'LL ESPECIALLY INVITE THE BOTH OF YOU...
...TO THE PRINCE'S HOMELAND OF PARADISO!
I'M SORRY, REI.
AND THANK YOU.

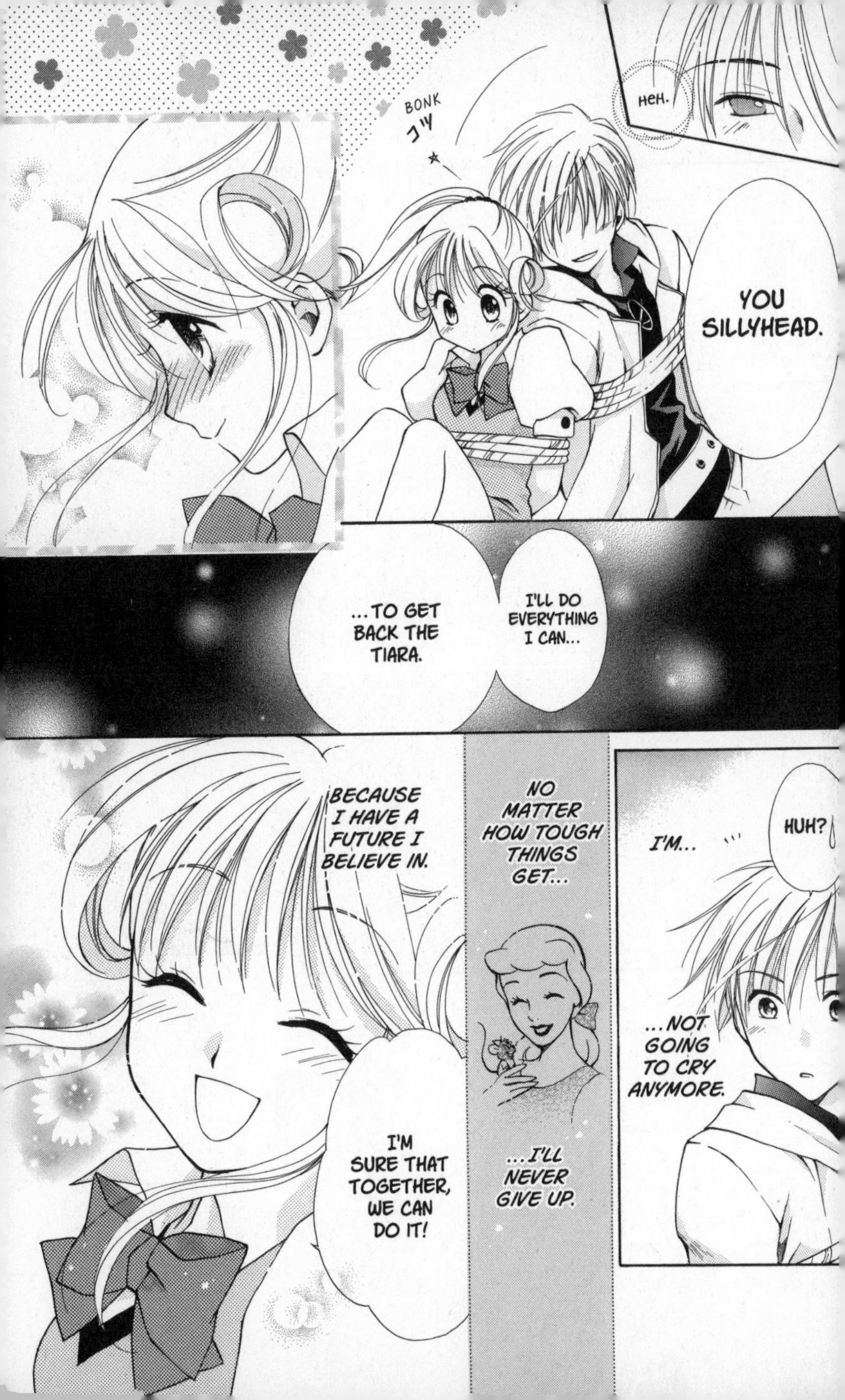
HEH.
BONK
YOU SILLYHEAD.
I'LL DO EVERYTHING I CAN...
...TO GET BACK THE TIARA.
HUH?
I'M...
...NOT GOING TO CRY ANYMORE.
NO MATTER HOW TOUGH THINGS GET...
...I'LL NEVER GIVE UP.
BECAUSE I HAVE A FUTURE I BELIEVE IN.
I'M SURE THAT TOGETHER, WE CAN DO IT!

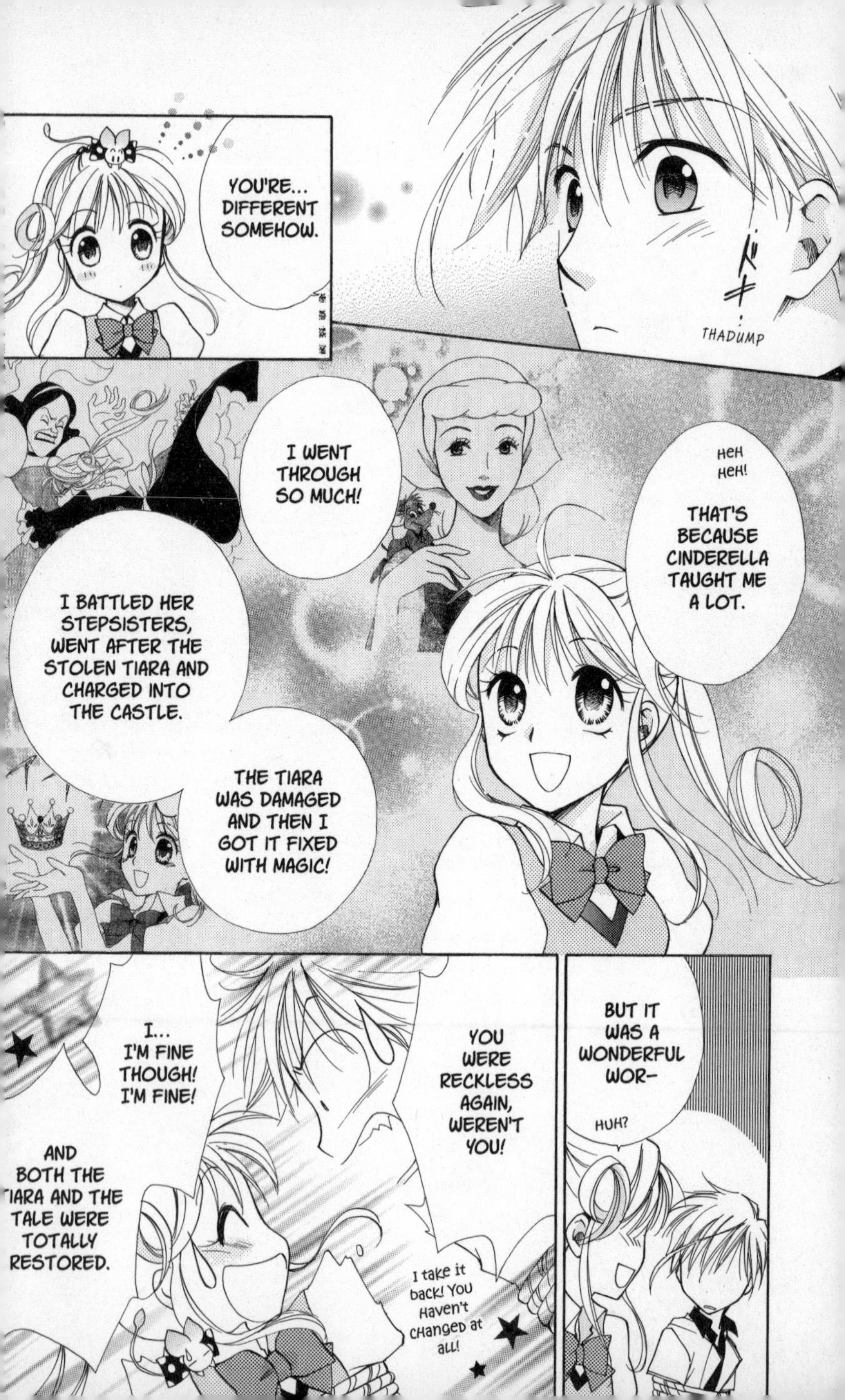
THADUMP
YOU'RE... DIFFERENT SOMEHOW.
HeH HeH!
THAT'S BECAUSE CINDERELLA TAUGHT ME A LOT.
I WENT THROUGH SO MUCH!
I BATTLED HER STEPSISTERS, WENT AFTER THE STOLEN TIARA AND CHARGED INTO THE CASTLE.
THE TIARA WAS DAMAGED AND THEN I GOT IT FIXED WITH MAGIC!
BUT IT WAS A WONDERFUL WOR-
HUH?
YOU WERE RECKLESS AGAIN, WEREN'T YOU!
I... I'M FINE THOUGH! I'M FINE!
AND BOTH THE IARA AND THE TALE WERE TOTALLY RESTORED.
I take it back! You Haven't cHanged at all!

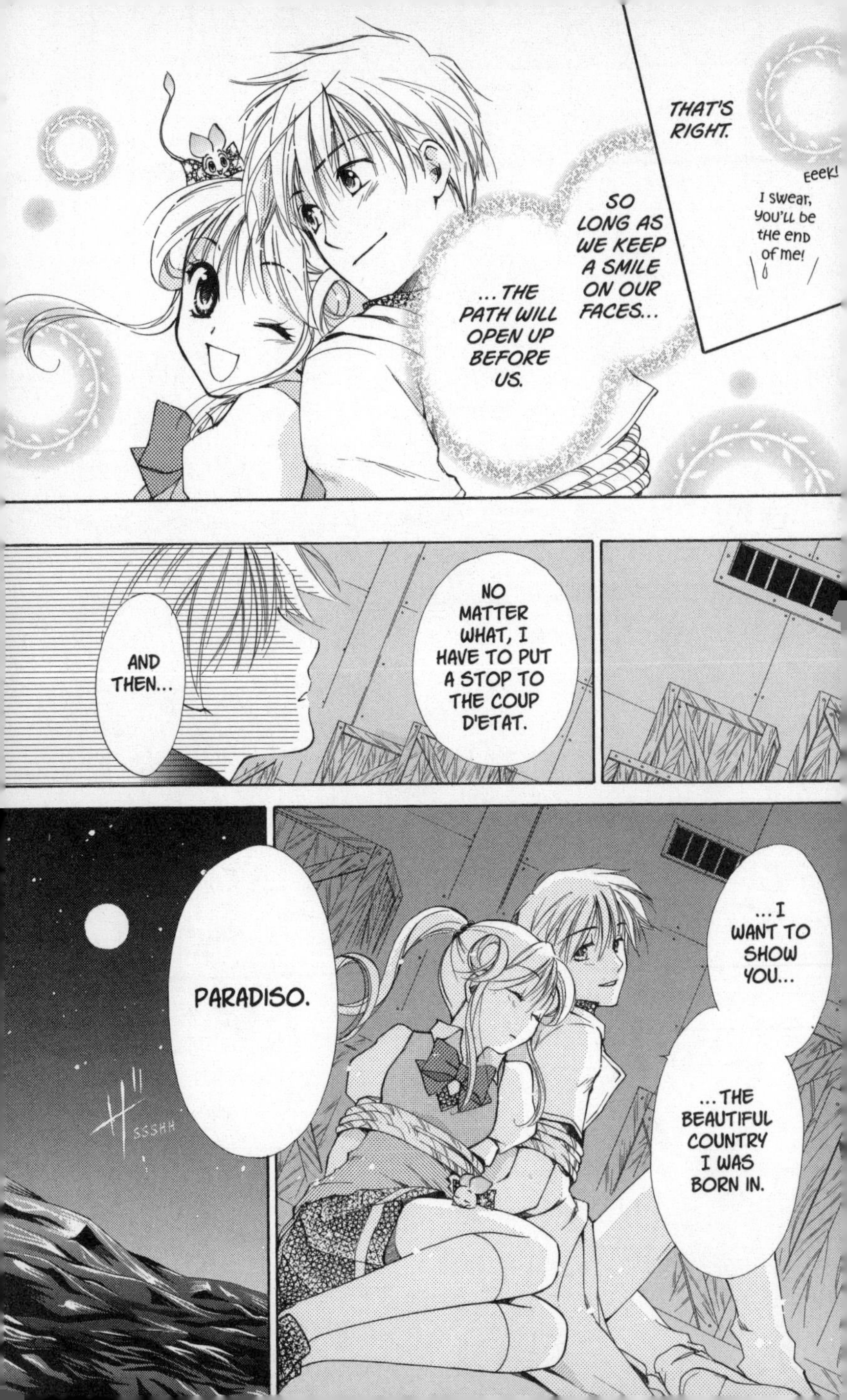
THAT'S RIGHT.
Eeek! I swear, you'll be the end of me!
SO LONG AS WE KEEP A SMILE ON OUR FACES...
...THE PATH WILL OPEN UP BEFORE US.
NO MATTER WHAT, I HAVE TO PUT A STOP TO THE COUP D'ETAT.
AND THEN...
...I WANT TO SHOW YOU...
...THE BEAUTIFUL COUNTRY I WAS BORN IN.
PARADISO.
SSSHH

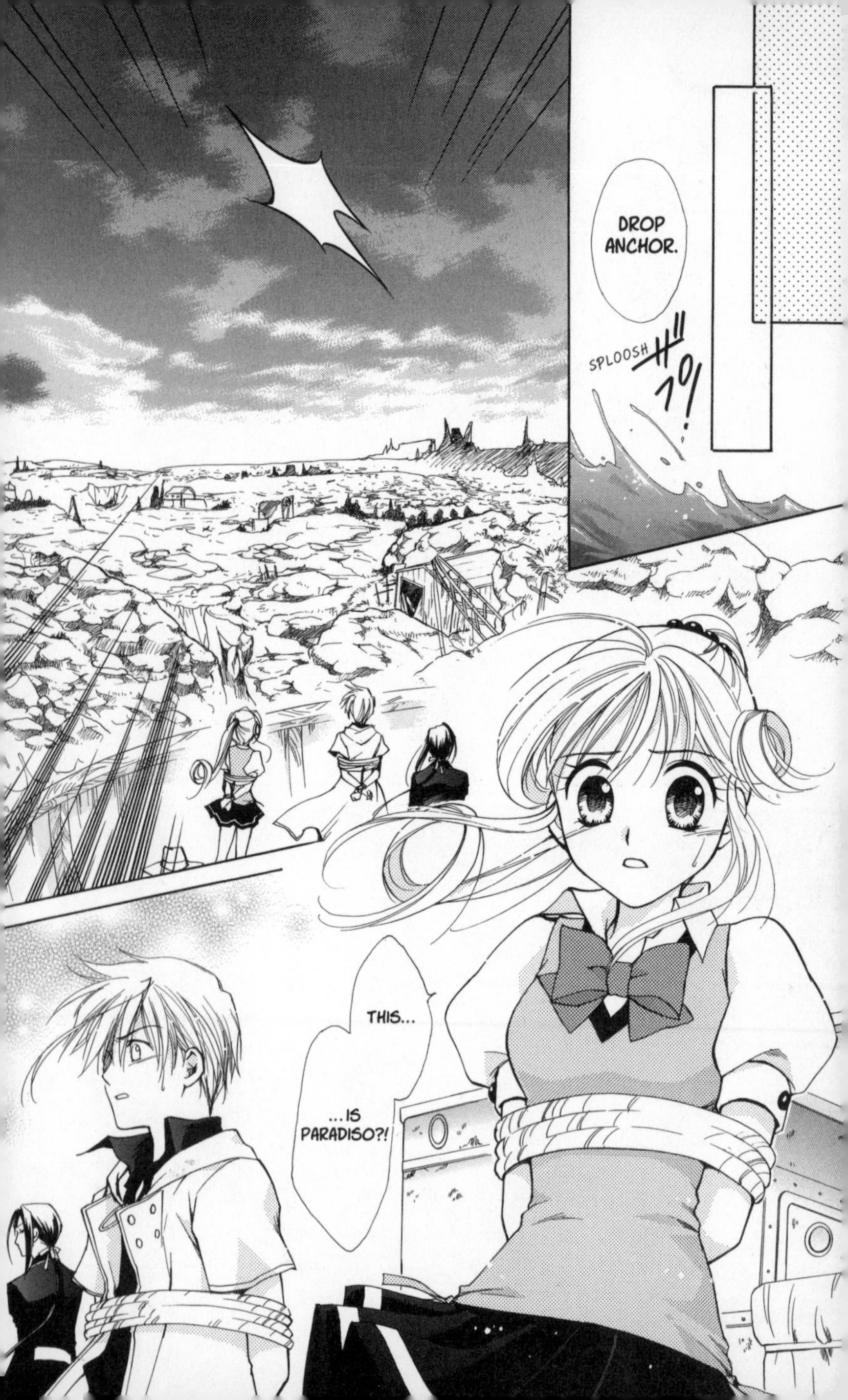
DROP ANCHOR.
SPLOOSH
THIS...
...IS PARADISO?!

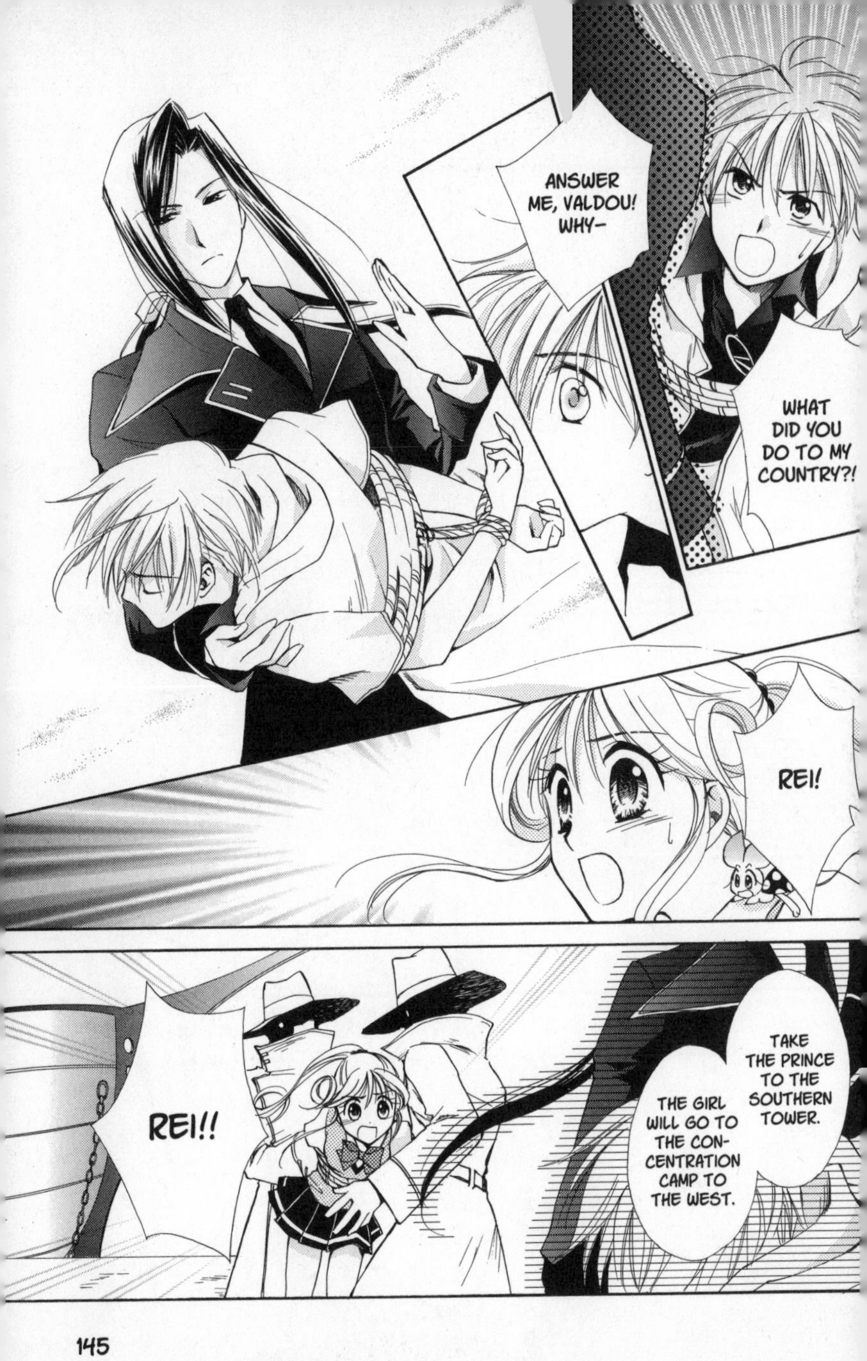
ANSWER ME, VALDOU! WHY-
WHAT DID YOU DO TO MY COUNTRY?!
REI!
TAKE THE PRINCE TO THE SOUTHERN TOWER.
THE GIRL WILL GO TO THE CON-CENTRATION CAMP TO THE WEST.
REI!!

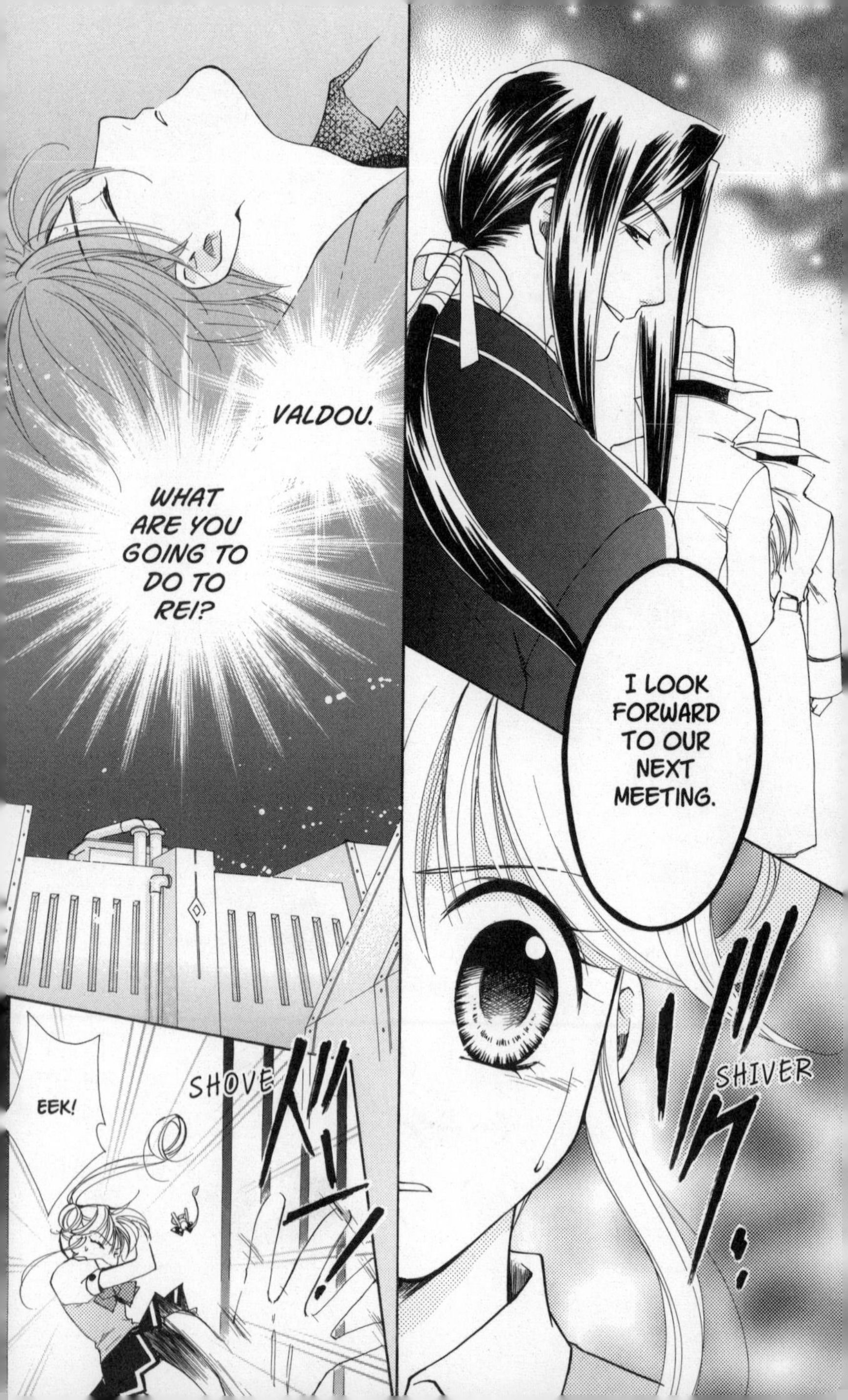
I LOOK FORWARD TO OUR NEXT MEETING.
SHIVER
VALDOU.
WHAT ARE YOU GOING TO DO TO REI?
SHOVE
EEK!

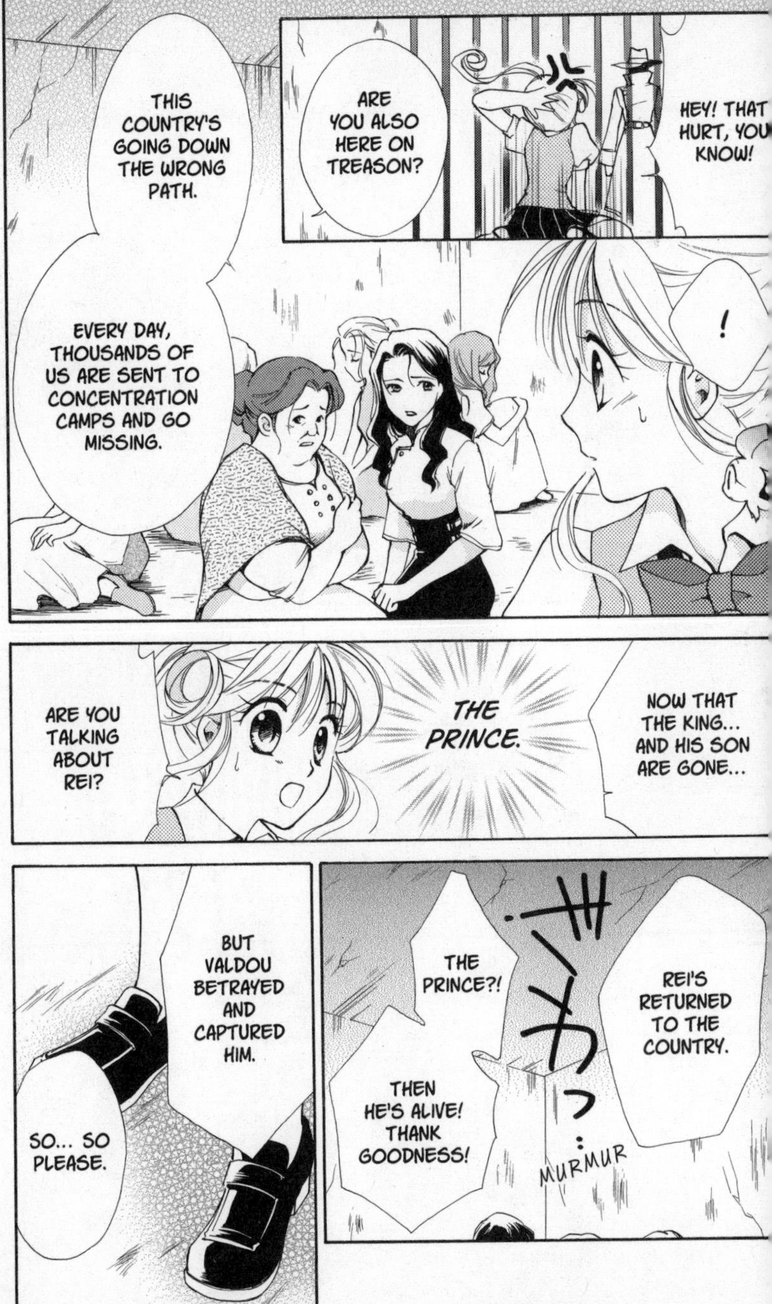
HEY! THAT HURT, YOU KNOW!
ARE YOU ALSO HERE ON TREASON?
!
THIS COUNTRY'S GOING DOWN THE WRONG PATH.
EVERY DAY, THOUSANDS OF US ARE SENT TO CONCENTRATION CAMPS AND GO MISSING.
NOW THAT THE KING... AND HIS SON ARE GONE...
THE PRINCE.
ARE YOU TALKING ABOUT REI?
REI'S RETURNED TO THE COUNTRY.
THE PRINCE?!
THEN HE'S ALIVE! THANK GOODNESS!
MURMUR
BUT VALDOU BETRAYED AND CAPTURED HIM.
SO... SO PLEASE.

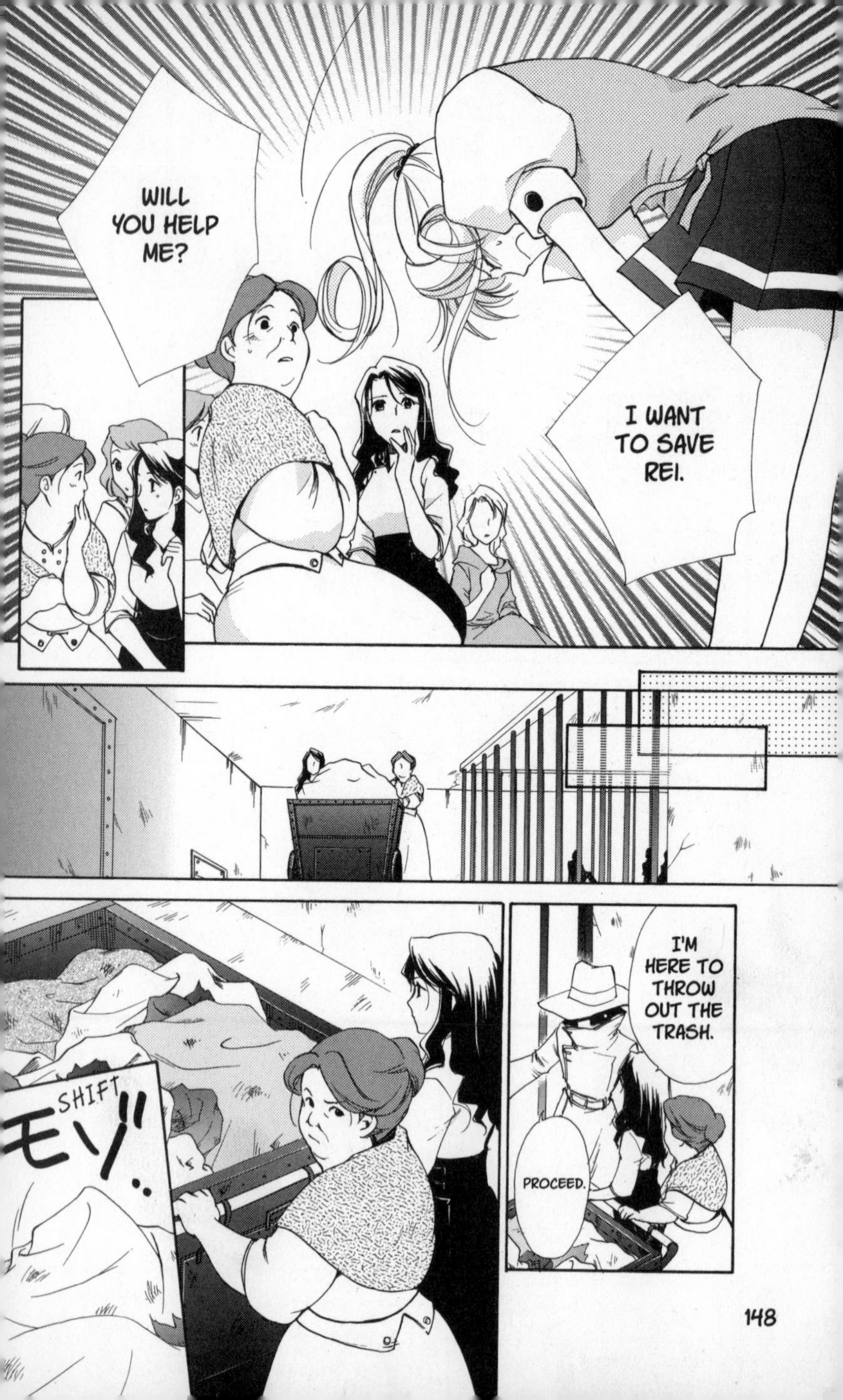
I WANT TO SAVE REI.
WILL YOU HELP ME?
I'M HERE TO THROW OUT THE TRASH.
PROCEED.
SHIFT
モゾ..

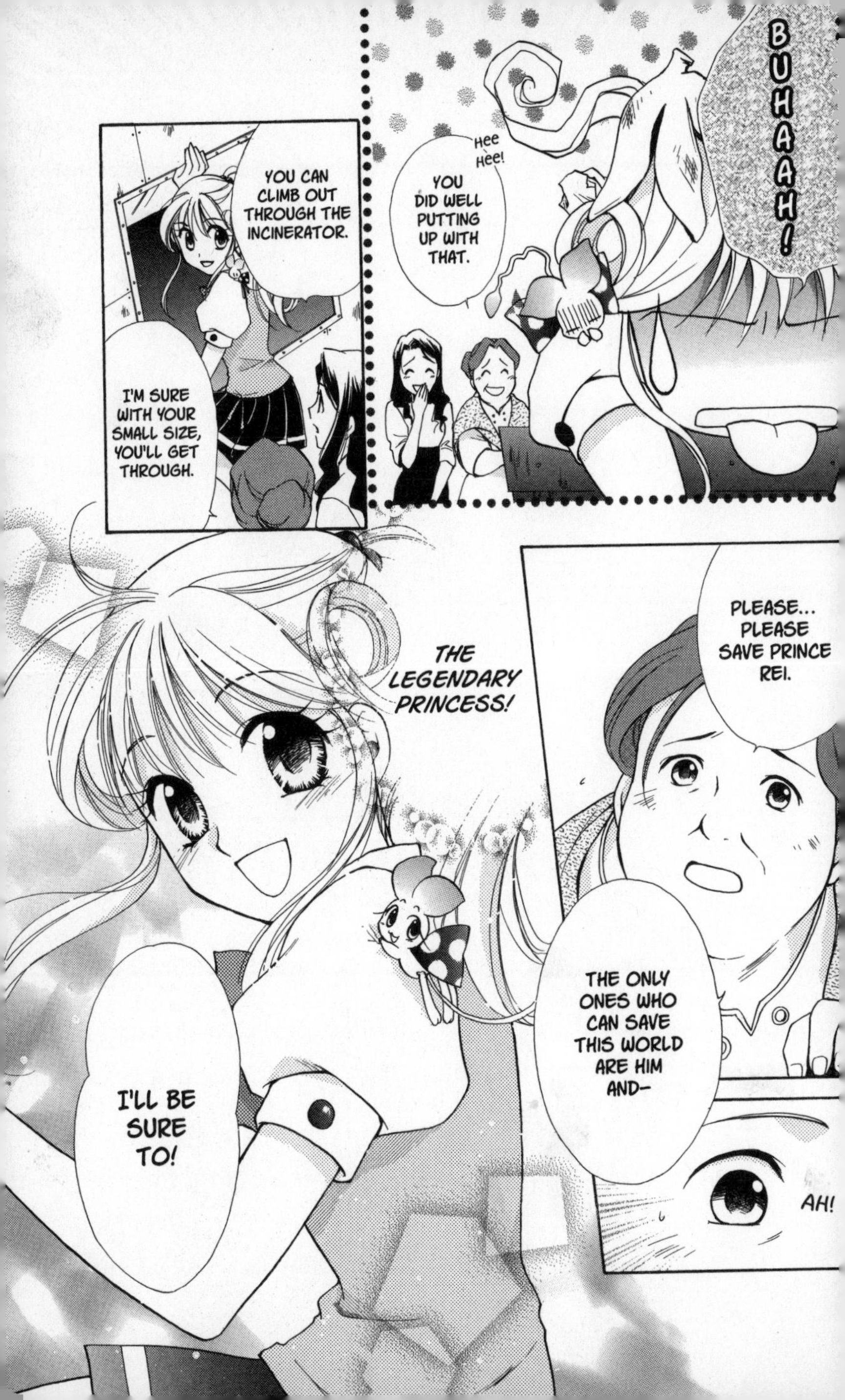
BUHAAAH!
Hee Hee!
YOU DID WELL PUTTING UP WITH THAT.
YOU CAN CLIMB OUT THROUGH THE INCINERATOR.
I'M SURE WITH YOUR SMALL SIZE, YOU'LL GET THROUGH.
PLEASE... PLEASE SAVE PRINCE REI.
THE ONLY ONES WHO CAN SAVE THIS WORLD ARE HIM AND–
AH!
THE LEGENDARY PRINCESS!
I'LL BE SURE TO!

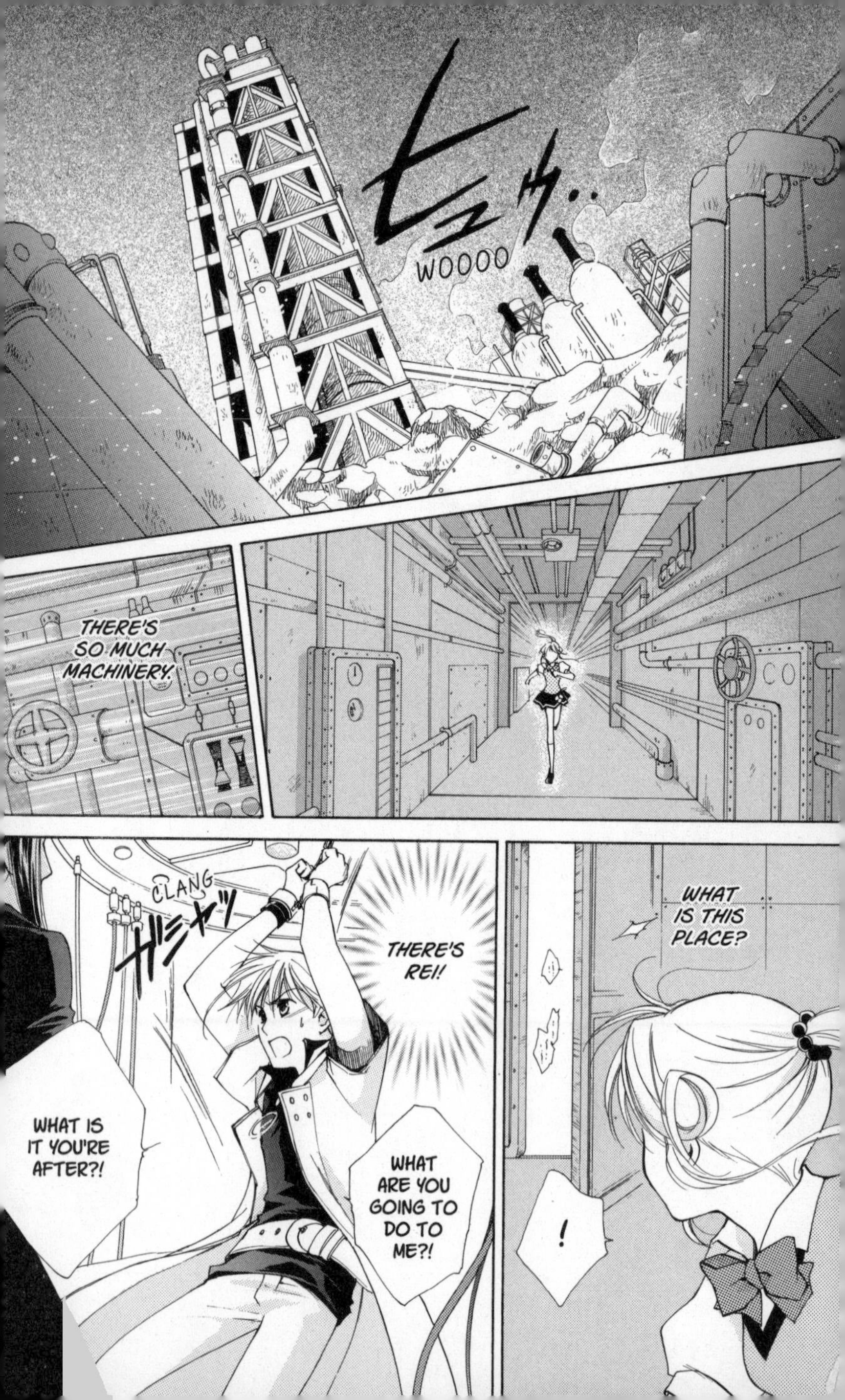
WOOOO
THERE'S SO MUCH MACHINERY.
WHAT IS THIS PLACE?
!
THERE'S REI!
CLANG
ガシャッ
WHAT ARE YOU GOING TO DO TO ME?!
WHAT IS IT YOU'RE AFTER?!

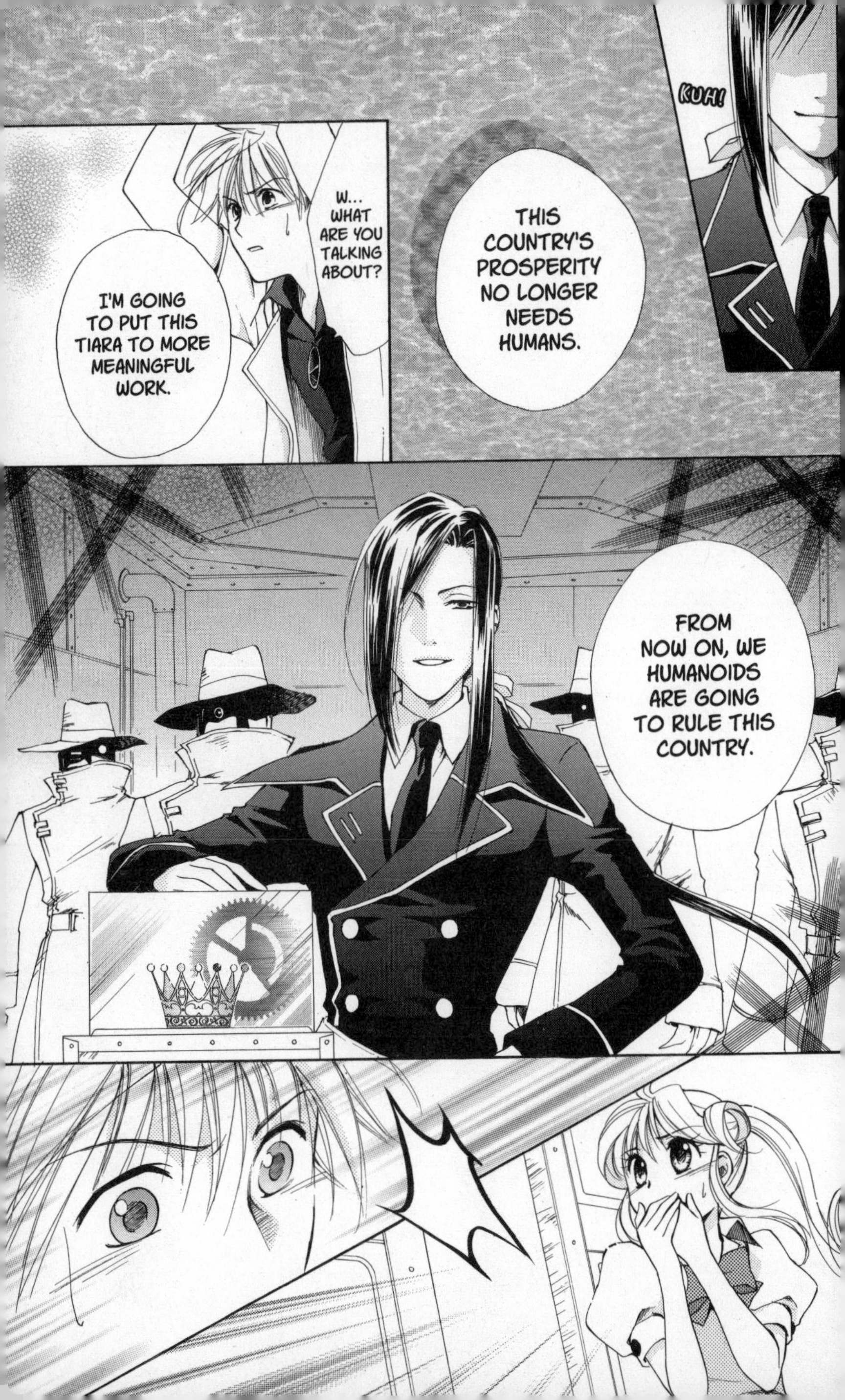
KUH!
THIS COUNTRY'S PROSPERITY NO LONGER NEEDS HUMANS.
W... WHAT ARE YOU TALKING ABOUT?
I'M GOING TO PUT THIS TIARA TO MORE MEANINGFUL WORK.
FROM NOW ON, WE HUMANOIDS ARE GOING TO RULE THIS COUNTRY.

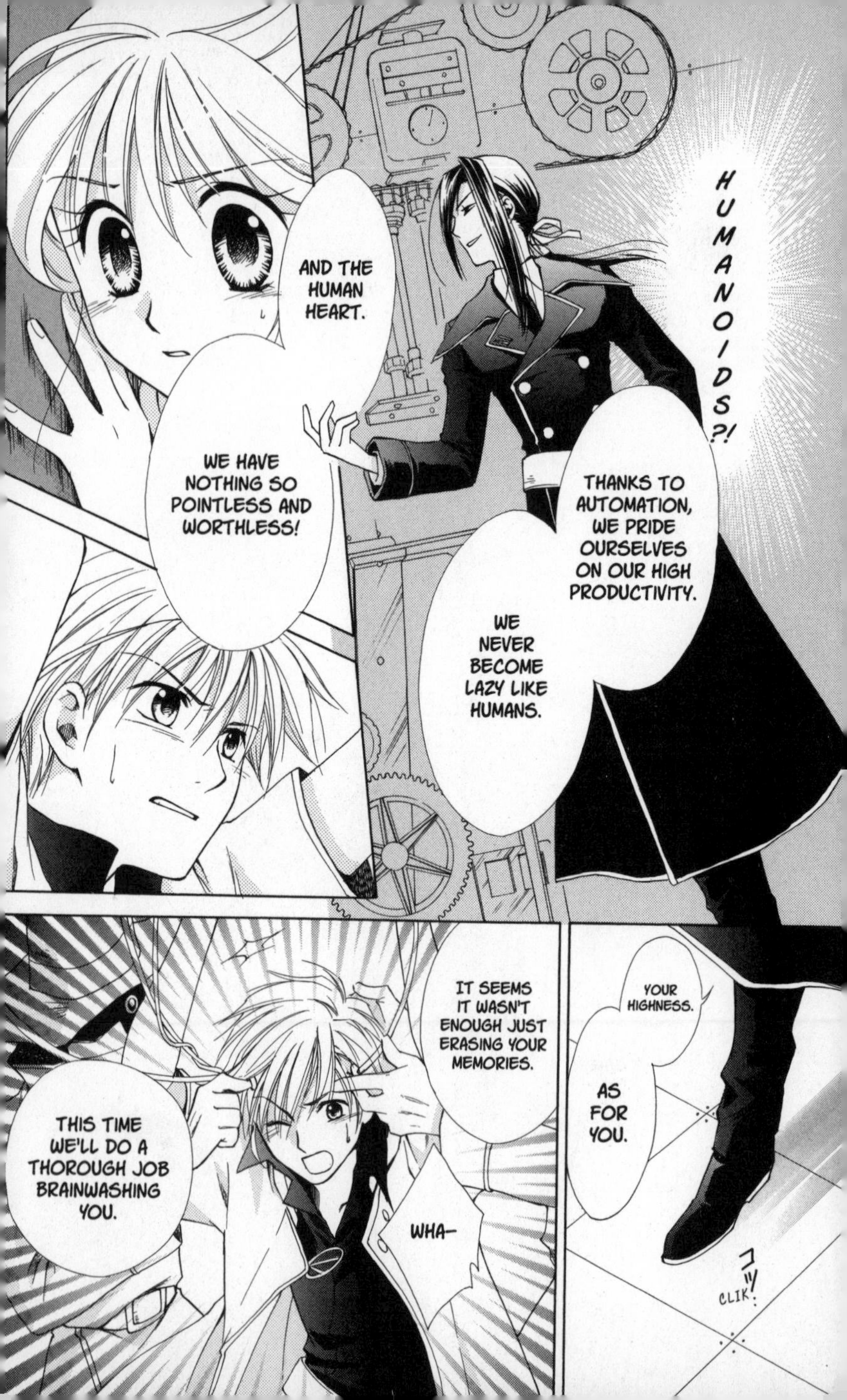
HUMANOIDS?!
THANKS TO AUTOMATION, WE PRIDE OURSELVES ON OUR HIGH PRODUCTIVITY.
WE NEVER BECOME LAZY LIKE HUMANS.
AND THE HUMAN HEART.
WE HAVE NOTHING SO POINTLESS AND WORTHLESS!
YOUR HIGHNESS.
AS FOR YOU.
コツ
CLIK!
IT SEEMS IT WASN'T ENOUGH JUST ERASING YOUR MEMORIES.
THIS TIME WE'LL DO A THOROUGH JOB BRAINWASHING YOU.
WHA-

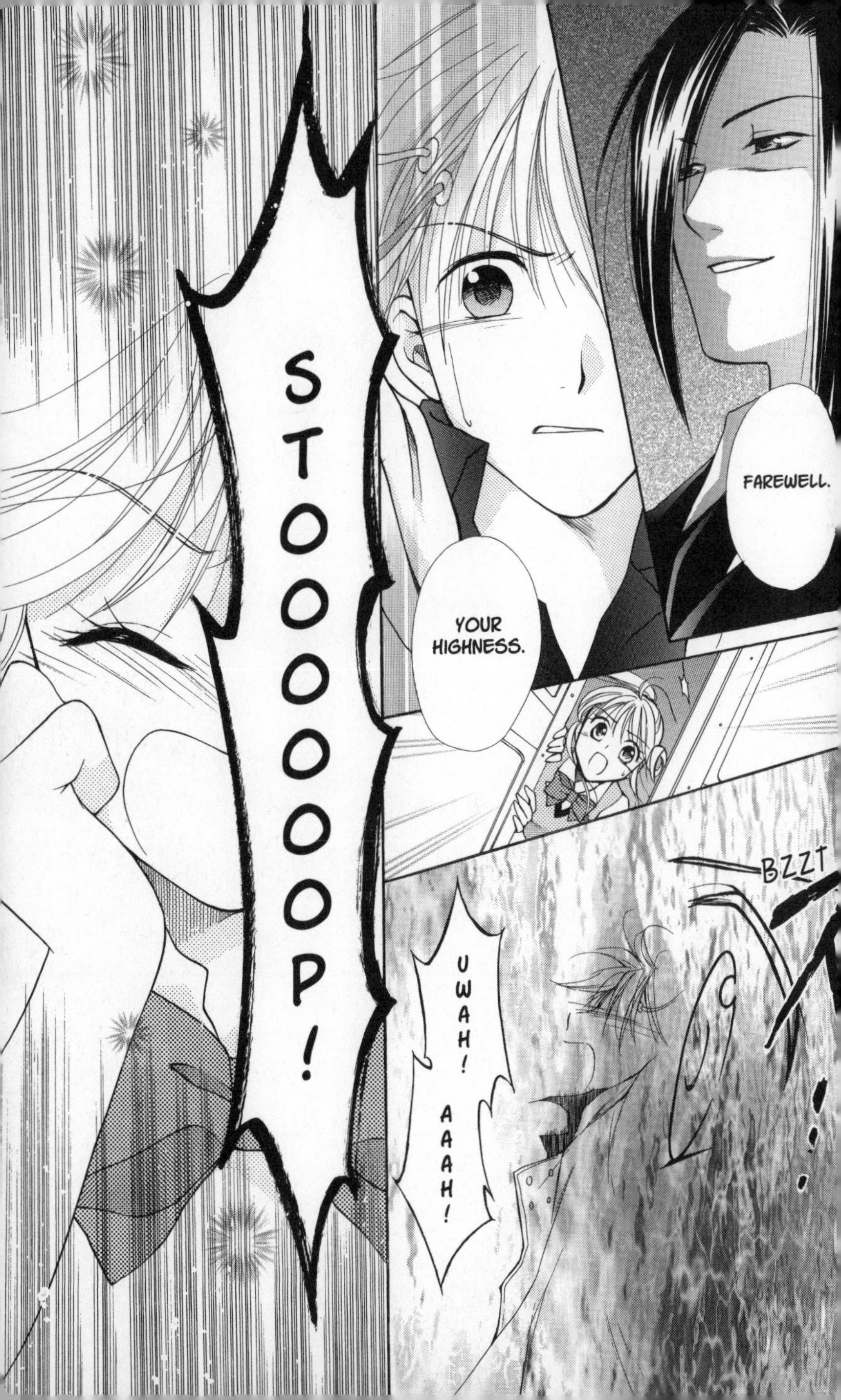
FAREWELL.
YOUR HIGHNESS.
BZZT
UWAH! AAAAH!
STOOOOOOP!

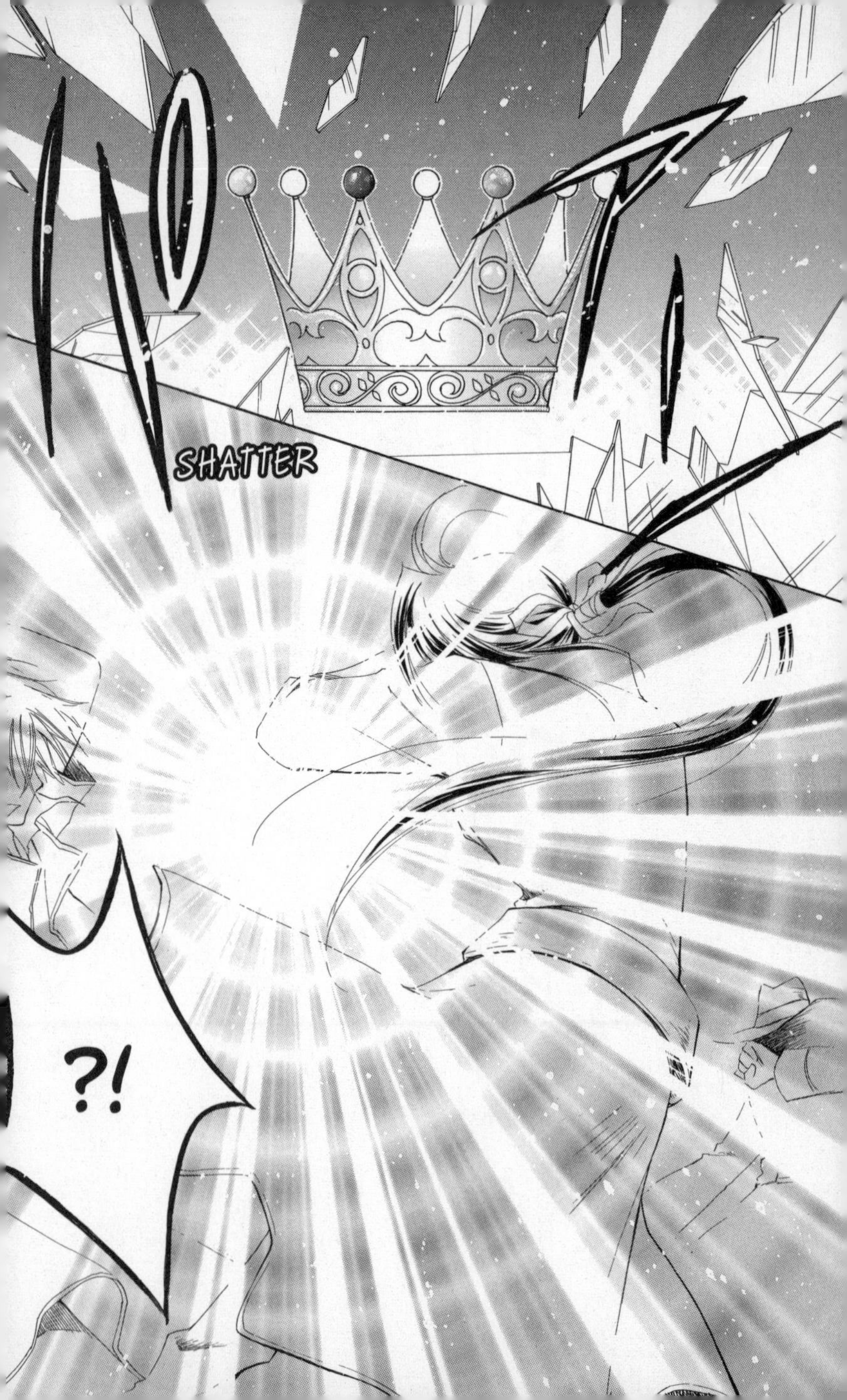
SHATTER
?!

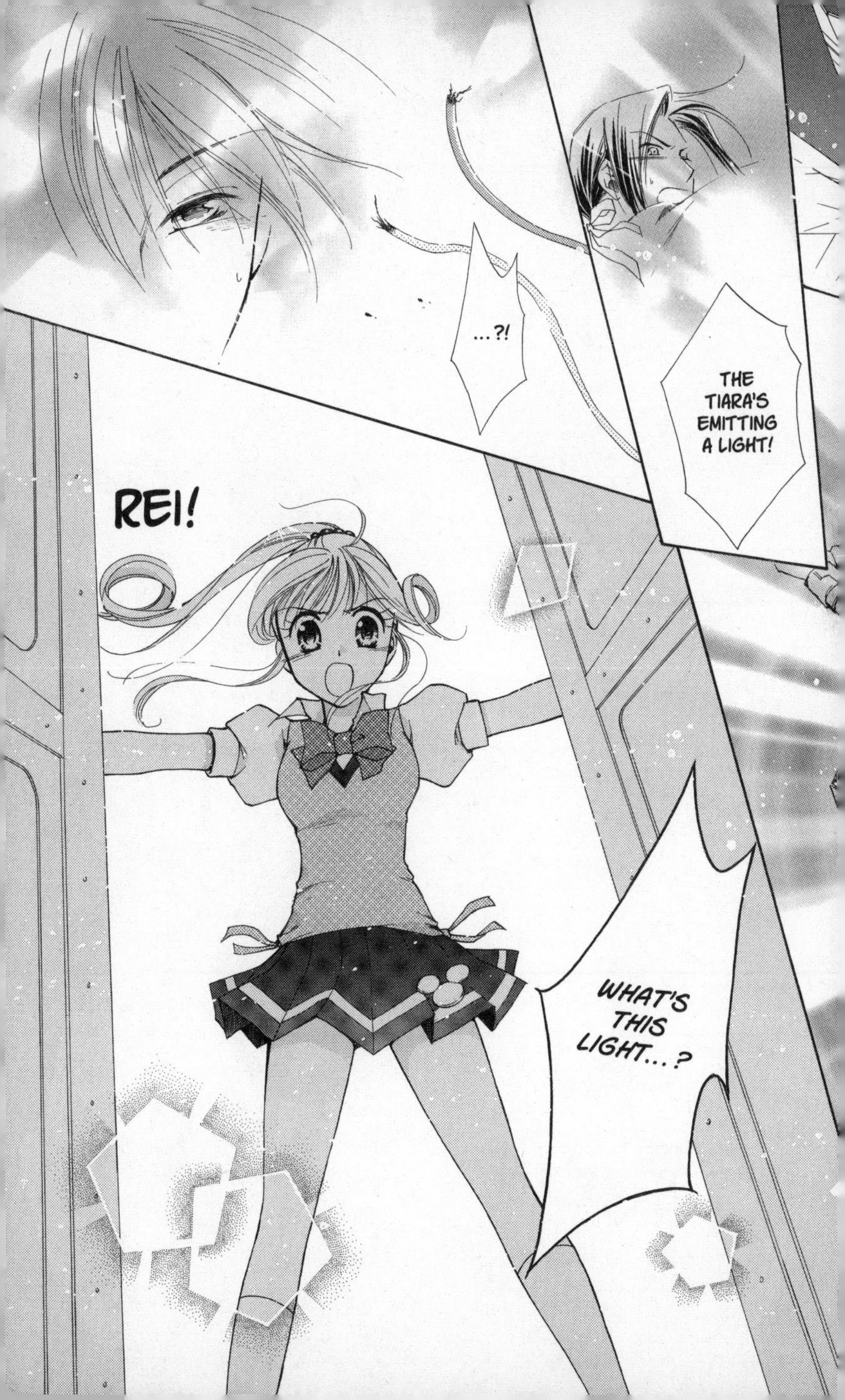
THE TIARA'S EMITTING A LIGHT!
...?!
REI!
WHAT'S THIS LIGHT...?

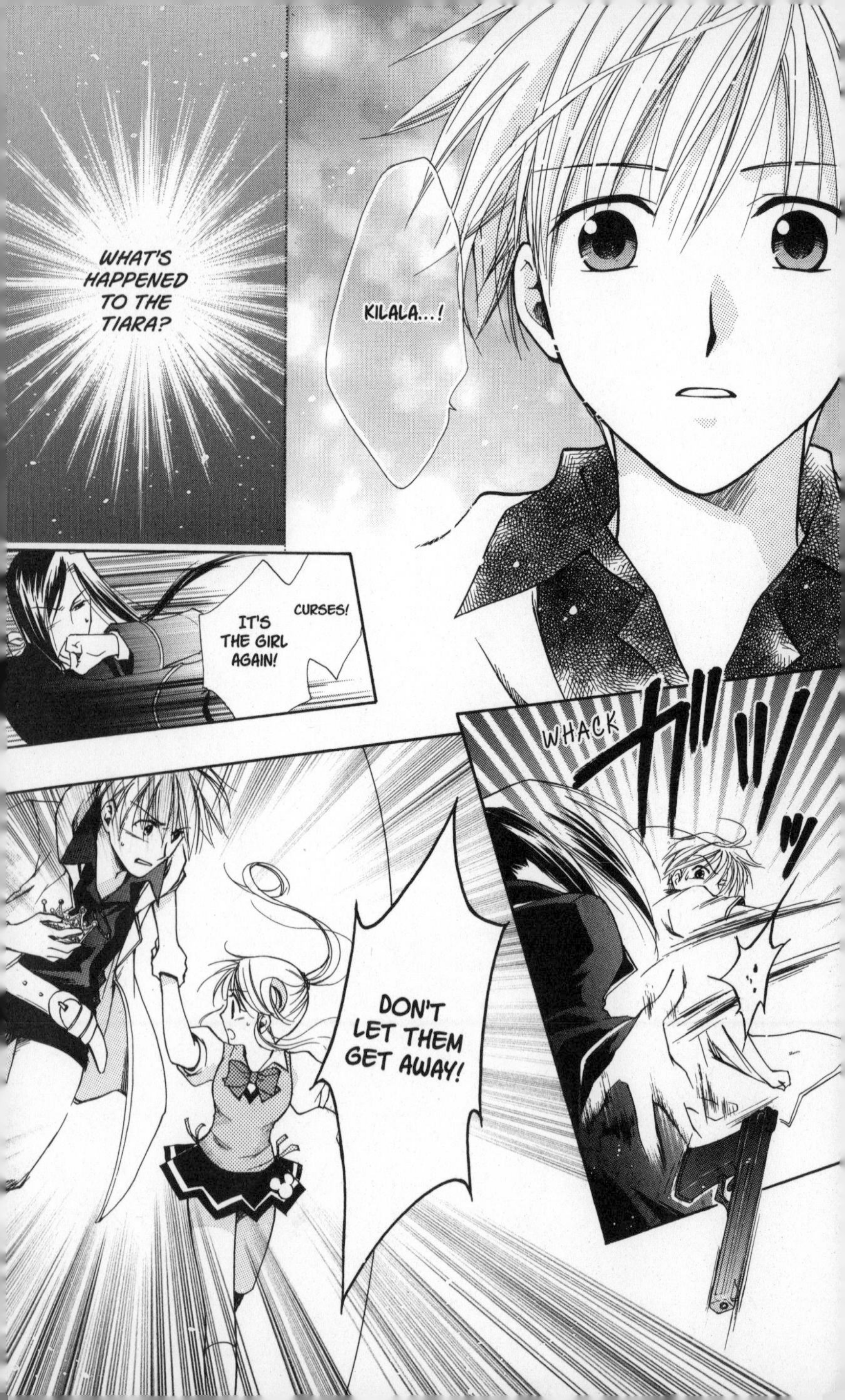
KILALA...!
WHAT'S HAPPENED TO THE TIARA?
CURSES!
IT'S THE GIRL AGAIN!
WHACK
DON'T LET THEM GET AWAY!

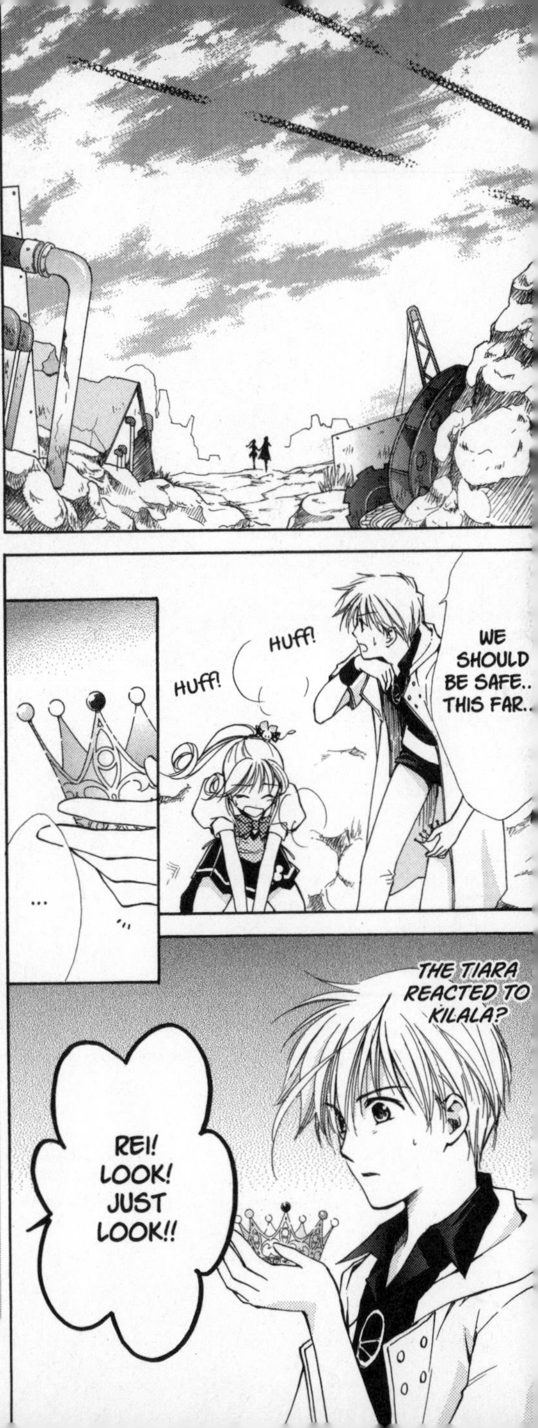
WE SHOULD BE SAFE.. THIS FAR..
HUFF!
HUFF!
...
THE TIARA REACTED TO KILALA?
REI! LOOK! JUST LOOK!!

Rika Tanaka

HELLO! THIS IS THE WRITER OF THE STORY, RIKA TANAKA. IN THIS VOLUME, KILALA FLIES TO THE WORLD OF CINDERELLA.

I ALWAYS FOUND IT VERY SAD HOW CINDERELLA IS BULLIED BY HER STEPMOTHER AND STEPSISTERS (;-;) AND THAT WAS MY MAIN IMPRESSION OF THE FILM. BUT AFTER REWATCHING THE MOVIE AGAIN, I REALIZED THAT SHE'S A SUPER OPTIMISTIC YOUNG LADY WHO NEVER STOPS BELIEVING IN HER DREAMS NO MATTER WHAT.

WHAT A LUCKY BREAK FOR HER THAT THE PRINCE FALLS IN LOVE WITH HER ♪ NAH, I'M JUST KIDDING. IT MUST BE HER POSITIVE HEART THAT ATTRACTS GOOD FORTUNE TO HER! I WROTE THIS ARC WITH KILALA BEING INSPIRED BY CINDERELLA'S "BEAUTIFUL ENERGY" AND WANTING TO MAKE HER SHINE EVEN MORE. DID YOU ALL PICK UP ON THAT? PLEASE LET ME KNOW YOUR IMPRESSION. ☆

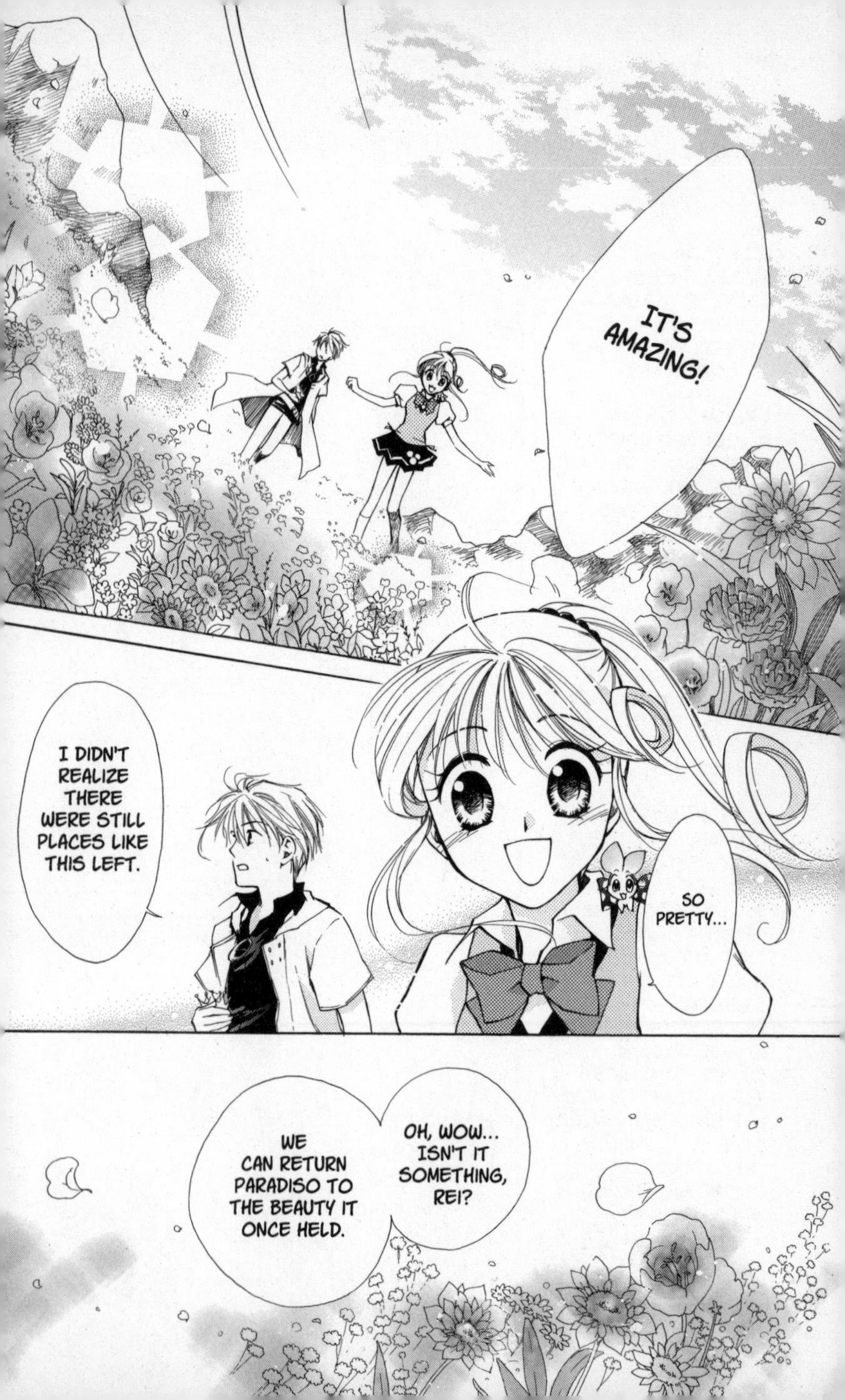
IT'S AMAZING!
SO PRETTY...
I DIDN'T REALIZE THERE WERE STILL PLACES LIKE THIS LEFT.
OH, WOW... ISN'T IT SOMETHING, REI?
WE CAN RETURN PARADISO TO THE BEAUTY IT ONCE HELD.

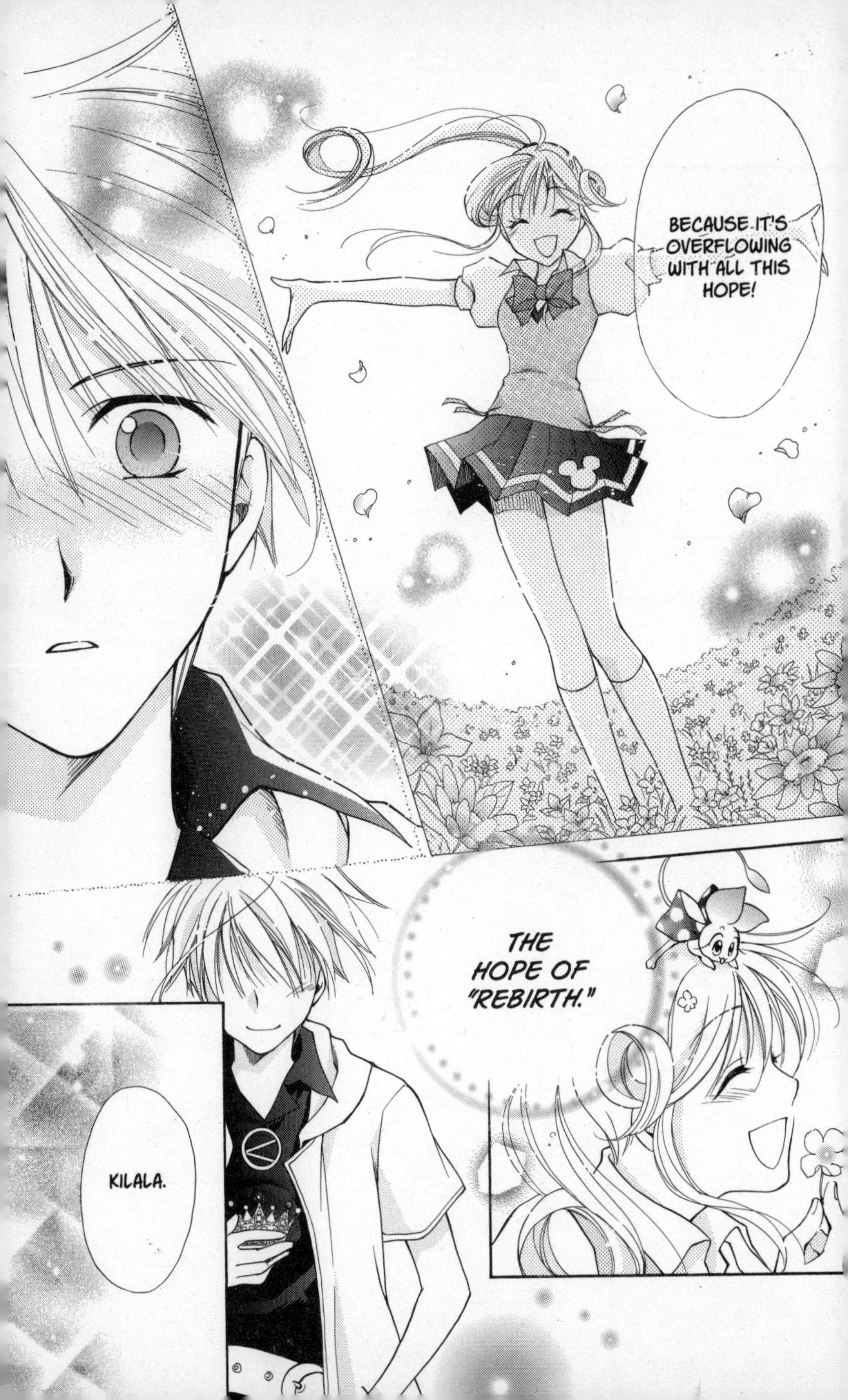
BECAUSE IT'S OVERFLOWING WITH ALL THIS HOPE!
THE HOPE OF "REBIRTH."
KILALA.

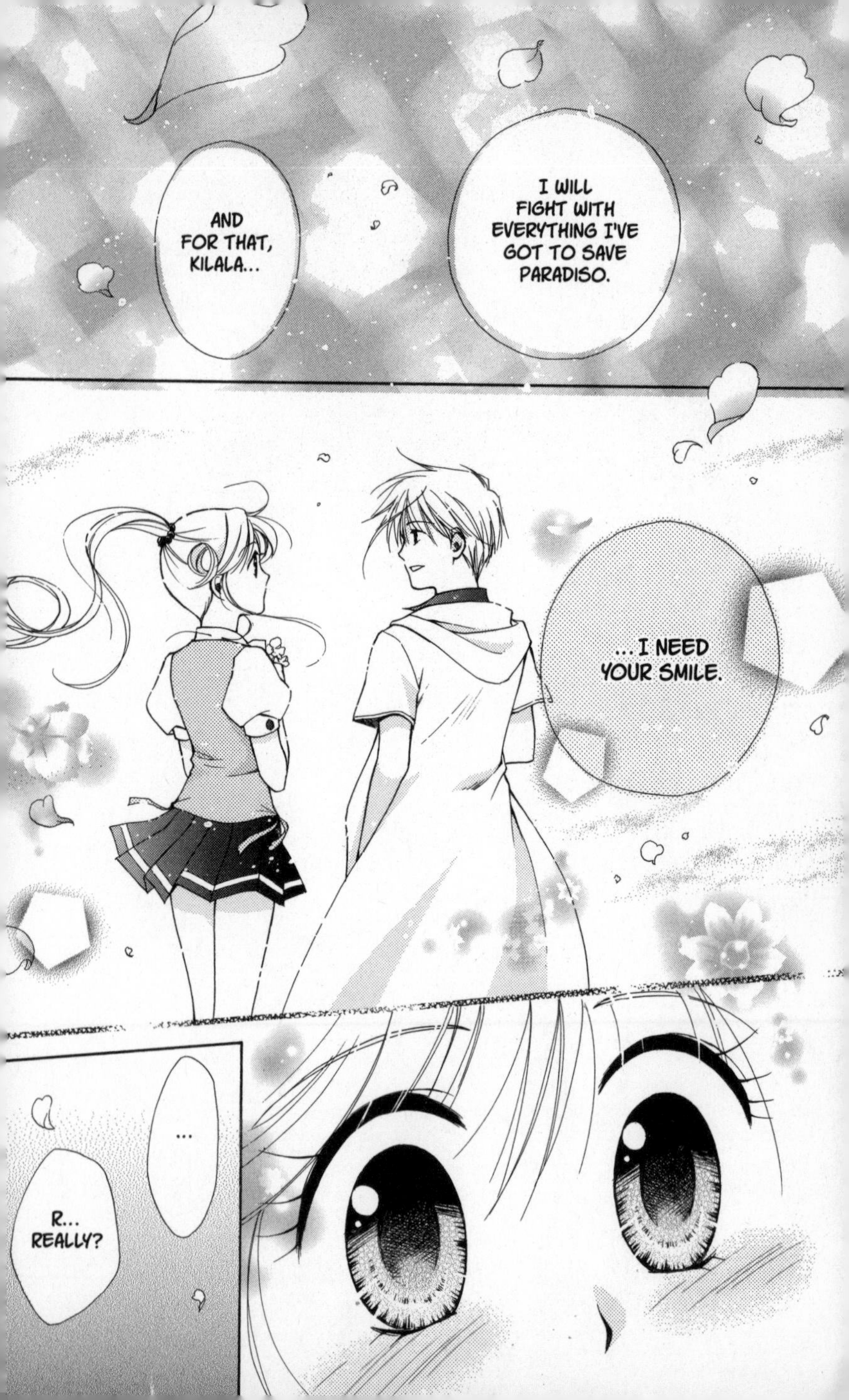
I WILL FIGHT WITH EVERYTHING I'VE GOT TO SAVE PARADISO.
AND FOR THAT, KILALA...
...I NEED YOUR SMILE.
...
R... REALLY?

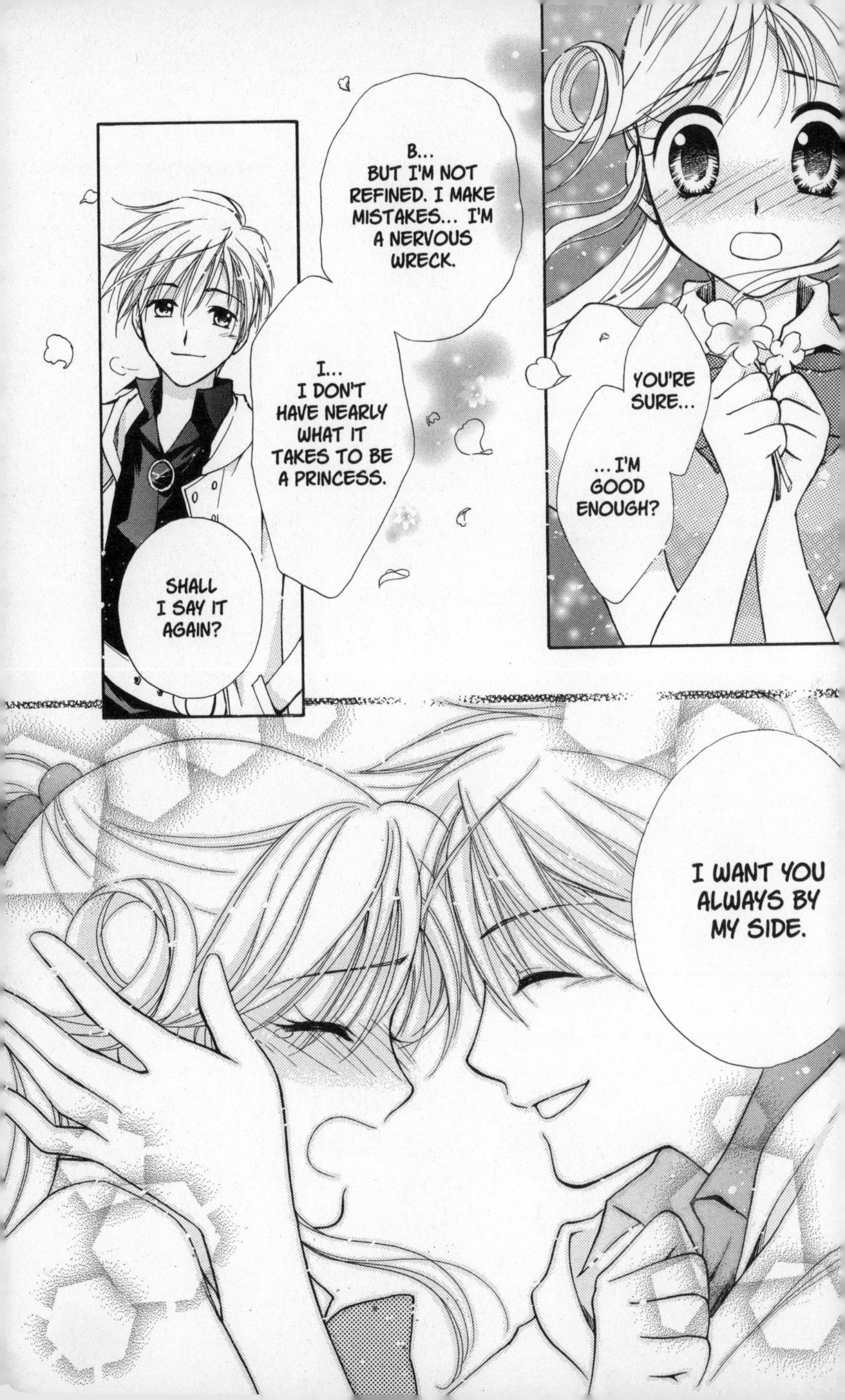
YOU'RE SURE...
...I'M GOOD ENOUGH?
B... BUT I'M NOT REFINED. I MAKE MISTAKES... I'M A NERVOUS WRECK.
I... I DON'T HAVE NEARLY WHAT IT TAKES TO BE A PRINCESS.
SHALL I SAY IT AGAIN?
I WANT YOU ALWAYS BY MY SIDE.

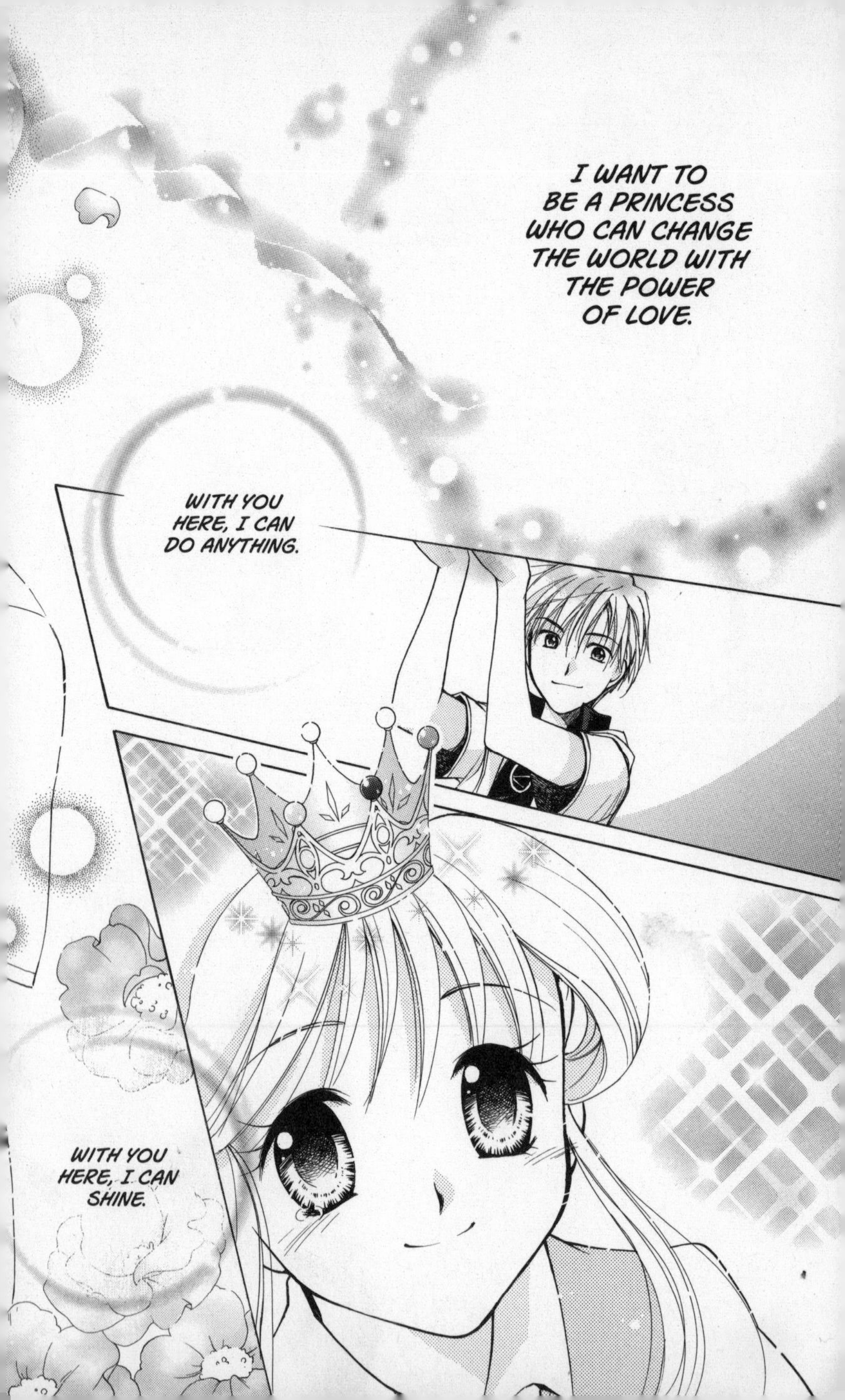
I WANT TO BE A PRINCESS WHO CAN CHANGE THE WORLD WITH THE POWER OF LOVE.
WITH YOU HERE, I CAN DO ANYTHING.
WITH YOU HERE, I CAN SHINE.

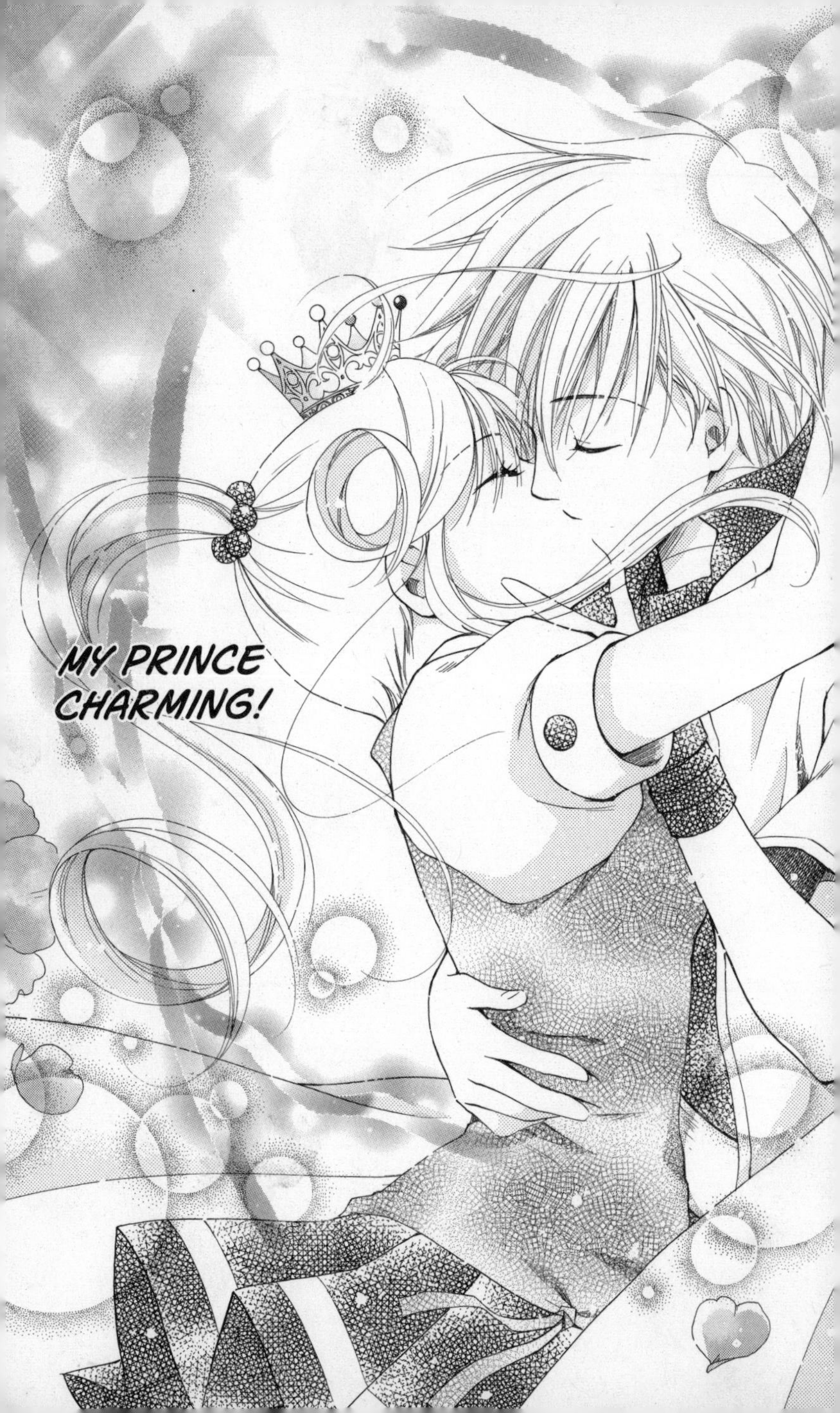
MY PRINCE CHARMING!

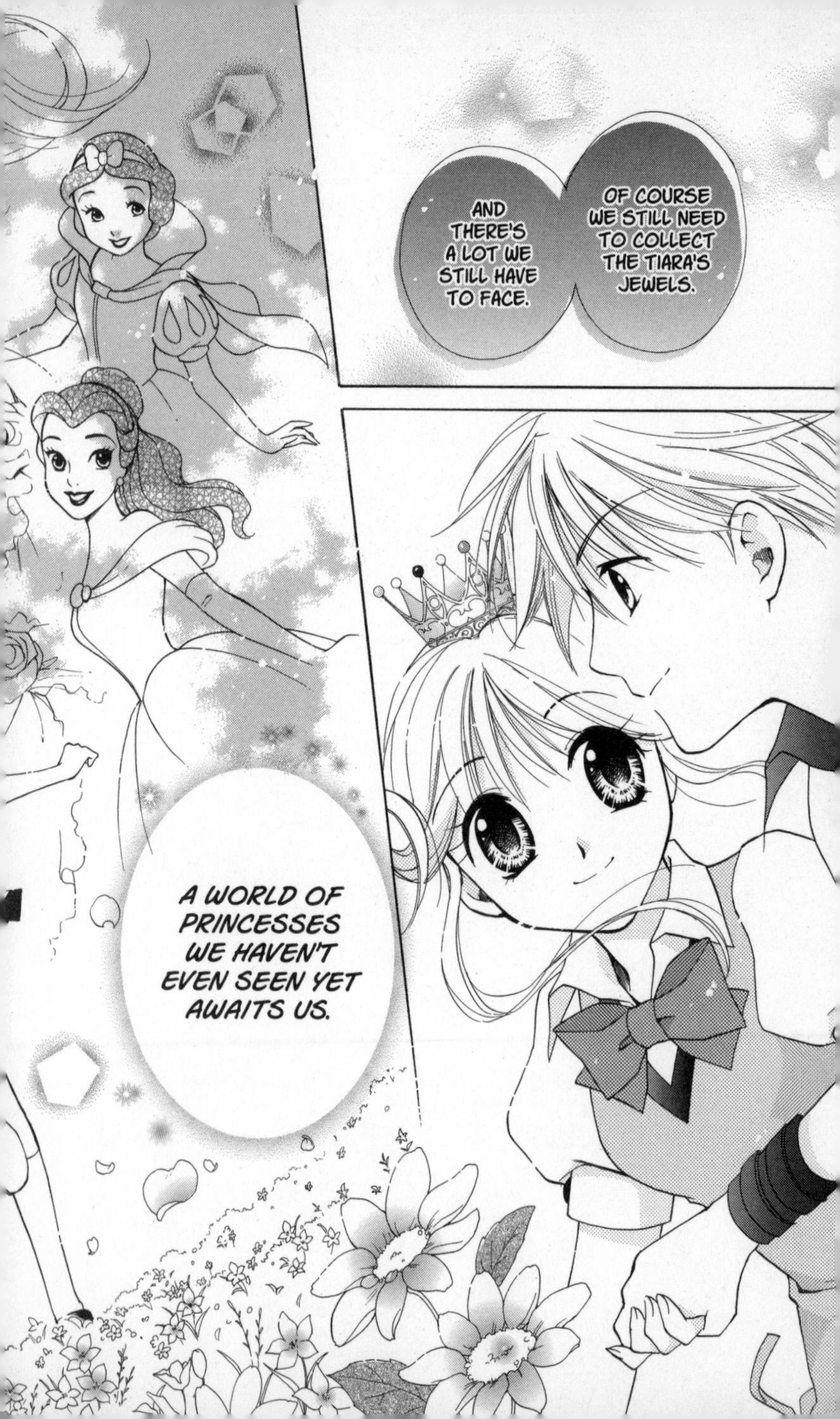
OF COURSE WE STILL NEED TO COLLECT THE TIARA'S JEWELS.
AND THERE'S A LOT WE STILL HAVE TO FACE.
A WORLD OF PRINCESSES WE HAVEN'T EVEN SEEN YET AWAITS US.

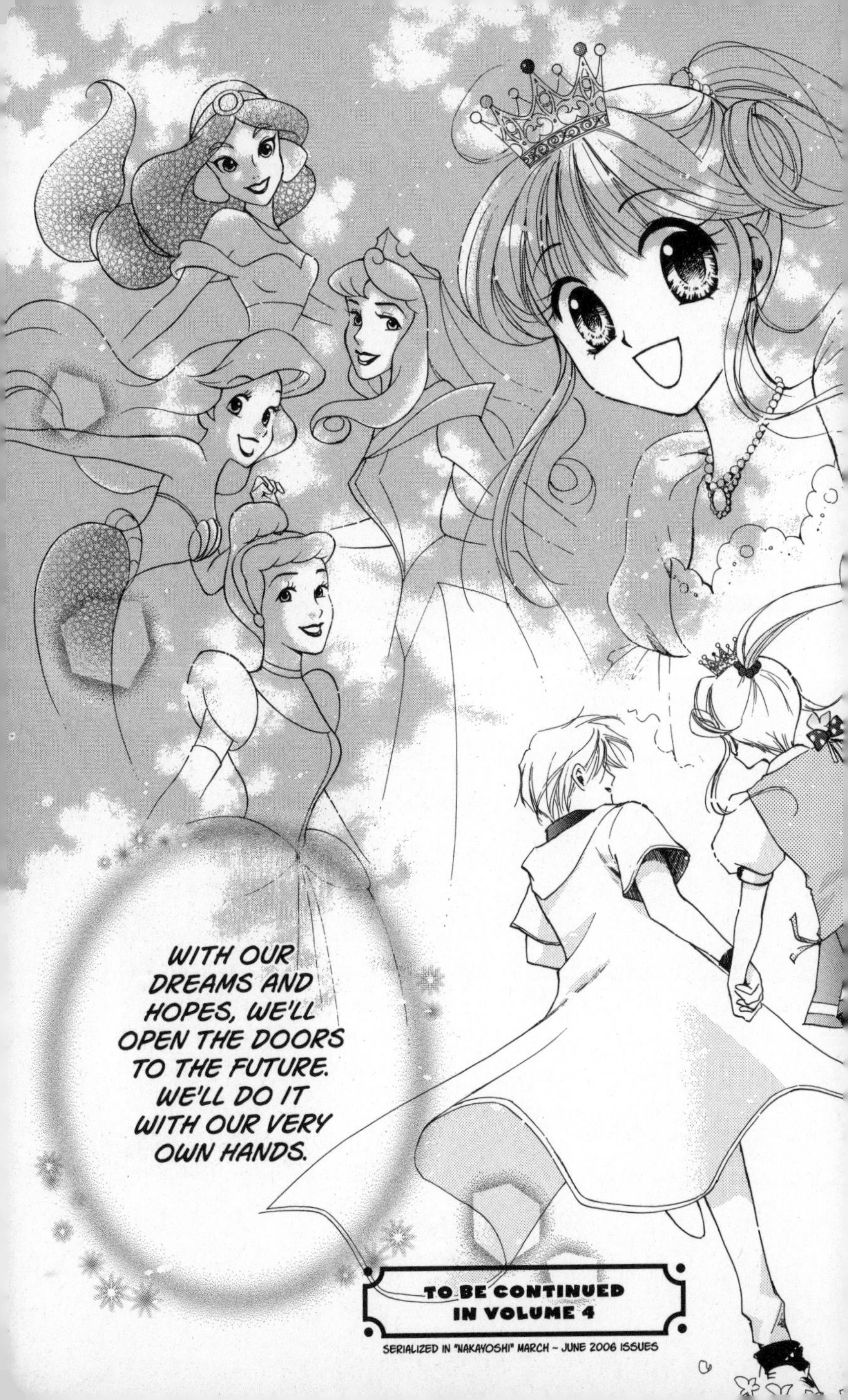
WITH OUR DREAMS AND HOPES, WE'LL OPEN THE DOORS TO THE FUTURE. WE'LL DO IT WITH OUR VERY OWN HANDS.
TO BE CONTINUED IN VOLUME 4
SERIALIZED IN "NAKAYOSHI" MARCH ~ JUNE 2006 ISSUES

PRINCESS

in Japanese

姫 means Princess in Japanese. It's pronounced "hime" ("hi" as in "heat" and "me" as in "melon")

Princess Aurora and Snow White are two princesses with "hime" in their name. Do you see where the character is?

白雪姫
SNOW WHITE

オーロラ姫
PRINCESS AURORA

You may not be able to tell by just looking at it, but this kanji (Chinese character) is actually composed of two parts!

女 and 臣

女 (onna) means "woman," while
臣 (jin) means "subject." A "woman subject" is a princess!

Other useful words the symbol of 女 appears in include:
娘 (musume) = daughter

What are women best at being?
嬉しい (ureshii) = happy

But, uh-oh, it's also in:
嫌い (kirai) = to hate

THANKS FOR READING!

IN THE NEXT VOLUME OF

Disney

Kilala Princess

Kilala and Rei are on a quest to collect
all the remaining gems for their tiara to save
their country, Paradiso. They fall into the world
of *Beauty and the Beast* and *Sleeping Beauty* and
encounter a villain in disguise and danger around
every corner. This time Kilala falls victim to a
curse that can only be broken by True Love's Kiss.
Will Rei rescue her in time to save Paradiso?

**JOIN KILALA AND THE DISNEY
PRINCESSES FOR MORE
ADVENTURES IN VOLUME 4!**

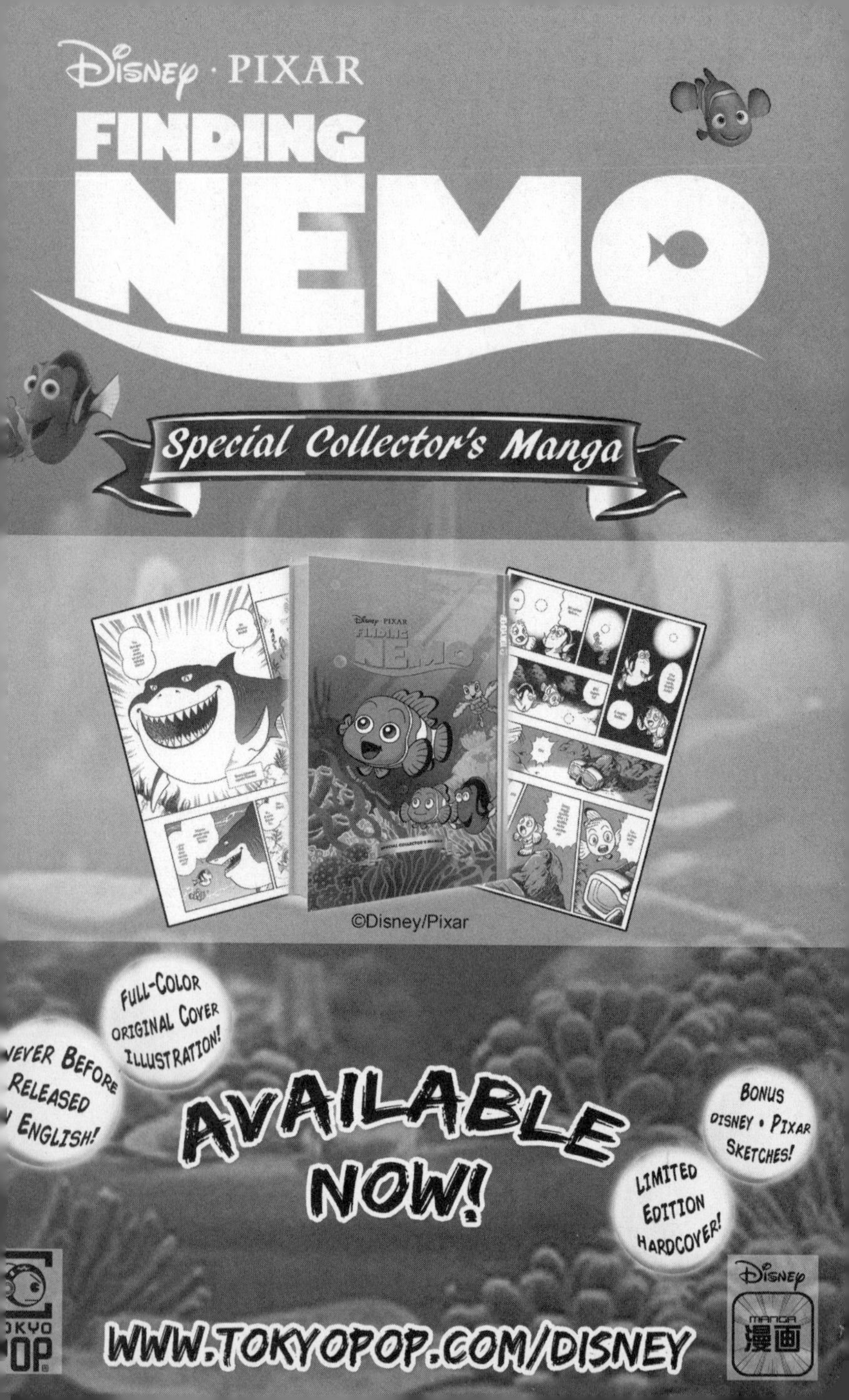
DISNEY · PIXAR
FINDING NEMO
Special Collector's Manga
©Disney/Pixar
FULL-COLOR ORIGINAL COVER ILLUSTRATION!
EVER BEFORE RELEASED ENGLISH!
AVAILABLE NOW!
BONUS DISNEY • PIXAR SKETCHES!
LIMITED EDITION HARDCOVER!
WWW.TOKYOPOP.COM/DISNEY

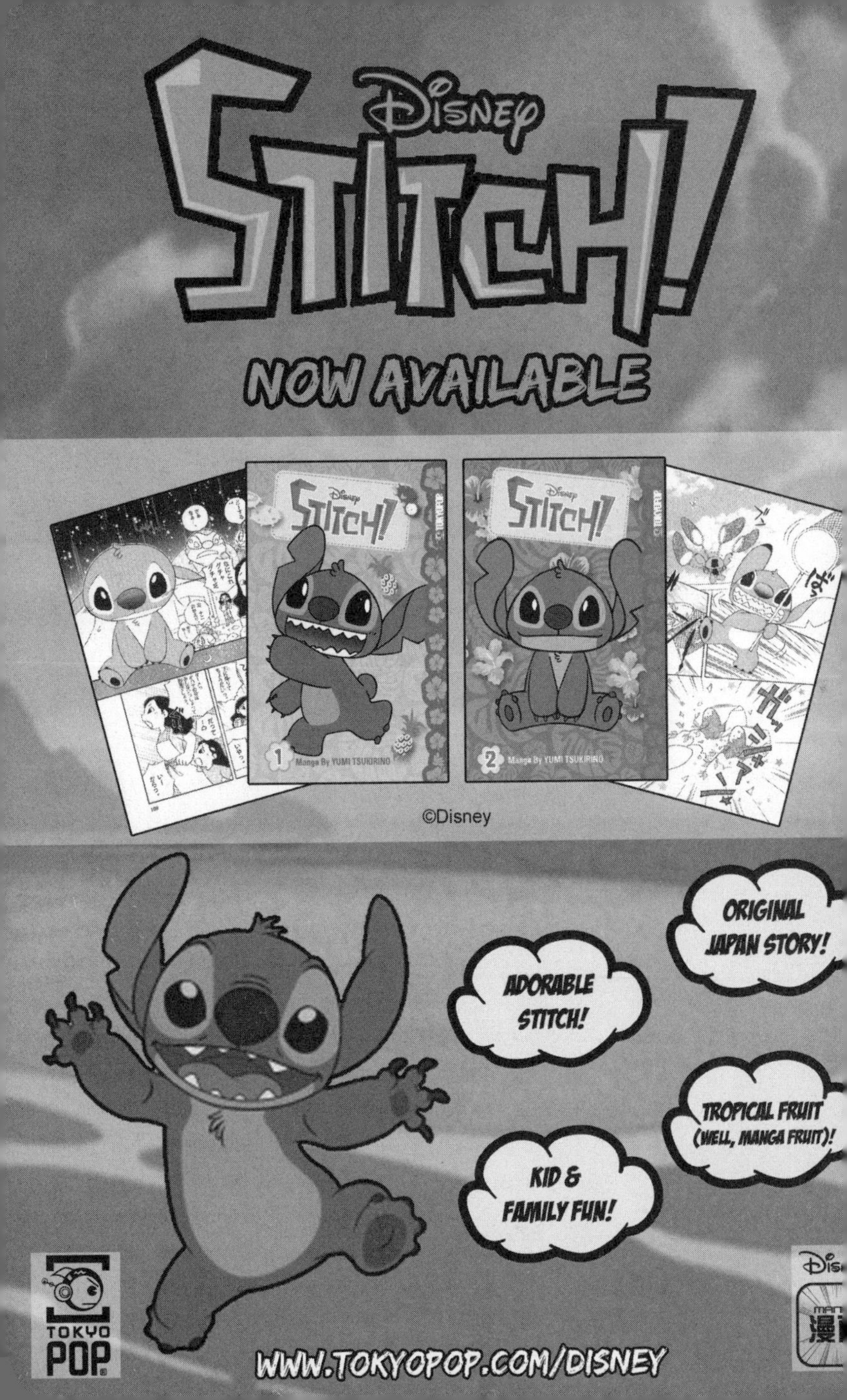
Disney
STITCH!
NOW AVAILABLE
Disney STITCH!
1 Manga By YUMI TSUKIRINO
Disney STITCH!
2 Manga By YUMI TSUKIRINO
©Disney
ORIGINAL JAPAN STORY!
ADORABLE STITCH!
TROPICAL FRUIT (WELL, MANGA FRUIT)!
KID & FAMILY FUN!
TOKYO POP
WWW.TOKYOPOP.COM/DISNEY

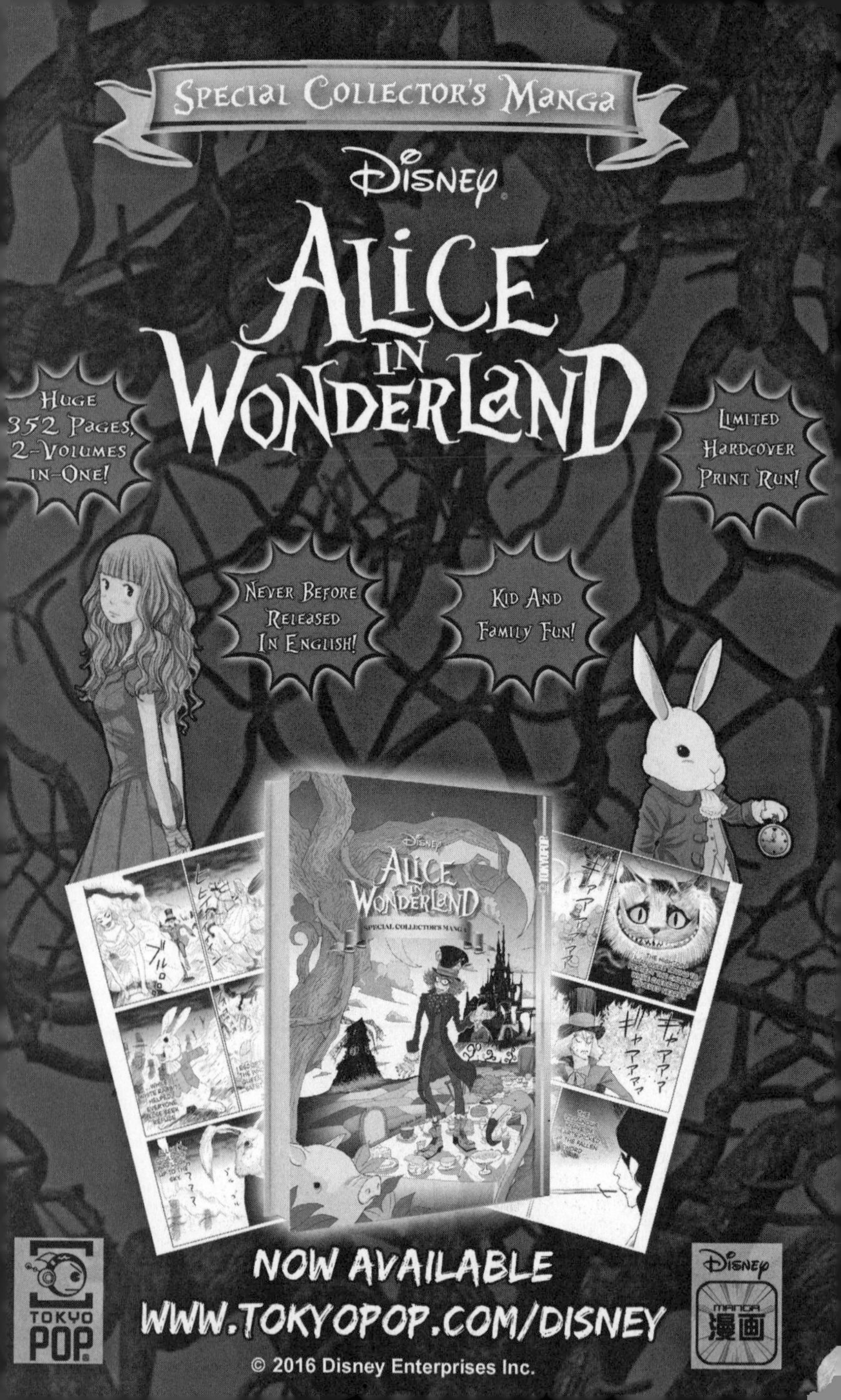
Special Collector's Manga
Disney
Alice in Wonderland
Huge 352 Pages, 2-Volumes in-One!
Limited Hardcover Print Run!
Never Before Released in English!
Kid and Family Fun!
TOKYO POP
NOW AVAILABLE
WWW.TOKYOPOP.COM/DISNEY
Disney MANGA 漫画
© 2016 Disney Enterprises Inc.

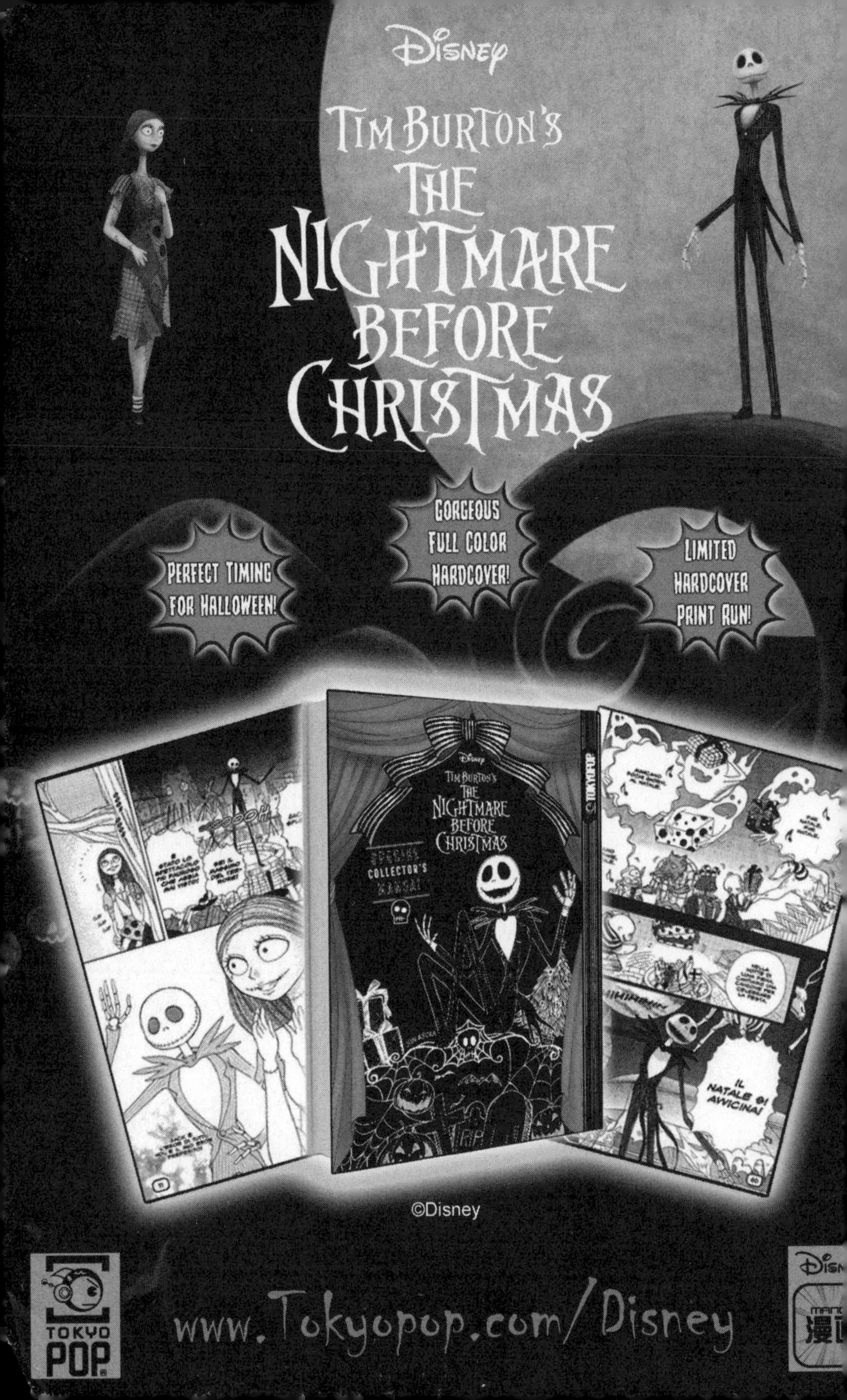
Disney
Tim Burton's
The Nightmare Before Christmas
Perfect Timing for Halloween!
Gorgeous Full Color Hardcover!
Limited Hardcover Print Run!
Special Collector's Manga!
IL NATALE SI AVVICINA!
©Disney
TOKYO POP
www.Tokyopop.com/Disney

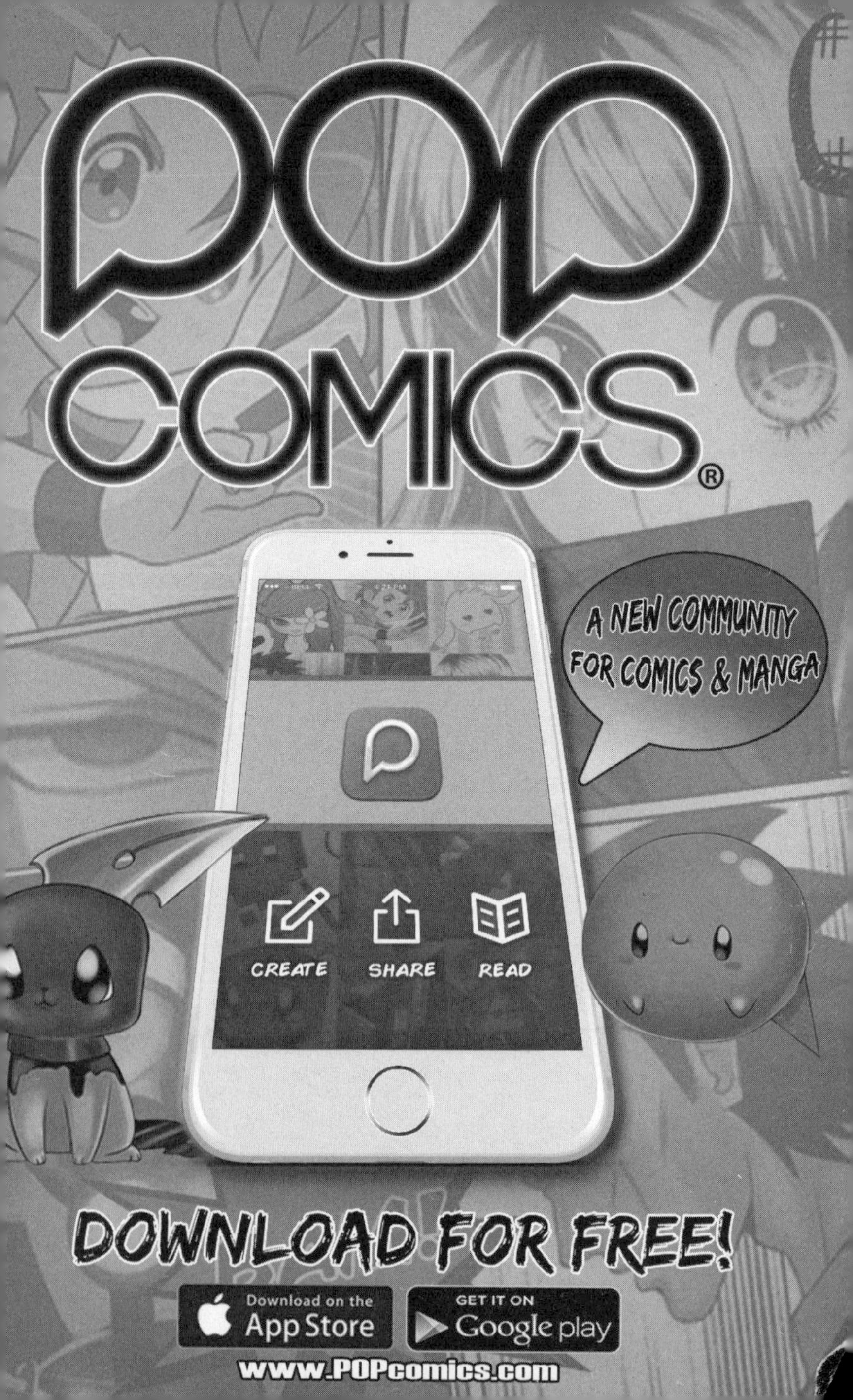
POP COMICS®
A NEW COMMUNITY FOR COMICS & MANGA
CREATE
SHARE
READ
DOWNLOAD FOR FREE!
Download on the App Store
GET IT ON Google play
www.POPcomics.com

Disney Kilala Princess
Story by Rika Tanaka
Art by Nao Kodaka

Publishing Assistant - Janae Young
Marketing Assistant - Kae Winters
Technology and Digital Media Assistant - Phillip Hong
Retouching and Lettering - Vibrraant Publishing Studio
English Adaptation - Christine Dashiell
Graphic Designer - Al-insan Lashley
Editor - Julie Taylor
Editor-in-Chief & Publisher - Stu Levy

A  Manga

TOKYOPOP and 🐾 are trademarks or registered trademarks of TOKYOPOP Inc.

TOKYOPOP inc.
5200 W Century Blvd
Suite 705
Los Angeles, CA 90045 USA

E-mail: info@TOKYOPOP.com
Come visit us online at www.TOKYOPOP.com

▪ www.facebook.com/TOKYOPOP
▪ www.twitter.com/TOKYOPOP
▪ www.youtube.com/TOKYOPOPTV
▪ www.pinterest.com/TOKYOPOP
▪ www.instagram.com/TOKYOPOP
▪ TOKYOPOP.tumblr.com

ISBN: 978-1-4278-5665-4

First TOKYOPOP Printing November 2016
10 9 8 7 6 5 4 3 2 1
Printed in the USA

STOP

THIS IS THE BACK OF THE BOOK!

How do you read manga-style? It's simple! To learn, just start in the top right panel and follow the numbers: